OUT IN THE OPEN

J B GLAZER

JBG Press

Copyright © 2014 J B Glazer

The moral right of the author has been asserted.

All rights reserved.
No part of this publication may be reproduced, stored in a retrieval system, or transmitted, in any form or by any means, without the prior permission in writing of the publisher, nor be otherwise circulated in any form of binding or cover other than that in which it is published and without a similar condition including this condition being imposed on the subsequent purchaser.

Published by JBG Press

ISBN 978-1-4952-7930-0

"Morning, Chicago Loop" by Doug Siefken, www.flickr.com/photos/siefken/2744217176
License at creativecommons.org/licenses/by/4.0/

Typesetting services by BOOKOW.COM

*For Madison and Dylan. Never be afraid to follow your dreams.
And to Josh, my dream come true.*

Books by J B Glazer

Out in the Open
I Should Have Said Yes

Lost and Found Series
In Search of Mr. Anonymous - Book I
Finding Forgiveness - Book II

The Elements Series
Into the Fire - Coming Fall 2020
Into the Light - Coming 2021
Into the Deep - Coming 2021

PROLOGUE

New York

I wheel in my suitcase, and I'm about to set it down in the hallway when I notice them—a pair of leopard-print kitten heels. I saw them on display in a store window recently and knew I had to have them, but they didn't come in my size. Silently I take off my own shoes and creep across the wooden floors, terrified that the pounding in my chest will give me away. I grip the handle of my bedroom door and pause, knowing I don't want to witness what I'm about to see, but my body ignores my screaming protests. I throw open the door and find Ben, my fiancé, in *our* bed with one of my coworkers, Claire. He looks at me, wide-eyed, while she attempts to appear demure.

"Lexi, I wasn't expecting you until tomorrow."

"Clearly. I came home early to surprise you, but I guess the surprise is on me." I hastily make my way from the room. I'm numb with shock, but my adrenaline is on overdrive, helping me put one foot in front of the other. I can't believe this is happening. The reality of his betrayal sinks in and the pain envelops me like a dense, dark fog. It's hard to think clearly, but I know I need to get the hell out of here.

"Let me explain," Ben pleads, following me as he attempts to put some clothes on.

"Oh, I don't think there's anything to explain. It's pretty clear what's been going on."

He places a hand on my arm. "Wait—let's talk about this."

"Don't touch me," I say, with such contempt that my voice is almost unrecognizable. "I don't want to see you—not now, not ever. It's over."

He runs a hand through his hair and looks at me miserably. "Please… wait," he says softly.

I look into his familiar hazel eyes, and I'm tempted, but I can't. I don't want to hear any explanation. All I know is that the man I thought I'd spend the rest of my life with broke my trust—and my heart. I look at him one last time then walk out of the apartment. It's weird how one defining moment can alter the course of your life so drastically. Just a few minutes ago, my life was perfect, and now I have no idea what my future holds or where to go from here. Once I'm outside I let the sobs escape and call my friend Jamie. Thank God she answers.

When she hears my voice, she says, "Lexi, what's wrong?"

"It's a long story. Can I come stay with you for a bit?"

"Of course. You can stay as long as you need."

I hail a cab and slam the door just as Ben runs down the front steps. He approaches my window, and I turn away as he presses his forehead against the glass, willing me to look at him.

"Ma'am?" the cabdriver says.

"You can go," I tell him as I meet Ben's gaze. Through my haze of tears, I see him mouth, "I'm sorry" as we pull away. I look back and watch his retreating figure until he fades from sight, and I wonder when we started to move in such different directions.

When I arrive at Jamie's, she's waiting in the lobby. "Lexi, what happened?" It's hard to get the words out, but I manage to tell her the gist. "I can't believe it. Ben, of all people!"

I can't believe it either. Everyone thought we were the perfect couple.

Ben and I met at a party my junior year of college at the University of Michigan. It was a *Casino Royale*-themed social mixer with his fraternity and my sorority. As an icebreaker, everyone received a playing card, and we had to mingle and find our match. I had the queen of hearts. I looked around the room and locked eyes with Ben. I remember thinking he was so good-looking, with his shaggy dark hair and hazel eyes. He came right up to me and asked me what card I had. I showed him and asked if we were a match.

"Yes," he replied. "I believe we are."

"You didn't show me your card," I pointed out.

He held it up and revealed the king of hearts. "It's close enough. Besides, you're destined to be my queen."

I laughed at his cheesy line, but thought he was cute, so I went along with it. "I don't think that's playing by the rules," I teased.

"Well, I'm in charge of this party, and I'm willing to bend the rules."

"Oh, you're in charge? I thought the social chair planned all the parties."

"You're looking at him."

"I thought Mark Bentley was the social chair."

"He was…last semester. Are you done with your interrogation?"

"Yes, I believe I am."

"Let me guess…You plan to go to law school."

"Nope, guess again."

"I like a challenge." Ben took my hand and led me to a table across the room. "Do you know how to play poker?"

"Yes, and I'm actually quite good."

"Let's play a hand and make a bet. If you win, you can find your real partner, but if I win, you have to go on a date with me."

"OK, deal." Inevitably I lost, though not intentionally because I always play to win. We were together ever since.

After graduation we moved to my hometown of Chicago. We spent a few years there, but then Ben was accepted to the Mount Sinai Medical Center residency program. It was a once-in-a lifetime opportunity, so I agreed to go to New York with him. It wasn't a decision I made lightly. I was uprooting my life and leaving a job I loved, not to mention all my friends and family. But I saw a future with Ben and didn't want to attempt a long-distance relationship.

The day before we moved to New York, he proposed. Even though I knew he was committed, it made me feel that much more confident about my decision. We had been packing, and Ben suggested we take a break and go out for dinner.

"I'm in a zone," I said. "Can't we just finish up then eat?"

"I'm starving. Come on. We can finish later."

He took me to my favorite neighborhood restaurant. I remember being annoyed because he was texting constantly throughout the meal and seemed distracted. When we got home, he fumbled around in his pockets and said, "Shoot, I forgot my keys."

"I have mine." I rummaged through my purse then unlocked the door. I went to hit the light switch, but to my surprise, the room was bathed in a warm glow of candlelight. Scattered rose petals lined the foyer, creating a path to a beautiful vase filled with a dozen red roses, each with a slip of paper attached. A card with my name on it was propped up on the table. I turned around to look at Ben, but he was gone. With shaking hands, I opened the envelope and pulled out the card, which read, "Twelve Reasons I Love Lexi Winters." I lifted the rose labeled "Number one" and read the slip of paper.

Number one: the way your smile lights up a room

I smiled in spite of myself and took out each rose in order.

Number two: *your compassionate nature*
Number three: *the fact that you listen to cassette tapes when you work out*
Number four: *the way you leave water bottles in each room so you'll never be thirsty*
Number five: *your drive and determination*
Number six: *how you always manage to see the silver lining*
Number seven: *your obsession with the Wolverines*
Number eight: *how you leave me love notes when you pack my lunch*
Number nine: *your willingness to watch hockey with me so we can spend time together*

> *Number ten: your addiction to Smart Pop and*
> *chocolate-covered pretzels*
> *Number eleven: the way you believe in me*

I realized there were only eleven roses in the vase. I turned around, and Ben was kneeling behind me, holding the last one. I looked into his shining eyes as he recited, "Number twelve: I love everything about you, but most of all, I love how you bring out the best in me. I knew there was something special about you from the moment I laid eyes on you at the mixer. Once I saw your card, I tossed the other queen of hearts from the deck because I knew then that I didn't want to share you. And I still don't. Lexi Paige Winters, will you do me the honor of marrying me?"

I stared into his earnest face and said, "Yes! Yes, I'll marry you." He lifted me and spun me around the half-empty room, his lips covering mine in a passionate embrace.

"Let's celebrate!" he said, going to the fridge then popping open a bottle of champagne that I didn't remember seeing earlier.

We'd packed all our glasses, so he handed me the bottle. I took a swig and savored the feeling as the sweet, bubbly taste warmed my insides. Then I handed it to him.

"I've got to call my family," I told him.

"Tomorrow. Let's savor this moment. Right now it's just about the two of us."

"OK," I agreed.

We finished almost the whole bottle, not a wise idea when we still had packing left to do. I started to gather up more things, but Ben lifted me into his arms. "It can wait until the morning. Besides, I have something better in mind," he said, leading me to the bedroom.

Between my excitement and the champagne, I couldn't sleep that night. I wandered into the living room, which was devoid of furniture. We'd sold most of it on Craigslist and donated the rest. I smiled when I saw the vase of roses on the counter. Because I hate clutter, I'm not usually one for keeping things, but I definitely wanted a memento from the evening. I found an empty box and scooped the flower petals into it. I wanted to dry out the roses, but there wasn't time before we left, so I carefully placed each one among the petals and labeled the box "Engagement." I added it to the pile of boxes and surveyed the room. The apartment seemed so empty without all our belongings, but my future felt full of promise.

"So what are you going to do?" Jamie asks, breaking my reverie.

"I don't know. I'll probably move back home."

"But what about The Studio? You can't leave your dream job."

The Studio is one of New York's premier advertising agencies. I work on the Aura account, a premium beauty manufacturer that prides itself on its eco-friendly image. I love what I do, and I'm in line for a promotion, but work is the furthest thing from my mind right now.

"I can't even think about going back there and facing everyone. They probably know by now considering Claire is the office gossip. Of course he had to choose *her*."

"Who is she? I've never heard you talk about her."

"She's the one who looks just like Megan Fox. God, I feel like such a cliché. Girl gets cheated on by fiancé with the younger, hotter coworker."

"Lexi, stop it. You don't have to make any decisions right now." Then she hugs me and says, "Don't worry. Things will turn out fine."

I manage a smile, even though I know things never will be fine again.

The next day I come back to our apartment when I know Ben will be at work. I pack up all my stuff and place my set of keys on the counter. I debate about leaving a note, but what would I say? I take a final look around and realize I forgot to do one thing. Slowly I take off my engagement ring and leave it on his pillow, where I know he'll find it. It's the first time since our engagement I've taken it off. I loved that ring, not because it was beautiful but because of what it represented: a promise and a commitment. I stare at my bare hand and feel like something is missing; I wish it were just the jewelry. My friends will say I should have kept the ring, but I don't want any part of him as a reminder. The scars on my heart are enough. I close the door without looking back, vowing never to let any man get the best of me again.

CHAPTER ONE

Chicago

It's been one month since I moved back to Chicago. I'm living with my best friend from high school, Liv. Luckily, Liv has a two-bedroom condo and was willing to rent me the extra room until I find my own place. I wasn't sure if I'd like the neighborhood. Her condo is on the Gold Coast, and I used to live in Lincoln Park, which has much more of a neighborhood feel. Turns out, though, that I like being close to downtown, and hopefully when I get a job, I'll be able to walk to work. I've interviewed with two agencies so far and have my third one today with Hartman & Taylor. From what I've read, it's the hot agency right now, so I applied. I also like that it's a family-run business. Two cousins, Bill Hartman and Stephen Taylor, started it. Bill is the president/CEO and Stephen is the CFO, though from what I understand, he's semiretired and more of a figurehead. Bill really runs the show. The position is an account director for a prestige European beauty brand that's looking to expand distribution into the States through department stores and specialty beauty outlets. I've worked on high-end cosmetics brands in the past, so this is right in line with my experience and interests. I considered applying to L&C, where I worked before I moved to New York, but I want to make a fresh start. And frankly people know I left to be with Ben, and I don't want them asking details about why I'm back.

"Good luck," Liv yells as I walk out the door. "You look great," she adds.

I'm wearing a charcoal-gray shift dress with a skinny belt, black patterned tights, and ankle boots. I accessorized with a mixed-chain layered necklace, simple drop earrings, and my silver Tiffany heart bracelet. It's kind of like my good luck charm. I bought it for myself when I got my first job and wear it to important occasions. I've styled my hair down, but I've loosely pinned back my bangs, which are growing out. I wanted to go for a sophisticated look with a slight edge, and I think I've pulled it off. That's one thing I love about this industry: You can wear clothes that express who you are. At my last agency, the creatives came to work wearing ratty, old T-shirts and ripped jeans. Not me—I always like to look put together. It's not a vanity thing. To be honest, I consider my looks average or maybe a bit above. You've got to work with what you've got, so I've perfected doing my hair and makeup, and I've acquired a great wardrobe. It's how you pull the whole package together that creates appeal.

I'm a bit nervous for the interview but feel a little better because I've done my homework. I Googled each of the people I'm meeting and checked their LinkedIn profiles. I head out, and make the fifteen-minute commute to Hartman & Taylor. Liv couldn't believe I was walking in heels. After living in New York, I've become accustomed to it. I practically live in heels. At five three, I'll take any extra height I can get. I arrive ten minutes early and give the receptionist my name. She tells me to take a seat and offers me something to drink. I accept a bottle of water and study the reception area. It's got a modern, Zen-like vibe. The floors are white, and the walls are made of rich wood paneling. The reception desk is white with frosted glass, and a lone purple orchid sits in the middle of it. The Hartman & Taylor logo is etched into a frosted glass half wall behind the desk with a water feature flowing behind it. Tall floor vases filled with bamboo flank each side of the desk. To the right of the desk is a large plasma screen showing a reel of work, and to the left is a gallery of print ads that are displayed in various-sized white frames.

A door opens, and a middle-aged woman walks over to greet me. She introduces herself as Judy Schaefer from HR. I remember my dad once telling me you can tell someone's character by the quality of his or her handshake, so I shake her hand firmly and smile, hoping to exude confidence. I follow Judy to her office, where she provides an overview of the position, benefits, and salary. She asks me a number of standard questions then runs through my interview schedule. I'm meeting with Morgan Hayes, executive director of account management, at nine; Simon Turner, group creative director, at ten; Michelle Adams, account executive, at eleven; and Jake Hartman, VP of business development, at eleven thirty. All were on my interview list but Jake Hartman. Although I didn't research him specifically, his name came up a bunch of times. I believe he's the nephew of Bill Hartman.

Judy leads me to Morgan's spacious corner office. Morgan stands to greet me and I immediately feel intimidated. She dresses impeccably, wears her dark hair in a sleek bob, and offers me a perfectly manicured hand. It makes me glad I thought to get my nails done yesterday. Her face softens as she offers me a warm smile, which puts me at ease. She explains that the agency was just awarded the Lumineux account. They're relatively unknown in the States, but it's our job to make that change. The first assignment is to create a new campaign for their anti-aging skin-care line. She goes on to say that because this is a new piece of business, Hartman & Taylor isn't fully staffed yet on the account. They've pulled various talent from within the agency, but they need a dedicated account lead with prestige experience, preferably someone from the outside who can offer a new perspective. Then she fires questions at me. I can tell she's fair but tough. She asks about my background, my client relationships—including which level of clients I worked with—and how many direct reports I had. Then she lays out various scenarios and asks me how I would handle each. I think I do a good job answering her questions. I'm well prepared, and I anticipated most of them, so I'm able to weave in the examples I'd thought of beforehand.

"Well, Lexi, it sounds like you have great experience. Just one last question: What brings you to Chicago?" she asks curiously.

Of course I'd expected this question. "It was a dream of mine to live in New York. I'm so fortunate I pursued it and was able to make that dream a reality. It's truly an amazing city, and I enjoyed my experience there, but Chicago is home. And for personal reasons, it seemed like a good time to come back."

Satisfied, she nods. "Now do you have any questions for me?"

I ask her about her management style and her role in the day-to-day work, their expectations regarding revenue for the account, and the size of the team I'd be leading. We talk for a few more minutes, and then Judy knocks on the door.

"Well, thank you for coming in, Lexi," Morgan says. "We'll be in touch soon."

"It was a real pleasure," I tell her.

Judy leads me to Simon's office. He looks me up and down, and I feel self-conscious under his intense gaze. As soon as Judy walks away, he says, "Thank God, someone who actually looks the part." I smile at him questioningly. "This is for a prestige beauty brand," he says. "We need someone the clients can relate to, not all the Forever 21s I've seen so far. You actually have a sophisticated sense of style." I like him already. He asks me a bunch of questions, namely about my relationship with the creative team. I tell him I view it as a partnership because it's very difficult to sell something if both parties aren't aligned. I also tell him I'm very supportive of a team pushing the envelope and going off brief as long as it delivers what the client has asked for.

"In my experience you can't successfully sell if you don't first give the client what they requested," I say. "It's important to deliver what they asked for then show them how it can be even better. This builds trust and makes them more open to the idea rather than being defensive, because we're essentially telling them they're wrong."

Simon nods and says, "I couldn't agree more." He asks me what some of my favorite campaigns are that I've worked on and why. I answer then ask him the same. Before I know it, Judy is back. Simon kisses both of my cheeks and says to Judy, "She's a keeper." I smile at him and say good-bye.

"Things seem to be going well," she says. She leads to me a conference room where Michelle is waiting. She introduces us and says she'll be back within a half hour. In the first few minutes of our conversation, I can tell that Michelle is a bright girl. We talk about her experience in her current role and what she'll be doing on the account. She asks me about my management style, which achievements I'm most proud of, and how I'd go about establishing relationships with a new group of clients. She's sharp, and we establish a good rapport. Soon the half hour is up, and Judy returns to take me to my final interview. "Mr. Hartman is finishing up a call," she says. "I'll take you on a brief tour of the office, and then we'll see if he's ready." I thank Michelle for her time and follow Judy out.

"I know you weren't originally scheduled to meet with Mr. Hartman, so I appreciate your being flexible. He travels a lot and happened to be in the office today, so I thought it would be good for the two of you to meet," Judy says as she leads me around.

I find it interesting that she's referred to everyone else on a first-name basis—either Jake prefers to be addressed formally, or she's fearful of him, neither of which I take to be a good sign. Judy informs me Hartman & Taylor occupies five floors of the building, which they're already outgrowing. She shows me the office where I'd be sitting, along with the conference rooms, kitchen, and brainstorming area, which takes up half the floor. It's meant to inspire creativity with a Ping-Pong table, pool table, meeting area with cozy couches and a TV, a library with magazines and books for inspiration, a huge bulletin board, a chalkboard wall, and a small kitchen. Pretty standard for an agency, though when I used to show my friends where I worked, they couldn't believe it. "This is what you do at work?" they'd exclaim. I always sensed they were skeptical that I actually worked hard. But I do. My career is very important to me. As we walk, Judy tells me there's a bar downstairs, Taylor Tavern, where people often gather, though it is not endorsed by the agency.

We head to Jake's office on the twenty-first floor. Judy introduces me to Joann Silver, his secretary.

"Is he ready?" she asks.

"Yes, go on in," says Joann.

I push aside my nerves and attempt to walk confidently into Jake's office. He's sitting behind his desk but stands to greet me. I offer him my hand and hope he doesn't hear my sharp intake of breath. He is *gorgeous*. He's tall, at least six feet, with a nice build and broad shoulders. I take in his icy-blue eyes, sun-kissed skin, and short golden-brown hair that's a bit longer on top with that perfectly imperfect messy look. He smiles and reveals a pair of dimples, causing the butterflies I just tamed to take flight once more, flapping their tiny wings insistently. I'm momentarily paralyzed, entranced by his good looks. Jake regards me with an amused expression, and I decide he has a sense of boyish charm about him. Even though he's very attractive, he seems approachable, and I bet that's a big factor in his success. I was expecting him to be older, but he looks to be in his late twenties. As he towers over me, I realize I misread Judy's reaction. She's likely not fearful of him; it's just that his looks are disarming. I sit down and take a deep, steadying breath.

"Nice to meet you, Alexandra," he says. "Thanks for meeting with me so last minute."

I manage to regain my composure. "Please call me Lexi." I see my résumé on his desk and try to make out the notes he's written beneath the "Alexandra Paige Winters" masthead.

"So, Lexi," he says, "why do you want to work for Hartman and Taylor? You're obviously very accomplished, having worked at top agencies in Chicago and New York. What makes you interested in us?"

Wow, he doesn't waste time for small talk. "You're right," I say. "I have worked at some of the top agencies. And it was an exhilarating experience to be a part of that success. But I've found that companies rely on the same formula to stay on top. They want to go with what's tried and true, which makes them averse to risk. I want to be part of a culture that's willing to try new things and learn from failure, push new and innovative ideas, and most of all, continually strive to be the best. I'm ready to take on a new challenge."

He regards me intently with his blue eyes, beautiful and vast like the ocean, but what lies beneath is a mystery. I ponder how he can find a shirt in the exact same hue when he interrupts my thoughts. "So tell me about yourself." Surprised by his change of tack, I pause. "I've read your résumé," he says. "I have a good feel for your professional experience. Now I want to know more about *you*."

"Well, I grew up in the northern suburbs and come from a close-knit family of five. I have two sisters, and even though I'm the middle child, somehow I'm the responsible one. I recently moved back here from New York, and I'm living with a close friend until I can find my own apartment. I love working with creative people, which is why I pursued a career in advertising. I thought I'd be a copywriter, but after a summer internship I decided I was a better fit on the account side. Plus I love trying to find a solution when one doesn't seem possible. I get energized when the client delivers a challenging brief that allows us to work through new solutions to solve their business problems. That's why I ultimately went into account management. It's the best of both worlds: I get to manage the work and relationships but still take part in the creative process." I hope I didn't share too much, but he seems satisfied with my response.

"Where in New York did you live?"

"Murray Hill."

"Do you miss it?"

"Yes, but this is home."

"What do you miss the most?"

"You'll probably think I'm crazy, but there was this great deli near my office that had the best soups. I went there practically every day."

Jake looks amused, and I wish I'd thought of something wittier. Then he smirks and says, "You know, we have great delis here too."

"None that I've found—not in the city at least."

"What about Cahan's?"

"I've heard it's good, but I never went because it wasn't near my office or apartment."

"There's this thing called delivery. You should try it sometime." I laugh, and he does too. Then he tells me he also lived in New York for about six months, right after he graduated from college.

"Why did you live there for such a short time?"

"I moved there to be close to a girl I was dating, but things didn't work out." I'm pleased about this revelation, although I have no intention of telling him about our shared history. "Anyway," he continues, "I always knew I'd come work here with my uncle, but she wanted to stay in New York, so we parted ways."

"How did you know you wanted to work for your uncle?"

"I practically grew up here. My dad traveled frequently, so I think my uncle tried to make up for his shortcomings. He attended my sporting events and helped me with homework, advice, that sort of thing. I'd often come to the agency after school and watch him work. I picked up a lot, and as I got older, he started formally training me."

"It must have been hard to go through high school without your dad around. What does he do?"

"He's a business consultant. He often traveled abroad and was gone for long stretches."

"Did it bother him that you wanted to work for your uncle?" I hope I'm not getting too personal, but he doesn't seem to mind.

"No, I think he was glad," Jake says. "We never discussed it much, but he once told me he regretted not being around enough for the family. He encouraged me to do something I love but advised me to think about the long-term implications. When you're in your late teens, you really don't think about how your career might impact your family life."

"That's good advice," I say. It makes me wonder whether he has a family, and I find myself hoping the answer is no. I look at his left hand and notice he isn't wearing a ring. "It must be nice working for a family business. My parents actually work together," I tell him.

"What do they do?"

"My dad is an architect, and my mom is an interior designer. His clients aren't required to use her services, but many of them opt to. She has a great eye."

"Why didn't you go into the family business?"

"Believe me, I thought about it. My younger sister Tara probably will follow in my mom's footsteps. But I wanted to do something I'm passionate about. If I had the skill, I'd have been a fashion designer. This is the next best thing."

Just then Joann pokes her head into his office. "Mr. Hartman, your one o'clock is here." Wow, it's already one? It doesn't seem like we've been talking for over an hour. Disappointment washes over me, and in that moment I resent Joann for the interruption.

Jake turns to me. "Do you have any further questions?"

"Just one. Would you still want to work here if it wasn't your uncle's company?"

He thinks for a minute. "This probably wouldn't have been my first choice right out of college," he says honestly. "But, if for some reason I did end up working here, I definitely would stay. It's a great group of people. We have some solid blue-chip clients, and we're growing. When I started here, the company had around a hundred and twenty-five employees. Now we employ more than five hundred and recently opened an office in San Francisco. I think there's still plenty of room to grow. In fact we're on a bit of a winning streak, and that brings momentum. It's an exciting time to be at Hartman and Taylor."

"Thank you so much for your time," I tell him.

"It was a pleasure to meet you, Lexi," he says, as he shakes my hand, letting his fingers linger a bit longer than necessary. Or perhaps it's just my imagination. Then he offers me another heart-stopping smile before he turns his attention to the man waiting outside his door.

As I walk out of Jake's office, I can't help think that our conversation felt more like a first date than an interview. And for the first time since I walked out on Ben, I'm actually open to the possibility.

CHAPTER TWO

I grab lunch and head back to my apartment. I'm just about caught up on *Grey's Anatomy* when Liv walks in. She's a teacher, and she has great hours.

"How'd it go?" she asks, flopping onto the couch next to me.

"I think it went well. The creative director seemed to take a liking to me." Liv raises her eyebrows. "Liv, he's gay."

"Oh, too bad."

Liv is on a mission to find me a man to help take my mind off Ben. I keep telling her I'm not ready to date anyone. "Lexi," she always says in exasperation, "I'm not saying you have to marry the guy—just go on one date. You need to find your rebound." As much as I protest, she keeps trying to fix me up, but I always turn her down. "What else?" she asks. "How did it compare to the other places where you've interviewed?"

"I really liked it. I think it's my top choice. The head of new business said it's a good time to join the company because they're winning a lot of accounts."

"Of course he'd say that. He obviously wants you to work there."

"Well, they have been getting a lot of good press. And I don't think he'd lie about it. His uncle is one of the founders, so he has the family name to uphold. He also happened to be adorable."

Liv perks up at this revelation. "Lexi, spill."

"There isn't much to tell. He looked to be in his late twenties, beautiful blue eyes framed by golden-brown lashes, strong jaw, good body, killer dimples, and no wedding ring." Liv knows I'm a sucker for dimples.

"Is that all?" she teases. "What's his name?"

"Jake Hartman."

"Let's go find out about Jake," she says, leading me to her computer. "Also, does the company have a policy on inter-office dating?"

"Liv, they haven't even given me an offer yet."

"I'm just sayin'," she replies.

We first look him up on Facebook, but there are many Jake Hartmans, and none look to be a match. Then she does a Google search and comes up with a number of hits. She skims a bunch of links then filters the search by image. And there he is up on the screen, looking all sexy.

"Lexi," she exclaims, "he's gorgeous!"

"I told you. I'm sure he has a girlfriend, or he's a player. A guy like that doesn't stay single for long." I close the window and shut the laptop. I don't want to think about Jake Hartman anymore. "What do you want to do for dinner?" I ask.

"Let's do sushi tonight instead of Sunday because I'll be out of town this weekend."

Since I've moved back, we've started a tradition of Sunday-night sushi. "That's right!" I exclaim. "The wedding is this weekend." Liv and her boyfriend, Jason, are going to Dallas for his friend's wedding. She and Jason have been dating for nine months now. I really like him and suspect they'll get engaged. It's one of the reasons I need to start looking for my own apartment. Liv always has had a boyfriend. Even back in high school, she typically was dating someone seriously. Although I didn't have many boyfriends, I had plenty of crushes, but I was always too shy to act on them. I'm kind of old-fashioned that way. I know a lot of bold girls who give out their number to guys who haven't even asked, or will go up to a cute guy in a bar and strike up a conversation. Not me. I think the guy should make the first move. I want to know he's interested first.

I like to take some credit for Liv and Jason's relationship. When they first met, she wasn't that into him. They were fixed up by a mutual friend after she'd gone through a bad breakup. Maybe that's why she's so intent on setting me up. I could tell there was something different about him, and I kept insisting she give him a chance. She was so hung up on her ex, though, that she didn't see she had a good thing right in front of her. At my urging, she agreed to go out with him again, and discovered the great qualities I recognized all along. He worships the ground she walks on, but he's not a pushover either. He's a defense attorney, and a good one from what I hear. He puts in a lot of long hours, so he and Liv spend only a few weeknights together. This works out for me because I get to spend more time with her, and I like having someone to do things with; it helps keep my mind off Ben.

That night I can't fall asleep. Inevitably my thoughts drift to Ben. I keep thinking back to when we were together, looking for signs of a red flag. The only thing I can think of is that I told him I wouldn't move to New York without a commitment. Perhaps he wasn't ready for marriage, but we'd been together seven years. Maybe that should have been a red flag in and of itself. But we were young when we met, and then he was busy with medical school and his residency. I'm a pretty good judge of character, and I thought he was one of the good ones, although I don't have much to compare our relationship to, given my dating track record. I went out with a few guys in high school—none seriously—and had many random hookups in college. During my sophomore year, I dated a guy for about six months, but then summer came, and we parted ways amicably. We lived far apart, and neither of us was up for a long-distance summer romance. Then Ben came along. He was the first guy who made me feel truly beautiful and loved. The memory of his romantic proposal plays over in my mind, and I wonder how things could have gone so wrong. I feel like I failed somehow, like I wasn't enough for him. It torments me that I don't know why he cheated, but I can't bring myself to talk to him. I'm just not ready yet; the hurt is still too raw. Deep down I know I'll never get back together with him, and the thought fills me with despair. But I could never be in a relationship with someone I can't trust, and I know I'd constantly doubt him. It's been four months since I ended things, and I really miss having him in my life. I tried to stay in New York after our breakup, but it proved to be too difficult; plus most of my friends and family are here. As the tears slide slowly down my face, I wonder whether this feeling will ever go away. I finally drift off to sleep, and Ben haunts my dreams.

I spend the next few days unpacking the last of my boxes—the ones marked "Miscellaneous" that I'd been avoiding. I put away the items I want to keep and toss the rest. Just as I sit down for a break, my phone rings. It's Judy Schaefer from Hartman & Taylor calling to offer me the job. I've already received offers from the other two agencies, but I've been holding out until I heard from Hartman. I probably should tell her I need to think it over, but I accept on the spot. There are only so many errands and so much unpacking I can do, and I get restless sitting around all day. I'm eager to get back into a routine. I start a week from Monday.

My first instinct is to call Ben, but I don't. Instead I call my parents to tell them the news, and then I call Liv. I catch her while she's between classes. "Congrats, Lexi! We'll have go out tonight to celebrate."

We agree to grab martinis at our favorite bar, Lux. I decide to cook a nice dinner to thank Liv for all her support. I don't know how I could have gotten through these past few weeks without her. I still feel like a ghost of myself. I peer in the mirror, and at first glance, I look the same—same long chestnut-brown hair, big almond-shaped brown eyes, olive skin, and slim build. But on closer inspection, I notice bags under my eyes even makeup can't hide; my skin has lost its luster; and clothes that once fit perfectly now hang loosely on my frame. I didn't have much of an appetite in the weeks after the "incident," as I now like to call it, and I'm still not back to my ideal weight. I make a mental note to add more protein to my diet. Then I look at my left hand, now bare, which serves as a constant reminder. I sigh in frustration and close my eyes. I start to think about Ben but push the thought from my mind. Everyone keeps telling me time heals all wounds, but I'm still waiting.

The week passes quickly. I'm totally unpacked, and the apartment is clean and stocked with food. On Sunday night I choose my outfit carefully so I won't have to waste time in the morning fretting about what to wear. I opt for a fitted, camel-colored pencil dress with exposed gold zippers in place of pockets. I accessorize with a skinny brown belt, suede Mary Jane pumps, and gold chandelier earrings. I don't sleep well and feel exhausted when the alarm goes off at six forty-five. I take a hot shower to wake myself up then blow out my naturally wavy hair until it's stick straight. Liv is always telling me I have such great hair because I can wear it so many different ways. It's amazing what you can learn on YouTube.

I grab a coffee at Starbucks then head to Hartman & Taylor. Judy told me to stop by her office at eight thirty so she could give me an ID badge along with a key to my office. I arrive right on time; being late gives me anxiety. She takes my photo for the badge and gives me a temporary card until it's ready. I head to my office and unpack the few personal items I have. My old office was filled with pictures of Ben and me. Now I have three simple framed photos: one of my family, one of my nephew Charlie, and the other of me with my friends. I stare at the picture and remember the night, one of my last in Chicago, when my friends threw me a going-away party. I hardly recognize the happy, carefree girl gazing back at me. Although it's only been months, it seems like a lifetime ago. My friends had the photo framed as part of my going-away gift, but now it only brings back painful memories. I make a mental note to replace it. Just then I hear a knock on my door. A pretty blond girl with warm brown eyes pops her head in.

"You must be Lexi," she says. "I'm Nicole. I sit in the office right next door."

"Hi. It's so nice to meet you."

We chat for a few minutes, and she offers to show me around. She introduces me to some people on our floor and gives me the lowdown on everyone. I can tell she's the type of person I would be friends with. Plus she seems like someone good to know because she's up on the latest company gossip. We're chatting outside her door when I spy Jake walking down the hall. Once again he's wearing a crisp, light-blue button-down shirt that brings out the color in his eyes, along with sterling silver cuff links. I find myself wondering if they were a gift.

"Hi, Lexi," he says. "I'm so glad you decided to join us. I see you've met Nicole."

The three of us chat for a bit, and I notice how easily he and Nicole banter back and forth. It's like they're old friends—or perhaps something more. Then Jake looks at his watch and says, "I gotta go meet with legal. If I don't settle this tagline dispute, Simon will have my head. See you, Lexi, Nicole."

"Bye, Jake," I tell him. "And good luck with that."

After he walks away, Nicole says, "Gorgeous, isn't he?"

I guess I'm not the only one who's noticed. "Yes," I reply with a laugh. "What's his deal?"

"I hear he goes out with a lot of girls, but he doesn't date anyone at the office. God knows, many have tried, but he has a strict rule about interoffice dating. It's kind of an unspoken thing."

"Oh," I say, trying to hide my disappointment. "Is there a company rule against it?"

"Only that you can't date your direct superior. Apparently there was an incident that happened a number of years ago—some girl claiming he sexually harassed her. From what I heard, she was hung up on Jake, and they had a fling. When he tried to end it, she freaked, and it was her form of revenge. Everyone around here knew it wasn't true, but ever since then, he won't date anybody at the office."

I too find the claim hard to believe. Jake doesn't seem the type; plus he probably can get any girl he wants. I plan to investigate further.

I go back to my office and check my calendar. I have a meeting with Morgan in fifteen minutes. I read through some of the materials she gave me then head to her office. She's talking with someone but motions for me to come in. "Lexi, this is Nigel Hughes. He's the head planner on our New Business team. Nigel, this is Lexi Winters. She just accepted the position on the Lumineux account."

"It's a pleasure," he says in a British accent as he shakes my hand.

"Lexi has a lot of beauty experience," Morgan says. "I'm sure she'd be a real asset on some of your upcoming pitches."

"I'll keep that in mind." Nigel looks me over, which makes me uncomfortable, but I hold his gaze. Then he turns back to Morgan and says, "I'll send you those numbers you asked for by the end of the day."

Once Nigel leaves, Morgan turns her attention to me. She shares her plans for the account and gives me background on all of our clients. The good news is that the company has an office in Chicago, which makes it much easier to establish and maintain a relationship with them. Plus it means less travel—not that I mind traveling, but constantly being on the road can be tiring. Morgan has made arrangements for the two of us to go to Lumineux's offices tomorrow so she can introduce me. She also arranged a lunch with my new team for this afternoon so I can get to know everyone.

The rest of the morning passes quickly, and my team and I head out to Riva's, a seafood restaurant at Navy Pier that overlooks Lake Michigan. Michelle is the only person there I've met. Morgan introduces me to Barb, our planner; Matt, creative director; Erica, art director; and finally Megan, our copywriter. It's a fun group, and everyone is very friendly. We spend a large part of the meal talking about our personal lives, and then Morgan gets down to business. We have our first briefing on Thursday, so she wants us to spend the next two days doing research to prepare. When I return to the office, I decide to set up meetings with each team member individually so I can learn more about their styles and experience.

The next day, Tuesday, Morgan brings me to meet our key clients: Paul, the marketing director, and Natalia, the brand manager. Paul recently came to Lumineux from Lancôme and is very seasoned. Natalia was based with Lumineux in France and recently moved to the States to help with the US launch. She has a beautiful European accent and is very polished. I can now see what Simon meant about wanting someone who looked the part. We talk about their challenges, goals, and vision for the business. I ask a lot of questions and take copious notes. Then I give an overview about my background and share some initial thoughts I have for the launch. Natalia latches onto one of my ideas but says we'll first need to engage the other agencies that will be helping with the launch. I suggest we arrange an introductory meeting and Paul asks for my help in setting it up. Overall it's a productive meeting, and I'm looking forward to working with them.

That night when I get home, I do another Google search on Jake. I'm curious about the sexual harassment claim and don't remember seeing anything about it when Liv and I did our initial search. I type in "Jake Hartman" and "sexual harassment." A number of links come up but none related to that topic. I scroll down and finally find a hit on page three. Clearly he had a good team in place to optimize the search results so the more favorable stories come up first. But that's the thing with the Internet—you entirely can't erase your past. I click on the link and scan the article. It doesn't give much information other than Hartman & Taylor planned to vigorously defend itself against a lawsuit brought by a former employee, Jessica Adams. The suit alleged that she received unwanted sexual advances from Jake Hartman, which resulted in a hostile work environment. I continue to scroll and find another hit. The story doesn't say much either, aside from the fact that the judge dismissed the case because the claims were unsubstantiated. I now understand why Jake won't date anyone at work. I can only imagine the embarrassment the case caused him and the company. I go back and read some of the other articles about him. Most of them discuss his success at Hartman & Taylor and the fact that since he took over the New Business team, the agency has more than doubled its client base. None of those articles mention the lawsuit. I bet he's had to work extra hard to make that stain go away. Before I go to sleep, I find myself thinking of Jake. It's too bad he's off limits. He definitely could be a nice distraction.

CHAPTER THREE

It's Friday, the end of my first week. Late in the afternoon, I'm heading back to my office when I bump into Jake.

"Hey, Lexi. How's your first week been?"

"Good, although it's felt like much longer than that. I've already had a few meetings at Lumineux's offices, and I just briefed my team on a new project."

"Sounds like you could use a drink. Want to head downstairs to Taylor Tavern?"

I'm flattered. "Yes, I definitely could go for a drink."

"Good. A bunch of us are meeting there at five. You should come."

I feel foolish for thinking he was inviting just me. I nod and say I'll see him there. Then I stop by Nicole's office.

"Are you going downstairs for drinks?" I ask her.

"Yes, you should definitely come."

"What's the deal with that place? Is it agency owned?"

"No, they just named in it our honor. And we get great drink specials, although on Fridays Hartman and Taylor always covers the first round. I have a few e-mails to finish up. I'll grab you when I'm done."

"OK, great."

I wrap up a few things and go to the ladies' room to freshen up. When I come back to my desk, Nicole is ready. We head downstairs at a quarter to six, and the bar is packed. She introduces me to a lot of people, and I do my best to try to remember their names. Everyone is very nice, and even people I don't work with make a point to come meet me. I guess there's something to be said for being the new girl. I spy Jake standing by the bar, talking to a well-dressed man. I recall from a photo on the company's website that it's Bill Hartman. I'm impressed he makes an appearance at happy hour. Jake catches my eye and motions for me to come over. I make my way to the bar and give him a shy smile.

"Lexi, I want to introduce you to Bill Hartman. Bill, this is Lexi. She just started on the Lumineux account."

Bill shakes my hand firmly and gives me a warm smile. "Lexi, I've heard great things about you from Ted Milton." I'm puzzled—Ted was my former boss in New York, so I don't know why Bill would be talking to him about me. Plus, I wouldn't expect someone at his level to get involved with hiring decisions. Seeming to sense my confusion, he says, "Morgan reviewed the list of candidates with me. Lumineux is an important client, and I wanted to know who we were considering for the position. I saw that you worked for The Studio, so I figured you'd know Ted. He and I go way back, so I called him. He gave you a glowing review."

I feel my cheeks redden. "Ted was a great boss and mentor. I learned much of what I know from him."

"Well, we're glad to have you."

"Thank you. I'm glad to be here."

"Jake, be sure to keep an eye on this one," Bill says, winking at me. "I've got to be heading out." He shakes my hand then pats Jake on the back.

After he walks away, I ask, "Does Bill always come out for happy hour?"

"He comes when he can. Why do you sound so surprised?"

"I don't know. I guess I'm not used to seeing senior-level executives mingling at these kinds of functions. They usually stick together—if they come at all."

"Yeah, I think he wants to be seen as approachable, and it gives him a chance to keep in touch with what's going on. Happy hour is a good place—drunk people who let their guard down."

"That's true," I say with a laugh. "I admire that he wants to stay close to his employees. It shows he cares about the people who work here."

"He does." The bartender hands Jake his drink. He takes a sip then asks me, "What would you like?"

You. The word almost slips out of my mouth, surprising me. Instead I say, "I'll have a vodka cranberry."

When the bartender serves it, Jake says, "We should make a toast: to your first week."

"Cheers to that," I say, and we clink glasses.

"I'm glad you decided to work here, because I know you had your choice of agencies. You're going to be a real asset."

"How did you know I had my choice of agencies?"

"Lexi, I have a lot of connections in this industry. I know you got an offer from each agency you interviewed at."

"Oh, well, Hartman and Taylor seemed like the best fit for me, and I had the best chemistry with the team."

Jake nods. "Chemistry is important." Our eyes lock, and I feel myself blush. Luckily he doesn't seem to notice. "When you're a leader, it can make or break your career," he continues. "And it's key to winning new business."

Nicole walks up to the bar. "Jake, you're monopolizing Lexi," she says. "Other people want to meet her. Come," she says, as she pulls me away.

"Bye, Jake," I say over my shoulder.

He holds up his hand and gives me a playful grin. I hang out for another hour or so then call it a night. I have to be up early tomorrow and want a clear head. I'm planning a benefit dinner in honor of my Aunt Lynne and have appointments with several vendors. Lynne was my mom's younger sister, and I was very close with her. She successfully battled breast cancer five years ago and was in remission. However, the cancer came back and her immune system was compromised from all of her previous treatments. She ended up catching pneumonia and passed away three years ago. My family put together a benefit in her honor, and it's become a yearly tradition. It's a big task, but I really enjoy planning it. I feel like it's a small thing I can do to help honor her memory; plus we're helping thousands of other women by raising money for a cure.

The next morning, my mom picks me up at eight. We have a full day of meetings, the first being with three florists to look at flower arrangements.

We had an initial meeting with each of them a few weeks back to give them a sense of what we were looking for. Today they're sharing their interpretation of our vision. All of them are beautiful, but a small local florist put together a stunning arrangement that outshines the rest. I take a photo of the centerpiece and text it to my sister, Jules. Even though she can't be here, I want her to feel like she's part of the process. She wanted to come today, but her husband Scott was invited to the Cubs game, and she had no one to baby-sit my nephew, Charlie. She's been very helpful, though. She works as a business consultant, and one of her clients is Starwood Hotels. She was able to secure us a great rate at the W, so we're having the event in their grand ballroom. Jules texts me back her approval and tells me she loves the arrangement. Next my mom and I meet with the caterer to discuss the menu and decide to go with a plethora of appetizer and dessert stations instead of a formal seated dinner. We sample all the foods and make our selections. My mom and I planned on going out for lunch, but we're both full, so we decide to do some shopping until our last appointment. We walk up Michigan Avenue, which is packed with tourists. I've gone down this street many times, but I try to view it from their perspective. As we're walking, my mom asks me about Ben and whether I've spoken with him.

"Not yet. He's still calling, but I'm not ready to talk to him."

"I understand you need time. But at some point, it would be good for you to hear him out."

"Mom, what's he going to say? 'I'm sorry I cheated on you'? What difference will that make? It's done and over. I just want to move on."

"I know you do. I just thought maybe it would help you move on—that's all." She changes the subject. "So have you met anyone interesting at work?"

"Yes, everyone is really nice, and I've made some new friends."

"Honey, that's wonderful. How are the men? Any potential suitors?" An image of Jake flashes through my mind but I'm hesitant to tell my mom. I don't even know how I feel about him yet. She senses my reluctance and asks, "Lexi, is there someone I should know about?"

"Well, there's one guy I'm attracted to, but I heard he doesn't date anyone at the office."

"What's his name?"

"Jake Hartman."

"Hartman? Isn't that the name of your agency?"

"Yes, he's the founder's nephew. Aside from being really cute, he's smart and very successful and has this charm about him. He runs the New Business group and has been responsible for a lot of recent wins."

"Well, you never know. Sometimes all it takes is the right person to come along to change someone's mind." I wish it were that easy. "Lexi, you deserve to be with someone who will cherish you. Don't forget that. I don't want you ever settling for someone. I know you worry, but you have your whole future ahead of you. He's still out there."

"Thanks, Mom," I say, and give her a hug. I hope she's right. I do worry; I'm twenty-seven years old and starting all over again. I thought I'd be starting a family within the next year, but instead I've started a new job and can't even think about dating anyone yet. Well, maybe one person, but he's off-limits. Maybe that's why I'm interested in him. He's an easy target, someone to lust after that I know won't ever return my affections. And I prefer to keep it that way.

We hit up Bloomingdale's, but I'm not really in the mood to buy anything. Soon it's time to head to our last appointment. We're meeting with a company to discuss linens. I know it sounds boring, but I love this sort of thing. It's weird having to do it again—I already planned so much for my wedding. At least this time it's for someone else. I'm able to get through it knowing it's for my Aunt Lynne, so I try to channel what she would want. We look at endless colors and textures of fabric before making our selections. Then my mom drives me home.

"Any big plans for tonight?" she asks me.

"No. I figured I'd be exhausted after today, so I'm just going to order in and watch a movie."

She tries not to look concerned. "OK, have fun. Thanks for everything today."

"Mom, I'll be fine. Love you."

I head upstairs, and I'm actually looking forward to a night of Thai food and *Twilight*. I've read all the books, but I haven't seen the movies. I get lost in the world of Edward and Bella.

CHAPTER FOUR

It's only week two, but already I have a three-day immersion with our agency partners. We're hosting the meeting at our offices because we're the only local agency. Natalia, Paul, and Laurence from Lumineux's research and development group will kick things off, and then each agency will share an overview of recent work, followed by a brainstorm session. The goal is to come up with a handful of ideas each agency feels good about that we can then ideate further with our respective agency teams. I stay late on Monday, working with Matt to come up with the right content to present. I also make sure the conference room has all the materials we'll need. We're starting promptly at 8:30 a.m. tomorrow.

I wake up early and arrive at the office a half hour before our start time. I check that breakfast has arrived, and then I wait in the lobby so I can greet everyone and show them to the conference room. We begin with an icebreaker exercise Natalia has thought up: two truths and a lie. Everyone has to share three facts about themselves, and then the group has to guess what the lie is. I find it hard to pay attention during these exercises because I'm always trying to think of my answer while the others are giving theirs. It kind of defeats the purpose in getting to know everyone. When it's my turn, I say, "I ran the Chicago marathon; my apple cobbler won first place at the North Shore Festival; and I have a horrible case of arachnophobia." Everyone guesses the apple cobbler, but I've never run a marathon. I actually hate running, and the thought of doing it for more than twenty miles is something I can't fathom. I tell the group I'll bring them my famous apple cobbler by the end of the week, and they can judge it for themselves.

The morning goes well, and we collectively come up with some interesting ideas. We've been brainstorming as a large group, so after lunch I suggest we break up into smaller cross-functional teams. I think people will be more willing to share out-of-the-box ideas they might be embarrassed about voicing in front of a new group of people. It seems to work, because we get much better ideas in the afternoon. Around five, Natalia thanks everyone for a productive day and dismisses us until dinner. I've made a reservation for the group at Gibson's, a renowned Chicago steakhouse. We first have cocktails by the bar then head upstairs to a private dining room at seven thirty. I'm seated next to Trey from the digital agency, and he entertains us with stories about his recent travels to Kenya. It was his wife's dream to go on an African safari, but he isn't the outdoors type.

"You're a good husband," I tell him.

"That, and now I see a lot more guys' getaways to Vegas in my future."

"Very strategic. Well played."

Eventually everyone shares information about their marital status, and surprisingly I'm one of the few single people at the table. It's not something I try to fixate on, but lately it's become a difficult fact to ignore. After dinner Natalia, Paul, and Laurence bid us good night, but the rest of the group is still up for going out. I take them to a nearby bar, and we stay there until past midnight. I'm not used to being out so late on a weeknight, but I feel like I should stay to bond with my new team. When I finally get home at 1:00 a.m., I sigh, knowing my alarm will be going off in five hours.

After several cups of coffee, I make it through the rest of the day then head to Taylor Tavern with the group for drinks. I leave on the earlier side so I can get to the grocery store to pick up ingredients for my apple cobbler. I bring it to our final session on Thursday, and everyone agrees it's award worthy—that, or they're just being nice, but it is one of my favorite recipes. We spend the day narrowing down the ideas from the past few days to our top three choices. Once Paul and Natalia are aligned, we're charged with blowing the ideas out into actual concepts and sharing them with the group in two weeks' time. It's been a very productive few days, but come Friday,

I'm exhausted. I spend the day getting caught up because it's been hard to do actual work with our days and evenings full.

Nicole pops her head into my office around five o'clock. "Do you want to head downstairs with me?"

I debate whether I should go. I want to, but I still have work to do, and I'm dead tired. "I don't know. I have two briefs to finish."

"OK. I'll give you a half hour. But you're coming. Plenty of people still want to meet the new girl."

I can't argue with that.

Nicole and I head downstairs at five thirty, and things are already in full swing. She introduces me to more people, and I end up bonding with her friend Courtney, who works on our automotive account.

"You're so lucky," she tells me. "I'd kill to get on a beauty account."

"Believe me, it wasn't always so glamorous for me. When I was an intern, my first account was for fertilizer, and then I moved up to a wireless provider."

"Sounds like fun," she says sarcastically.

"Tell me about it. Try coming up with a unique campaign for a commodity when the client wants to simply focus on plan features. Then I got a job at an agency that was looking to fill an account executive role on the KandE account."

"I've heard of them," Courtney says. "They make tween nail and cosmetics products. My niece is a big fan."

"It was a really fun account to work on. Even though the target consumers were younger, the job paved the way for me to get into beauty. What about you? How long have you worked at the agency?"

"Two years, both on automotives."

"Then you should be up for rotation soon."

"Yep. I'm keeping my ears open for any new business wins."

"At least you work on a luxury car account. That must be nice."

"True," Courtney says, "but all I can show for it is a free car wash, and I don't even have a car. What about you? Do you have any product samples I can test out?"

"You're in luck. A shipment actually came this morning. Stop by my office next week, and I'll give you some."

"Thanks, I'm a total beauty-product junkie."

As we're talking, Ross walks by and gives Courtney a curt nod. A look of distaste crosses her face. I think back to what Nicole told me; I believe he works in our finance department and is a close friend of Jake's.

"What? You're not a fan of Ross?" I ask.

"Not particularly."

"Why's that?"

She rolls her eyes. "He hasn't hit on you yet?"

"No, should I be offended?"

She laughs and shakes her head. "I guess he can't help it. He's one of the few straight men in a sea of eligible ladies. He's hooked up with more people here than I can count, but he always manages to end things in a way that's to his advantage."

"What do you mean?"

"I can't explain it, but somehow he sweet-talks his way out of things and ends up remaining on good terms with each girl afterward."

"I guess he has to, or he'd have a lot of enemies at this agency."

"Let me tell you, he's one smooth talker. Watch your back."

"Thanks for the tip," I tell her.

"I take it you're single?"

I nod. "What about you?"

"I've been dating someone for about three months. It's just reached the point where we're not seeing other people."

"That sounds promising."

"I hope so," she says, but I can't help notice how her eyes search out Ross. I have a feeling she was one of his victims and hasn't gotten over it. I'll have to ask Nicole for details later.

After a while I decide to mingle and make my way over to Michelle. I haven't really gotten to talk to her outside of work. She's always so serious around me, so I try to get her to open up. Now that she's had a few drinks, my efforts seem to be working. She tells me about her boyfriend and how she's annoyed that they just bought a place together but he hasn't proposed.

"Maybe he has something in the works," I offer.

"I don't know. I probably shouldn't have agreed to move in with him."

"Give it a try, and see how things go. If he's willing to live with you, he's obviously willing to make a commitment."

"That, or he just wants cheaper rent," she says, laughing. "What about you? Have you ever lived with someone?"

I haven't told anyone at work about my situation, but I don't want to lie. "Yes, when I was in New York."

"Oh, did he move here with you?" I shake my head. "Sorry. I didn't know."

"It's OK. Why would you?"

Nicole approaches us and asks why we look so somber. "I hope you're not talking about work," she says.

"No, we're talking about our relationships."

"Oh, good. Anyway, I could use a change of scenery. Let's take this party elsewhere."

I look at my watch. It's already six forty-five, and I realize I haven't had dinner. "Do you mind if we get something to eat first?"

"The guys just ordered a bunch of appetizers. Go share with them."

I'd rather not eat greasy bar food, but I don't want to drink on an empty stomach. I make my way over to their table and see that Jake's there. "Hey, Lexi. Have some," he says, motioning to the food. He introduces me to the other guys at the table, and one of them offers me a buffalo wing. My eyes water because it's so spicy.

"I like a girl who can eat wings," says Ross.

I'm about to make a surly reply, but I hold my tongue. Fortunately the waitress comes by with a plate of sliders and sweet potato fries. I can deal with that. After we eat, I ask if I can help with the bill. I get a resounding no.

Nicole comes over and says, "OK, where are we going next?" Someone throws out the name of a karaoke bar, and everyone gets excited about this idea. I'd rather die than sing karaoke.

"I think I'm going to head home," I say.

"Come on, Lexi. You can't eat and run," says Ross.

"I don't do karaoke."

"Well, you can watch us make fools of ourselves. Let's go."

Reluctantly I follow them. I figure I'll hang out for a song or two then make my escape.

We head into the bar, and it's packed. Then we find a table near the back and place our drink orders. Someone also ordered a round of shots, so I decide it's a good thing I don't have to be up early tomorrow. Two kamikazes later, all the girls decide to go up and sing "I Will Survive."

"Come on, Lexi," says Nicole, taking me by the hand.

What the hell? At least I'll be in a big group. We sing the song, and it's actually quite fun. A couple of the guys go up to put their names on the list, and I notice Jake has stayed behind.

"Not into karaoke?" I ask him.

"Definitely not my thing," he says, shaking his head.

"Me either, but I still did it."

"Well, then you won't mind doing it again."

"Nope, once is enough."

He inclines his head toward the stage. "I think they just said your name."

"What?" Sure enough, a voice is calling me to come up on stage. "Someone must have put my name on the list."

"That they did. It's a Hartman and Taylor inauguration ritual. Here," he says, handing me another shot.

I down it and, mortified, make my way to the stage. Cheap Trick's "I Want You to Want Me" starts up. I'm grateful my college roommate's boyfriend was into eighties music. At least it's a song I know and like. If I'm going to do this, I figure I'll put on a show. Even if I can't sing, I can dance. Everyone is cheering for me, and I get really into it. Then some guy gets up onstage with me, so I serenade him. Who knew I could karaoke?

When the song ends, I walk back to the group, and everyone applauds. I catch Jake's eye and he's watching me with an unreadable expression, which I find unnerving.

"Why didn't anyone warn me?" I ask.

Courtney throws her arms around me. "Every newbie has to sing that song. Hands down, that was the best rendition I've heard yet."

"That's great. I just hope it doesn't show up on YouTube." Then I look at Jake and say, "Your turn."

I'm parched, so I walk over to the bar to get some water. While I'm waiting, the guy I serenaded approaches me. He's wearing a very tight shirt and conveniently has left the top buttons undone.

"Hi. I'm Tony. What's your name?"

"Lexi."

"Lexi, that was some dance you did there. You can show me those moves any time."

"Thanks," I say, attempting to walk away.

"Hey, what's the rush? You sure seemed interested when you were dancing with me onstage," he says, grabbing my arm.

At that moment, Jake walks over. "Is there a problem?" he asks, looking at me.

I don't want him to think I can't take care of myself, so I say, "No. It's nothing I can't handle."

Tony looks at Jake, sizing him up. "What's it to you?"

"She's with me," Jake says, placing a protective hand on my shoulder. I'm acutely aware of his touch and the feel of his warm hand against my bare skin.

"Dude, you're a lucky man. She's smokin' hot." He looks back at me and says, "Nice meeting you, Lexi. I hope you'll sing for us again."

As we make our way back to the group, I say to Jake, "Thank you. You didn't have to do that. You're lucky he was so agreeable."

"Lexi, that guy was totally shady. And don't worry—I could have easily taken him on if I had to, but I figured he couldn't put up much of an argument if he thought you were with me."

"That's true, but I owe you one."

He looks thoughtful and leans into me. "Maybe someday I'll find a way for you to repay me."

My face grows hot. It seems like there's innuendo in his comment, but perhaps my judgment is clouded from a few too many cocktails. Feeling bold, I ask him to dance.

"This kind of place isn't really my scene," he says. "Perhaps some other time."

I try to downplay my embarrassment. "So you won't dance, and you won't do karaoke. I made a fool of myself up there. The least you can do is return the favor."

Before Jake has a chance to reply, a girl bumps into him, spilling her drink on his shirt. She apologizes and offers to pay for his dry cleaning, which he refuses.

"You should put some club soda on it," I tell him. "I'll go get some." I walk over to the bar before giving him a chance to reply. When I return, he starts to protest, but I tell him it'll help prevent the stain from setting. I lightly place my hand on his shirt and dab at the spot with a napkin, taking in his well-sculpted chest beneath my fingers. I do my best to ignore how nice his body feels as I work. "There. It looks like I got most of it."

I meet his gaze, and he's staring at me with an intense expression. "Thanks," he says in a husky voice. "Here. Let me have the rest of that." He takes the club soda from my hand, brushing his fingers against mine, and I shiver as a spark of energy passes between us. I fumble to come up with something to say, but I'm saved by Nicole, who walks over and informs us she's leaving.

"Are you coming, Lexi?"

"Yes, I'll be with you in a few." I turn my attention back to Jake. "Looks like you're off the hook."

"I guess we're even then," he says.

"I guess so."

I find myself wanting to stay. I look at Jake, imploring him to ask me to, but he doesn't.

Instead he smirks and says, "Thanks for the show."
"Glad you enjoyed it. Have a great weekend."
"You too, Lexi."
I walk out into the night, feeling more hopeful than I have in a long time.

CHAPTER FIVE

It's been about a month since I've started at Hartman & Taylor. I'm fully immersed in the business and just sold my first campaign. I'll be traveling next month on a photo shoot to Paris. I love my job! Granted, I'll be working most of the time, but I'm hoping I'll be able to do some sightseeing. When I traveled Europe after I graduated, I never made it to Paris, but it's a destination that's at the top of my list. I call Liv from work to tell her the news.

"Get out! Can I come with you?"

"Seriously, you could if you can get away. You'd get free lodging."

"Lex, I'd love to. I'm sure the tickets are super expensive, though."

"I'll look up airfares and let you know. Do you have miles?"

"I do, but I'm saving them—just in case."

I know she's referring to her honeymoon. She and Jason probably will get engaged soon. "Save them. You can go to Paris with Jason."

"Can you imagine? What a romantic honeymoon that would be."

I actually wanted to go to Paris for my honeymoon, but Ben couldn't get that much time off work. We were planning to go to Hawaii instead. After Liv and I hang up, I scour the web for cheap flights to Paris but don't find any. I text Liv the news and tell her I'll keep looking. I hear a knock on my office door, and it's Michelle. "I'm heading downstairs for happy hour. You coming?" I'm tempted by the thought of seeing Jake, but I've spent a lot of late nights at the office this week preparing for our campaign presentation. "I think I'll pass today. Have a great weekend." I'm looking forward to a night of relaxation and getting caught up on my TV shows. Having a backlog stresses me out.

The next morning I get a call from my friend Brian. He's been bugging me to see him since I've been back in town. We've been friends forever, since we were in grade school. Liv always thought we'd get together, but he's like a brother to me. I never could look at him in a romantic light. He wants to know if I can meet for brunch. I don't have much going on, so I agree. He recently moved to Lincoln Park, and we decide to meet in his neighborhood so I can see his new apartment. I take the El to the Fullerton stop and walk the familiar route to his place. It's right by Clark and Fullerton, not far from where I used to live. He opens the door to greet me and gives me a big hug.

"You look great, Lexi," he says, studying me. "Perfect as always."

"And you look terrible," I say. He laughs. "Seriously, you look really good," I tell him.

He's grown out his hair, and he's tanner. Something else is different, but I can't quite put my finger on it. His apartment is nice, with a great view of the lake. He shows me around, and then we then head to brunch. People are milling about on this beautiful spring day that feels more like summer. We weave through the crowd and make our way to the restaurant, which is packed. There's a short wait, but luckily we get a table outside. He fills me in on what he's been up to, and I do the same. He asks if I've spoken to Ben, and I tell him no.

"Lexi," he says, "don't you think you ought to talk to him?"

"No," I reply tersely. "I have nothing to say."

"I just thought it might help you get some closure—you know, understand what happened and why."

"What's to understand? He cheated on me with someone I thought was a friend. I'm not sure any explanation would help me feel better." Suddenly I'm suspicious. "Did he put you up to this?" They became good friends when Ben and I were together and used to hang out a lot.

"No," he says. "He's called me a few times to see if I've heard from you, but that's it. I swear."

"I believe you," I reassure him.

"I just want to see you happy. Are you dating anyone?"

"No, I'm not ready."

Brian nods. "Don't rush it. You'll know when the time comes."

I hope so. Then I ask him about his love life. Turns out he's been seeing someone for the past month, and he seems really into her. I'm very happy for him. Brian's a good guy but hasn't had the best of luck with relationships. He's such a sweetheart, and I think he always fit into the "friend" role. When I was younger, I didn't like nice guys. I always was attracted to the bad boys who inevitably would break my heart. I told him that once we were older and wiser, girls would be knocking down his door. There comes a point when you realize you want the nice guy.

"I'd like to meet her sometime," I tell him.

"We'll see how things go. If we're still dating in a few weeks, we could all meet up," he says.

"I'd like that."

Much to my protest, he pays for brunch. We walk back toward his place and I hear someone call my name. I turn around, and it's Jake walking with an adorable little girl. I'm struck by their strong resemblance and wonder about the nature of their relationship. She has golden-brown hair, big blue eyes, and a smattering of freckles on her nose. She crosses her arms over her Hello Kitty shirt, and I get the feeling she isn't happy about the interruption.

"Hi, Lexi. This is my niece, Hailey," he says. "Hailey, this is Lexi. We work together."

Feeling relieved, I bend down and shake her hand. "Nice to meet you," I say. "And this is my friend, Brian."

Brian and Jake shake hands, and Brian gives Hailey a little wave. "Well, it was nice meeting you both," says Brian. Then he looks at me and says, "I'm going to take off, OK?"

"Sure. Go ahead."

"Thanks for coming my way. Take care, Lexi," he says, as he envelops me in a big hug.

I turn back to Jake and Hailey. "I love your light-up shoes," I tell her. "Do you think they make them in my size?"

She regards me for a moment then says, "No, you're too big."

"Oh, that's too bad. Where are you guys off to?" I ask.

"We're going to the zoo," Hailey says.

"Oh, the zoo, I love the zoo!"

"Really? What's your favorite animal?"

I think for a minute then reply, "The monkeys. I love the monkey house."

"Me too," she says. "My favorites are the penguins."

"The penguins are great. Have you ever seen the zookeepers feed them?" She looks at me with big eyes and shakes her head. "Well, hopefully you'll get a chance to see them today." I look at Jake and say, "It's nice of you to take your niece to the zoo."

"My sister is pregnant and could use the break. Besides, I love spending time with my favorite niece," he says, smiling at her.

Could he be any cuter? "Well, have fun."

"Will you come with us?" Hailey asks.

"Hailey," says Jake, "I'm sure Lexi has plans." He looks at me, and I tell him I was just going to go to the gym.

"But what if I have to go to the bathroom?" Hailey asks Jake.

"I'll take you," he says.

"But then we'll have to go in the men's room," she says, pouting.

"She makes a fair point," Jake tells me.

I try to read the situation. I can't tell whether he really wants me to come or whether he's trying to placate Hailey. The thought of spending an afternoon with Jake is rather tempting, so I say, "I'll tell you what, how about I come with you for a little while?"

"Yeah!" says Hailey.

The three of us head toward Lincoln Park Zoo. I'm glad I wore something suitable for walking around in—a striped maxi dress and Tory Burch flip-flops.

"You look different," says Jake.

"Probably because I'm not in heels."

"That's it," he replies. "You definitely look shorter."

"Thanks," I say sarcastically. "Where do you want to start?" I ask Hailey as we approach the zoo.

"The penguin house," she says.

Hailey leads the way, and we go inside. We're watching the penguins through the glass when a zookeeper enters the exhibit. "Lexi!" Hailey shouts. "Look! She's going to feed the penguins!" The zookeeper tosses fish, and Hailey watches, fascinated. "I'm so glad you got a chance to see," I say, kneeling beside her. I look at Jake, and he's watching me, but I can't read his expression. Embarrassed, I look away.

I wonder whether I should go, but Jake hasn't said anything, and I'm having a really good time. We walk through some more exhibits, and then Hailey says she wants to get a snack.

"How about ice cream?" asks Jake.

"Yes," she says. "I want ice cream."

We find a vendor selling cones. "Lexi, do you want one?" Jake asks.

"Yes, I'll have chocolate please."

"Me too," says Hailey.

Jake also gets one for himself, and we find a bench. "It's refreshing to see a girl eating ice cream," he says.

I'm not sure how to take his comment, but I'm guessing he means it as a compliment. "I have a sweet tooth," I tell him. "Chocolate is my vice."

"I'd never guess," he says, looking at me.

"Why do you think I'm headed to the gym later?" I tease him. "Life's too short not to eat dessert."

"I couldn't agree more," says Hailey.

We all laugh. "What about you?" I ask Jake. "What's your vice?"

He thinks for a minute. "Coffee. I need at least three cups a day to function. And beautiful women," he adds, looking right at me. I blush, although I don't know if it's a compliment. He didn't say *I* was beautiful.

"Will you braid my hair?" Hailey asks after we've finished our cones.

"Sure. Do you want a French braid?"

"No, I want it like yours."

I'm wearing my hair down with a headband braid at the crown. I rummage in my purse and produce a brush. I braid Hailey's hair then show her the end result in my compact.

"I love it! Don't I look pretty like Lexi?" she asks, turning to Jake.

"Yes, you look very pretty."

Hailey smiles at her reflection then says, "I have to use the bathroom."

"Let's go look for one," I tell her.

"Wait," says Jake. "Give me your cell number, just in case."

We exchange contact information, and I'm secretly pleased I have his number. We return a few minutes later, and Jake says we have time for one last exhibit.

"I want to go on the merry-go-round," Hailey informs us.

"OK, let's go," says Jake.

We head toward the merry-go-round, and I offer to take their picture. "Here, give me your phone," I tell him.

"Just use yours and text it to me," he says, as he tries to keep up with Hailey, who's determined to ride on the panda. Once she's seated, I take their photo and send it to him, but I can't bring myself to delete it.

We head back toward the entrance.

"Where do you live?" I ask Jake.

"Not that far from here—in a brownstone on Orchard. But my sister is picking us up at the entrance. It's a bit of a long walk for Hales."

"Well," I say, "it was so nice to meet you, Hailey. Thanks for letting me spend the afternoon with you."

"Wait, I'll drive you home," Jake offers.

"That's not necessary. I can take the El."

"Really, it's no problem."

For some reason, I hesitate. The thought of being alone with him makes me nervous.

"Come on," he says, "It's the least I can do. My sister has an SUV so we can all fit."

"OK," I agree, because I don't want to make a big deal out of a simple gesture. I wonder if he'll invite me in. Jake's sister pulls up a few minutes later. She's very pretty, with light-brown hair and the same icy-blue eyes.

"Kate, this is Lexi. Lexi, this is my sister, Kate."

"Hi," I say as I climb into the car.

"Lexi and I work together," Jake says. "We ran into each other on the way to the zoo, and Hales insisted she come along."

Kate laughs. "Hailey can be very persuasive."

We chat on the short drive home. I ask Kate when she's due and she tells me November, which I'm guessing puts her at about twelve weeks.

"Are you going to find out the sex?" I ask her.

"No, we want to be surprised. How about you? Do you have any children?"

"No, but I adore kids. I have a nephew who's a little younger than Hailey."

"I'm four and a half," she says from the backseat.

"That's old," I tell her.

"Do you see him often?" Kate asks.

"Well, I was living in New York until recently. But now that I'm back, I'm going to try to see him at least twice a month. I need to get my fix. It's so nice to see the world through his eyes. Everything is fun and games."

Kate nods. "It's fun, but it's also exhausting."

We pull up in front of Jake's place.

"It was nice to meet you, Lexi," says Kate.

"Bye, Lexi!" says Hailey from the backseat. "Thanks for coming with me to the zoo."

"Anytime," I tell her. "It was fun."

"I just need to grab my keys," Jake says after Kate drives away. "Come on in. I'll give you a tour."

Jake's place is fabulous. It's a three-story townhouse with huge windows and lots of sunlight. It has a vintage charm, yet it's been updated, and it has a nice contemporary feel. He shows me around, starting with the kitchen. It has white cabinets with black granite countertops, stainless-steel appliances, and a beautiful glass tile backsplash accented by sage green walls. An island with hanging glass pendants separates it from the family room, which has black leather couches and a large plasma TV mounted above the fireplace that's finished in the same tiles as the kitchen.

"I love your place," I tell him as we walk upstairs. "Did you decorate it yourself?"

"No. Kate helped me."

I'm relieved he didn't say it was an ex-girlfriend. The second level has two bedrooms and two bathrooms. He shows me the master, with its huge king-size bed, and I wonder how many women he's taken here. I push the thought from my mind. "Here. You'll like this." He shows me his immaculate walk-in closet, which looks like something out of a California Closets ad. I look around in awe and decide it's larger than my first apartment.

"Can I move in?" I ask. Jake gives me a funny look. "Just kidding. Haven't you lived with anyone before?"

"No, you?"

"Yes," I say, but I don't elaborate.

We walk up to the third floor, which is a loft he's turned into a den. It's a guy's space with a deep couch and two black leather recliners, a big flat-screen TV, and a small bar complete with a fridge.

"I bet you're popular on game days," I remark.

"Pretty much," he says. "I'm a huge sports fan and love having the guys over."

"What's your favorite sport to watch?"

"Basketball, but football is a very close second."

"I like football too. But only if the Wolverines are playing."

"That seems to be the sentiment of most people who go to U of M."

"It must be in our DNA." I look around at his memorabilia and spy a photo of him in a team uniform. "Did you play any sports in high school?"

"Basketball and golf. You?"

"Tennis and dance."

"Were you any good?"

"I was on the varsity tennis team all four years," I tell him. "I wasn't outstanding, but I was pretty good. I spent most of my summers at tennis camp. Do you play?"

"I've never had formal lessons, but I'm not bad."

"Well, then I'm challenging you to a match."

He looks at me for a moment and hesitates. "I'm usually pretty busy on the weekends. Come on, I'll drive you home."

I feel like an idiot for suggesting it. We just had such a nice time today, and he seemed to be dropping hints that he was interested. Maybe I read the whole situation wrong. He opens the garage and unlocks his car. It's a black, two-door BMW convertible.

"Nice car," I tell him.

"Thanks." He smiles. "I bought it when I was promoted to vice president. I figured I'd been working hard and should treat myself."

I get in, and he pulls out of his garage. "Aren't you going to put the top down?" I ask.

"You're OK with that?"

"Of course. It's a beautiful day."

"I wasn't sure. Most girls are concerned about their hair getting messed up."

I put on my sunglasses and enjoy the sensation of the wind blowing through my hair as he speeds down Lake Shore Drive. "Take the Oak Street exit," I tell him. I give him directions to my building, and he pulls up in front. Suddenly I feel awkward. It's not a date, but I don't know what to say. Fortunately Jake goes first.

"Thanks for joining us. I'm sure you hadn't planned on spending your day with a four-year-old."

"No problem. It was fun. I hadn't been to the zoo in a long time."

"Any big plans for tonight?"

"Well, I'm off to Zumba now then drinks with friends later."

"Zumba," he says. "Isn't that like Latin dancing?

"Yeah, it's a Latin-inspired dance fitness program. I'm not one for lifting weights or running. I like doing classes, especially anything that involves dance."

"Yes, I saw that," he says with a smirk. I feel myself redden and ask him about his plans for the evening. "Just a typical Saturday night out," he responds.

I want to ask him what that entails, but judging by his vague answer, I don't think he wants to tell me. I thank him for the ride and wave as he drives away. I let out a deep sigh as the realization hits me: I definitely have a crush on Jake Hartman.

CHAPTER SIX

I poke my head in Nicole's office on Monday morning.
"How was your weekend?" I ask her.
"Great," she says. "I went out with Danny."
I rack my brain. "Remind me—which one is Danny?" Nicole is always going out with some new guy; it's hard to keep up.
"He's the one I met at the gym."
"Right. How was it?" She goes on to tell me he took her to a trendy new restaurant, where she ran into someone else she's currently seeing. "Was it awkward?" I ask her.
"Actually, I was glad. It makes me look more desirable."
I laugh. "That's a good perspective."
"So," Nicole says, changing the subject, "have you read *Fifty Shades* yet?"
"Not yet, but it's on my list."
"I just started reading it this weekend, and I'm almost done. You can borrow mine."
"You're almost done? Isn't it like five hundred pages?"
"Yes, but trust me, it's a fast read. You've got to read it—it's life changing."
"Really?"
"Yes, really.
"OK, just let me know when you're done."
Nicole gives me the book the next day. I give her an amused look. "I told you, life changing," she says. I read it on my commute home, attempting to hide the cover. So far I don't see what all the hype is about. I stay up the next night reading and finally get to the good stuff. I see what Nicole means; I can't put it down. I usually don't take a lunch break, but I'm so

engrossed in the book that I decide to sit outside the next day. I head toward the Wrigley Building and find a grassy spot overlooking the river. I don't want anyone reading over my shoulder, so I try to find a somewhat secluded area. This proves to be difficult during lunchtime on a beautiful day. Then I see a large planter that can serve as a bench right near the water. It's perfect. I watch as an architectural cruise boat goes by—I've never been on one and realize I should take advantage of everything Chicago has to offer. As I take in the picturesque backdrop, I resolve to take a lunch break more often.

I'm in the middle of a steamy sex scene when a shadow blocks my sun. I look up and see Jake.

"Hey," I say, startled. "What are you doing here?"

"I was on my way back from a client meeting and saw you. Whatcha reading?"

I'm embarrassed but don't want to lie because he can probably read the cover. "*Fifty Shades of Grey.*"

He smirks. "How is it?"

"It's…" I pause, searching for the right word. "…enlightening."

"I just don't get it. What's all the hype about?"

"Let's put it this way: It's more descriptive than anything I've ever read. Wanna take a look? Maybe you could learn a thing or two," I say, feigning innocence.

"Trust me, Lexi. I don't need a book to teach me anything. I'm doing just fine on my own."

"I'll take your word for it," I say, "unless you want to prove it to me."

"I can have a contract drawn up tomorrow."

"Bring it on, Hartman."

He regards me with interest. "Tell me, would any girl ever really agree to such a thing?"

"You know the premise then?" He nods. "Jake, if there really was a Christian Grey, believe me, I'd sign anything he asked me to without hesitation."

Jake looks at me, surprised. Then he turns serious. "Lexi, any guy would be very lucky to have you." Our conversation is interrupted by Darrien, who works in our media division.

"Hey, Jake, Lexi. You're looking fine as always."

"Thanks," I tell him. "You too. You've been working out, I see."

He gives me a very satisfied smile. "That I have. So what are you two discussing?"

Jake looks at me. "We were talking about Lexi's taste in books."

I narrow my eyes at him.

"Oh, what are you reading?"

"*Fifty Shades of Grey.*"

He gets a big grin and says, "I'd be your Christian Grey anytime. You have a need, you call me."

I laugh. "I'll keep that in mind." I'm not offended by his comment; he's actually a really good guy.

Darrien turns to Jake. "I've been meaning to talk to you. Do you have a minute?"

"Sure. I'll head back with you. Enjoy your book, Lexi."

"Oh, I will," I reply. As they walk away, I reflect on our conversation. I'm on cloud nine.

The feeling, however, is short-lived. I come back to the office, and there's an issue with Pierre, the photographer we wanted to book for the shoot—rather, the photographer Natalia insisted we use for the shoot. He is now slated to be out of the country and won't be available. I tell Natalia we can have new choices to her within a few days, but she won't hear of it. She wants to postpone the photo shoot until we can find a timeframe that works for the photographer. I tell her we need to rework our timeline to see what it'll do to our launch date. My dreams of going to Paris fade before my eyes. Michelle reworks the timeline to accommodate the photographer's schedule and shows it to me. It's extremely tight, and we'd need the sun, moon, and stars to align to make it work. It's doable, but it gives us no wiggle room in the event something goes wrong, and inevitably it will. I find Matt to discuss a plan of action. I really like having him as my creative counterpart because he has a maturity and quiet sensibility about him. We both agree that we need to find another photographer. Now that we know the kind of style Natalia is looking for, we can find a suitable alternative. I e-mail her and say we're working on a revised timeline, along with a few other options, so she can make an informed decision. We set up a conference call for Wednesday afternoon.

Over the next day or so, Matt works closely with Kim, our art buyer, and strides into my office with a triumphant expression. "We got it," he tells me. "John Paul is my recommendation." He shows me a portfolio from a local French-American photographer that has the romantic style Natalia is looking for; plus he has experience with beauty brands. He has some shots that look to be the European countryside, but Matt tells me they were shot in his studio, and he creates the background effects in postproduction.

"You're kidding," I exclaim. "How did you find him?"

"Kim used him at her previous agency and said he's great."

"Let me talk to Kim about pricing, but given that we're eliminating travel costs, I can't imagine him coming in higher than Pierre."

Kim e-mails me an estimate later that afternoon; it's one-third the cost of the original shoot. I have Matt pull some photography samples, and we put together a presentation with our new recommendation. On a hunch, I ask Kim to have John Paul available during our call in case Natalia wants to speak with him. I talked to him yesterday, and he was very reassuring. I got the sense he totally understands what we're looking to accomplish.

We call Natalia at our scheduled time on Wednesday. We start out by having Michelle share the new schedule and assure her that while it's doable, it won't allow room for any rework. Natalia is very agreeable and says she wants to proceed. "That's great," I say, "but we have one more option. I'm e-mailing it to you now." Once she receives the file, Matt goes through a brief bio of the photographer and shares some of the samples that capture the essence of our campaign.

"What do you think?" I ask her.

"His style is very nice."

"Yes, we thought so too. Plus he's one-third the cost of Pierre." Now I know we have her. "He's available right now if you'd like us to conference him in. Perhaps it would give you a greater comfort level if you could speak with him."

"Yes, that is a very good idea."

We patch him in, and he's very charming. He totally wins over Natalia, and she gives us permission to book him. As much as I'm upset about not going to Paris, I'm thrilled we've found an alternative that will make our timeline work. The last thing I need is for everyone to be stressed, because it always ends up compromising the work. I thank everyone for their flexibility and help in finding a solution. Then I go back to my office and shoot Morgan an e-mail with an update. For the most part, she lets me be autonomous, but I like to loop her in when any potential issues may arise. She e-mails me back, thanking me for following up and for finding a solution that will keep the project moving forward. I text Liv that Paris is out, and she replies with a sad-face emoticon. I do intend to get there, someday.

I spend the next few days focused on lining things up for the shoot. We need to find talent and a stylist and decide on looks for wardrobe. At least we no longer have to scout locations. Our first priority is casting a model for the print ad. Natalia wants to use the same talent for TV and print to establish a consistent look for the campaign. We've agreed on a dark-haired brunette of ambiguous ethnicity with blue eyes and fair skin. She should have somewhat of an ethereal quality, although we can accomplish a lot of that in hair and makeup. The decision is ultimately Natalia's, but Matt and I will work closely with her to make sure we're comfortable with the decision. We've been at it all morning. The plan is to make a clear yes or no decision for each girl then narrow down the yeses. So far there are only a handful of girls in that pile. Natalia has a very discerning eye, and Matt is very picky. I understand the importance of getting it right—this campaign will be the first impression US consumers have of the Lumineux brand. I watch as each model receives instructions then poses accordingly for her shot. It's amazing how some of them look so average when they walk in, yet they transform themselves in front of the camera.

During a ten-minute break, I head outside to check my messages. The conference room is freezing, and I want to warm up. It's a beautiful day, so I take off my jacket and enjoy the sensation of the warm sun on my skin. I'm wearing a satin halter tank that has a bold floral pattern, along with white fitted boot-cut pants. I mindlessly tie my hair into a loose knot while I play my messages. I spy Jake walking into the office, carrying his lunch.

"Hey, Jake," I call out to him.

"Lexi, I didn't recognize you."

"It's the hair," I say, once again letting it fall around my shoulders.

He studies me for a minute and says, "It's not the hair. It's the pants. You usually wear skirts or dresses."

"Oh, I guess I do," I reply, surprised that he noticed.

"Are you in the casting meeting?"

"Yes. We're on a break."

"How's it going?"

"It's going well. We've seen a few possibilities, but I'm still waiting for someone to wow me. We'll be starting up again in a few minutes—I'll head upstairs with you."

"After you," he says, motioning for me to go first through the revolving doors.

"What's your take on revolving doors?" I ask, as we're waiting for the elevators.

"My take on it?" he says, confused.

"I mean from an etiquette standpoint. I've heard mixed ideas about it. One philosophy is that the guy should go first so he can push the door, and the other is that he should allow the girl to go first, as is customary."

"I've never thought about it. I guess I've always had it engrained in my head that ladies go first, so I think that's the safer bet. Some girls may get offended if you push the door for them. What do you think?"

"I agree with you. I don't mind guys having nice manners, but I don't want them doing something because they think I can't do it for myself. And I'm definitely capable of pushing my own door."

The elevator opens to our floor, and we part ways. "Good luck with the rest of your meeting. I hope you find someone who wows you," Jake says.

I already have, I think as I watch his retreating back.

By Friday I'm ready for the weekend to begin. Tomorrow is my volunteer day at the children's hospital. I applied for a position there shortly after I moved back. I love kids, and it breaks my heart to see anyone that young experience any kind of pain. I wanted to do something that would allow me to help them with the healing process, and in a way, it's helped me heal too. I primarily work in the outpatient clinic, interacting with patients and their siblings in the waiting areas. I get to help them with art projects, games, reading—essentially anything to keep them entertained and their spirits up. Occasionally I get to help out in a one-on-one capacity, which I enjoy because I get to form more of a bond with the patients.

I wake up early on Saturday morning and head to the hospital. As it turns out, I'll be visiting the infant and toddler rooms today because their regularly scheduled volunteer has come down with the flu. I pick up some crayons and construction paper from the nurses' station and make my rounds. I typically only stop in rooms that have the door open. I'm about to pass one, but I hear the sound of laughter coming from inside. I lightly knock and am greeted with "Come in!" I poke my head around the curtain and see a sweet-looking little girl lying in bed, laughing at an episode of *Curious George*. Her mother appears to be asleep on the sofa.

"Hi. I'm Lexi. I just came by to introduce myself and see if you could help me with something."

"What?" she asks curiously.

"I need to make a picture for my nephew's birthday, but I don't know how to draw."

"What kind of picture?"

"I don't know. He likes fish and dinosaurs, so maybe something with one of those."

"I can help you," she informs me.

"Great. Thanks. I have some crayons and paper here. What's your name?"

"Molly."

"That's a pretty name. How old are you, Molly?"

"Three."

"Well, in your opinion, which do you think my nephew would like better?"

"I think the dinosaur. I'm going to draw a T. rex."

"That would be perfect."

I sit as Molly draws the picture. She is very animated and asks me a lot of questions. I'm careful not to ask her about her diagnosis, but she offers it to me.

"I'm here because my body has a bug. It's not supposed to be there so the doctors had to take it out."

"Oh, no. That's too bad. I hope you get better soon."

"Me too, but I have a secret."

"What's that?"

"I'll get better because I have superpowers."

"You know, I thought there was something special about you. What's your superpower?"

"I have superhuman strength. I'm just here because the doctors say I have to stay. Otherwise I'd go home."

"Do you have any brothers or sisters who live at your house with you?"

"I have a big sister. She's five."

"Well, I bet she comes and visits a lot."

"She does, and she brings me treats," she says.

"That's very nice of her. Sisters are special friends. I have sisters too."

"You do? What are their names?"

"The older one is named Julia, but I call her "Jules" for short, and my younger sister is named Tara."

"I like that. My sister's name is Emma. She's coming by to see me later. She had to go to a birthday party this morning. I wish I could go to a birthday party," she says with a forlorn expression that tugs at my heart.

"When's your birthday?"

"May twenty-fifth."

"That's coming up soon. Maybe you can have a party for your birthday."

"But what if I'm still here?" Molly asks.

"Well, that doesn't mean you can't have a party. Everyone can bring the party to you."

She seems excited about that. I see her mom stirring and realize I should make my way to see other patients. I briefly introduce myself and tell her that Molly and I have been chatting and that she's a delightful little girl. She and Molly thank me for stopping by.

"Will you come again?" Molly asks.

"Sure. I'm here about three times a month, so I'll stop by on my next visit."

"Thanks, Lexi. And I'm inviting you to my party."

"When is it?"

"May twenty-fifth."

"Oh," I say. "That makes sense. I'll be there."

On the way out, I put an appointment in my calendar to stop by and see Molly again. I make the rest of my rounds, and I'm about to head to the elevators when I hear someone call my name. I turn and see Molly's mom.

"Hi. I'm Rachelle. Thank you for spending time with Molly. She seems quite taken with you."

"It was my pleasure. She's a special girl. And I'd like to stop by on her birthday. Can I give you my number so you can let me know when it's a good time to come?"

"Sure. I hadn't thought about throwing her a party. Isn't that terrible? I've been so focused on her diagnosis because this is all so new—it's a lot to take in. Molly has leukemia and had to have a tumor removed. She'll start chemotherapy in a few weeks."

I don't know what to say as I hand her my phone number. "Well, I hope she's feeling better. She's a brave girl."

"She is." Rachelle smiles at me. "Anyway, I think a party is a wonderful idea. I just have to check with the doctors to make sure she can be around other kids once she starts her treatment."

"I understand. Please keep me posted, will you?"

"I certainly will. Take care, Lexi."

"You too."

On my walk home I think about Molly and her positive outlook in the face of adversity. I realize I could learn a lot from her. I pledge that I too will find my inner strength.

I'm feeling nostalgic after my visit with Molly. I call Jules and ask her if I can see Charlie tomorrow.

"Of course. He was just asking about you. Scott has some stuff to do around the house, so we'll come to the city. We could go to the Shedd."

"That would be great! Charlie loves the aquarium. Should I meet you there?"

"No. We'll pick you up. Is nine OK?"

"Sure. I don't have any big plans tonight."

"No hot date?"

"No hot date. Believe me, you'll be the first to know when I do."

"OK, see you tomorrow."

"See you."

I hang up and feel a bit better. I know Jules worries about me—my whole family does. They used to check in constantly, but at least that's somewhat subsided. I love my family, and I'm grateful to be close to them again, but sometimes I need my distance.

I wake up the next morning and grab a quick workout at the gym in my apartment building. I'm downstairs in the lobby by eight fifty. There's something to be said for going to bed early. When the car pulls up, Charlie spies me and waves enthusiastically. I hop into the backseat.

"Hi, Char. I've missed you!"

"Auntie Lex, guess where we're going."

"Where?"

"To the aquarium. I can't wait to see the sharks! Did you know there are more than three hundred and fifty different kinds?"

"I did not know that. When did you get to be such a smart kid?"

He shrugs and rattles off more facts until we arrive. The three of us walk in, and Charlie heads right for the huge Caribbean reef tank filled with sea turtles, eels, sharks and colorful fish of all sizes. He stands there mesmerized, even though he's seen it many times. We spend the morning exploring the various exhibits and decide to catch a dolphin show at eleven, followed by lunch. We eat at the in-house café so we'll have time to do some more exploring. Charlie is especially excited about the jellies, a special exhibit I haven't seen before. This time it's my turn to be mesmerized. By the time we get to the car, Charlie is passed out in his stroller.

"Looks like we've tired him out. Will he transfer?"

"He usually does," says Jules as she lifts him into his car seat.

On the ride home, I watch him sleeping peacefully. "Thanks for coming out this way today," I tell my sister. "I needed a hug from Charlie."

"Anytime. Did something happen?"

"Not really." I briefly tell her about Molly. "I guess it put things into perspective for me. As bad as my problems seem, I have my health and my family. I'm lucky for that."

"Yes, you are, but it doesn't diminish what you're going through. It's tough losing someone you love."

"I know, but when I think about the pain Molly's family must be experiencing, I feel bad wallowing in self-pity.

"I don't think you're wallowing—in fact just the opposite. I'm very proud of you and the way you've handled things. You've held your head up high and landed an awesome job, and you haven't lost your righteous indignation."

"What?" I ask sharply.

"Exactly," she says with a laugh. "I just mean you're still you. I love that you haven't let Ben get the best of you."

"I guess," I say somewhat skeptically.

"Believe me, when you're ready to date, you'll have the boys eating out of the palm of your hand."

"I highly doubt that."

"Just you wait. You'll see."

I sure hope she's right.

I wake up on Monday and feel achy all over. I chalk it up to a hard workout over the weekend and hop in the shower. I find myself sneezing all day at work, and my throat feels scratchy. I know the feeling all too well, but I don't have time to get sick. I must have caught something from being at the hospital; I'll have to up my vitamin regimen until I build my immunity. I rummage through my desk for some Tylenol. I take two and make it through the rest of the day. I sleep terribly that night even though I'm exhausted. In my career I've rarely taken a sick day, but I decide I'm not doing anyone any favors by going into the office. I send Morgan and my team an e-mail saying that I'm home sick and tell them to call my cell if they need anything. I scan my schedule to see which meetings I have planned and notice there's one with Joann, Jake's secretary, on the calendar. It's customary for her to meet with new hires to discuss their background and interests so she can add them to the new business database, a tool the agency uses to match talent to pitch opportunities. I was supposed to meet with her early on, but the meeting got postponed. I send her a note that I'm out sick and ask her to reschedule. I spend most of the day in bed; it's the most rest I've gotten in as long as I can remember.

The next morning I still feel like crap, so I decide to work from home, fully intending to be in the office tomorrow. But when I wake up the following day, my head feels like it's about to explode. I haven't seen my doctor since I moved back to Chicago, but the office is willing to fit me in with the nurse practitioner, which I'm glad about. I've known my doctor for years and don't want to go into any details about my personal life. During my appointment the nurse asks me about my symptoms and examines me. It turns out I have a sinus infection. She prescribes me antibiotics and assures me I should be feeling better within twenty-four hours.

"Do you think I can go back to work tomorrow?" I ask, feeling guilty for having stayed home three days.

"That's entirely up to you. But don't push it."

I get home, and there's an e-mail from Simon, saying word has it that I'm terribly ill. I e-mail him back and tell him not to be so dramatic; I hope to be back tomorrow. As I read through my other messages, my landline rings, interrupting me. It's Roland from the front desk of my apartment building, calling to tell me I have a delivery.

"I wasn't expecting anything. Do you know what it is?"

"Some guy just hand-delivered a bag from Cahan's Deli."

I go downstairs and peer into the bag. There's a challah roll and a white Styrofoam bowl that appears to contain soup. Puzzled, I go upstairs and empty the bag and find a note inside.

Heard you were sick. This is hands down the best chicken noodle soup and rivals anything you'll find in your New York delis. Feel better. —Jake

I put down the note and smile. He remembered our conversation from my interview. Joann must have told him I was sick. I taste the soup; it's delicious. I send Jake a text to thank him and admit that while the soup is up there, it's still a close second. I try not to read too much into the gesture, but I can't help think he doesn't go around sending soup to all of Hartman & Taylor's sick employees. Then again he really urged me to try Cahan's, so he could have seen it as an opportunity to do something nice for me. Or perhaps he *is* interested in me. This thought fills me with hope. Jake Hartman is just what the doctor ordered.

CHAPTER SEVEN

THE following week I have my first business trip. I'm going to a beauty trade show in Las Vegas that will offer a look at major trends to expect in cosmetics, hair, nails, and skin care. I've attended this event every year with a number of my coworkers, but Hartman & Taylor has opted to send me as its sole agency representative. I don't mind, because I know a lot of the vendors that will be there and already have received many dinner invitations. It's an action-packed three days filled with hundreds of exhibitors on the showroom floor, speeches from prominent industry leaders, and educational seminars on the latest in beauty. My nights are filled with cocktail hours and trips to the casino. On Thursday night, one of my old vendors invites me to see Cirque du Soleil's *O*, and I gladly accept. It's a spectacular show with unimaginable and breathtaking acts. I go clubbing with the group afterward, even though I have an early flight in the morning. I figure I can sleep on the plane; plus I made arrangements with Morgan to work from home because I had a feeling I'd need to recover. The timing isn't ideal because it's what would have been my bachelorette party weekend, and I have big plans. Originally I would have spent the weekend in the Hamptons with my girlfriends. Of course I cancelled the trip when I called off my engagement. Instead, Liv planned a girls' night out with my high school and college friends, and my best friend from New York, Jamie, is coming in. I'm so excited to have everyone I love in one place. I spend Friday afternoon putting together a presentation that captures what I learned from the trade show, along with the implications for our account. I take a nap and am out cold until I'm awoken by Liv coming home from work. We head to the airport to pick up Jamie and spend a low-key evening catching up in anticipation of our big night out tomorrow.

The next day my friends come to our apartment, and we spend the morning lounging by the pool. Liv informs us she made a lunch reservation at the Zodiac Room at Neiman Marcus, one of my favorite places. I haven't been in a long time and realize I was last there for one of my bridal showers. I try not to dwell on it; the purpose of this weekend is to have fun and get my mind off the would-have-been wedding festivities. We have a nice lunch followed by some shopping on Michigan Avenue. Afterward everyone comes back to our apartment, where we hang out until dinner. Liv made a reservation at Casa Maya, a fun, upscale Mexican restaurant that, ironically, is filled with bachelorette parties. I've never been, but I've wanted to try it. We order a round of their famous margaritas, and Liv makes a toast: "To Lexi…and new beginnings." "Cheers!" everyone says, as they clink glasses. I look around at my friends and feel grateful to have such an amazing support system. I've been dreading this weekend because it's a reminder of what could have been, but surprisingly I'm having a fabulous time. Then the waiter brings another round of drinks.

"We didn't order these," I say.

"It's from the gentleman by the bar," he tells me.

I look over, and a cute guy raises his glass to me.

"What should I do?" I ask Jamie. "Should I go thank him?"

"Definitely. He bought eleven drinks. That deserves a thank-you. I'll go with you."

We make our way through the crowd to the bar. The guy is standing there with a few of his friends. He looks to be in his early thirties and is better looking up close. He has short dark hair, brown eyes, and a goatee. I'm usually not a fan of facial hair, but he pulls it off. He's wearing jeans, a white T-shirt, and a black leather jacket. He has a cool, laidback vibe about him.

"Thanks so much for the drinks," I tell him.

"It was my pleasure. Are you ladies celebrating something?"

"No, just a girls' night out."

He extends a hand and introduces himself. "I'm Ian, and these are my friends, Blake and Aidan."

"I'm Lexi, and this is my friend, Jamie."

We all shake hands.

"Are you guys eating here or just getting drinks?" Jamie asks.

"We're having drinks while we wait for our table," Ian says. "We're waiting until one opens up next to you beautiful ladies."

Oh, he's quite the charmer. "Have you eaten here before?" I ask him.

"Nope, first time. You?"

"Same," I reply.

"So, Lexi, what do you do?"

"I work in advertising for Hartman and Taylor."

"Advertising, huh? Must be a pretty cool job."

I nod. "I love what I do, and I'm fortunate to work with a great group of people. What about you?"

"I'm a bond trader at the Chicago Board of Trade."

It's an impressive job, but I find it hard to ask him about it. I don't know the first thing about trading.

"So have you worked on any campaigns I would know?" Ian asks.

"I don't think you're my target audience. I've worked mostly on cosmetics and personal care accounts. My ads run in magazines like *Vogue* and *In Style*."

"Then you assumed right—I probably have not seen any of your ads."

"You don't strike me as the *Vogue* type."

I glance at Jamie, who's flirting with Blake. The hostess comes over and tells Ian and his friends that a table has opened up. I look back to where we're sitting, and sure enough, the table next to us has emptied. We walk back over, and I introduce the boys to my friends. I motion for Jill, Melanie, Sara, and Emily—my single friends—to come sit by me at the end. We spend the rest of our dinner talking as a group, and then we all agree to head over to Century Club next. Jill and I stop by the bathroom on the way out to freshen up.

"What do you think of Ian?" she asks me.

"He's cute and nice enough."

"But..." she says.

"There's no 'but.' I don't know him well enough to make a judgment." That's only half true. I usually can tell right away whether or not I click with someone. "What about you? Any of them catch your eye?"

"Blake is cute, but Jamie seems into him."

"I'll talk to her. She's only in town for the weekend, but you live here."

"Thanks," she tells me.

We all walk the few short blocks to Century Club, and there's a wait to get in. "I'll be right back," Liv says. She struts to the front of the line and talks with the guy at the door. I see her smile and gesture toward us. The guy shakes his head. She comes back over and tells us the girls are welcome but the guys have to wait.

"Go ahead," says Ian. "We'll meet you inside."

"Are you sure?" I ask him.

"Yeah, I don't want you standing in line on account of us."

I feel guilty, but we head upstairs. I'm not surprised to find that the place is packed mostly with girls. We head to the bar and grab some drinks. I know I'll be feeling it in the morning. I lost count of how many margaritas I had at the restaurant. Maybe four? I've toned down my partying since college because I like to be in control, but tonight is an exception. We find an empty couch in the corner and grab it. The place has a cool ambiance. It's very loungy, with a retractable glass roof that opens to the city skyline. We sit for a while, admiring the view, then hit the makeshift dance floor. The DJ is playing high-energy club music. It kind of makes my head throb, so I pound down my drink, thinking it'll help. The guys finally make it upstairs and join us. Ian dances with me, and he's got some good moves. Normally I'd be into him, but I know I won't go home with him if he asks. I probably should. I've only slept with three guys: my prom date in high school, the guy in college I dated my sophomore year, then Ben. I really should see what else is out there. I decide to take a break from dancing, and Ian follows me. We're sitting on the couch, talking, when he asks if he can take me out sometime.

"I'd love to, but I recently broke up with someone, and I'm not ready to date yet."

He nods and asks, "Was it serious?"

"Yes. We were engaged. Tonight actually would have been my bachelorette party."

"Well, when you decide you're ready to date, let me know. I'll give you my number."

Pretty bold move, but I don't want him to feel bad, so I put his number in my phone. Plus you never know—once I decide I'm ready to date, maybe I'll call him. We stay and dance for a while longer. I look at my watch; it's 2:00 a.m.

"Should we call it a night?" I ask Liv.

"Up to you. I'll go whenever you're ready."

We gather the group, and I say good-bye to Ian. "Lexi," he says, kissing my hand, "it was a real pleasure." I have to say, he's a standup guy. He could have been a total ass when I said I wouldn't go out with him.

"See?" says Liv. "There still are good guys out there."

"I know. I'm just not ready yet."

Later, as I lie in bed, I can't help think that it's not that I'm not ready to date—it's just that the right person hasn't asked me yet. I fall asleep, and for once I dream of Jake instead of Ben.

The next morning I wake up with a pounding headache. I go to the kitchen to get some Tylenol and find Jamie fast asleep on the couch. I go back to bed and wake up at eleven. It's a dreary day, so I'm not very motivated to get up. Eventually the three of us make it out for brunch, and I feel much better after a cup of coffee, a big omelet, and hash browns.

"What should we do today?" Liv asks.

Jamie wants to do some shopping so I suggest we hit up Armitage Avenue, my favorite area in my old neighborhood. This is her first time in Chicago, and Armitage is a great place where you won't find the same stores that are in every mall in America. Plus she's having dinner with a friend who lives near there. We step outside the restaurant, and I notice that the temperature has dropped. As we walk to the El the skies open up and it starts to pour. Luckily, we're only a few blocks away from my apartment building. We run back and get changed, then watch a few *90210* reruns until the rain stops. The sun has come back out, so we take the Red Line to Armitage and spend the rest of the afternoon shopping. Finally we drop Jamie off at her friend's place. I give her a big hug and thank her for making the trip this weekend.

After we see her off, Liv says, "I'm starving, let's have dinner." We decide to go to Sushi Maki. It's one of my favorite restaurants and used to be a neighborhood staple.

We walk in and give the hostess our name. She tells us it'll be a few minutes for a table. Liv and I are standing at the front, waiting, when Jake walks in.

"Lexi," he says, "what are you doing in my hood?"

"Hi." I smile at him. "A friend of mine from New York was in town, so I wanted to show her around. Jake, this is Liv, my roommate. Liv, this is Jake. We work together."

Liv shakes his hand. "Nice to meet you," she says, playing it cool.

"Are you picking up or eating in?" I ask him.

"Picking up, but I haven't placed my order yet. They're usually pretty quick."

"I know—I used to order from here all the time."

"You should join us," Liv says. "I haven't had the chance to meet any of Lexi's coworkers yet."

"It's nice of you to offer, but I don't want to intrude."

"Oh, it's no problem." Liv turns to the hostess and says, "It'll be a party of three."

"Right this way," she replies, leading us to a table.

"I see you did some shopping," says Jake, motioning to our bags.

"Yeah, it was my friend's first time here, so we took her shopping on Armitage. How was your weekend? Anything exciting?"

"Nah, pretty low-key. I went to the gym, hung out with some of the guys. That pretty much sums it up."

The waitress comes to take our drink order. Jake orders a beer, and Liv and I both tell her we'll have water.

"No drinks?" Jake asks.

"I drank enough last night to last me through the week," I tell him.

"Oh? Big night out?"

"A bunch of us went to Casa Maya for dinner then Century Club," Liv informs him. "They have killer margaritas there."

"I've been," says Jake. "Cool place."

The waitress returns with Jake's beer and asks us if we're ready to order.

"We haven't looked yet. Can you give us a few minutes?" I ask. After she walks away, I turn to Jake. "What do you typically order here?"

"All the rolls are good. My favorite is the Red Dragon maki. Do you want to split some?"

"I don't eat sushi," I tell him.

"Really?" He seems surprised. "What do you eat here?"

"I usually get chicken teriyaki. I don't like seaweed or most fish, but I'll eat some whitefish as long as it's mild. The two of you are welcome to share some rolls, though."

He and Liv agree on a selection. "Have you had sashimi?" Jake asks me.

"No, I haven't."

"You can try one of mine. There's no seaweed, and I ordered one with sea bass."

"OK. I'll try it," I tell him.

We decide to share edamame as an appetizer.

"So, Jake," Liv says, "what do you do at Hartman and Taylor?"

"I work in the New Business group. We essentially try to bring in new clients for the agency."

"Lexi tells me you've been winning a lot of accounts. What's your secret?"

He smiles. "No secret really. We just have a talented group of people, and I know the right questions to ask."

"Oh?" she says. "Like what?"

"Well, I'm pretty good at reading people, and I listen to what our clients want. I try to let them do most of the talking and probe when I pick up what

I think is interesting information. People love to tell you about themselves. I ask them about their work, accomplishments, that sort of thing. They're always happy to share anything that makes them look good. Once they've done that and feel comfortable, I can get at what I really want: their goals, challenges, and what keeps them up at night."

"Sneaky," says Liv.

"It's a smart strategy," I tell him. He gives me a somewhat embarrassed smile that makes my heart race. Yes, I'm sure he's successful because of his strategy, but he underestimates the power of that smile. The waitress brings our appetizer, and I notice that Jake offers the bowl to us first.

"Do you and Lexi work together?" Liv asks.

"No," I tell her, even though she already knows the answer. "I haven't worked on any pitches yet."

"Actually," says Jake, "I just learned of a lead for a fragrance company. I'm not sure if it'll pan out, but if it does, I'd love to pick your brain."

"Sure," I tell him. "I'd be happy to help. I used to work on new business pitches at my old agency from time to time. It's nice to work on something different. Plus I have a lot of prestige experience that I'm sure will apply."

When the waitress brings our meals, Jake puts a piece of sashimi on my plate. "Try it," he says. I take a small bite. Jake laughs. I take a bigger bite.

"What do you think?"

"Not bad," I tell him.

He gives me a satisfied smile. "Want a roll?"

"Now you're pushing it."

Then Jake turns his attention to Liv. He asks her what she does, and she talks about her teaching.

"What grade do you teach?"

"High school English."

"That must be challenging. Kids these days have access to so much information on the Internet. How do you know if their work is really their own?"

I've often wondered the same thing.

"We have a program that helps track that sort of thing. Plus we do a Google search on the topic and know most of the common papers kids copy. Once the students learn that, they figure it's easier to write the papers on their own than risk getting expelled."

"Kids can get expelled for plagiarizing?" Jake asks.

"Yes, we need a strong incentive for them not to do it."

I'm so glad Liv and Jake are getting along. She can be judgmental, and trust me, no guy wants to experience the wrath of Liv.

"You two seem like you've been friends for a long time," Jake comments. "How long have you known each other?"

"Since our freshman year in high school," I tell him. "Liv and I met in first-period algebra. We bonded over our hatred of quadratic equations."

"Yeah." Liv rolls her eyes. "It was the only subject Lexi wasn't good at."

I ignore her comment. "When I decided to move back to Chicago, Liv offered to rent me one of her bedrooms."

"It must be fun to share that history and now live together," he says.

"Yes, although I'm actually moving soon."

"Why's that?"

"Liv is moving in with her boyfriend."

"How long have you been dating him?" he asks her.

"Nine months, but when you know, you know. I figure there's no use in wasting time."

"I agree," Jake says. He turns to me and asks, "So where are you moving?"

"Within the building. It's a one-bedroom a few floors down. I love the neighborhood, and the timing worked out with the lease. Now I've just got to pack and figure out if I should hire movers."

"How much stuff do you have?"

"Not a lot. All the furniture is Liv's except my bed, dresser, and nightstand. I figured I could walk a lot of the stuff down and maybe recruit Simon to help me with the bigger pieces."

He looks at me and says, "You're joking, right?"

"No," I tell him.

"You mean Simon as in Simon Turner?"

"Yes, why?"

"I'll help you. My brother Nick and I can do it."

"I appreciate the offer, but I don't want to put you out."

"It's no problem. Trust me, you don't want Simon helping you if you want your stuff to arrive in one piece."

I laugh. "OK, as long as it's not too much trouble."

"None at all. When are you moving, and what time do you need us?"

"A week from Saturday. Is nine thirty too early?"

"No, that's fine."

I thank him, and then the waitress brings us the check. Jake motions for her to bring it to him. Liv and I take out our wallets, but Jake tells us to put them away. We protest, but he insists on picking up the bill.

"Thank you. That was very generous," I tell him.

"Yes," Liv agrees, "Thanks, Jake."

I glance toward the entrance, and my heart sinks. I spy Heather Hendricks, a totally annoying gossip from my high school days. I try to avoid making eye contact with her, but she sees me and makes a beeline to our table.

"Lexi!" she exclaims. "So good to see you! Hi, Liv. And who's this?" she asks, turning to Jake.

"Heather, this is Jake," I say, offering no further explanation.

She takes his hand, gives him a huge smile, and bats her eyelashes at him. I want to vomit, not only in response to her ridiculous gesture, but because I know what's coming. She turns her attention back to me. "I've been wondering if I was going to run into you, Lexi. I heard you were back in town. I was so sorry to hear about your broken engagement. And so soon before the wedding, you poor thing. Tell me, is it true you walked in on him?"

I sit there for a second, speechless. Then Liv pipes up. "It's a good thing Lexi realized things weren't right before the wedding. She's doing great—in fact she already has guys banging down her door. Now tell me about you. Are you married?"

Heather shakes her head. "No."

"Engaged?" Liv asks.

"No," she says again, a bit more uncertainly.

"Well, are you dating anyone seriously?

"I'm dating someone," Heather says a bit crossly.

"Well, I hope it works out. It's so hard to meet quality guys at our age. Anyway, it was *sooo* good to see you. Take care," Liv says brightly.

Heather storms away from our table. There's an awkward silence. Liv spies one of her students and says, "I have to go say hello. It may be a few minutes—the mom's a talker."

I walk outside and Jake follows me. I will myself not to cry; I don't like people to see me being vulnerable.

"You know, Heather's jealous of you," he says.

"What? Why do you say that?"

"She obviously was trying to get to you. No normal person would say that to someone. Clearly she was trying to get a rise out of you, or she's just so insecure that it was the only thing she could do to make herself feel better."

"She was always a social climber."

"So you were engaged, huh?"

"Yes," I tell him.

"Is that why you moved back here from New York?"

I nod. "I haven't told many people at work. I'd prefer to keep it that way."

"I understand. Your secret is safe with me. Just curious—why don't you want people to know?"

"It's kind of embarrassing. I feel like I failed, and I'm not used to failure. I just wanted to come back and have a clean start. I don't want people talking about my personal life or pitying me."

"I wouldn't look at it as a failure. Relationships just sometimes don't work out the way we planned. Maybe it happened because you were meant for something different."

I smile. "You sound like Liv. She's always telling me everything happens for a reason. I'm still trying to figure out what that reason is."

Jake looks like he wants to say something but doesn't. "Have you talked to him since you left New York?"

"No. After I caught him in the act I pretty much stormed out of there."

He looks surprised. "Don't you want to know what happened?"

"Honestly, no. I'd rather not hear it. There's nothing he can say that will change what happened or make it better. I'll talk to him when I'm ready. He calls me all the time and has left several messages, but I haven't returned any of them."

"Do you think you'd ever reconcile?"

"It's doubtful. I never could trust him after what he did. Besides, if he really wanted to get back together, he'd have to do something big."

"What do you mean?" Jake asks.

"You know, like a grand gesture to show me how much I mean to him. Phone calls are easy—he'd need to do something that really proves he's serious."

"What kind of gesture?"

"I don't know, but I'll know it when I see it."

Liv is back, and the discussion is over.

"Come on. I'll drive you guys home," Jake says.

"You don't have to do that," I tell him. "It's totally out of your way."

"I don't mind. It's only a ten-minute drive at this hour." I try to protest, but he hands his ticket to the valet. "I drove here because I was out doing errands. I have my car anyway." The valet pulls up a few minutes later, and Jake opens the passenger's-side door. "Come on. Get in." Liv climbs into the back and lets me take the front seat. I'm pretty quiet on the ride home.

Liv tries to break the tension by saying, "I guess Lexi told you about Ben then? Can you believe the nerve Heather has?"

"You did a nice job of putting her in her place," Jake responds.

"She deserved it."

Liv changes the subject and chats up a storm the rest of the way home. I think she's trying to make up for my lack of conversation. I'm grateful to her and only half listen to what she says. I can't believe Jake knows about my engagement. I don't know why, but I didn't want him to know. Finally he pulls up in front of our building.

"Thank you for the ride and for dinner. It was very unnecessary, but I appreciate it," I tell him.

"It was so nice meeting you, Jake," Liv says.

"Same here. Thanks for letting me join your dinner. See you tomorrow, Lexi."

Once we're out of the car, Liv turns to me and asks if I'm OK. "Yes," I tell her. "I'm fine."

"Good," she says. "Now let's talk about Jake. You didn't do him justice. He's totally gorgeous but so down to earth. I think he likes you."

"I don't know. I keep getting mixed messages from him."

"Well, he didn't have to drive us home."

"True, but he's a nice guy. He could have just done it to be polite."

"I don't think so. There's polite, and then there's totally going out of your way. Plus he offered to help you move. Don't give up on him yet."

She doesn't have to tell me twice. I know I won't.

CHAPTER EIGHT

THE week passes quickly. Every day I come home from work and pack. Since I have Jake and Nick helping, I decide it'll be easier to put my stuff in boxes rather than going back and forth with small loads. I carefully label each box with its contents and which room it belongs in; I figure it'll make unpacking that much easier. I decide to take the day off on Friday so I can finish up without having to pull an all-nighter. On Thursday I swing by Jake's office to make sure we're still on. I knock, and he smiles when he sees me.

"Lexi," he says, "are we still on for Saturday?"

"Yes, I was just about to ask you the same thing."

"Nine thirty. I've got it."

"Thank you so much. I owe you one."

"Actually I think that makes two. I also saved you from shady karaoke guy."

"No, we called it even, remember?"

"That's right. Seriously, you don't owe me anything, but as I was telling you at dinner, I could use your help with this fragrance pitch."

I take a seat. "Do you have a brief?"

"Here." He hands it to me.

I read through it and ask to borrow a pen. Then I write notes and some questions in the margins. I tell him my thoughts, and he asks if I'd be willing to work on the project with him if he clears it with Morgan.

"Absolutely," I tell him.

"Thanks, Lexi."

"Now we're even," I say, standing up. "See you Saturday."

"Bright and early," he says as I walk out the door.

On Saturday I wake up at 7:00 a.m. then eat a bowl of oatmeal, take a quick shower, and throw on a bright pink tank top and a pair of Lululemon capris. I pile my hair in a bun then pack my last box. My phone rings just as I'm finishing. It's Roland, my favorite doorman, announcing Jake and Nick's arrival. "Send them up," I tell him.

There's a knock on my door a few minutes later. I open it and Jake says, "Your movers have arrived." He looks so cute. It's rare that I get to see him in casual clothes. His hair is still damp, and he's wearing a light blue T-shirt—which I swear he did on purpose to bring out the color of his eyes—khaki cargo shorts, and sneakers. Nick looks very much like Jake but with darker, longer hair. Good looks definitely run in the family. Jake makes introductions.

"Lexi, this is my brother Nick. Nick, this is Lexi."

"Hi," he says, giving me a slow, lazy grin.

"Thank you so much for helping," I say, trying not to sound flustered.

"No problem," says Nick. "Where's all your stuff?"

I lead them to my bedroom and show him the furniture and pile of boxes.

"You've labeled all your boxes?" Nick asks.

Now I'm embarrassed. "Yeah, I figured it would be easier to unpack that way. What can I say? I like things organized."

"Nothing wrong with that," Jake says. "It's why you're such a good account person."

He and Nick agree to move the heavy things first then my boxes. I tell them I've reserved the freight elevator so they can pack in as much as they want before we head down.

"Great, now you, out of the way," Jake says.

He and Nick take apart my headboard and bed frame first. I watch as they expertly work and notice that Jake is very good with his hands. They move the frame out then the mattress. Next is the dresser. As Jake lifts it, I see the definition in his arms as he strains against its weight. I allow myself to check out his body, lingering on his shorts.

"Lexi," he says, breaking my reverie, "we're ready to go downstairs."

Crap. I hope he didn't notice me staring at him. I steal a glance at Nick; he gives me a wink, and I know I've been had. Embarrassed, I follow them and help carry some of the lightweight boxes.

"How many boxes of shoes do you have?" Nick asks me.

"I didn't count. Maybe five."

He rolls his eyes. "Girls and their shoes."

"Shoes can make or break an outfit," I tell him. "Plus you need shoes for lots of different occasions. There's formal, casual, heels, flats, boots—and you need to have all those shoes in a variety of colors."

"OK, I get it." He opens the box and takes out a pair of five-inch platform sandals. "You can walk in these?"

"You'd be shocked to know they're quite comfortable."

He studies a pair of my stiletto heels. "These can be used as a weapon," he says.

I laugh. "Good point. I'll keep that in mind."

I unpack while Jake and Nick finish carrying in the rest of my stuff. They're done by eleven thirty.

"Thank you both so much. Please—let me buy you lunch."

"No, that's OK," says Jake.

"Come on. I insist. You did me a huge favor. There's a great restaurant at the end of the block." He looks uncertain. "They have amazing burgers," I say, trying to tempt him.

"Sold," says Nick.

I look at Jake. "It's not the Ritz. Let me buy you a burger."

"OK," he says, relenting.

We walk down the street and sit outside to take advantage of the beautiful late-spring day. The waitress arrives, and I order Jake and Nick a beer and an iced tea for myself.

"So," I ask them, "who's older?"

"Me," says Jake, "by three years."

"It's nice that you guys are so close in age. Were you friends growing up?"

"Yeah, Jake was always cool," says Nick, "although we're closer now that we're older."

"How old?" I've always been curious to know Jake's age.

"I'm twenty-six," says Nick.

The waitress brings our drinks, and then I turn my attention back to Nick. "So what do you do?" I ask him.

"I have my own computer consulting company. We do support, repair, network design, installation—that sort of thing—for small and medium-size businesses."

"Wow. How did you get into that?"

"I went to MIT and helped out at the computer lab there. After I graduated I decided I didn't want to work for someone else. By the way, if you need help getting anything hooked up, you can call me," he says, handing me a business card.

"Thanks. Your parents must be so disappointed. Clearly you're a couple of slackers," I tease.

"Actually all my parents want is for one of us to get married so they can have grandchildren," says Nick.

"I take it you're not married?"

"Nope, but I'm thinking of proposing to my girlfriend."

"Oh, that's so exciting! When are you going to do it?"

"Soon. She just got a job offer in Boston. So I'm thinking I'll propose then move there with her."

"It's great that you're willing to relocate for her."

"I'm not sure it'll happen, because she's interviewing here too, but I can take my business anywhere. What about you? Would you move for the right person?"

"Been there, done that."

"Sorry," he says.

"That's OK. It was the right decision at the time. But I don't think I'd do it again." I feel Jake's eyes on me as we're talking. "Anyway, how are you going to propose?"

"I don't know. I have a few ideas. I just feel like everyone places so much emphasis on the engagement. It's a lot of hype to live up to."

"Don't worry about what everyone else thinks. Do what you think would make her happy. What are your ideas?"

"Well, I was thinking of taking her to dinner and putting the ring in the dessert."

"Cliché," says Jake.

"What else?" I prod.

"I was going to decorate our apartment with rose petals and candles."

"That's romantic," I tell him, trying not to think of Ben's proposal.

"What do you think?" he asks me.

"Well, you could take her back to the place where you went on your first date or somewhere else that has meaning to you both."

His eyes light up. "We met at a wine shop."

"Well, you could tell her you're going to a party and stop there on the way to pick up a bottle of wine. You could have a special label printed, or you could bring the wine to a restaurant."

Nick seems excited about the idea. "Thanks, Lexi. I can work with that. Apparently Jake here isn't going to deliver, so the pressure's on me to carry on the Hartman name."

He gave me the opening I've been waiting for. "You aren't dating anyone then?"

"Nah, no one special," says Jake.

"He's a serial dater," Nick informs me. "Most girls don't make it past two dates. Except what's her name…Ashley," he says. "Is she the one with the great—"

"Nick," Jake says in a warning tone, "that's enough."

Damn, I wanted to hear more about Ashley.

"So what about you?" Nicks asks. "A pretty girl like you must have a boyfriend."

I turn red with embarrassment. "Nope, I'm not seeing anyone seriously. I just got out of a long-term relationship," I add, feeling the need to justify myself. The waitress arrives with our bill. Jake tries to intercept it, but I don't let him. "It's my treat," I say firmly. "You both did me a huge favor."

"All right," Jake says grudgingly. "But just this one time."

I hope that means there'll be a next time.

The following week I receive an e-mail from Jake saying that Morgan has approved my involvement in the pitch as long as it doesn't conflict with my Lumineux responsibilities. I assure him I can balance both, but if it becomes an issue, I'll definitely let them know. I don't hear back, but I receive an invite to the briefing for the following day, so I assume everything is fine. I'm excited to be working on the pitch. There's an energy that comes with the challenge of putting forth your absolute best work. While I've worked in beauty, I've never worked on a fragrance account. It's a more risqué category, so I'm interested to see how the creative team will push the boundaries. Plus I'll get to work with Jake. I send my team an e-mail to let them know that I'll be helping with the pitch but reassure them Lumineux is my priority. Michelle writes back that she's always wanted to work on a pitch, and if we need any support, she's happy to help. I tell her I'll keep that in mind and let Jake know as well; I'm sure he's always looking for willing volunteers.

I attend the briefing the following morning. Jake makes introductions then talks about who else we're pitching against, the strengths they'll play up, and where he sees the biggest opportunities. Everyone is listening with rapt attention. I love seeing him in action; he knows how to command a room. Then he turns the briefing over to Nigel, the planner I met in Morgan's office. As Nigel's talking, I read ahead and am pleased to note that most of the comments I shared with Jake are accounted for.

When Nigel gets to the deliverables section, Jake interjects. "For the first creative review, I want to see how your ideas translate in print only." Mark, one of the art directors, asks why they can't focus on the TV spot. "Print will better showcase the viability of the idea. You can think through what the spot will be, but if your idea can't translate to print, we'll have a problem. You shouldn't need to rely on a spot to sell your idea."

"Should we bring storyboards to the meeting to share after the print ads?" Mark asks.

"No, but you can develop storyboards once we align on a direction so you won't waste your time on ideas that may not end up in front of the client."

Simon speaks up. "It's the right approach. It'll make sure only the strongest ideas survive. If we find we can't articulate the idea succinctly in print, it's not a big idea—it's a spot."

Mark relents, and Nigel finishes going through the brief. Simon then assigns three different creative teams to work on the project. There's nothing like a little friendly competition to up the stakes. "OK then," says Jake. "The first review is a week from today."

I want to tell him I thought the meeting went well, but Mark beats me to it. I take my time gathering my things while he and Jake are immersed in conversation. Looks like I'm not his only admirer.

Later that afternoon I stop by Jake's office. He's on a call and seems irritated. I'm about to walk away, but he gestures for me to come in. "Thanks for your interest. Feel free to get in touch if things change." He hangs up and says to me, "That was a waste of time." I look at him questioningly. "I got a call from a potential client, but they have no budget and essentially wanted us to work for free."

"Seems like a good deal to me," I joke. "I stopped by to tell you Michelle expressed interest in helping with the pitch."

"Oh, I didn't know she had a desire to work on new business."

"I didn't either. I told her I'd mention it to you in case you need extra help now or with any projects down the line."

"Do you think she'd be valuable on this pitch?"

"She probably could help with the competitive analysis," I tell him. "I can have her pull work for our key competitors and map out the various territories they're playing in. It might help us identify whether any white-space opportunities exist."

"That's a great idea."

"Do you want me to have her talk to you?"

"No. You can engage her as you see fit. There's no need for me to get involved. But I'll definitely keep her in mind for future assignments."

"OK, sounds good."

"How do you think the briefing went?" Jake asks.

"I think it went well. I really liked your approach with focusing on print first. It's a good way to evaluate the work."

"Thanks." I'm about to leave, but he changes the subject. "So how's your new place?"

"It's good. I was nervous about living by myself, but so far things are fine. I can't remember the last time I didn't have a roommate."

"Well, if you need any help getting your computer hooked up, I can ask Nick."

"Thanks, but I don't have a personal computer."

He looks at me, surprised. "I would have pegged you to be up on the latest technology."

"I have my work laptop. If I ever need access to a computer, I can bring it home."

He looks from me to my dated BlackBerry and says, "So you have no computer, and your smartphone basically can't surf the Internet."

"It can, sort of."

"You should at least get an iPhone."

"I know, and believe me, I want one, but I need an actual keyboard. I don't know how you can type on that thing."

"What about an iPad?" he suggests. "At least the keys are bigger."

"I'd like an iPad. I guess I just haven't seen the need to buy one. I feel like technology is replacing so many things in our lives—like books, for instance. I'd never get an e-reader."

"Why not? You wouldn't have to lug books around. Plus it's greener. What do you do with your books when you're done with them?"

"I keep them in case I want to read them again."

"And *do* you?"

"Well, no, but there's something appealing about physically turning the pages. It wouldn't be the same experience on a screen."

"Trust me, if you read a book on one, you won't want to go back."

We're interrupted by Joann buzzing Jake to let him know he's expected at a meeting.

"Thanks for the chat. It was enlightening," he says. "See ya, Wilma."

It takes me a minute to realize what he meant. I think he just called me Wilma Flintstone. Now that's a first.

CHAPTER NINE

Friday is a hectic day of back-to-back meetings. I'm about to head out to lunch when my cell phone rings. It's a number I don't recognize, and I debate letting it go to voice mail. I decide to answer, and I'm glad I do. It's Jason calling to ask me if I'll help him pick out a ring for Liv.

"Absolutely! I'd be honored to help. When do you want to go the jeweler's?"

"Is tomorrow OK?" he asks somewhat sheepishly.

"Tomorrow's fine."

"Sorry it's last minute. I wanted to do it on my own, but I'm freaking out because Liv is so particular."

"Don't worry. I know exactly what she wants."

"I figured you would," he says with a laugh. "Can I pick you up at ten?"

"Sounds good. See you then."

I can hardly contain my excitement the rest of the day. I'm seeing Liv tomorrow night, and I pray she doesn't call me to make lunch plans.

Jason is downstairs promptly at ten the next morning.

"How was the commute?" I joke, assuming he slept at Liv's.

He laughs. "The commute was easy. It was getting out of there early that was tough."

"Where does Liv think you're going?"

"To play basketball with the guys."

"I see you planned ahead," I say, taking in his workout attire.

"I am playing basketball, just not until later."

On the ride over, I ask him if he knows how he's going to propose. We've talked about it in the past, but he's never been happy with any of the ideas he's come up with. He excitedly tells me his plan.

"On the day she throws a quiz for her class, I'm going to include my own version. It'll be full of questions about my feelings for her—things like 'When did Jason know Liv was the one?' and 'What's Jason's favorite quality about Liv?' That sort of thing. The last question will be 'Will you marry me?' I've already worked it out with one of her coworkers. She's going to slip it into Liv's grading pile."

"Jason, that's a brilliant idea. Liv will love it!"

"I know," he says, beaming. "She's been suspicious every time we've gone out lately. I want to do something that'll really throw her off. She does most of her grading after school, so I'll have to take off work early so I can be there. I guess I'll hide out in the hallway."

I laugh, picturing him nervously pacing the halls. "I wish there was a way you could film it. I know she'd love to see it later…and me too."

"You know, that's not a bad idea. I'll look into it."

When we arrive at the jeweler's, Jason shows me the setting he has in mind. It's actually close to what Liv wants, but I make a few suggestions. He then chooses a beautiful princess-cut stone. The jeweler starts to talk about clarity and carat sizes, so I conveniently glance around the shop so they can discuss the details in private. Jason motions me back over and says he wants me to see how it looks put together. The jeweler places the stone on the platinum ring, which is set high with a tapered baguette on either side. Jason asks me to try it on so he can see how it looks. I usually see that as bad luck, but I figure I've already had one broken engagement. What harm could it do? I slip the ring on my finger and admire it.

"It's perfect," I tell him. "When are you going to propose?"

"In the next few weeks. I've got to get my act together and write the quiz. Then I need to time it with when Liv actually gives one to the class."

"I can't wait! You guys are a great couple," I tell him sincerely.

"Thanks. I'm glad she has a friend like you. You're one in a million, Lexi Winters."

That evening my friends and I are headed to a hot new lounge called Blu. I'm wearing a gunmetal-gray, one-shoulder jersey mini dress with subtle embellished details at the shoulder. I pair it with sky-high-stiletto, peep-toe, black-patent-leather pumps and a Michael Kors metallic leather clutch. I flat-iron my hair pin straight then shake it out by the roots to give it some volume. Once I'm ready, I knock on Liv's door.

She takes one look at me and says, "You look hot! Ugh, I need to change."

"You look great. You know I love that tank. I'd maybe pair it with your black mini instead. It'll dress it up a bit."

She puts the skirt on and says, "I wouldn't have thought to wear the two together, but you're right, much better."

We head downstairs, and I text Jill and Melanie that we're on our way. When our cab pulls up to the club, there's already a line out the door. We wait about ten minutes, and then Jill and Melanie arrive. I motion for them to come over. Jill holds up her finger in a "one-minute" gesture and walks up to the bouncer. She flirts her way to a spot at the front of the line. We walk in, and I'm amazed. The ambiance is very cool—the perfect blend of lounge meets club. Long leather benches are interspersed throughout the floor. Pendant lights of various lengths hang above, casting a soft, warm glow in the dimly lit room. There's a high dome ceiling lined with horizontal glass tubes creating an accordion affect. The walls are concave and made out of a waved textured material, giving the appearance that we're in a fishbowl. But the bar is the main attraction. Blue pendant lights hang above, giving the bar a bluish cast. Behind it are two wide floor-to-ceiling acrylic tubes that house an aquarium filled with large blue fish. In the center are white glass panels that also go up to the ceiling with niches that house various-colored backlit bottles. The whole place has a swanky, chic vibe.

After checking out the main level, we walk upstairs to the rooftop deck. The bouncer tells us it's closed because they're preparing for a private event. I'm bummed; it's a beautiful night, and I would have loved to hang out up here. We head back downstairs and chat by the bar for a while. I turn to my friends. "I have to use the restroom," I tell them. "I'll be right back." I find my way, but there's a long line. The girl in front of me says there are more washrooms downstairs, so I follow her. We walk down a long hallway lined with portholes that house abstract art. The restrooms are straight ahead, but I notice another doorway to my right, which I assume is the VIP lounge because it's roped off. I glance inside and spot a group of good-looking guys. Upon closer inspection, I see that one of them is Jake. He's engaged in a conversation with a very pretty blonde and doesn't see me. He looks super cute in a black sport coat with a fitted black-and-gray crewneck shirt underneath, along with dark jeans. I feel my face redden; he always has this effect on me. I decide not to interrupt him and get in line for the bathroom. I thought I'd escaped the line by coming down here, but apparently everyone else had the same idea.

A few minutes later someone behind me says, "Come here often?" I recognize the voice as Jake's.

I turn around. "Hey, I saw you earlier and was going to come say hi."

"Why didn't you?"

"Well, I'm not a VIP. Plus you were engrossed in a conversation."

"Oh," he says. "You're a VIP in my book."

"Such a smooth talker," I tease.

"Who are you here with?"

"Liv and some other friends of mine from high school. You?"

"A few buddies from college. One of them actually owns this place."

"Really?"

"Yeah, he always wanted to own a bar."

"I love the ambiance. It's so different from most clubs I've been to and has a really cool vibe."

"You want a tour?" he asks me.

"I'd love one," I say just as it's my turn in line. "Can you give me a minute?"

"Sure. Would you like me to hold your drink?"

"I don't know. Are you trustworthy?"

Jake laughs then leans in close and says, "That's debatable."

Flustered, I open the door to the ladies' room. When I come out, he's waiting for me with my drink in hand. I take it from him and pretend to inspect it. He turns serious and says, "I wouldn't trust me either." He looks at me intently, probably trying to read my reaction, and I feel myself turn a deep shade of red once more.

"Are you in line?" A girl motions to us, breaking the tension.

"No. Go ahead," Jake says.

"Don't you have to go?" I ask him.

"No. I was just coming to talk to you." I smile. "How about that tour?" he says, lightly touching my back, letting me lead the way. "Have you been upstairs to the rooftop yet?"

"We tried, but it's closed for a private event."

"I'll take you."

We head up two flights of stairs. Then Jake talks to the bouncer, who tells us we can have a quick look around. I walk outside and take in my surroundings, letting out a contented sigh.

"Impressive, isn't it?" Jake says.

"Yes. I feel like I'm somewhere else."

Large cabana-style seating areas are surrounded by billowing white curtains and tropical-looking potted plants. In the center are three long white tables lined with chrome barstools. Votive candles in various sizes run the length of each table. I walk to the edge of the rooftop and check out the spectacular view of the city. I'm so bummed this area is off-limits—if it weren't for the Chicago skyline, I'd swear I was on vacation. We head back downstairs to the main level, where Jake shows me the private office, which has TV screens monitoring every floor.

"Wow. I never think about security when I'm at a bar," I say. "It's kind of creepy how they can see your every move."

"I never thought about it that way. Let's go," he says, and momentarily takes my hand to lead me through the crowd.

I feel disappointed when he lets go. "I probably should go find my friends. I'm sure they think I got lost."

"I'd love to meet them. Why don't you join us in the VIP room?"

"Will I be able to get in?"

"I have connections here." Jake smirks. "Just tell them you're with me."

"OK," I say, liking the sound of that.

I go gather up Liv, Jill, and Mel.

"We've been looking for you!" Liv exclaims.

"Sorry. Jake's here, and he invited us to the VIP room. Apparently his friend owns this place."

"Thank God I finally get to meet your crush!" Mel says excitedly.

"Don't breathe a word of it."

"Obviously," she says, rolling her eyes.

We head to the VIP lounge. I tell the bouncer I'm with Jake, and he lets us right in.

We step past the rope, and I can see why Jake and his friends like to hang out here. It's a large open space flanked by two seating areas and a bar in the back. The walls are covered in pale-blue, glass-beaded wallpaper and lined with modern sconces. The seating areas are semiprivate, with floor-length, rich chocolate-brown curtains surrounding them, creating a cocoon. Inside are brown leather sectionals with light-blue modern throw pillows in various sizes and geometric patterns. A large, low, square table sits in front, with raised leather panels on either side that I assume can be used as extra seating. Above hangs an elegant chandelier that starkly contrasts the otherwise modern surroundings. To the back is a floor-to-ceiling bar finished in a deep mahogany; glasses of various colors, shapes, and sizes are displayed on backlit panels. The fish theme continues, as the base of the bar is another aquarium. The overall effect is very chic and modern. I spot Jake, and he waves us over.

"His friends are totally cute," Jill whispers to me.

"Hi," I say as I approach him.

"Lexi, meet my friends. This is Zach, Ethan, and Brad. He's the owner. And this is Lexi. We work together."

"Hi," I smile at each of them. "These are my friends, Jill and Melanie, and you know Liv of course," I say to Jake.

Everyone exchanges hellos, and then Brad offers us some champagne. "No, that's OK," I say.

"Come on. It's on the house," he tells me.

"Who are we to say no to that?" Liv pipes in.

"OK," I relent. "Thank you."

We accept the champagne, and Brad raises his glass in a toast. Then I turn to him and say, "I'm impressed. This place is amazing. How did you decide you wanted to open a bar?"

He tells us the story about how he used to be a lawyer but hated it, and owning a bar always had been his dream. He managed a bar in college, so he was familiar with how to run one. He had some connections and got the financing, and the rest is history. I can tell Jill is interested in Brad; she inundates him with more questions. Somehow Melanie, Zach, and Ethan get into a conversation, leaving Liv and me to talk to Jake.

"Do you guys come here a lot?" I ask him.

He nods. "Most weekends we do."

"I can see why."

"How do you all know each other?" Liv asks.

"We're friends from college."

"Oh, were you in the same fraternity?"

"No, we were in a band together."

"You were in a band?" I ask in disbelief.

"Yep, I played guitar and sang backup."

"Really? Do you guys still play?"

"No. We tried, but once we started working, we got too busy."

"That's too bad. I'd love to see you play."

In actuality it's probably a good thing. Watching him play would put me over the edge; I have a thing for musicians.

"What about you?" Jake asks. "Do you have any hidden talents aside from dancing?"

I raise my eyebrows. "What are you talking about?"

"Karaoke night…you put on quite a show."

"Oh, that," I say. "Yeah, thanks for warning me I had to go onstage."

"Lexi did karaoke?" Liv asks incredulously.

"I did. I'm surprised you remember," I say to Jake.

"It's hard to forget. I had to go home and take a cold shower."

"Oh," I say, embarrassed, although secretly I'm extremely pleased. I feel Liv elbow me in the back and hope Jake doesn't notice. Jill and Melanie turn their attention back to us.

"I'm sorry, but did I just hear that Lexi did karaoke?" Jill asks.

"This seems to be a big deal." Jake smirks at me.

"Oh, Lexi doesn't do karaoke," says Mel.

"She does now. Why don't we sit down?" Jake says, motioning toward the sofa. "Lexi can put on another performance for us."

I narrow my eyes at him. "You need to give me at least two more of these," I say, tapping my champagne glass.

"That can be arranged." Jake motions for Brad to come over with the bottle and tells him I need a refill.

"What am I, the bartender?" Brad jokes as he tops off my glass.

He and Ethan join us on the couch, and we're packed in tightly. The room is buzzing, but all I can focus on is the sensation of Jake's thigh brushing against mine. I do nothing to move it, and he doesn't move his leg either. Liv is talking to Jake, but I'm having trouble concentrating on what she's saying. I'm distracted, sitting so close to him. I look at my friends, who are deep in conversation with Jake, and feel a sense of elation, which I'm sure is helped by the champagne. Suddenly I realize I don't have any recent photos with my friends.

"Will you take our picture?" I ask Jake.

"Sure," he says.

I hand him my phone, and we get together for a pose.

"Let me see how it turned out," I say, and he shows me the photo.

"Does it meet with your approval?"

"Yes." I smile, happy that I finally can replace the picture in my office. Jake asks to see my other photos; he scrolls through my phone and lands on the one of him and Hailey. Crap, I forgot that was in there.

"You still have this," he comments.

"Oh, I didn't realize I still did."

A small smile plays at his lips, but he keeps going, asking me who various people are. Then he comes to the one of Ben and me. It's my last picture of the two of us together; I couldn't bring myself to delete it. I got rid of all the other ones after I found out he cheated, but I've always loved this picture. It's from our engagement party. One of my friends must have captured it when we weren't looking. It's a close-up, candid shot of the two of us smiling at each other.

"Is this your ex?" Jake asks.

"Yeah, I must have forgotten to delete it," I say as I take back my phone.

"How about one of the two of us?" he suggests.

"OK."

I hand my phone to Liv. Jake puts his arm around my shoulder, and I lean into him. She snaps the photo and looks at it. "It's a good picture," she tells us.

Jake and I study it; it really is a nice photo. He's wearing a mysterious expression that makes him look very sexy.

"Why don't guys ever smile in photos?" I ask him.

"I don't know." He shrugs. "We could take another one," he offers as he pulls me close to him.

"No, that's OK," I say, suddenly feeling self-conscious.

"Text it to me," Jake says. "Do you still have my number?"

"Yes, I still have it. As you can see, I obviously don't make a habit of deleting things."

He studies me for a minute then says, "I'm going to get another drink. Do you want something?"

"No, I'm still good with the champagne."

Jake, Brad, and Ethan head to the bar, and I turn my attention back to my friends.

"What do you think?" I whisper.

"He's adorable," says Jill. "And he definitely seems into you."

"I don't know…You think?"

"Yes, he's been watching you all night. I've been paying attention."

"This is how he is," I say. "He flirts with me but never follows through on anything. It's so frustrating."

"Well, maybe your luck will change tonight," offers Mel.

"I'm not holding my breath. Let's talk about something else. They're coming back."

Brad hands us each a shot glass and says, "On the house."

"Thanks," I say, eyeing it skeptically.

"It's our house specialty—the Blu Bonanza."

I don't want to know what's in it. We all raise our glasses in a toast. It's actually not that bad, although I already feel myself becoming more buzzed. Then Brad entertains us all with stories about the bar and some of the crazy things people have done to get kicked out.

Suddenly Liv stands up and says, "I'll be right back" then walks over to a less crowded area with her phone. She returns a few minutes later. "I'm headed out. Jason is picking me up. He'll be here in a few."

"OK, I say, standing. "Thanks for coming out." I hug her, and she gives me a look and instructs me to call her later. She says good-bye to Jake, and I realize the others have all gone to the bar, and it's just the two of us. Suddenly I feel nervous.

"Do you want to go hang out with your friends?" I don't want him to feel like I'm monopolizing his time.

"I'm fine here. Do you want to sit? It must be hard standing in those shoes."

"Oh, these are the ones Nick liked. Like I told you, they're comfortable."

I sit anyway. Jake sits right next to me, even though there's plenty of room, and casually puts his hand around my waist. The noise level in the bar has increased, so he leans in close to me. My heart pounds in my chest as his hand lightly strokes my back while we're talking. I try to focus on our conversation and not let myself get distracted by the sensation of his warm touch as his fingers caress my bare skin.

"Your friends seem nice," I tell him. "I think Jill is into Brad. Is he a good guy?"

"He is, but he's definitely a player."

Are you a player? I want to ask. But instead I say, "I should probably go warn her."

"She'll be fine. Stay with me," Jake says, reaching for my hand.

Just then the blonde Jake was talking to earlier comes over. "Jake, I've been looking for you everywhere!" She sits down next to him; I can tell he's annoyed.

He introduces us. "Lindsay, this is Lexi."

"Hi," I say. I can tell she's sizing me up. She turns her attention back to Jake and puts her hand on his knee.

"I'm bored. Let's go back to your place," she purrs at him.

I feel very uncomfortable. Jake senses I'm about to stand up and tightens his grip on my waist, forcing me to stay seated.

"I'm sorry you're bored," he says, removing her hand, "but I'm catching up with Lexi here."

She stares at him incredulously. "Whatever. Don't expect me to come by later."

He turns to me and rolls his eyes.

"Is that one of your groupies?" I tease. Then I look at him seriously and say, "Don't let me get in the way if you want to go home with her."

"Actually I'd rather stay here and hang out with you."

"OK." I smile at him. I can't believe he blew off going home with Lindsay so he could stay and talk to me. I feel insanely happy.

"I like your dress," Jake says, lightly touching the fabric on my shoulder. He slides his hand down the length of my dress, grazing my breast, and rests it on my knee. I raise my eyebrows at him.

"You don't mind, do you?" he asks in a low voice.

"No," I say, meeting his gaze.

He stands up, and I stand up too, thinking we're leaving. "Wait here," he says, then closes the curtains to our seating area, giving us complete privacy. He makes his way back toward me wearing a determined expression that makes my heart beat wildly in my chest. Is he going to kiss me here, in the middle of the bar? He looms over me and takes the drink out of my hand. I feel the color rise in my face, and my breathing becomes ragged. Jake tilts my chin so I meet his gaze and leans in close when suddenly the curtains part and Brad walks in. "Sorry, dude," he says to Jake, "but Maurice just informed me there's a girl here looking for you. She says you work together, and she's on her way down."

Jake's demeanor immediately changes. He fully opens the curtains and moves to the other side of the couch, putting some distance between us. I look at him questioningly, but his flirty smile is gone, replaced with a cool stare. Then I see a brunette talking to the bouncer, and I'm guessing she's looking for Jake. She makes eye contact, and he motions her over.

"Jake, I thought I'd find you down here."

I recognize the woman as someone we work with.

"Kelly, good to see you."

"I told you I'd make it here one of these days. You look familiar," she says, turning to me.

"Lexi works with us," Jake says.

"Kelly," she says, offering her hand. I shake it, and then the two of them engage in a conversation, making no effort to include me; I feel like a complete outsider.

"Well, it was nice meeting you," I say to Kelly. Then I turn to Jake. "I think I'm going to head out."

"OK," he says. His face is impassive, and he doesn't make an attempt to stop me.

"See you Monday," I say.

He gives me a curt nod in response.

I head over to find Jill and Melanie. "I'm going to go," I tell them. Melanie says she'll come with me, but Jill decides to stay. I find it ironic that she'll probably hook up with Brad. "Call me later," I whisper to her.

I catch Jake's eye as I'm walking out, but he looks away. Why do I feel like I'm always dealing with Jekyll and Hyde with him? It's as though tonight never happened, and we're back at square one.

During the cab ride home, tears of disappointment sting my eyes. I know Jake would have kissed me if Kelly hadn't walked in. But his reaction to seeing her is what kills me. It's like whatever he felt for me immediately switched off. How can he just change his emotions like that? I don't think I'm reading things wrong; I can sense he's into me. But I feel like we're on the edge of a cliff, and something always seems to get in the way, pulling him back. I'm not sure what else I can do to push him over the edge. And I don't know how much more I can take trying.

On Monday Jake stops by my office.

"Hey," he says, giving me a slow smile.

"Hi," I say, doing my best to look nonchalant.

"How was the rest of your weekend?"

"Fine. I'm actually busy at the moment. Do you need something?"

He seems caught off guard. "No. Just wanted to see if you wanted to have lunch. I have some thoughts on the pitch I want to run past you."

"I'm actually slammed today. I feel like I haven't been able to focus on my own account lately, so I need to get caught up." In actuality I could go to lunch with him. But I'm still pissed about his blowing me off Saturday night, so I'm not ready to jump at the chance to have lunch with him.

"I understand. Look, if you feel like the pitch is taking up too much of your time, let me know. I don't want you to neglect paying work."

"I can handle it," I tell him somewhat coolly. "I know how to budget my time. That's why I'm not going out to lunch."

"OK. Let me know when you come up for air, and I can share my ideas then."

"Fine. See you later."

He hesitates in the doorway then says, "See you."

I stay at work late that night then head to the gym to blow off some steam. It's past eight when I get home. I make myself a quick dinner and take a shower. After I blow-dry my hair, I check my Gmail account and see I have a message from Jake. Curious, I open it.

From: jake.hartman@yahoo.com
Sent: June 9, 2014; 9:34 p.m.

To: lexi.winters@gmail.com
Subject: Apologies

Lexi,

I feel I should apologize for Saturday night. It was a very pleasant surprise running into you, and I enjoyed hanging out with you and your friends. I'm sorry the night got cut short. Kelly is an old friend of Brad's and mine, and I've been telling her to come by to check out the place. Anytime you and your friends want to stop by, you're more than welcome.

—Jake

I'm not sure how to respond. I'm sure he sensed I was upset with him this afternoon. I decide to be brief.

From: lexi.winters@gmail.com
Sent: June 9, 2014; 9:42 p.m.
To: jake.hartman@yahoo.com
Subject: Re: Apologies

Jake,

You don't have to apologize. Kelly probably did me a favor because I had to be up early the next morning. It was fun hanging out with you too. Thanks for the VIP treatment.

See you tomorrow,
Lexi

p.s. How did you get this e-mail address?

I think I know the answer, but I want to see what he says. Almost immediately I get a reply back.

From: jake.hartman@yahoo.com
Sent: June 9, 2014; 9:45 p.m.
To: lexi.winters@gmail.com
Subject: Re: Apologies

It was on your résumé.

> From: lexi.winters@gmail.com
> Sent: June 9, 2014; 9:47 p.m.
> To: jake.hartman@yahoo.com
> Subject: Re: Apologies
>
> I didn't realize you kept them on file.
>
> From: jake.hartman@yahoo.com
> Sent: June 9, 2014; 9:49 p.m.
> To: lexi.winters@gmail.com
> Subject: Re: Apologies
>
> Company policy. Although I keep personal copies of all candidates I'm interested in.

I try not to read into his response.

> From: lexi.winters@gmail.com
> Sent: June 9, 2014; 9:51 p.m.
> To: jake.hartman@yahoo.com
> Subject: Re: Apologies
>
> Well, then I consider myself lucky that I was up to your standards. I'm really happy at the agency and think the change was just what I needed. And now I should get some much-needed sleep. Good night.
>
> From: jake.hartman@yahoo.com
> Sent: June 9, 2014; 9:54 p.m.
> To: lexi.winters@gmail.com
> Subject: Re: Apologies
>
> Sweet dreams.

I smile and log off. I'm wired and not ready to go to sleep, so I call Liv. I give her a rundown of what happened and ask for her advice.

"Lexi, I don't want to see you get hurt again. It sounds like Jake is into you, but he can't make up his mind. I don't want you sitting around waiting for him. I think he's comfortable flirting with you, but it seems that anytime there's an opportunity to take the relationship further, he hesitates. It makes me wonder what his intentions are."

"I know, and I'm being careful. I just want to see where things go."

"OK, you know what's best for you. Just know that if he hurts you, he'll have me to answer to."

We say good night, and I toss and turn, thinking of Jake before I fall into a dreamless sleep.

CHAPTER TEN

THE following afternoon I attend the first-round creative review for the fragrance pitch. Each team shares a different campaign idea. I can tell Jake isn't pleased, and I don't blame him. It's not that the work is bad; it's just very expected. He and Simon go back and forth, and the meeting gets very heated. Jake tries to appease Simon and tells him the work is very strong creatively, but he's looking for a winning idea, which he hasn't seen yet. Then he pulls up a bunch of ads from the competition along with Michelle's analysis. He shows him how our work is playing in much the same territory and says we need to get to a differentiated idea. Simon finally agrees but puts the burden back on account management and planning to find something that'll provide them with new inspiration. It's an intense meeting.

"Can I make a suggestion?" I ask. All eyes turn to me. "We need to take a step back and start with our consumer. We need to reevaluate why she wears perfume in the first place."

"To get the guy," says Ari, one of the art directors.

"That may be the end goal, but I don't think it's why she wears it. I like to think of perfume as an accessory, just like clothes or makeup. Perfume is the last thing she puts on to boost her confidence. She wears it for herself more so than for others. It makes her feel in control, sexy, and empowered, and that's what guys find attractive. It's her secret weapon."

"I love it!" says Simon. "It conjures up images of Angelina Jolie in *Mr. and Mrs. Smith*. We could take that idea in a lot of different directions."

Nigel nods. "We should take the discussion to a focus group to confirm the insight, but I think Lexi's on to something here."

The rest of the meeting turns into a brainstorming session around my "secret weapon" idea. When we leave, everyone is jazzed.

Jake looks at me and says, "You were amazing in there. I was ready to pull my hair out, but you gave the team the inspiration they needed. Thank you."

"You're welcome. It probably didn't hurt that I was the only woman in the room."

"True." Jake laughs. "I didn't think about that."

"You may want to get a female art director on it," I tell him. "It would help to have a woman's touch. This weapon idea needs to be spot on, or it could end up a disaster."

Jake agrees and says he'll talk to Simon.

When I come home that night, Liv says she wants to set me up on a date with her cousin's friend, Jason.

"Really, his name is Jason?"

"I know. It must be meant to be. If he's anything like mine, you're in luck." She goes on to say he recently moved to town and is looking to meet new people. I tell her I'm not ready, but she cuts me off. "Lexi, if Jake asked you on a date, would you go out with him?"

"Yes," I tell her without hesitation.

"I know," she says quietly, "but he hasn't asked, and he's had plenty of opportunities. I hate to see you waiting for him when it doesn't seem like he's going to come around. I don't want you missing out on meeting someone else. Whatever rule he's made for himself about dating girls at work, he seems to be sticking to it. And while he seemed into you Saturday night, when push came to shove, he didn't pull the trigger."

I know she's right. "OK." I sigh. "I'll do it."

I tell Liv to let Jason know to keep things low-key. After we hang up, I think about Jake and wonder if our relationship is simply a game. He's been a safe bet to lust after, which makes me question whether my feelings for him are real or whether he's more of a distraction from Ben. As I reflect on our encounters, I realize my feelings for him are genuine. And while he seems into me, perhaps I'm an easy target for him as well. He's a sharp guy, so he must know I'm interested. When he basically groped me at Blu, I told him I didn't mind. I just wish I knew what game he was playing and what the rules are. One thing I'm certain of: Jake definitely isn't playing fair.

Jason calls the following Monday, and we make plans for dinner and a movie that Thursday. I figure a weeknight won't be as much pressure as a Saturday-night date. He offers to pick me up in a cab, but I tell him I'll meet him because I live in the opposite direction. I appreciate the offer, considering neither of us has a car, but I feel more comfortable this way.

The week passes quickly, and soon reality hits that I'm going on my first date since my breakup with Ben. I can't believe I agreed to this. I haven't dated in years, and I have no clue what the rules are these days. Plus it's an acknowledgment that I'm moving on. As much as I need to, taking the step is like admitting that things with Ben are completely over. And that's something I haven't wanted to face. I rifle through my closet and fret about what to wear. I call Liv for moral support, and with her help, I decide on a sheer, three-quarter-sleeve printed blouse with a camisole underneath; skinny jeans; and nude platform heels. I straighten my hair and do a deep side part with side-swept bangs, which are now more like long layers. Liv stops by to wish me good luck.

"Lexi, you look great! He won't know what hit him."

"Thanks," I tell her. "And thanks for pushing me to do this. I know it's the right thing, I just wish I weren't so nervous."

"You'll be fine," she reassures me. Then she gives me a hug along with instructions to text her with updates.

"I'm sure he'll love that—me texting at the table."

I go downstairs, and Roland turns on the cab light for me.

"Big night out?" he asks.

"I have a date."

He whistles. "Good luck."

I'll definitely need it. A cab pulls up, and I'm on my way. Jason and I made plans to meet at an Italian restaurant across from the movie theater. He said he'd meet me out front. I time it so I'm about five minutes late; I don't want to be the one waiting. Sure enough, the cab pulls up, and I see him standing in front of the restaurant. He's just as Liv described: tall, dark, and handsome. I figured she was just saying that to get me to go, but I'm pleasantly surprised. I get out of the cab and approach him.

"Jason?" I ask.

"That's me. You must be Lexi."

"Yes. Hi."

"Hi. It's nice to meet you. I put our name in but wasn't sure if you wanted to sit inside or out."

"Definitely out. It's a beautiful night."

After a few minutes, we follow the hostess to the patio. Our waiter comes right away with the specials and asks for our drink order.

"Do you want to share a bottle of wine?" Jason asks.

"I'd love to, but then I'd fall asleep during the movie. I'll just have a glass."

I order a sauvignon blanc, and he gets a merlot.

"I hear you've been living back here for a few months now," Jason says. "How's it going so far?"

"It's good. To be honest, it feels like I never left. It's nice to be close to my old friends and family, of course, but sometimes I miss the energy of New York. Don't get me wrong—Chicago has a great restaurant scene and night life, but there's no place like New York."

"I totally agree," he says. "I debated moving here, but there was an opportunity with my company I couldn't pass up."

He tells me he works for a market research firm, and Chicago is a key market. I discover my agency uses some of their services. The waiter returns with our wine, and we place our order. Jason opts for the salmon special, and I order rigatoni with vodka sauce, one of my favorites. I take a sip of wine and feel more relaxed. Jason is nice and very attractive, with warm brown eyes and a mop of wavy hair, which he totally pulls off. He seems sincere, but I kind of get a player vibe from him. He has a confidence that borders on cocky. He definitely would have been my type in the old days but not so much now. Still it's just one date, and I figure it's good practice. We talk easily over dinner, and I give him the lowdown on where to go and what to avoid in the city. We bond over our favorite places in New York and debate which is better: New York or Chicago-style pizza. Of course he thinks New York is better, and I prefer Chicago.

"You haven't tried Lou Malnati's then," I say.

"Nope. We'll have to go for pizza on our next date."

"OK, you're on." I guess I just agreed to a second date. I excuse myself to use the washroom so I can text Liv.

>   Me: Going well so far. Already made plans for a second date. Cute and nice, but not sure he's boyfriend material.

She texts back immediately.

>   Liv: What do you mean he's not BF material?
>   Me: He just seems like a player. Gotta go. I'll call you when I get home. Xo

When I come back, Jason says, "We probably should get going soon." He pays the bill, and I offer him money, which he refuses. He instructs me that he's going to buy the movie tickets also and not to protest. We're seeing some new action-adventure film, and there's a long line. I'm waiting inside for him when Jake walks in with a tall blonde. I can't pretend not to notice them because he's already spotted me.

"Lexi, hi," he says. "This is Ashley. Ashley, this is Lexi."

She offers me a tight smile. "I'll be right back," she tells Jake.

"So I finally get to meet the infamous Ashley," I say. I'd rather I didn't. She looks like a Barbie doll.

Jake shrugs. "We're just hanging out. She's fun but not my type."

"What's not to like? She's tall, blond, and gorgeous." And she has a killer body, but I decide not to mention that.

"I prefer brunettes," he says, looking at me.

Oh.

Just then Jason, with our tickets in hand, finds me. I introduce him to Jake and feel very awkward. Fortunately we aren't seeing the same movie. Barbie comes back, and we say good-bye. I spend the whole movie thinking about Jake and Ashley. Damn him, my first date in ages, and somehow he's right there with us.

After the movie, Jason offers to share a cab with me back to my place. I decline because I'm not certain whether he has ulterior motives. After giving him a chaste kiss on the cheek, I thank him for a nice night, and he says he'll call me. Then I go straight to Liv's apartment.

"How was it?" she asks.

"Good, not as bad as I thought it would be." I recount the evening's events and tell her about my run-in with Jake.

"It's weird that he made that brunette comment to you."

"I know, right? I can't decide if he's playing mind games. It's like he senses I'm trying to move on, so he has to say something to reel me back in."

"Lexi, I know you don't want to hear this, but I think you need to put yourself out there. It's obvious you can't move on until you know where things stand with him. Let him know you're interested and see what happens. At least then you'll know, and either you can be together or you can move on."

"I'll try. But subtle is more my style."

"Make sure you're not too subtle. Guys are idiots."

The relief I felt at having made it through my first date is replaced with apprehension about confronting Jake. But I know I need to do it. It's time.

On Monday morning I have a mandatory sexual-harassment training seminar. It's a requirement for new hires, and all other employees must attend a yearly refresher. I have a feeling it was part of the settlement with Jake's lawsuit. I head to the conference room a few minutes before the meeting starts. The company has hired an outside consultant to lead the session. When he begins to speak, I'm struck by the monotone sound of his voice. It brings back images of Ben Stein from *Ferris Bueller's Day Off*. How did this guy land this job? I do my best to pay attention and try to stifle a laugh when he says, "I want everyone to bring their A game today. This is an important topic, and we all must drink the Kool-Aid." Fortunately a number of videos break up the morning. I can't believe I have to sit here for three hours. The scenarios they're laying out are so obviously in poor taste that I can't imagine anyone actually doing such things. I probably shouldn't make light of the situation. The reality is that these things happen, which is why we're here in the first place. I make it through the morning and head back to my desk. Nicole catches me as I'm walking past.

"Lexi, I wasn't sure you were in today."

"I'm here. I was just in that sexual harassment training."

She rolls her eyes. "Did you have Weber as your instructor?"

"Yes, he's been here before? I can't believe they invited him back."

"Tell me about it. All I could think about when he was talking was 'Bueller? Bueller?'"

I stifle a giggle. "I was thinking the exact same thing! And can you believe all his trite business phrases?"

"Did he say he wanted everyone to drink the Kool-Aid?"

"Yes, and what about the 'elephant in the room'?"

"Nope, he used 'moose on the table with us.'"

We laugh hysterically. Jake pokes his head in my office and asks us if we are OK. "Yes. Let's take this discussion offline," says Nicole, and we laugh even harder.

Bewildered, Jake says, "I just wanted to ask Lexi her thoughts on something for the pitch."

"Go for the low-hanging fruit," Nicole says, and we convulse into giggles.

"I'll stop by later," Jake says.

I wipe my eyes. "Now is fine. I'll take one for the team."

Nicole snickers. "Remember Lexi, there is no 'I' in team."

Jake comes into my office and closes the door. Usually I'm the one coming to see him.

"What's up?" I ask.

"Simon previewed the print with me."

"How does it look?"

"I want to get your opinion. I asked him to leave a copy with me. He reluctantly agreed as long as I promised not to pass it around. So you never saw this."

"OK," I say as he flips over the board. I study it for a minute and say, "It's a bit literal."

"That's what I was thinking. I wanted to see if you were on the same page before I give him my feedback. I try not to laugh at his use of "on the same page." "What?" he asks.

"Nothing. It's just that my morning has been ripe with clichés. Anyway, I think it's a good start. I'd just urge him to push the thinking further. This is what I'd expect to see based on the insight. Maybe we can offer a range—start with ideas that are close in then some that take more liberties in their interpretation of the insight."

"I like that approach. I'll circle back with him," he says to me with a smile.

"Run it up the flagpole," I reply.

He's about to leave but then asks, "How was your date?"

"It was good," I tell him. "How about you? How's Barbie?"

He laughs. "I told you, it's nothing serious. What about you? Will you go out with Justin again?"

"It's Jason." Now's my chance. "That depends," I say.

"On what?"

"On whether or not I get any better offers," I respond, looking pointedly at him.

He regards me for a moment but doesn't say anything. I feel the atmosphere in the room change and watch as his playful smile is replaced with a look of discomfort. He takes a deep breath and says warily, "Lexi, I think—" But my phone cuts him off.

"I have to take this," I tell him. It's only my mom, and I could have let it go to voice mail, but frankly I don't want to hear what he has to say. I already know—his silence spoke volumes.

I'm typing angrily on my computer when Simon knocks on my door.

"Hi. I came by to show you the latest ads," he says.

I'm glad Jake previewed the work with me so I can half-heartedly listen to his pitch. I give my input then continue to type my e-mail.

He walks over and closes the door. "Are you going to tell me what's wrong, or will I have to get you a new computer?"

I manage a smile. "Si, I'm done."

"Why? What happened?"

I recount last night's events and my conversation with Jake earlier. Simon and I have formed a close bond and he knows about my feelings for Jake.

"But Lexi, you don't know what he was going to say. And maybe he didn't get your hint."

"Oh, he got my hint all right. And I could tell he was going to say, 'I think I gave you the wrong impression' or something to that effect. For my own sanity, I need to put some distance between him and me."

"That's probably a good idea—make him realize what he's missing."

"I'm not doing it to play games; I just think it's time I face reality. Jake doesn't date anyone at work, and as much as I'd like to think I'm an exception, I'm not."

"My dear, everything is a game," he says.

Well, I think, *this is one I no longer intend to play.*

After Simon leaves I think about what he said and know I'm right. Even though it was subtle, Jake definitely picked up on my insinuation. To be honest, I wasn't expecting that reaction. I used to think I was fairly good at reading people, but Jake is a mystery to me. I definitely feel like we have a closer relationship than he has with the other girls at work. He seems more flirtatious with me and throws out hints that he's interested with his "any guy would be lucky to have you" and "I prefer brunettes" comments. And don't even get me started on that night at Blu when he almost kissed me.

But Liv is right—he's had plenty of chances to ask me out, and he hasn't. So even if he is interested, he clearly doesn't like me enough to bend his rule. Hard as it will be, I know I'm doing the right thing.

Jake is in San Francisco at the beginning of the following week, which gives me the excuse I need. When he returns, I stop dropping by his office. Instead I e-mail him whatever updates I have on the pitch. I also try to avoid going to his side of the floor so I won't run into him. On Thursday he stops by my office.

"Hey, Lex. Long time no see."

"Hi. I'm actually about to head to a meeting."

"I'll walk with you."

"I'm going to stop by the ladies' room first. See ya later."

The next afternoon I'm in the kitchen getting a Diet Coke when he walks in and approaches me.

"Hi, Lexi. What's up?"

"Hi," I say, barely glancing at him. Fortunately Michelle walks in, so I engage her in a conversation.

Jake grabs a soda, pauses, and says, "Are you going to happy hour tonight?"

"No, I won't be there."

"Why? Do you have a hot date?" Michelle teases.

"As a matter of fact, I do." With that I stride out the kitchen without looking back. I don't mention that my date happens to be with my four-year-old nephew.

Scott, my brother-in-law, picks me up after work. His office is in the city, so he's driving me to their house. He and my sister have a date night, so I'm baby-sitting for them. I haven't seen Charlie in a few weeks, and I miss him. When I walk in, he jumps up and down. "Hi, Auntie Lex!" It's nice having someone who's always happy to see you.

After Jules and Scott head out, Charlie and I play a bunch of games, and then I heat up a frozen pizza for us. Afterward I give him a bath, and he insists on bathing all his fish toys. When I finally get him to bed at eight, he's out like a light, which gives me a chance to go through my notes on the cancer benefit my mom and I have been planning. It's a few weeks away, and everything is taken care of for the most part. I just need to finalize the gift bags and raffle prizes. A lot of Hartman & Taylor's clients have offered to donate items for the bags. It's a win-win; we get free merchandise, and they get a sampling opportunity with a desirable audience. I anticipate we'll have around 175 people in attendance, but I plan for 200 bags. I don't want to worry about not having enough; plus people likely will take extras.

I must have dozed off, because the next thing I know, Jules is gently shaking me.

"How was your night?" I ask her and Scott.

"Great," Jules says. "It was so nice to be able to have adult conversation. Thanks, Lex."

"No problem. I love seeing Charlie. He's such a great kid."

"How was he? Did he give you any trouble?"

"None at all. He insisted on bathing all his toys, but I had him down by eight."

"Perfect. He loves when you come here."

"Probably because she gives him her undivided attention," Scott jokes. "Come on. I'll drive you home."

Scott and I make small talk on the ride back. He and I have become close, and I think he's a really good guy. My sister got very lucky.

"So are you dating anyone?" he asks.

"I went on a date recently."

"How'd it go?"

"It wasn't as bad as I thought it would be. He was good-looking and nice, but I can't tell if there's a spark, ya know?"

"Give it time. You've just come out of a long-term relationship, so have some fun. You deserve it."

"Thanks. I'll try."

Maybe Scott's right. I always look at every guy as a potential boyfriend. I probably should go with the flow and see where things lead instead of analyzing everything to death like I always do.

We make good time to the city; it's late enough that there isn't any traffic.

"Thanks for the ride. See you at the benefit."

"Take care, Lexi. And thanks for sitting for us."

I wave as he drives off. Roland is at the door and gives me a wink.

"Was that your date?"

"No." I laugh. "That was my brother-in-law."

"Well, you deserve a real gentleman," he says.

I agree. Now I just need to find him.

—•◆•—

The next week I get back to focusing on my own account; I've been so busy working on the fragrance pitch that I haven't been giving it as much attention as I'd like. I spend the next few days at Lumineux, going over the options from our shoot as well as some new opportunities we'd like to pursue. It keeps me focused, and I haven't had much time to think about Jake.

I'm on an all-agency call to share the status of our projects when my cell phone rings. I see that it's Rachelle, Molly's mom, so I put my office phone on speaker and mute it. Michelle is leading the call and already has given our update, so I figure it's fine to answer my cell phone. "Hi, Rachelle. Is everything OK?" I can tell from her voice that it's not. She informs me Molly has taken a turn for the worse. I try to reassure her and tell her kids are resilient, but in my heart, I don't believe it. I ask her if I can visit Molly this weekend.

"I'm sure Molly would love to see you, but now isn't the best time."

"I understand. Please let me know if things change."

"I will. Just so you know, we're still planning on having a birthday party for her next weekend. She was so disappointed when I had to cancel in May because of her treatments. This is one thing she has to look forward to, and I don't want to take it away from her."

"I'll be there. Text me once you know the details."

"Thanks, Lexi. I will."

"Give Molly a hug for me."

We hang up, and I close my eyes. *Not Molly.* My eyes fill with tears, and I do my best to suppress them, but it's no use. I'm usually not a crier, but I've shed more tears these past few months than I have in my life. You'd think I'd be prepared and have a box of tissues in my office, but I don't. I do my best to wipe my eyes and collect myself. Then I make my way to the restroom, and as luck would have it, Jake is standing outside the door, talking to Ross. Damn it. If I turn around, it'll look like I'm avoiding him. I walk past them with my head down and mumble a hello. I hate when people see me cry, and few actually have. Jake lightly touches my arm, and I look up into his concerned eyes.

"Hey, are you OK?"

"I'll be fine."

"Did something happen with Ben?" he asks quietly.

"Not that it's any of your business, but no. I volunteer at the children's hospital, and one of my patients isn't doing well."

He seems surprised. "If you need to take some personal time, I can cover the review this afternoon."

"No, I'll be fine," I say again. I walk into the restroom and leave him standing in the hallway. Thankfully it's empty. I splash cold water on my face and take some deep, steadying breaths. When I emerge a few minutes later, Jake is gone. I head back to my office and attempt to lose myself in my work.

I'm very quiet at the review that afternoon. No one seems to notice, or they're too polite to say anything. After the meeting, I make a beeline for my office. Even though I have a lot more to do, I decide to call it a day. I'm not being very productive, and mentally I can't be here anymore. I pack up my things to leave when there's a knock on my door. I look up to see Simon standing in my doorway.

"I came to see how you were doing," he says, closing the door.

"How did you know I needed checking on?"

"Jake stopped by. He seemed concerned about you."

For once I'm glad Jake meddled in my personal business; I could really use a friend right now. As he pulls me into a hug, I feel tears prickling my eyelids again. This time I don't hold them back. I cry not just for Molly but for all the things wrong in my personal life. When did things become such a mess? Simon rubs my back and tells me everything will be fine. I wish I could believe him.

"What happened?" he asks. "Jake said something about a patient."

"Molly's mom called me earlier and said she isn't doing well. It doesn't sound good." I sob again. "I'm just not cut out for this. I get too personally invested."

"I know it doesn't seem like it right now, but it's one of your best qualities. I also think it's one of the reasons you're so successful. You take a personal interest in people, which not only makes them open up to you but also makes you want to deliver the best outcome possible."

"Yeah, maybe I'm successful in my professional life, but my personal life is a disaster."

"I know things aren't in a great place with Jake right now, but from where I'm sitting, it's pretty one-sided."

"What do you mean?"

"I mean the current status of your relationship is your choice. If he had a say, I don't think you'd be on nonspeaking terms."

"We're not on nonspeaking terms. I just don't go out of my way to talk to him. Besides, he's had plenty of opportunities to take our relationship further, but he hasn't acted on any of them. You know all of this."

"I know, but I still think he cares about you. Why else would he send me to check on you? You should have seen him when he came into my office. He seemed pretty concerned."

"Simon, I'm not saying he doesn't like me. But it's obviously not enough, or we'd be together. I have plenty of other issues going on in my life that I don't want to deal with it anymore."

"Look, I know things are tough right now, but they'll turn around soon."

"How do you know?"

"Because the only way to go from here is up."

"I hope you're right. I can't imagine things getting much worse."

"Will you be OK?"

"Yes," I lie, not wanting to burden him with my overwhelming sense of sadness.

After Simon leaves, I call Marta at the children's hospital and tell her something has come up with my schedule, and I won't be able to honor my commitment any longer.

"I'm sorry to hear that," she says. "You've been an asset here, and the door is always open if you change your mind."

I thank her and tell her I'll definitely let her know if things change, but I highly doubt they will. I'm not in the right frame of mind where I can constantly deal with this kind of heartbreak. I still want to give back, so I decide to focus my energy on something else: the Make-A-Wish-Foundation. There are countless deserving kids waiting to have their wishes granted, and I'd like to play a part in making them a reality. Ever since I was a little girl, I always believed wishes come true. Even if it can't happen for me, I'm hell-bent on making sure it happens for someone else.

CHAPTER ELEVEN

The following week is a busy one. I get the initial retouched images back from John Paul and work with Matt to narrow down our top choices. We share our recommendations with Natalia, and after much negotiation, we align on a direction. On Thursday I stay late to catch up on all my unread e-mails. I'm ready to call it a night and walk past the conference room on my way out. I see the creative team hard at work on the fragrance pitch. Simon catches my eye and motions for me to come in.

"Want to see our progress?" he asks.

"Sure. I'd love to." The pitch is two weeks away, and the work looks amazing. I offer a few minor comments, but otherwise I tell them it's perfect.

"I agree." I turn around to find Jake standing there, having just brought in dinner for everyone. "You're welcome to stay and eat something," he says.

I debate what to do because I'm hungry, but I find it best not to be around him. "That's OK. I'm actually headed to the gym. One last thing," I say, turning to Simon. "This may be pushing it, but given that the creative is almost done, it might be a good idea to prepare some thought starters for how we'd extend the campaign into other channels such as digital and mobile. They can be in white-paper format, and you don't even need to share them. Just have them in your back pocket in case they ask."

"We're already on it. Jake offered the same suggestion."

"Great minds think alike," says Ari.

I manage a small smile. "Have a good night, everyone."

"Bye, Lexi," the group choruses.

I'm waiting for the elevator when Jake approaches me. "Did I forget something?" I ask him.

"No. I was just wondering if I did something to upset you."

I stare at him for a moment. "No, Jake, you didn't do anything."

That's the problem.

The next morning I stop by Simon's office to congratulate him on the exceptional campaign and see he's in a meeting with Jake. "Sorry. I didn't mean to interrupt. I'll find you later." I walk away before either of them has a chance to respond.

That afternoon Simon comes by my office and closes the door. "I had a very interesting conversation with Jake," he informs me.

"Oh? What'd he say?"

"After you walked out of my office, he asked me if you were acting different. And I said, 'Different how?' He mumbled something about how you seemed angry with him. Then he started talking about how he doesn't date anyone at the office, and he thought everyone knew it was an unwritten rule."

"What did you say?"

"I said, 'I know, but Lexi's different.' And then he said, 'Believe me, I know.'"

"He said that?"

Simon nods. "Yep."

Thank God. At least I know I'm not crazy. "It still doesn't change anything," I say. "He might be interested, but it's obviously not enough for him to act on. If he really liked me, he'd do something about it."

"I just thought you'd like to know."

"Well, thanks for telling me."

Later that day I get a text message from Rachelle, reminding me that Molly's party is this weekend. I reply that I'll be there and ask her to send me the details. I've visited Molly a few times since our initial meeting and feel like we've formed a special bond. I know she's into superheroes, so I go online in search of the perfect gift. When I was growing up, Wonder Woman was my favorite heroine. I find a retro-looking costume and see that they have it at Toys "R" Us. I call Liv and ask her if I can borrow her car tonight.

"Sure. Where are you off to?"

"I have to pick up a birthday gift at Toys "R" Us."

"I'll go with you. There's a Jewel across the street, and I have to do some grocery shopping."

"Wanna grab dinner first?" I ask her.

"Sure. Let's meet in the lobby at six thirty. Will that work for you?"

"I think I can be out of here by then."

Liv and I grab dinner at a great place around the corner from our building that serves soups, sandwiches, and salads. I'm a bit obsessed with their grilled chicken panini.

"Have you talked to Jason recently?" Liv inquires.

"He called the other day. He wants to go out again."

"What did you say?"

"I said yes. We're going out Tuesday night."

"Good. Where are you going?"

"I'm not sure. He said something about a wine bar."

"Are you excited?"

"I'm looking forward to it. But honestly I'm a bit nervous. I don't know the rules anymore. What happens on date number two?"

"Well, considering most people seal the deal on date three, you could kiss him."

"Whatever happened to taking things slow? I can't imagine sleeping with someone after only three dates. It's hardly enough time to know someone, let alone feel comfortable being intimate."

"I agree," Liv says. "But you should kiss him. You need to get over the hurdle of kissing someone other than Ben. It may as well be Jason."

We finish our sandwiches and walk to the parking garage. On the ride over, I muse about kissing Jason. I'm not against it, but I'm not exactly for it either. I find him attractive, but I don't feel a connection with him. Perhaps it's normal at this stage of the dating process. Although when I think about the time when Jake almost kissed me, I definitely envision sparks flying. I'm glad I didn't have any direct encounters with Jake today; it's exhausting trying to ignore him.

Liv and I arrive at Toys "R" Us, and I find the costume.

"What do you think?" I ask her.

"I like it, but do you think you should get her a princess dress instead? All the girls these days are into princesses."

"No, she's into superheroes. She's a bit of a superhero herself."

Liv looks at me a bit quizzically and says, "Then I'm sure she'll love it."

I buy the outfit and a gift bag, then tag along with Liv while she shops. I end up getting groceries for myself too. It's rare that I have access to a car, so I typically buy only what I can carry. We get back to our building and load our bags on the luggage cart. We help each other unload, and then I bring the cart back down to the lobby.

"How are things going, Lexi?" asks Roland.

"Same old, same old," I tell him. Sometimes status quo is good, but I'm yearning for a change.

On Friday I briefly stop by happy hour. I don't want to overdo it because Molly's party starts at ten, so I have to be up early. I see Jake hanging out by the bar with Ross. We make eye contact, and he holds my gaze until I look away. As much as I try to avoid him, my eyes keep casting glances in his direction. Not once has he looked my way. I notice that he doesn't approach any of the girls, but plenty search him out. I watch as he flirts with them, knowing he used to act that way with me. A seed of doubt is planted: Perhaps I'm not that different after all. I sneak out quietly after staying for an hour so people won't give me a hard time about leaving. It proves to be successful.

When I get home, I keep busy by doing final preparations for the benefit; I can't believe it's next weekend. I'm double-checking the invite list when my cell phone rings. I look at the caller ID and see that it's Ben. I'm tempted to answer but decide against it. He leaves a message, and I try to ignore it, but my curiosity gets the best of me. I call my voice mail and tense as I hear his familiar voice. "Hi, Lexi. I was just thinking of you and wanted to see how you were. I know your benefit is next weekend, so I'm sure you're busy preparing. If you get a minute, I'd love to talk to you. Please call me. I miss you." For a minute I get a horrible feeling he'll show up uninvited to the benefit. But I immediately dismiss the thought; he knows how important this event is to me, and I don't think he'd want to compromise it. My phone rings again, and irritated, I check to see who's calling. This time it's Jules.

"Hi, Jules. What's up?"

"Hi, Lex. I know it's last minute, but our sitter canceled for tomorrow night, and we have plans with Scott's coworkers. Would you be able to watch Charlie?"

"Of course. That's the best offer I've had all day."

"Thanks. I owe you. We've been trying to get together with them for weeks, but something always seems to come up. I would have felt terrible canceling."

"I didn't have plans anyway. And it actually works out because I'll already be in the suburbs for a birthday party."

"Whose party are you coming out this way for?"

"It's a long story," I say. "I'll tell you when I see you."

"OK, can you be here by five?"

"Sure. The party is in the morning, so I'll just come by afterward. Tell Char I'm excited to see him."

"I will, and believe me, he'll be thrilled you're coming."

I'm in a much better mood knowing I'll get to see Charlie. He's the only man in my life right now.

—◆◆—

I wake up early on Saturday morning, shower, wrap Molly's gift, and print the directions. I'm a bit nervous about going to the party because I don't know what kind of condition Molly will be in. I figure I'll stop by briefly to make an appearance. Liv was nice enough to let me borrow her car. I find Molly's house and hear animated voices coming from the yard. I take a deep breath then head out back to discover a large inflatable bounce house and various activities set up. Molly sees me and runs over to me.

"Lexi, you made it!"

"Hi. I wouldn't miss your party for the world. Happy birthday!" I study her, taking in her frail features and the bandana that hides her hair loss, but her eyes are still full of life.

Rachelle comes over and introduces me to her husband, Jeff, and various friends and family members. Everyone is really nice, and I end up staying longer than I intended. Rachelle and I have a moment alone, and I ask her about Molly's prognosis. Her eyes tear up as she tells me she isn't responding to the treatments as they'd hoped. "It isn't good," she whispers. Although it's what I suspected, I'm very upset by this news but put on a brave face. "I think it's time for cake," Rachelle says, dabbing at her eyes. Then she calls everyone over to sing "Happy Birthday." "Now close your eyes and make a wish," she says before Molly blows out her candles.

"I wish I could star on TV," she says, then blows them out in one breath.

"Molly, you're not supposed to say your wish out loud, or it won't come true," says Molly's sister, Emma.

The hairs on the back of my neck stand up. Fate works in funny ways. While things may not be meant to be with Jake, now I realize I was brought into Molly's life for a reason. Not only do I have the means to make a TV spot, but it's also weird that I was thinking about volunteering at the Make-A-Wish Foundation, and now I'm here to witness Molly's wish. I do think our meeting was meant to be, because I'm probably the one person who can help make her wish come true.

On Monday I stop by Morgan's office.

"Do you have a minute?" I ask her.

"Sure, Lexi. Come on in."

"I was wondering if the agency does pro bono work."

"Yes, we do, although Bill has to approve it. What's on your mind?"

I tell her about Molly's wish. "My initial idea was to film her and create a pretend commercial. But there are so many other inspirational patients like her that I was thinking we could capture their stories as well. I did some research and found that a handful of other patients from the hospital had a wish granted through the Make-A-Wish Foundation. We could capture each of their testimonials and weave together an emotional spot on behalf of the foundation."

Morgan studies me for a moment then says, "I like the idea. Let me run it past Bill, and I'll get back to you. I have a contact at the Make-A-Wish Foundation, and I'm sure he'd be thrilled to partner with us. Are you sure you have time to take this on in light of your other commitments?"

"Yes. I'll be able to get it all done. The pitch is almost over." It'll be a lot of work, but it's worth it. I leave her office feeling encouraged.

Morgan e-mails me the following day and says that Bill is onboard. She tells me to work with the head of each department to determine who has capacity to work on the project. She's also reached out to her contact at Make-A-Wish, and he's very interested in working with us. She arranges a conference call for later in the week so we can discuss a joint vision for the project. I decide not to tell Molly about it yet; I don't want to get her hopes up in case it falls through. Once I'm confident, I'll discuss it with Rachelle first to make sure she's comfortable with the idea. I suspect she will be. How can she not be over the moon about having the chance to fulfill her daughter's wish?

The rest of the day passes uneventfully. I leave shortly after five to get ready for my second date with Jason. Once I'm changed, I head downstairs to wait in the lobby. This time I accepted his offer to pick me up. The cab pulls up in front of my building, and Jason slides over in the backseat. He doesn't get out to open the door for me, which Jake would have done. I'm irritated with myself for even comparing the two, and I make a point not to let thoughts of Jake infiltrate my evening.

"You look nice," he says.

"Thanks. So do you."

He's wearing a fitted, long-sleeve, button-down black shirt with a black-and-white plaid pattern on the rolled-up cuffs; jeans; and black leather sandals. His wavy hair is slicked back, as though he just got out of the shower.

I notice his face is a bit scruffy, like it was on our last date. It makes me wonder if I'm not worth the effort of shaving or if he thinks it gives him sex appeal. I notice he's left his top two buttons undone, so I decide it's the latter. We make small talk in the cab until we arrive at our destination. He's chosen a relatively new wine bar in Lincoln Park.

"I thought we were going for pizza," I tease him.

"That was my plan, but you look too nice for pizza."

"Thanks, although that's a cop-out. You're just worried you'll actually like deep dish."

"It so happens that I chose this location because there's a pizza place a few doors down. If you're still hungry afterward, we can stop in for a slice."

"Deal."

When we walk into the bar, it's fairly crowded, but we're able to get a table. It's a charming place, with rustic-looking stone walls that have built-in wooden wine racks. An entire wall has been finished with chalkboard paint that showcases the wine list. There are rows of closely packed tables, and upon closer inspection, I notice the bases are made out of large wine barrels. The lighting is very dim and accented only by candelabras that flank each corner of the room. Empty wine bottles create a piece of artwork behind the bar.

"What's your preference? Red or white?" Jason asks.

"Red is fine. Do you like Cabernet?"

"Yes. And let's order some appetizers."

"OK. Do you want to get the cheese-and-fruit platter?"

"Done. Let's get a flatbread too, your pick."

"The margarita one looks good."

The waitress comes by, and Jason chooses a bottle of Cabernet and puts in our appetizer order. "So how have things been?" he asks.

"Fine. Work has been crazy, but I like being busy."

"What are you working on?"

I tell him about the pitch and my Make-A-Wish spot.

"What inspired you to want to do pro bono work?"

"I volunteer at Lurie Children's Hospital. I met a patient there, and she told me her dream is to be on TV."

"Wow. It's lucky she met you."

"I know. I figured it must be fate. What's the likelihood of her meeting someone who can actually make her wish a reality?" To be honest I've never been a big believer in fate, but lately I'm starting to change my mind.

"How did you get into volunteering?" Jason asks.

"I don't know. It's something I've started recently. I love kids, and I've always wanted to give back and do something meaningful. I applied at the hospital when I moved here, but it's kind of hard with my work schedule. So I decided to focus on Make-A-Wish instead. I would love to grant wishes and help kids feel that all is not lost. No child should have to give up hope."

"That's very noble of you."

I feel like the conversation has turned serious, so I try to lighten the mood. I ask Jason how his job is going and whether he's met any interesting new people. He entertains me with funny stories about his boss, who sounds like an overbearing micromanager. He keeps topping me off, so it's hard to keep track of how many glasses I've had. I excuse myself to use the restroom and feel a bit dizzy when I stand up. I'm definitely buzzed and plan to slow down my drinking. Jason seems like a nice guy, but it's only our second date, so I want to keep a clear head.

When I return to the table he says, "So Liv's cousin told me you used to be engaged."

And there it is. I wondered if he knew. "Yes, I was. Things didn't work out, though, which is why I moved back here."

"I take it things didn't end well?"

"I wish I could say it was amicable, but no."

Jason is quiet for a moment then says, "Look, you're smart, successful, and compassionate, and I find you very attractive. But it's obvious you're still getting over your ex; you kind of give off a closed-off vibe. I just moved here, and I'm looking to meet new people. I guess what I'm trying to say is that I like you, but the timing seems off. I'd normally ask you out for a third date, but then we'd be heading in a direction I'm not sure either of us is ready for."

Wow. At least he's being candid, which is refreshing. "I appreciate your honesty. Dating after being with someone for so long is definitely a new experience, but I'm glad I got to share it with you."

He smiles and says, "The pleasure was mine."

I guess this means there won't be a third date, which leaves me feeling very relieved. Jason pays the bill, and we head outside to wait for a cab.

"You know what'll help you get over your ex?" he says.

"What?"

"Getting past the hurdle of a first kiss with someone new."

I stare at him incredulously. Does he really think I'm going to kiss him after we've established we aren't going out again? But then I think, *Why not?* I'll need to do it sooner or later, so now is as good a time as any. I nod, and he leans in and kisses me. His lips are surprisingly soft and inviting, and while it's a nice kiss, I don't feel anything. "Something to look forward to when you're ready to date," he says. I manage a smile and thank him for a nice evening. Perhaps the kiss was a bad idea. I was hoping it would somehow fill a void, but it's left me feeling emptier than before.

I take my own cab home and reflect on his comment that I'm closed off. I decide that's not the case; it's just that my heart belongs to someone else.

The Make-A-Wish project is a go, and the foundation has approved our storyboard. When I call Rachelle and tell her the news, she's overjoyed.

"Thank you, Lexi. You don't know how much this means to Molly, to all of us."

"You're welcome. I'd love to tell her about it."

"Let me put her on the phone."

When I tell Molly she's going to star in a TV commercial, she's quiet for a few moments. Then she says, "Lexi, does this mean I'm going to die?"

Her reaction stuns me. "No, that isn't what it means. It just means you made a wish, and I'm helping to make it come true."

"Are you like, my fairy godmother?"

"Something like that. Now can I tell you what the commercial is about?"

"Yes," she says, sounding more like herself.

I do my best to be enthusiastic as I describe the spot. "You'll get your makeup done, and we'll pick out a special outfit for you, which you can keep afterward."

When she chats about what she wants to wear, I know she's excited about the idea.

Jake stops by my office the next morning.

"Hey. How are things going?"

"Fine. You?"

"Good. I haven't seen you in a while, so I wanted to check in."

"Well, as I said, everything's fine." I go back to typing.

"I heard about the Make-A-Wish spot. Everyone's talking about it. It's really impressive that you took the initiative to make it happen."

"Thanks. And don't worry—I'll still be able to get the pitch done."

"I wasn't worried about it."

"Good."

"I just want to let you know that I think what you're doing is very admirable."

"Well, Molly's a special girl." I look up and meet his gaze. I haven't truly looked at him in weeks, and he's as handsome as ever, although I detect a hint of sadness in his eyes. I feel myself weaken and don't want to be susceptible to his spell. "See you later," I say, effectively dismissing him from my office.

My phone rings later that afternoon; it's Liv. I haven't heard from her boyfriend Jason since we went ring shopping, and I've been nervous every time she's called me.

"Lexi," she practically screams when I answer, "I'm engaged!"

"Congratulations! I'm thrilled for you. Tell me everything." I close my door and listen intently as she tells me all the details.

"So I was sitting here grading quizzes, and when I got to the last one, I saw Jason's name at the top. It was like an out-of-body experience. I knew what was coming, but I couldn't believe it. I started reading, and the questions were all about our relationship and his feelings for me. The last one was his asking me to marry him, which I barely could read because I was crying so hard. Then he was in the room and got down on one knee."

"Liv, that's one of the best proposal stories I've ever heard."

"I know. I never realized he was so creative."

"I can tell you he put a lot of thought into it. He told me his idea. You should have seen how proud he was. How's the ring?"

"It's gorgeous! Exactly what I wanted. Thanks, by the way."

"Did he tell you I helped?"

"No," she says, "but I assumed."

"Can I stop by on my way home from work? I want to give you a congratulatory hug. And we must go out tonight to celebrate."

"I'd love to, Lex, but I'll have to take a rain check because Jason planned a dinner with our families. But you definitely can stop by to see the ring."

"How sweet is he? You've got a good man."

"I know," Liv says. "I lucked out. I can't wait to see you later."

"Me too! Love you."

"Love you too."

I'm ecstatic for Liv; it's nice to see one of my oldest and closest friends so happy. I send Jason a text congratulating him and ask him where they're going for dinner. I want to arrange to have a bottle of champagne sent to their table. He texts me back, saying they'll be at Spiaggia, so I call the restaurant with my request and provide my credit card information. After that I call it a day. I've been on an emotional roller coaster all week, and I'm looking forward to going home.

CHAPTER TWELVE

On Friday Michelle pops by to see if I want to head downstairs with her to happy hour.

"Thanks for the offer, but I'm going to pass today. I have that benefit tomorrow and need to go home and do some final preparations."

"I forgot that was tomorrow. I'd like to donate. Can I bring you a check on Monday?"

"Sure. That's very thoughtful. You can bring a check or donate online."

"Oh, I can donate online? I'd rather do that."

"The link is on the sheet outside my office."

"Perfect. I hope it goes well. Have fun!"

"Thanks. Have a great weekend."

I go home and find I don't have that much to do. I make a few calls to confirm delivery times then make myself a frozen dinner, as I'm not in the mood to cook. My phone rings, and I see that it's my younger sister, Tara.

"Hey, Tar. What's up?"

"Hi, Lex. I just wanted to see how you're doing and if there's anything I can help with."

"Thanks. I think everything is pretty much taken care of."

"Do you want me to come early to help you set up?"

"Sure. I could use your eye." I ask her about college and her love life. She tells me she's dating a new guy. "Are you going to bring him to the benefit?"

"No. We've only been going out a few weeks."

"Well, keep me posted."

"I will. See you tomorrow." I wish my love life were as active as Tara's. Every time I talk to her, she's going out with someone new.

I wake up early on Saturday and head straight to the hotel. I spend the day setting up and making sure everything is in order. I'm glad I have Tara to give input; she's great with space planning. She's one of those people who think best visually. I, on the other hand, work best when I write things down. I head home late in the afternoon to run some last-minute errands and get ready. When I return to the hotel, I spy Jules, Tara, and my parents talking with the DJ. I wander over and give them each a hug and tell them the place looks fantastic.

My mom beams at me and says, "Lexi, you made most of the decisions."

We chose square tables with three different-size flower arrangements in tall, clear vases. They're all in various shades of pink, my Aunt Lynne's favorite color. Interspersed are small votive candles in square, glass holders. The tablecloths are white satin with a silver organza overlay, and both fabrics are also draped behind the dance floor. We rented matching silver-backed ballroom chairs with white seat cushions. I wanted to create an elegant yet fun affair, so we brought in various-size lanterns that are suspended from the ceiling over the dance floor. The lighting is soft and gives the room a warm, pink glow. Tables are set up at the back of the room with appetizer stations, which later will turn into a dessert bar. I walk around and read the placards to double-check that the menu is right.

Jules comes over and says, "Everything looks perfect. Aunt Lynne would have been proud."

I look around and know she would have loved this event. Ironically it's almost like I planned a wedding. I wonder if I'll ever plan another event like it.

Slowly people start to arrive. Liv and Jason, Simon, Sydney, Jill, Melanie, and a few friends from college are coming. I didn't mention the benefit to that many people at work because the tickets cost $250. Instead I put a sign-up sheet outside my office with a note that said donations were welcome. Jill and Melanie are my first friends to arrive.

"Lexi," Mel exclaims. "You look fantastic!"

"God, I'd kill to have your body," says Jill.

"And I'd kill to have your height," I reply. "You all look great too."

"I love your dress," says Mel. "Very regal."

I'm wearing a deep-purple, V-neck, floor-length satin gown that fits me perfectly. It's the first dress I've ever bought that didn't need alterations. I had my hair done this afternoon; Marco styled it down in soft, loose waves. Afterward I went to buy new mascara at Nordstrom, and the woman ended up doing my makeup. She gave me smoky eyes and pale-pink, glossy lips. It's a bit more dramatic than I'm used to, but I'm happy with the effect. Just then I spy Simon walking in.

"Simon, thanks for coming," I say, throwing my arms around him.

"Lexi, you're like a sexy Greek goddess," he responds, holding me at arm's length so he can admire my dress.

"Thanks," I say with a laugh. "You look nice too."

He's wearing a black pinstriped suit with a lavender tie and matching handkerchief. I introduce him to my friends.

"We've heard so much about you," says Jill.

"Come. Let's get a drink," I tell them.

We make our way to the bar, and things are in full swing. There's a large crowd on the dance floor, and others are mingling by the food stations. As I look toward the entrance, my heart drops. In walks Jake looking very sharp in a three-piece suit. I had no idea he was coming.

I glance at Simon, who shrugs. "I may have mentioned something to him," he says innocently.

Jake spies us and makes his way over to the bar. "Hi, Lexi, Simon," he says.

"Hi," I say, not able to keep the surprise out of my voice. "I didn't know you were coming. I checked the guest list today, and your name wasn't on it."

"I bought my ticket at the door. Simon told me about the event; I figured we should have representation from the agency."

Of course he has to make it about work. God forbid he should want to come on his own accord. Jake says hi to my friends, and I introduce him to Jason. I'm surprised they haven't run into each other before, especially since Jason lives down the street from him.

As we're talking, my mom comes over. "Jill, Melanie, Sydney, so good to see you," she says warmly.

"Mom, these are two of my coworkers, Simon and Jake."

"Wonderful to meet you. I've heard so much about you both." Jake looks pleased, but I'm ready to kill her. "It's just that Lexi speaks so highly about all her coworkers," my mom says, trying to recover.

"Nice to meet you, Mrs. Winters," says Jake. "Now I see where Lexi gets her good looks."

"Aren't you sweet?" my mom says. "Please call me Anne." Then she turns to me. "Lexi, I could use your help at the gift-bag table." As I follow her, she remarks, "Jake's adorable. He's obviously very smitten with you, or he wouldn't have come."

"I don't think so. He said he wanted to represent the company."

"Well, he could have sent someone else. He didn't have to come personally. Plus Simon is here."

She has a point, but I'm sick of trying to analyze his intentions.

The night flies by, and I'm busy chatting with my parents' friends and putting out small fires. I've hardly had a chance to talk to my friends, so I make my way over to them. Jill, Melanie, Sydney and Liv are standing at the dessert table. "This cake is to die for," says Jill. "Have a piece." I accept a slice of white chocolate cake drizzled with raspberry sauce and taste it. It's divine.

"How are things going?" Liv asks.

"Good. Only a few issues, but nothing I couldn't handle."

"I can't believe Jake showed up," she whispers to me.

"I know, me either. I've been doing my best to ignore him these past few weeks. I don't know what to make of it."

Just then the DJ puts on "Run" by Matt Nathanson. I love this song and haven't heard it in a long time. I feel a tap on my shoulder and turn around.

"I believe I owe you a dance," says Jake.

"Yes, I believe you do," I reply, thinking back to when he turned down my invitation at the karaoke bar. That feels like ages ago, yet here we are, still in the same place. I set the cake on a nearby table, and he takes my hand, leading me to the dance floor. He pulls me close as we begin swaying to the music, but I try to maintain some distance.

"So," he says, "it's a great event."

"I'm happy with the way everything turned out. I won't know what to do with myself once it's over. I've spent so long helping my mom plan it. But don't worry," I tell him a bit sarcastically, "not on company time."

Jake ignores this comment. "When did your aunt pass away?"

"Three years ago. She was fifty-one."

"I take it you were close to her?"

"Yes, and my mom and Lynne were super close. We spent all our holidays together and I saw her all the time. She always wanted a daughter but had three sons, so she treated me like I was one of her own. It's still hard."

"I'm sorry," he says sincerely. We continue our dance in silence, and then he comments, "You don't stop by my office anymore."

"I've been busy." I look around at the other couples on the dance floor. I look everywhere but at Jake.

"Hey," he says, taking my chin in his hand so I'm forced to look at him. "I like when you stop by my office. I've missed our talks." He pauses then says, "I've missed you."

Oh. I don't reply because I'm not sure what to say. He looks at me, trying to gauge my reaction, but I remain silent. "I feel like I owe you an apology. I'm sorry I've been giving you mixed signals," he says quietly.

Finally he's being honest with me. "Just make up your mind already," I respond.

"Lexi, I made up my mind a long time ago not to get involved with anyone at work. But then you came along, and it's taken all my willpower not to change it." I don't know how to take his comment. Obviously he hasn't given in yet. Then he says, "You look beautiful tonight, Lexi. And it's not just because you're dressed up. You're so passionate about this benefit and everything you do that you have this glow. I'm in awe of you." *Whoa.* I meet his gaze and smile at him, a shy smile. "There it is," he says. "I've missed that smile."

Suddenly I'm so tired. I'm tired of being aloof and constantly not acting like myself so he won't think I'm into him. I'm not bitchy by nature, and it's exhausting. I feel myself relax in his arms. I think Jake senses it too, because he holds me tighter, and his touch is strong and reassuring. I've never been this close to him before. He's intoxicating—a mix of something comforting and familiar with the promise of something new. His face is inches from mine, and it takes every fiber of my being not to pull him in for a kiss. As we dance, all my senses are heightened; I smell the distinctly earthy scent of his aftershave, feel the rise and fall of his chest with each breath, and practically touch the heat that emanates from his body. I listen to the music, and as the words wash over me, all I can think is how fitting the lyrics are. *Yes, Jake. I know that it's wrong, but still I run right into you.*

"What's this song?" Jake asks.

"'Run' by Matt Nathanson."

"I like it," he whispers in my ear.

I shiver, and he pulls me even closer, resting his cheek against mine. As the song ends, I reluctantly pull away, but Jake doesn't let go of my hand. Instead he pulls me back toward him, and I feel vulnerable under his intense gaze, which is broken when my mom walks up to the podium and asks for everyone's attention. As she begins her speech, I want to listen, but I'm so distracted. Jake is holding my hand, in public, while gently caressing my back with his free hand as she speaks. I'm freaking out. I catch Liv's eye, and she gives me a knowing look. She and I have so much to discuss later. I turn my attention back to my mom, who's talking about my aunt and how much she would have loved to be at this party. Then she thanks me and says that she couldn't have put together such a successful event without my help. She asks me to come up on stage. Jake slowly unravels his fingers from mine and gives me an encouraging look. Nervously I walk up to the podium. I didn't plan on speaking, so I'm not prepared. I wish my mom had mentioned that she wanted me to say a few words. I'm not one of those off-the-cuff speakers; I like to have what I'm going to say planned out.

"Thank you all for coming to the Third Annual Lynne Sachman Benefit. It means so much to my family and me to have your support behind such an important cause. In the United States, breast cancer claims the lives of almost forty thousand women annually, and a new diagnosis is made every three minutes. But thanks to generous people like you, there are survivors. Your donations will help fund programs that give patients access to quality care and also will help fund research to find a cure. If I have a daughter someday, my dream is that she'll never know the terrible effects of this disease. Thank you from the bottom of my heart for helping to make a difference. You've touched not only our lives but also those of countless other women."

Everyone applauds as I make my way back to my friends. I'm stopped along the way by many well-wishers, telling me what a great event this is and how touching my speech was. Finally I find the table where my friends are sitting.

"Great speech, Lexi," says Liv.

"Yes," my friends echo in agreement.

I look at Jake, and he smiles at me. "You never cease to amaze me," he says.

I blush and can't erase the smile from my face. The DJ announces it's the last song.

"That's our cue," says Jason. "I like to leave before the crowd." He looks at Jake and says, "Hey, want a ride home? You're on the way."

Jake looks uncertain then replies, "Yeah, sure."

Liv hugs me and whispers, "I'm going to kill him."

"Don't worry," I whisper back. "As you've said, guys are clueless."

Simon stands up and says he's leaving too. I give him a huge hug and thank him for coming. Jake is standing right next to him. He says good-bye to me, and I lean in and give him a soft, lingering kiss on the cheek. I can tell he's surprised by the gesture.

"Thank you so much for coming," I tell him. "It means a lot to me."

"I'm happy I came," he says.

I watch them walk out and feel slightly worried. What if this was my only chance with Jake? I'm sure he'll come to his senses in the morning, and we'll be back to where we started: nowhere.

I stop by Jake's office on Monday morning.

"Hi." I smile at him nervously.

"Hi," he says, beaming back at me.

I instantly feel relieved. "I wanted to say thanks again for coming on Saturday, and I wanted to give you this. You won the silent auction for the iPad."

"Oh, I hoped you were coming by because you wanted to see me. Why don't you hold on to it? It's actually a gift for you."

"What do you mean?"

"I bid on it for you. I already have an iPad." I stare at him incredulously. "Welcome to the twenty-first century, Wilma."

"I can't believe you bought me an iPad."

"I didn't buy it. I donated to a worthy cause and happened to bid on an item you needed."

"I can't accept it," I tell him.

"That's fine. Do with what you want with it. The funds are already going to one worthy cause—why not let it solve another?" He has a point. He senses I'm relenting and says, "You'll love it. I take it you have Wi-Fi?"

"Yes," I reply, rolling my eyes. "I have Wi-Fi. Thank you," I say, turning serious. "This is very generous of you."

"I told you, it's for a worthy cause. And I don't mean you."

"Gee, thanks," I say sarcastically. His phone rings, interrupting our conversation.

"I have to take this. See you later," he says in a somewhat questioning tone.

"See you," I affirm.

I leave his office and sense things are different between us. Or maybe it's just that I'm different. The benefit seems to have been a turning point in our relationship. I walk back to my office with a renewed sense of hope.

I'm in a meeting with Michelle when Simon stops by my office. "Come in," I tell him. "We're just finishing up." Once Michelle leaves, Simon closes my door and sits down. "I've been meaning to stop by to thank you again for coming on Saturday," I say. "It's just been such a crazy day that I haven't had the chance."

"It was my pleasure. How do you think things went?"

"I think they went well. The proceeds from the silent auction exceeded what we raised last year."

"That's all well and good, but I meant with Jake."

"Oh," I smile. "That seemed to go well too."

"I noticed."

"He bought me an iPad."

"What do you mean?"

"He bid on it in the silent auction—for me." He looks confused, so I add, "One time we were talking about technology, and I made a comment that I didn't have an iPad but would like one."

"Interesting. Are things back on then?"

"I think so. I can't explain it, but things feel different between us. I don't know…Maybe it's just me resuming how I was acting before. I can only hope there's a different outcome this time."

"Trust me—you and Jake getting together is inevitable."

"I don't know. This is what we do. He flirts; I get my hopes up; and then he backs off. Do you really think it's for real this time?"

"Lexi, I may be gay, but I'm not blind. That boy has it bad for you."

I laugh. "Tell me, what should I do?"

Simon looks thoughtful for a minute then says, "I think you need alcohol. Lots of alcohol."

CHAPTER THIRTEEN

On Tuesday morning Jake stops by my office. He seems stressed.

"Hey, everything OK?" I ask.

"Nigel's wife went into labor three weeks early. He's not coming to San Francisco."

"Oh, that's too bad. What are you going to do?"

"I was hoping you would come."

"Me? You want me to present?"

"Yes."

"But Jake, I'm not a planner."

"I know that, but you're familiar with all the work, and you helped uncover our key insight. You attended the research sessions, so you know our consumer. You're closer to it than any planner I could pull in. Plus, with your background, you have the right credentials. I've already cleared it with Morgan."

I stare at him, debating what to do. "OK then. I'll do it."

Jake gives me a big smile. "Thanks, Lexi. I knew I could count on you."

"When are we leaving?"

"Thursday morning. We have the next day or so to bring you up to speed on what you'll be presenting. The deck is pretty much locked, although you're welcome to make edits so it's more your style. I'll put some time on your calendar this afternoon so we can review it."

"OK. Let me clear my schedule. I'll see you later."

I can't believe I get to go to San Francisco for the pitch—and with Jake. It's a high-profile client, and this is a huge opportunity for me. I stop by Michelle's office to let her know I'll be unavailable the rest of the week. We run through the status of her projects and I tell her the key things that need to happen while I'm out. I'm glad I can trust her to handle them.

Jake, Simon, and I meet that afternoon, and they walk me through the pitch deck. I have a few suggestions, but otherwise it's in really good shape. Jake and I discuss how we'll divide up the content. He's going to open up the meeting, handle introductions, set up the assignment, then turn things over to me and Simon. Next we review the final print ads, and they look amazing. The team also boarded up our concept for the website, digital media, and outdoor billboard. The white-paper ideas for social media and promotional extensions are going into the presentation. I look at Simon and tell him what an incredible job the team did. It's a smart, sexy campaign, and I'd be shocked if we didn't land the account.

"What do you think?" I ask Jake. "You do these pitches all the time."

"I think we have outstanding creative. If they judge us on the work, we'll win hands down. The only issue will be cost. We're up against some smaller shops, and they'll be very aggressive with their pricing. I also think chemistry is important, which is another reason I wanted to bring you. You and Simon are a good team and play off each other's strengths. Plus I think they'll relate to you. Knowing my luck, they'll want to put you on the account. Then Morgan will really have my head."

"Let's not get ahead of ourselves. We can worry about that when we win it."

"I'm glad you're optimistic," Jake says. "Why don't you take the day off tomorrow? Take some time to go through the deck so you're comfortable with it. We can rehearse one last time Thursday night."

"Are you sure?"

"Yes, I think you'll be able to focus better at home. There are too many distractions here."

I can't argue with that. We make a plan to meet at the office on Thursday morning then head to the airport together.

"I'll have Joann book your plane ticket. Simon and I are planning on staying through the weekend. I have to be there for a meeting on Monday, and Simon has friends in the area."

"I'll stay through the weekend too. I've never been to San Francisco before."

"You, my dear, are in for a treat," Simon tells me.

I spend all evening going through the presentation. I wake up the next morning and review it again. I'm really very comfortable with the content. I decide to take a break and make an appointment for a mani/pedi that afternoon and throw in a bikini wax. I tell myself it's because I might go to the pool. I come home and pack, then go through my notes one final time. I don't want to overdo it and sound rehearsed. We're leaving on a 1:00 p.m. flight, so the plan is to have an early dinner then do a final run-through.

The next morning Jake, Simon, and I meet to do a dress rehearsal. Jake plays the role of the client and throws a bunch of questions my way. I do a fairly good job answering them, but he gives me some suggestions. It's fun to see him in his element. I can tell he's pumped about this pitch. He radiates a positive energy that's kind of contagious.

"We probably should get going," he says. "Let's meet in the downstairs lobby in five."

I go to the ladies' room, grab my suitcase, and head downstairs. I can't believe I'm going on a business trip with Jake. I know it's for work, but I'm excited nonetheless. Jake ordered a town car, and it's waiting for us. The driver takes our bags, and we get in. Simon and I are in the back, and Jake is in the front.

He turns around and hands me my ticket. Then he looks at me apologetically. "I tried to get you in first-class with us, but it was too expensive so last minute."

"Don't worry about it. I'll be fine in coach. Just don't forget about me when you're sipping your champagne and eating ice cream."

"Not these days," says Simon. "We'll be lucky if we get a bag of peanuts."

"At least you'll have more leg room."

"Like you need it," he says, and I narrow my eyes at him.

Jake gets a call and is on his phone the entire ride to the airport. Simon and I chat in the backseat. After we check in and get through security, we decide to grab lunch.

"Where should we go? Chili's?" I tease Simon. He wrinkles his nose at me. "Hey, there's nothing wrong with Chili's," I tell him.

"I was thinking more along the lines of Wolfgang Puck."

"Of course you were. It's a good thing I didn't suggest the food court."

We eat lunch then head to the gate. We only have about five minutes before we board. I use the restroom one last time, and when I get back, they call first-class to board. "That'd be us," says Simon. I wait another ten minutes before my row is called. When I walk past Jake, he grabs my bag.

"Is there anything you need in here?" he asks me.

"No. I have a separate carry-on. Thanks." I watch as he effortlessly lifts my bag into the overhead bin. "It's nice to see there are still gentlemen out there," I say, giving Simon a look.

He shrugs. "I knew Jake would offer."

I make my way back until I find my row. I have a window seat, and miraculously no one is next to me. There's an older man in the aisle seat, but he's already put on his headphones. Good, I can stretch out a bit more and not have to worry about making polite conversation. It's a long flight, so I brought a book and some magazines. I love reading and haven't had a lot of time to lately. We're about midway through the flight when Jake comes by.

"Is this seat open?" he asks me.

I nod, and he sits down. "Slumming?" I ask him.

He laughs. "I feel bad that you're stuck all the way back here. I figured I'd keep you company for a bit."

"That's nice of you," I say.

"What are you reading? The next book in the Fifty Shades series?"

"No, that's old news." He feigns disappointment. "I finished all three a long time ago. I'm now reading *The Choice*."

"What's it about?"

"Did you ever see the movie *Sliding Doors*?" Jake shakes his head. "Well, it's kind of like that. Basically it's about the choices we make and how one decision can change the course of your life entirely. This girl is torn about where to go to college: Does she accompany her boyfriend or go to the school of her choice and be on her own? The first part of the book follows her life where she chooses the same school as her boyfriend. The second shows how things turn out when she charts her own course. She ends up meeting a new guy, but the twist comes toward the end, when her two lives collide, and she has to choose between the two."

"Which does she choose?"

"I don't know. I haven't gotten to that part yet."

He stares at me intently then asks, "Who do you think she should choose: the old boyfriend or the new guy?" Suddenly I get the feeling we're no longer talking about the book.

"Well, the old boyfriend is the safe, reliable choice. But I think she should pick the new guy."

Jake nods. "Let me know how it turns out."

I ask him about the kinds of books he likes, and he tells me mostly non-fiction. "What are you reading now?" I ask him.

"A biography about JFK. I also like memoirs because they give me a glimpse into what people's lives were really like. Have you ever read one?"

I shake my head. "I usually read fiction. I guess I feel like everyday life is hard enough— sometimes it's nice to read a book and know you're escaping reality."

"That's understandable," he says. "Speaking of, have you talked to your ex yet?"

"Not yet." I try to change the subject. "What about you? How are things going with Barbie?"

"I haven't seen her in a while. She doesn't interest me that much."

"Oh, what does a girl have to do to interest you?"

"She has to be smart and accomplished, have a sense of humor, share some of my interests, and have a goal for herself."

"What about Ashley? Doesn't she have a goal?"

"Her goal seems to be marrying someone rich to take care of her," he says with a laugh. "Not the goal I had in mind."

"You didn't mention anything about looks," I point out.

"I figured that was implied. I have to be attracted to someone to get to the other stuff. What about you?"

"Well, as you said, I need to find the person attractive, but it goes beyond that for me. There needs to be a spark."

"A spark?"

"You know, chemistry. I've been on many dates where I thought the guy was nice looking, but something was missing. Right away I need to feel a connection with someone that makes me intrigued, excited, and wanting to learn more. I need to get a *feeling* about someone. After that he needs to be goal oriented, confident but not cocky, secure in who he is, and not take himself too seriously. He also can't be afraid of commitment and has to have a good relationship with his family."

"Is that all?" Jake teases.

"Oh, and one more thing—he needs to have nice manners. Call me old-fashioned, but I like a guy who's a gentleman."

"I wouldn't have pictured that. You seem to be sort of a feminist."

"I know, and I am in many ways. Like I wouldn't want a guy to order for me at a restaurant, but there are certain things I still feel a guy should do." Just then the fasten seat belt sign comes on, and the captain announces we'll be landing in about thirty minutes.

"That's my cue," Jake says.

"Thanks for keeping me company."

"Anytime," he says, and makes his way back to his seat.

I try to get lost again in my book, but my thoughts keep drifting to Jake.

When I get off the plane, he and Simon are waiting for me. Jake has my bag and won't let me take it.

"Jake, I can pull my own suitcase."

He shakes his head. "You can check one thing off your list," he says with a smirk.

"Well, it's a start, but it probably shouldn't count because I gave you an unfair advantage."

Puzzled, Simon looks at us. "What are you guys talking about?"

"I'm just trying to keep up with Lexi's high standards," Jake says.

I try to hide my smile. We head to the car rental desk, and Simon informs us he wants to get a separate car. He plans to visit some friends on Saturday in the Bay Area. I assume he'll invite me to tag along.

"Lex, you can come with me. Jake likely will be on the phone the whole time."

"You know me too well, Simon," he replies.

We arrive at the hotel and check in. Our rooms are all on the seventh floor. I hope this is a sign of good luck. Before we part ways, we agree to meet for dinner in a half hour. I decide to freshen up and change. It's beautiful out, so I throw on a color-block tunic dress with platform espadrille wedge sandals. I put my hair half up, reapply my makeup, and I'm ready. I happen to be the first one downstairs. I take a seat on the couch in the lobby and wait. A well-dressed businessman comes and sits beside me.

"I thought the men were usually waiting for the women," he says to me.

I smile. "You're right. Something is wrong with this picture."

He extends a hand to me. "I'm Todd."

I shake his hand. "Lexi."

"Are you here on business?" he asks.

"Yes. I just arrived. You?"

"I actually leave tomorrow."

I look up and spy Jake getting off the elevator. He sees us and makes his way over. "Sorry to keep you waiting," he tells me.

"No problem. I was just chatting with Todd here."

Todd looks from me to Jake. "Well, Lexi, it was nice meeting you. I'll be at the bar later if you care to meet for a drink."

"OK. Nice meeting you too." After he walks away, Jake raises his eyebrows at me. "What? He just struck up a friendly conversation. He pointed out that usually the men are waiting on the women."

He laughs. "Leave it to Simon to be ready last."

On cue, Simon gets off the elevator. "I just talked to my friend, and he told me there's a great seafood place within walking distance. Is that OK with you, Lexi?"

"I'll be fine."

We head to the restaurant and decide to sit outdoors. We split a bottle of wine, and I feel very relaxed considering we have a huge presentation tomorrow. I ask Simon about his friends, and he reveals they were the ones who set him up with his partner, Lance.

"I still have to meet him," I scold Simon.

"I know, and I tried. I invited you to our dinner party, but you turned me down."

"Fair point, but it was last minute, and I already had plans." I don't mention I was baby-sitting for my nephew that night. "I'd really like to meet him."

"Lance is a great guy," says Jake.

"You've met him?" I ask incredulously.

"Yes, at last year's holiday party."

"Oh, we're allowed to bring dates?"

"Not to the company-sponsored party, but inevitably there's always an after party, and a lot of people bring their significant others."

"Probably not the best idea," says Simon.

"Why? Are there scandals that go on?"

"Usually. Free alcohol and work events don't mix well."

"Give me some names," I tell him.

He thinks for a minute and says, "Sharon and Mike from accounting."

"I don't know them. Tell me about someone I would know."

"OK. Nicole and Derrick."

"No way. She never told me!"

"Maybe she doesn't remember," Jake says, smirking.

"Don't tell him that," I say. "I don't think he'd take it as a compliment."

The waiter arrives with our meals. Simon takes a bite and says, "This is divine. Try some, Lexi."

Even though this restaurant is known for its seafood, I refused to order fish, which Jake and Simon gave me a hard time about. I take a bite and make a face. They both laugh. I knew I'd be safe with pasta.

"So what other scandals should I know about?"

Jake gets a funny look, and I realize it's probably best to change the subject.

"That's about it," says Simon.

"Is the holiday party a big deal then?" I ask him.

"Oh, yeah. Everyone gets decked out to the nines. The company rents out an entire auditorium, and people from the agency put on a performance. They'll be sending out an e-mail soon about auditions."

"You have to audition?"

"Yep, it's a major production. They usually spoof a Broadway musical. Last year it was *Phantom of the Opera*. People spend all their free time rehearsing. Crazy if you ask me."

Jake breaks in. "It's a company tradition, and it's considered a big honor to be in the show."

"Do you know what musical they'll be doing this year?" I ask him.

"I do," Jake says, "but I was sworn to secrecy."

I bat my eyelashes at him and say seductively, "Come on. I promise not to tell anyone."

"Nope. You'll have to beat it out of me."

"There are other ways," I say, and innocently sip my wine. I can see Jake smile from the corner of my eye. "So is it all entertainment?"

"Mainly, although Bill and Stephen give an update on the state of the business first."

The waiter comes and asks if we want dessert.

"Come on, Lex," says Simon. "Share something with me."

"Twist my arm. Of course you know I'm always in for dessert. But it has to be something chocolate."

He rolls his eyes. "Would I have it any other way?"

The waiter brings a sinfully delicious slice of flourless dark-chocolate cake. The three of us share it, and I'm stuffed. We walk back to the hotel and decide to meet in Jake's room in ten minutes for a final run-through.

I knock on his door ten minutes later, and for once I'm the last to arrive. Jake is sitting at the desk with his laptop. He wants to go through the presentation one last time because he's made some changes. He reads them aloud, but it's hard for me to follow without seeing the deck. I move behind him and lean over his shoulder so I can see the screen. He smells just like he did the night of the benefit. My head is practically level with his, and I see a hint of stubble on his cheek. If he were to turn toward me, our lips would meet. This is very distracting, so I return to my chair. We spend the next hour and a half going through the presentation and possible questions. We're ready. I'm glad we're done because my neck is killing me. I absent-mindedly massage it while we're talking.

"What's up with your neck?" Simon asks me.

"You try sitting in coach for more than four hours."

"Here. Let me help." He comes up behind me and kneads his fingers into my neck. It hurts at first, but it's a good kind of pain.

"Mmm," I moan. "You've been holding out on me." I stretch my legs out on the ottoman and let my head fall forward. I close my eyes and give in to the moment. When I open them, Jake is staring at me; I feel self-conscious under his gaze. "Thanks, Simon. I feel much more relaxed."

"Good. I'll be right back," he informs us.

I look at the clock. It's ten, which means it's midnight Chicago time. I'm exhausted, and my back is getting stiff from my having sat in one place for so long. I stand and slowly stretch, putting my arms behind my back and arching my chest. I look at Jake, who's watching me intently.

"You're making it really difficult," he says in a low voice.

"What?" I ask, puzzled.

"To resist you."

Oh. Suddenly I'm really nervous.

Simon comes back and says, "I'm going to turn in."

Jake looks at me. "What about you, Lexi? Are you staying?" His blue eyes bore into mine.

"I'm going to turn in too," I find myself saying. Disappointment registers on his face, but he quickly hides it. "I'm tired, and I need to have a clear head for tomorrow," I add.

Jake nods. "OK, see you tomorrow."

Shit, what did I just do?

Simon and I leave his room, and I look at him. "I think I just blew it."

"What do you mean?"

I tell him about Jake's comment. "I think he was propositioning me when he asked me to stay."

"Well, why didn't you?" Simon asks.

"I don't know…I panicked. As much as I wanted to, the timing wasn't right. We have a huge meeting tomorrow, and I don't want to be off my game. The last thing I need is for things to be awkward between us and for that to come across. Shit, what if he thinks I'm not interested?"

"Lexi, he might. Face it—you're going to have to make the next move."

I sigh. "I know." As much as I'm against doing it, I don't think Jake will try anything further after tonight.

That night I have trouble going to sleep. I may just as well have slept with Jake; I probably would have gotten more rest. I toss and turn all night, worried about how he'll act toward me tomorrow. He didn't overtly ask me, but I know the meaning behind his question. All I've wanted was for Jake to give me a sign he's interested. Now that he has, why the hell didn't I take him up on his offer? I was just caught so off guard and freaked out. On the bright side, maybe he is finally ready to forget about his rule. I just hope it's not too late.

We meet in the lobby the next morning. I purposely arrive five minutes late so I don't have to be alone with Jake. My plan worked; he and Simon are waiting for me.

"'Morning," I say.

"Good morning," they respond.

Jake seems to be his usual self, but then he says, "You drive with Simon. I have some calls to make."

"Oh, we're taking two cars?"

"Yes. I have business to take care of afterward at the agency, so I'm not coming back to the hotel."

"OK," I say, wondering whether he really has calls to make or whether he's avoiding me.

"Nervous?" Simon asks.

"A little," I admit.

He looks and me and says, "You'll be fine, and you look perfect as usual. Love the shoes."

"Thanks." I give him a smile. I'm wearing a fitted black jacket with a white ruffle blouse, slim-fit black pants, and hot-pink stilettos for a pop of color. I added a statement necklace but kept the rest of my jewelry simple. My hair is pulled back into a low bun, but I kept the top loose so it looks more casual.

"You have everything?" I ask Simon.

"Of course," he says. "Let's go. We'll see you there, Jake."

Once we're in the car, I turn to Simon. "Do you think he's avoiding me?"

"It's hard to say. Try not to worry about it. Focus on the pitch, and then we'll plan your art of seduction."

I smile. He used our tagline for the campaign. How appropriate.

We arrive fifteen minutes early, and the receptionist asks us to take a seat in the lobby. Twenty-five minutes later, she shows us into the conference room. It's show time. We have an hour for the presentation followed by a half hour of Q&A. Jake handles introductions and opens up the meeting. He really is so charismatic and knows how to captivate a room. Then it's my turn to share our strategic approach to the assignment. My voice comes out much more confident than I'm feeling. I go through my slides, and Simon interjects here and there to build on what I'm saying. Jake is right—we do make a good team. Next, Simon shares the creative. I try to read the room while he's presenting. The clients primarily have poker faces, but I can tell the design director loves the print campaign. Simon picks up on it too and shares some details about the photography style he envisions and the list of photographers he has in mind. He gets through all the work, and then Jake reviews the staff plan and cost proposal. The clients ask a lot of questions about our fee structure, and then they ask if we're the team that will be working on the business.

"That's up for discussion," Jake says. "We hand-selected a very talented group of individuals to work on this campaign. We felt it was important they had a certain style to bring the work to life in the way Simon envisioned. In light of that, many of the art directors would stay on if you choose to go with this direction."

They ask a number of other questions, most of which we anticipated. Then they throw us a curveball. "Do you think your campaign pays off the name of the perfume?"

Simon jumps in. "Yes, I think we've definitely paid off the notion of Enchantress but in an unexpected way. Many of our initial ideas were in the direction of a fairy tale. But we didn't want to go with the first thing that came to mind. We wanted to go deeper and push the boundaries creatively."

Michael, the company's marketing director, nods and says, "I like the direction you've taken the work. I guess we were expecting something a little softer, like the fairy-tale angle."

I get an uneasy feeling. Have we totally missed the mark? Jake seems to be thinking the same thing.

He tries to appease Michael and says, "We definitely could go the fairy-tale route. However, we believe our approach will strongly resonate with our consumer."

"Yes," I say. "Speaking from the perspective of your target audience, who doesn't love a fairy tale? But the thing about fairy tales is there's usually a damsel in distress who needs rescuing in order to get her happily ever after. I don't like to think of myself as a victim at the mercy of someone else. I want to have some ownership and a hand in making my own destiny. That's why I like our approach. It makes me feel empowered and in control instead of helpless, but I still get my happy ending."

The clients stare at me and nod. Simon again jumps in and says, "Lexi is right, although there are some things we can do creatively to soften the work without losing the integrity of the idea. For instance we could add a faint lipstick kiss by the logo. And maybe our spokeswoman is draped in white bed sheets. That will add more drama given the dark background. We also can play around with different lighting."

Michael seems excited by the idea. "So you're flexible then?"

"Absolutely," says Simon. "We're open to making adjustments so everyone is comfortable as long as we don't lose the intent behind the concept."

"That's fair," he says. "Thank you all for coming. It looks like you spent a lot of time and effort on the work. It's a beautiful and arresting campaign. We should have a response out to all of the agencies within the next month."

We all shake hands and thank them for their time.

All three of us are quiet on the elevator ride down to the lobby.

Once we're out of the building, Jake says, "Great job in there, both of you. Whatever happens, I'm proud of the work and the way you handled their questions. It was a tough crowd, but I think we made a strong showing."

"Do you think we had the right strategy? It seemed like they were expecting something safer," I say.

"I think we brought them something they weren't expecting to see. But you both managed to dismiss their concerns and show them why this is the right campaign. Lexi, I loved how you reminded them of their target when you gave your perspective on fairy tales. You made the idea seem outdated and irrelevant, but you did it in a way that wasn't insulting."

"Thanks." I smile at him. "You both were great too. Simon, I think you won Michael over with your suggestions." I turn to Jake. "I've never seen you present before. You definitely know how to work a room."

"A skill I've perfected over time. You should see my uncle. I learned from a master."

"How do you think it went?" I ask Simon.

"I definitely think we have the design director in our court, though I'm not sure how much influence she has. I saw a few smiles from the others when I flipped over the print ads. I think they loved it."

"Really?"

"You have such little faith. Do you think they want to go with some outdated fairy-tale approach? Sex sells."

"I'm glad you're so confident," I tell him.

"This is your first pitch. Trust me—unexpected is good. No client wants to go with an expected idea, especially in this category."

"I agree with Simon," Jake says. "I'm going to call the office to let them know how things went. Are we still on for dinner?"

"Yes," I say.

"I actually decided to meet up with my friends tonight," Simon says. "So you two are on your own."

Jake fidgets with his car keys and seems uncomfortable.

"Is that OK?" I ask him.

"Yeah, no problem. What time is good for you?"

"I don't know. Seven?"

"Sure. See you then. Oh, by the way, I made massage appointments for both of you at the spa this afternoon. You deserve some relaxation. It's on me."

"Thanks," I say. "That's really nice of you."

"Yes, Jake. You are a saint."

Jake smiles. "See you at dinner, Lexi."

"See you." As Simon and I walk back to the car, I give him a suspicious look. "Do you really have plans tonight?"

"Yes. I thought you should take your own advice and get started on this seduction plan. You're the one who said you want a hand in making your own destiny."

"I did say that, didn't I?"

"Yep. So how do you plan to do it?"

"I'm not sure, but I'm taking your advice. It'll involve alcohol—lots of alcohol."

He laughs. "Good girl. Now, my dear, I have some calls to make."

Simon phones the office and gives the creative team an update on how the pitch went. I'm lost in my own thoughts about Jake. Now that the pitch is over, I need to focus on my plan for tonight.

CHAPTER FOURTEEN

When Simon and I get back to the hotel, I call the spa.

"Hi. This is Lexi Winters. I'm calling to confirm an appointment."

"Yes, Ms. Winters. We have you down for our signature massage at two followed by a paraffin mani/pedi."

"Um, great. Thanks."

"Oh, and Ms. Winters, all services and gratuity have been taken care of."

I thank her and hang up. I can't get over the fact that Jake paid for my services. I really don't think he's writing this off as a business expense. I call Simon, who answers on the first ring.

"I just called the spa, and Jake treated me to a massage and mani/pedi."

"He is generous. I have a massage and facial."

I laugh.

"What? You shouldn't neglect your skin."

"OK, see you down there," I tell him. "Actually, do you want to meet for a quick bite first?"

"Yes. Let's meet in the lobby in ten minutes."

I quickly check my e-mail then head downstairs. Simon and I decide to eat outside by the pool. We order salads and split a bowl of fruit.

"I could get used to this kind of treatment," I tell him.

"Tell me about it."

"Is Jake always this generous?"

"He's good to his staff. I hear he gives out great gifts at Christmas. I've only traveled with him a handful of times. Now that I think of it, he does always pick up the tab, but it's usually business-related expenses."

I digest this news and decide to change the subject. "So tell me about these friends of yours. Who are you going to visit?"

"Shane and Elizabeth. They were the ones who introduced me to Lance. I lived next door to them when I first moved to Chicago, and we were very close. They moved out here a few years ago, so I called them up when I knew we were coming. They were delighted."

"That's great. It's nice that you keep in touch. Do they have any children?"

"No, they tried to for years, but Elizabeth was never able to get pregnant. They were going to adopt, but the plans fell through. I think that's why they moved—to get a fresh start."

"Stories like that break my heart. Do you think they'll try to adopt again?"

"I don't know…maybe. They're older now, in their midforties."

I try not to think about the fact that my biological clock is ticking. This was never a factor for me before, but now that I'm no longer with Ben, it's something I have to consider. I know I'm only twenty-seven, but who knows how old I'll be when I meet someone and settle down?

Sensing my mood, Simon says, "Lexi, you're young. And who knows, after this weekend you just may have yourself a baby daddy." I punch him lightly on the arm.

We head to the spa for our appointments. After checking in we each receive a locker key and go to change. I blow Simon a kiss. "See you later." I head into the changing room and find a big, white, fluffy robe with a matching pair of terry-cloth slippers in my locker. I put them on and head into the waiting room. It's dimly lit; soft classical music is playing; and the air is filled with the sweet fragrance of jasmine. Immediately I feel more relaxed. I love going to the spa; it's just something I don't do that often. I regularly treat myself to nail appointments but never at a place like this. A woman in a white smock comes in and calls my name. I stand up, and she introduces herself as Monica. I follow her down the hall into one of the treatment rooms. She tells me to undress and lie down on the table. After she leaves I do as she says and slip under the sheets, which are heated.

This is heavenly. She knocks and comes in; then she gets to work putting a cucumber mask over my eyes. She asks me if there are any particular areas that are bothering me.

"My neck and shoulders are a bit stiff."

"Do you sit behind a desk?"

"Mainly, yes."

"OK. I'll put some extra focus there. But we'll start on your front first."

I find myself relaxing as she works. After a while she has me roll onto my stomach.

"My, you are tense," she says as she works on a knot in my back.

"I've been under a lot of stress lately."

"Just try to relax and picture the tension rolling off your body."

I do as instructed and make a concerted effort not to think about this evening. A short while later she pats my back and informs me she's finished. She tells me to dress, after which she'll take me to my next appointment. I stretch luxuriously, put my robe and slippers back on, then head to the locker room to change. When I emerge, Monica is waiting for me.

"Thank you. That was wonderful."

"You're welcome. Enjoy the rest of your stay."

I certainly intend to. She takes me to Trina, who's doing my mani/pedi. She tells me to go choose a color. I decide on Essie's "You Don't Know Jacques!" for my toes and "Angel Food" for my hands. I find an issue of *Us Weekly* and catch up on celebrity gossip while my feet are soaking. Trina adds some orange peel and flower petals to the water. Does it get any better than this? I'd text Jake, but I think they frown upon people using their cell phones in here. An hour later my nails are drying when a fiery redhead who looks to be about my age sits next to me.

"I love your color," she says, eyeing my toes.

"Thanks. I've gotten it on my fingernails but never my toes before. I wasn't sure if I should do this or something brighter."

"No, I like it. It's a good choice."

"Thanks. Are you here for a special occasion?"

"A wedding. It's tomorrow."

Just then one of the nail technicians calls her name. "Have you chosen your color?" she asks.

"Yes, I want what she has."

I smile at her. "Have fun at the wedding."

I dry for about twenty minutes then head upstairs. I decide to take a short nap before getting ready for dinner. I place a wake-up call for five and also set my cell-phone alarm, just in case. This is one time I definitely can't afford to oversleep. I need to look perfect. After channeling our target consumer for the pitch these past few weeks, it's my turn to play the temptress.

I must have fallen asleep, because the phone wakes me up from a dream. I take a long shower then carefully blow-dry my hair. I decide to wear it down with a center part, but instead of flat ironing it, I use a big round brush. I want full, sexy hair. For my makeup I do smoky eyes in a bronze palette with nude glossy lips. Now I need to choose the perfect outfit. Of course I packed lots of options. I decide on a short chiffon halter dress that's a deep coral color. It's always brought me good luck; plus it looks great with my tan. I wonder if it's sexy enough, because it has a high neckline, but I figure the back is open; plus it's cinched at the waist, which gives it a very flattering fit. I pair it with gold stiletto sandals, chandelier earrings, and a cuff bracelet. As a finishing touch, I add my secret weapon, a dab of Emporio Armani, on my neck and wrists. I throw my phone, lipstick, some cash, and my hotel key in a clutch. I double-check my reflection in the mirror and fluff my hair. Satisfied, I make my way to Jake's room. We didn't discuss an actual meeting place, so I figure I'll stop by on my way to the lobby. I'm ten minutes early, but I'm too antsy to sit and wait in my room. I probably should have raided the minibar beforehand to calm my nerves. But I didn't want to meet him smelling like alcohol, so I figure I'll just get drunk at dinner.

I knock on Jake's door, and he opens it, shirtless. He's on his cell phone, and I can see he's in the process of getting ready. He's wearing black pants with a black belt, and his button-down shirt is laid out on the bed. He mouths, "Sorry" and mimes someone talking. I nod, thankful for the distraction. Wow, does he have a nice body. His chest is perfectly sculpted, with just a sprinkling of golden chest hair. He has very defined pecs and a distinctive six-pack. His boxer briefs are peeking out of his waistband, tempting me with what lies beneath. He has wide shoulders, and his arms are very muscular and toned. He's trim and fit but not overly built. He's perfect. I'm not sure he notices me staring because he's distracted by his conversation. He walks over to the bed and picks up his shirt to put it on.

"Don't," I hear myself say. Before I lose my nerve I close the distance between us until I'm standing in front of him. Tentatively I place my hands on his stomach, just above his waistband. His eyes bore into mine, and we stand there for a moment, staring at each other.

"Nick, I'm going to have to call you back." He ends the call and tosses the phone on the bed. "That's not fair," he says.

Shit, this isn't the reaction I expected. "What?" My voice is barely a whisper.

"I'm standing here half naked, and you're fully dressed."

"Oh," I say, and let out the breath I didn't realize I'd been holding. Up until now he's been a fantasy. Someone safe to lust after knowing he would never cross the line. But things between us are about to get real. And I'm all in. I turn around and lift my hair. Slowly Jake undoes my zipper. My dress falls to the floor at my feet. I step out of it and turn around. Still in my stilettos, I stand facing him in a lacy, skin-colored, strapless, push-up bra and matching thong. I pray he can't see that I'm trembling. Perhaps I should've ditched the heels, because I worry they won't support me. I take a steadying breath to calm my nerves, which are on over-drive knowing what's to come. I haven't been with anyone since Ben. And frankly, I never thought I'd want someone as much as I want Jake in this moment.

His eyes sweep over me, taking in every detail. I've never felt more exposed—or more desired. "Lexi, you are so incredibly beautiful." Grabbing my face, he pulls me toward him and kisses me earnestly. God, he's such a good kisser. I knew he would be. His tongue seeks out mine, and I respond, pouring all my pent-up desire and longing from the past few months into the kiss. It's a deep, passionate embrace. I don't think of anything but him and this moment. Things heat up quickly. He moves his mouth down, kissing my neck then shoulder while his hands move to explore my body. He gently strokes my arms and back then expertly unfastens my bra. He caresses my breasts with his hands then his mouth, his tongue circling my nipples. I let out a small groan. His touch is driving me crazy with need. My hands are in his hair, and then I nibble his ear and neck, softly breathing warm air on his skin. I work my way down, lightly touching his pecs. I kiss his chest and slowly glide my tongue down the length of his body until I reach my target. I want him—all of him.

I hover at his waistband and peek up at him. His eyes are closed and his head in thrown back as though he's savoring the moment. He's usually so composed and I love seeing him come undone. Encouraged, I keep going. I undo his belt buckle and zipper then slide his pants and boxers down. I take him in my hand, stroking him slowly at first, but then I increase the pace and intensity. "Lexi," he breathes. My name sounds like velvet on his tongue. I continue to pump his shaft as I ease the tip of his erection into my mouth. He exhales sharply and presses one hand against the back of my head. I keep going, taking him as deep as I can. "Baby, that feels so good. But now it's your turn." He pulls me to my feet and kisses me again. His hand slides over my panties, lightly teasing me, arousing me. Then he slips his hand inside and continues his exploration, leaving me quivering from his touch. His slides my panties down and I step out of them, giving him full access. His fingers expertly move in and out, stroking me at just the right rhythm. I let out a moan. He places his lips against my ear and whispers, "You feel so good. And your mouth is pure heaven. Now I'm going to return the favor." My skin breaks out in goosebumps despite the heat between us. He sinks to his knees then uses his tongue to stimulate me, leaving me wet with want. I let out a cry then his lips find mine again and he pushes me back so I'm lying on the bed. He covers my body with his, and I feel him boring into my thigh. My hips press against him in response. I'm so ready.

He looks at me and says, "Are you sure you want this?"

I nod. "I've never been more sure of anything. I should be asking you that question."

"Believe me, Lexi. I want you."

He leans over and grabs a condom from his wallet on the nightstand. I watch in anticipation as he puts it on then he eases himself inside me. He starts with slow, deep thrusts, and I savor each one, but he quickly increases the pace. I match him, thrust for thrust, with everything I've got. I've fantasized about this moment for so long, and I want him to want me as much as I want him. As he moves on top of me, he stimulates me with his hand, and I feel myself building.

"Come on, Lexi. Let yourself go," he whispers seductively in my ear.

I do. It's as if I'm falling as my orgasm consumes me. He goes right over the edge with me. We take a few minutes to catch our breath, and before I can process what happened he pulls me close. He kisses me again, tenderly at first, but soon our kisses take on an urgency. Desire builds within me once more. My body responds to his touch as though he's a puppeteer pulling the strings. I've lost all control and I'm just along for the ride. God, I'm ready for him, and from what I can feel he's ready for me too.

He flips me over and tells me to lie flat on the bed. I hear the rip of a condom wrapper then he's inside me again. This time it's much deeper, more intense. Sex with Ben was good, but this is different. This is hot, raw. He's lying directly on top of me, his face hovering inches from mine. I close my eyes and inhale deeply, his familiar earthy scent filling my lungs. I feel the beads of moisture on his skin, mixing with mine, his warm breath in my ear. I've never been more turned on. He pulls out then thrusts back in, teasing me, torturing me. Over and over again. He intensifies his thrusts, which puts me over the edge. I climax again, and he finds his release moments later. He rolls me over so I'm facing him, and traces his finger lightly against my cheek. I close my eyes and enjoy the sensation, letting out a satisfied moan.

"I love the noises you make," he says. "They turn me on."

I smile, glad for the compliment but also somewhat embarrassed. "You happen to turn me on too if you couldn't tell."

"Nope, I couldn't tell," he teases.

"Maybe we should do it again so I can enlighten you."

"While I love that idea, we'll never make it to dinner," he says with a laugh.

Suits me just fine. But I keep that thought to myself. He looks into my eyes and cradles my face in his hands. "You're amazing, you know that?"

"I'm glad you think so. To be honest I wasn't sure how you felt about me."

"If that was any indication, now you know."

I smile. "But if I hadn't initiated things tonight, would you have made a move on me?"

"Yes," he says without hesitation. "I was just planning to wait until after dinner."

"Oh," I say, embarrassed once more.

"But I'm *very* glad you did," he says.

"I didn't think you ever would," I tell him. "You're extremely hard to read. Sometimes I thought you were interested in me, but you're so hot and cold. Then last night I thought maybe my luck had changed. You just caught me by surprise, and I didn't want to be off my game for the pitch. I was worried you'd changed your mind."

"I definitely didn't change my mind. And believe me, I was interested… *am* interested. I've wanted you since the day you walked into my office."

I'm completely shocked. "Really?"

"Yes. I could tell there was something different about you. You're smart, strong-willed, and easy to talk to, and you have this aura about you. I was drawn to you. But I made a pact with myself a long time ago that I never would date anyone at work again. I'm sure you heard the rumors."

"I've heard a little bit."

"Well, there was this girl Jessica who worked on the Smart Beverages account. She got pulled in to help with a pitch I was working on. We started to have what I saw as a harmless fling. But she was very needy, and I wasn't that into her. I tried to be honest and break things off. I wanted to be a standup guy instead of leading her on, but she freaked out and told me she was going to hit me where it hurts. I didn't know what she meant, but a few days later, she accused me of sexually harassing her. I was devastated. I'd worked so hard to get where I was at the agency. When my uncle hired me, I told him I didn't want any special privileges or treatment. I wanted to work hard and move up on my own accord, not because I was the founder's nephew. I didn't want people to treat me differently or not take me seriously. I felt like I was just beginning to establish myself. Even though people at work knew it wasn't true, there's always that doubt. If someone accuses you of something, people think there must be an ounce of truth to it. I vigorously defended myself, and she didn't have any claims or witnesses to back her story."

"What about your uncle? How did he react?"

"He was very supportive," Jake says. "But he talked to me about the importance of separating my professional and personal lives. That's why it took me so long to come around. I felt so conflicted. I know you're nothing like Jessica, but I've spent a long time trying to undo that damage. I sensed you were into me, but then you pulled away. That really killed me. I knew I was sending you mixed signals, and I felt I needed to make a decision to be fair to both of us. Then I came to the benefit, and it hit me how beautiful you are, inside and out. Once I held you, I knew there was no turning back." He takes a deep breath. "This is a big step for me. I want to be with you, but I'm not ready for people to know yet. Do you mind if we keep this between you and me for now?"

"Of course. I understand. But what about Simon? I think he may suspect something."

"OK, just Simon. You two are really close, huh?"

"Yes, and he'd know if I lied to him. Believe me, he'll ask me about this weekend."

"What will you tell him?"

"That it was very memorable."

"Well, I plan to make a lot more good memories," he says with a wicked smile. Then he asks, "What about you? When did you know?"

"That day at the zoo. If I wasn't getting out of a long-term relationship, it probably would have been sooner, but I felt something, seeing how great you were with Hailey."

"Looks like we have a lot of lost time to make up for." Jake pulls me up from the bed. "Come on. Let's have dinner, and then we'll get started."

"Sounds like a plan to me."

I go to the bathroom and freshen up. Really I just need a few minutes to collect myself. It's still surreal to me that I had sex with Jake. And that I'm officially moving on. I look like a mess, so I attempt to smooth out my hair and wipe away the smudges of mascara under my eyes. So much for all that time I spent getting ready. Jake comes up behind me and puts his arms around me. "You look perfect. Let's go."

On the way down, he tells me he made us a reservation at a cool sushi restaurant he found this afternoon. "I checked—they have chicken," he says. I smile, happy that he remembered. The restaurant is within walking distance, and he takes my hand. "We don't know anyone here," he says, kissing my fingers.

Dinner is lovely. Jake is really playful and carefree. I've never seen him like this before. After we order he says, "I want to know everything about you."

"What do you want to know?"

He fires questions at me. "Favorite color?"

"Purple."

"Favorite flower?"

"Hydrangeas."

"Favorite movie?"

"*August Rush.* You?"

"*Pulp Fiction.* Ideal vacation?"

"Relaxing on a tropical beach—white sand, clear turquoise water."

"Favorite memory?"

"I'd say our recent activity just about tops my list."

"Doesn't count. Something from your childhood."

"Hmm, I guess it would be my Sunday girls' day. When I was growing up, my dad golfed on Sunday mornings, so my mom, Aunt Lynne, Jules, Tara, and I would spend the morning together. We'd dress up, and my mom would do our hair and makeup. My aunt would cook what she called a fancy meal, and we'd have a ladies' lunch. I always looked forward to it. What's your favorite childhood memory?"

"When my dad taught me how to fish. It was a rare weekend away with just the two of us."

"I can't picture you as a little boy. What were you like growing up?"

"I was a good kid," he says. "Of course once I got to high school I got into trouble from time to time."

"What kind of trouble?"

"Nothing too serious. Skipping school, fighting, that sort of thing."

"I don't picture you as being the violent type."

"I wasn't. It's just that this guy hit on my girlfriend."

"Oh, how noble of you. Did you have a long-term girlfriend in high school?

"I dated someone my junior year for about nine months but aside from that nothing too serious. Don't get off track. I'm trying to learn about *you*. Favorite concert?"

"Dave Matthews Band. He played at this tiny venue when I was in college, and it was really intimate. What about you?"

"U2, their Elevation tour. Favorite person at work?"

"You, obviously," I say with a laugh.

"Aside from me."

"Simon. You?"

"After you, my uncle."

"Speaking of," I say, "are you going to tell him about us?"

"Honestly I haven't thought that far ahead. But yes, when the time is right, I'll tell him."

I nod, absorbing this news. I'm not sure how I feel about Bill knowing I'm sleeping with his nephew, but it's not up to me. Our food comes, and I devour my chicken.

"Hungry?" Jake asks me.

"I've worked up quite an appetite."

"Good, and I suggest you finish that. You'll need your energy for later."

A delicious chill works its way up my spine at the thought. Once the waiter clears our plates, he asks if we'd like to order dessert. "Yes," Jake says, looking at me with desire. We'll take whatever you have that's chocolate. To go," he says, not taking his eyes off me. I feel myself blush and give him a big smile in return.

"Right away, sir," the waiter says. He returns with the check and a bag with our dessert. Jake pays the bill and takes my hand. As we walk back to the hotel, I have trouble keeping up with Jake.

"In a hurry?" I tease him.

"Yes. I'm hungry for my dessert," he says, as he corners me against the wall of a building.

"You can have it now," I say, as I pull him in for a kiss.

A heated make-out session ensues, and I get so lost in the moment I forget we're out in public. "You're going to get us arrested," he jokes. "Let's go so I can take advantage of you properly."

"I hope there's nothing proper about it."

At first I think I've shocked him into silence. To be honest I've shocked myself with this uncharacteristic boldness. But the smile that lights up his face is priceless—as is the determined look on his face as he races back to the hotel.

I'm breathless when we get back to his room. I attempt to compose myself as he opens the bag. But's it's a bit difficult when I'm already worked up knowing what's to come.

"Chocolate cake," he says.

"One of my favorites."

"We probably should take off your dress so it doesn't get messy." He helps me out of my dress, bra, and panties, and I slowly undo each button on his shirt. He removes his pants and instructs me to lie down on the bed; I do as he says. He breaks off a piece of cake and feeds it to me.

"Delicious," I say, licking his fingers. "Aren't you going to have some?"

"Yes, of this." He takes out a container of chocolate syrup and dips his finger in it. He rubs it seductively on my lips and kisses me.

"Mmm," I say. "It's delicious."

Then he pours the syrup over my breasts and in a trail down my stomach. "I want to explore every inch of you," he says. He takes his time licking it off and works his way toward my belly button. I writhe in anticipation. I've never had someone eat food off my body before. It's very erotic. His tongue finds my sweet spot, and I groan. He slowly tortures me, his tongue working its magic.

I'm lost in the sensation, and just when I'm close to the edge, he enters me. This time, it's slow and sensual. My body responds to his, and I match his rhythm. I feel myself building again; my body is already so sensitized from his touch. I finally give in, saying his name as I climax. I'm not always one to have an orgasm from sex—I envy those girls—but with Jake I have a good track record so far. I find him so damn attractive, and my body just seems to work with his. He comes loudly and lies on top of me, catching his breath. I'm exhausted.

After a few minutes, he says, "Let's go get a drink."

"Really? Aren't you tired?"

"Nope. I'm just getting warmed up." I stare at him and raise my eyebrows. "Lexi, now that I've had you, I can't get enough."

I kiss him in response. "OK, one drink."

We get dressed and head back downstairs. On our way to the bar, we pass the ballrooms. There's a party going on in one of them, and Rihanna's "We Found Love" is playing.

"I love this song," I tell Jake.

He takes my hand. "Come on. Let's check it out."

It appears to be a corporate event because there's a table outside with a bunch of nametags on it. Jake picks one up and hands it to me. "Here, you can be Aubrey Stuart. I'll be David Kim." I smirk at him. "Free drinks and music—what's not to like?" he asks. We walk into the room. The dance floor is packed, so we decide to get a drink first.

"What would you like?" Jake asks me.

"I'll have a vodka cranberry."

He orders a gin and tonic for himself and hands me my drink. We find a highboy and rest our drinks on it. I survey the crowd—it looks to be a lot of middle-aged men and women. I wonder what kind of company this is. We're chatting when a pretty blonde comes over and asks Jake to dance.

"I would, but I don't think my girlfriend would like it very much," he tells her.

After she walks away, I say, "Sure, blame me. So I'm your girlfriend, huh?"

He smiles at me. "I don't want to share you with anyone else."

I beam at him in return. Maybe it's a combination of the alcohol and adrenaline, but I suddenly have a burst of energy. "Let's dance," I say, taking him by the hand. We find a spot among the crowd and dance for the next half hour. They're playing great music, and I'm in my element. I dance seductively for Jake, pressing my body into his. The song "Good Life" by OneRepublic comes on.

"I love this song," I say, "but it's weird to dance to. Is it fast or slow?"

"Slow. Definitely slow," Jake says, pulling me close. His hands caress my naked back, sending shockwaves through me. He kisses me under the dim lights of the dance floor—a slow, sensual kiss filled with lots of promise. "Do you know how much I want you?" he whispers in my ear.

I laugh and reply, "I can kind of feel it."

"Let's go," he says.

On our way to the elevators, we pass a unisex bathroom. Jake pulls me in and locks the door behind him.

"In here? Really?"

"You don't know what you do to me," he says in a low voice.

Oh, but I do. My desire for him is overwhelming. He grabs me in a passionate embrace. His kisses are urgent, and his hands explore my body until he finds what he's looking for. He yanks my panties down, and I can feel his smile when he discovers I'm ready for him. I'm heady with lust, and this territory we're heading into is both terrifying and exhilarating. I unbuckle his belt and unzip his pants. He instructs me to wrap my legs around him. My back is against the wall, and I'm holding on to the handicap bar with one hand for support; the other is around his neck. If you had told me I'd be having sex in a public restroom, I'd have been horrified, but it's actually hot. I can tell Jake thinks so too from the dirty words that leave his mouth as he pounds into me. Jake's thrusts are quick, and I tilt my pelvis up to meet him. He moves harder and faster, and I hold on tightly. I feel the strain of his muscles as he works to hold me up. He thrusts into me hard and comes, just as there's a knock at the door.

"It'll be a few minutes," he calls out in a raspy voice. I attempt to stifle a giggle.

He slowly eases his grip then gently sets my feet on the floor. We take a few minutes to catch our breath.

I'm about to pull my underwear on, but he drops to his knees. "I want to pleasure you," he says. I don't know that I can relax in a public place, especially knowing someone could be right outside, so I shake my head. "Come on," he says seductively and slowly tortures me with his tongue. I lean my head back and give in. My body, already stimulated, responds to his touch, and I come quickly. He gives me a satisfied smile and kisses me. I taste myself on him and pull away. He looks at me with a devilish grin and slowly licks his lips, then kisses me again, deeper this time. Finally he pulls away then leans his forehead against mine. I'm exhausted; I can't believe that just this morning we were giving the pitch, and then all this.

"Can we go to bed now?" I ask, yawning.

"Yes, let's go."

I'm relieved the hallway is empty when we exit.

"Maybe your screaming scared them off," he teases.

"My screaming? More like your swearing."

"Touché."

Jake practically has to carry me back to the room. He helps me undress, and I'm out the second my head hits the pillow.

CHAPTER FIFTEEN

The next morning I wake up and wonder whether it all was a dream. I open my eyes and feel relieved to find myself in Jake's room. I glance at the clock and see that it's 11:15 a.m. It's been a long time since I've slept this late. I stretch luxuriously and get out of bed. Jake left a note saying he went downstairs to make some calls. I decide to take a quick shower. I run the water and let the room get steamed up. I smile, thinking about last night; I can't believe we had sex three times. When I was with Ben, we did it on average twice a week. Just as I'm about to get into the shower, I hear the door open, and Jake enters the bathroom.

"Good morning." I smile at him.

"It is indeed," he says, eyeing my naked body. "Whatcha doing?"

"I was about to take a shower," I say, stating the obvious. "I felt a bit dirty after last night's activities."

"You might want to wait on that," he says, as he peels off his shirt. "I'm about to get you dirty again. Then we'll shower together."

And that makes five.

Afterward I ask Jake if I can borrow a shirt so I can go get my suitcase. He offers to do it for me, so I give him my room key. "You might as well move all your stuff in here anyway," he says.

I quickly blow-dry my hair and ask him what we're doing so I'll know what to wear.

"Well, I was initially thinking we'd drive up to Napa. But since it's so late, I figured we could just hang out by the pool."

"Sounds perfect. I've never been to Napa, so we'll have to go another time."

"Definitely," he says, as he pulls me into another embrace.

I rummage through my suitcase to find my swimsuit and cover-up. I choose my new turquoise bikini, a purchase that was supposed to be for my honeymoon. When I saw it, I knew I had to have it. I love the color, and it has cute gold rings as straps that tie behind the neck, along with matching details on the waistband of the bottom piece.

Jake looks at me admiringly. "I don't know what I did to deserve you."

I smile at him. "Ditto."

"Are you hungry?" he asks.

"Starving."

We go downstairs and decide to eat on the terrace. Jake looks amused as he watches me scarf down my omelet.

"What? I told you I was hungry. You've been giving me quite a workout."

A satisfied smile slowly spreads across his face. "Better get used to it." I definitely could.

After breakfast we find a pair of lounge chairs next to the pool. Jake goes to get towels, and I pull out my book and sunscreen. Jake watches as I apply it, and then I hand it to him so he can do my back. "With pleasure," he says. A waiter comes by and takes our drink order. I've found my nirvana: sun, pool, drinks, and Jake.

After a while he asks me if I want to take a dip in the pool, but I shake my head.

"Come on. Come with me."

"I don't feel like getting wet."

He looks all pouty, so I agree to put my feet in the water. As I'm about to sit down, he grabs me and throws me into the pool. I grab his legs and pull him in too and splash him.

"Looks like you're all wet after all," he says, and kisses me.

"You bet I am."

He catches my meaning. "Patience—we just got out here," he says, but I can tell he's pleased.

We splash around in the pool some more then get in the hot tub. I feel so relaxed sitting in Jake's lap while he massages my shoulders. "I think I'm in heaven," I murmur. He nuzzles my neck. Another couple that looks to be about our age gets into the hot tub with us, so I slide over.

The girl says to me, "You and your boyfriend are so cute."

"Thanks," I reply, blushing.

"How long have you been together?"

"Um, since this weekend."

She laughs. "That explains it. I'm Pam by the way."

"Lexi. Where are you guys from?"

"Arizona. We came in for my friend's wedding. It's actually here at the hotel."

"It's a beautiful place to get married," I say.

"Yeah, they're going to have the wedding outside at sunset."

I look over, and Jake is engaged in conversation with Pam's boyfriend. "What about you?" I ask. "How long have you been dating?"

"He's actually my fiancé. We got engaged about four months ago. The wedding is next month."

"Wow, so soon."

"Yep," she says, patting her stomach. "I wanted to be married before the baby arrives."

"Oh, congratulations. I wouldn't have known. You're not really showing yet."

"That's the goal. I want to fit into my wedding dress. Anyway, Mike and I have been together since college. We knew we were going to get married anyway; the baby part just happened sooner than I expected."

"It happens," I tell her, not really knowing what to say.

"I screwed up the pill one time. I didn't think much of it; I guess I should have."

"Well, at least you're with someone you care about and know will be there for you and the baby."

"That's true," Pam says, looking over at Mike. He moves over and sits next to Pam, wrapping his arms around her.

"Good luck," I tell her, as I get out of the hot tub. Jake follows me back to our lounge chairs.

"What was that about?"

"She's pregnant, and they're getting married next month."

"Wow. I had no idea."

"I know, me either. She was nice but got a bit personal. She basically told me she screwed up her pill, and the pregnancy was an oops. Who knows? Maybe she was playing me. When you're pregnant, you're not allowed to go in a hot tub." Jake gives me a questioning look. "I once had a pregnancy scare with Ben. It totally freaked me out. I've been very strict about taking the pill ever since."

"Are you still on it?"

"Actually I am. I guess it's such a part of my routine that I didn't think about going off it."

Jake smiles and says, "Good. I hate using condoms."

"Hold on. Have you been tested recently?"

"Lexi, I haven't been in a committed relationship for a long time. I got tested back then, and everything was fine. I've used condoms with all my partners since. But to be sure, I'll get tested when we get home."

"OK. Thanks. I will too. I've only had unprotected sex with Ben, but at this rate, it's probably a good idea that I get checked," I say a bit crossly.

"We'll go together," Jake says, taking my hand in his. "Come on. Let's go upstairs."

And we bring the count to six.

I'm still tired, so I take a late-afternoon nap. Jake nudges me at close to five-thirty, and I take another quick shower to wake myself up. I decide to wear a blue peplum dress with tan ankle-cuff heeled sandals. Jake takes my hand as we head downstairs, and even when I wear my heels, he still towers over me. We stop by the concierge for restaurant suggestions and choose an Italian place near Fisherman's Wharf. Before the waiter takes our drink order, he asks to see our IDs. I can't remember the last time I was carded; I guess I should be flattered. We decide to split a bottle of red wine.

"Let me see your ID," I say, taking it from him. I study his picture then his stats. "Your birthday is coming up."

"Yep, the big three-oh. Let me see yours." I hand him my license, and he looks it over. "That's a good picture of you."

"Thanks. Yours is good too. So is your life everything you thought it would be by the time you turned thirty?"

Jake contemplates this for a moment then says, "Yes and no. Career-wise, it's on track with my goals, but I thought I'd be married by now. When you're younger, thirty seems so old."

"That's very true. Are you OK with how things turned out?"

"Yes. It's made focusing on my career easier. Fewer distractions, I guess. But it would be nice to have someone to share it all with. I'm glad you're here with me now," he says, taking my hand.

I feel a warm glow inside. He doesn't ask me the question—he probably knows life didn't turn out the way I expected. "Well, we'll have to celebrate your birthday," I tell him, making a mental note to plan something.

Two glasses in, I feel a bit buzzed, which gives me the courage to ask Jake about his past. "Earlier you mentioned you've used condoms with all your partners. Have there been a lot of them?"

"Yes," he says honestly.

"Are we talking double digits?" He nods. "Triple digits?"

"No, nothing like that."

"Do you know how many girls you've been with?" I suddenly feel self-conscious and wonder how I measure up.

"Does it matter? None of them really meant anything. They were all flings. Now that I'm with you, I don't need or want to be with anyone else."

"You always say the perfect thing."

"Lexi, I'm by no means perfect."

"I didn't say you were, just that what you said was perfect—although I do think you're perfect…for me."

"I'm glad," he says, pulling me in for a kiss. "So what about you? What's your past?"

I'm embarrassed to tell him. "I've only been with four guys, including Ben."

"You say that like it's a bad thing."

"It's not, although in hindsight I wish I hadn't put so much pressure on being with the right guy. I guess I wasn't one to sleep around unless it was with someone I cared about."

"That's very admirable," Jake says, "and it's the way it should be. I just haven't met anyone in a long time I've wanted to commit myself to. It's a very different experience being intimate with someone you care about."

"Different how?"

"Different better. It takes the relationship to a new level. It's not just about sex. It's about connecting with that person."

"Oh," I say, smiling at him. The check comes, and I try to take it.

"Don't even think about it."

"Jake, I don't expect you to always pay for me. Let me do something nice for you."

"Let me make this clear. I appreciate the offer, but I want to take you to dinner. I won't let you pay, not now, not ever. And besides, this one's on Hartman and Taylor."

"Fine, but I will insist on certain occasions that I pay, like your birthday."

"OK. You can take me out on my birthday."

"I guess I'll have to find another way to show you my appreciation," I say, rubbing my leg against his under the table.

"That I won't argue with. Let's go."

On the cab ride back to the hotel, I thank Jake for an amazing weekend.

"It's not over yet," he says.

"I know, but it's back to reality tomorrow."

"What time's your flight?"

"Around noon."

"I'll drive you to the airport," he says.

"Thanks. How long do you have to stay in San Francisco?"

"All week."

It's weird—I've only spent the past two days with Jake, but I'm going to miss him. "That feels like a long time."

"I know, but let's do something when I get back on Friday. I land around five o'clock. Can I cook you dinner?"

"You cook?"

"Well, I can grill."

"It's a date. I'll bring dessert."

"I take it you bake?"

"Yeah, I'm a decent cook but a much better baker. I used to watch my grandmother when I was growing up. She left me all her recipes, and I've gotten pretty good at it. Whenever we have family get-togethers, I'm always designated to bring the dessert."

"I look forward to testing out your skills," Jake says. "Do you want me to pick you up?"

"No, it would be out of your way, and you'll have dinner to prepare. I can take a cab."

"Are you sure? I'm happy to drive you."

"No, it's fine really. Plus it means I'll get to see you sooner rather than having to wait while you sit in traffic."

"I can't argue with that."

Good. I have an idea and want to surprise him. We arrive back at the hotel and work our way up to number seven.

My cell-phone alarm goes off at eight the next morning. Jake is lying in bed beside me, asleep, which gives me a chance to study him. I know he's under a lot of pressure at work, so it's nice to see him looking so peaceful. I sneak out of bed and get ready. I finish packing then gently nudge him. He opens his eyes and looks at me sleepily.

"Why are you dressed?" he mumbles.

"I have to get to the airport, remember?"

"Oh, what time is it?"

"Eight forty-five."

"Good. We don't have to leave here for another half hour. Come back to bed."

And that makes eight. Once we're dressed we go downstairs so I can check out. I kind of feel bad having the company pay for a room I really didn't use, but I wasn't about to check out early and not have a matching flight. I don't need to raise any questions. Jake drives me to the airport, and we're both quiet. It was such a magical weekend; I'm nervous how things will be once we're home and back to reality. Jake pulls up to the terminal. He gives me a long kiss and strokes my hair. "You'd better get out of this car, or I'm going to make you miss your flight," he says. He takes my bag and places it on the sidewalk. He gives me a big hug and another kiss. "Have a safe flight."

"See you Friday." I walk into the airport and check in. The woman at the counter informs me I've been upgraded to first-class. Being with Jake does have its perks. Once I get through security, I don't have that much time before my flight is scheduled to depart. I make it to the gate with only a few minutes left until boarding. I decide to text Liv.

Most amazing weekend ever. Sealed the deal with Jake. Eight times. Xoxo

Almost immediately, my phone rings.

"Lexi!" she practically screams. "Why didn't you call me earlier? How did this happen? How was it?"

"Amazing! Sorry for not calling you, but I was pretty much with Jake every minute."

"Are you OK? Were you thinking about Ben?"

"The funny thing is, Ben never crossed my mind. You'd think I would've been comparing the two, but I didn't think of him at all—other than the fact that we didn't have sex as much, and it wasn't as good as this."

"Oh, Lexi, I'm so happy for you."

"Shit, they're calling my group to board."

"OK. Let's do sushi tonight. I need a full report."

"Sounds good. We can figure out where to go when I get home."

"Oh, no. I need details. We're ordering in."

I laugh. "See you later." Once I'm on the plane, I get settled into my seat and send Jake a quick text.

Thanks for the first-class treatment. Looking forward to Friday.

I lean back in my seat, close my eyes, and fall asleep with a huge smile on my face. When I land, there's a text from him.

You deserve to be treated like royalty. Miss you already.

I hug myself with glee. He misses me too. I text Liv that I'm back in town, and she tells me to come up to her apartment once I'm settled.

Roland greets me as I walk into the lobby. "You have a package, Lexi. I'll bring it to you." Hmm, I didn't order anything. He returns with a large box. Once I get upstairs, I lift the lid and unwrap the tissue paper to discover a stunning arrangement of purple hydrangeas. I read the card: "Beautiful flowers for a beautiful girl. Thank you for an unforgettable weekend." I smile and call to thank Jake. He answers on the first ring.

"Thank you for the gorgeous flowers. It was a nice surprise to come home to."

"You're welcome," he says. "I'm glad you like them."

"You have a very good memory."

"Didn't I mention that?"

"Nope, you forgot that detail," I say.

"Well, I do. So watch it."

"I promise to be on my best behavior."

"Actually, I like your naughty side," he says, and I laugh. "So what are you up to?" he asks.

"I'm going to have dinner with Liv: Sushi Sunday."

"Where are you going?"

"Just her place."

"Uh-huh," he says knowingly.

"Don't worry. I'll keep some things to myself."

"I'd love to be a fly on the wall for that conversation."

"I bet you would," I tell him. "So what are you doing tonight?"

"Nothing really. I'll probably order room service and go to bed early. You're not the only one who's tired."

"Wish I could be there with you."

"Me too."

"Good night, Jake."

"'Night, Lexi."

I unpack my things and get ready to spill.

The next morning it's business as usual. Simon stops by my office at ten, his customary arrival time at work. He closes my door.

"So…anything I should know about?" I can't help the huge smile that lights up my face. "I knew it!" he practically shouts. "How was it?"

"Best weekend ever."

"I meant the sex."

"I know. I did too."

He grins. "Do tell."

And so I do, leaving out most of the juicy details of course. "Jake's not ready to go public yet, so you can't tell anyone. He said I could tell you, though."

"Your secret is safe with me."

Simon stands up to leave, and I give him a big hug. "Thanks for hanging in there with me—and for your part in helping to move things along. If you hadn't backed out of dinner on Friday, who knows what would have happened."

"Well, I'd like to take some credit, although even if I had joined you on Friday, you would have been just fine. As I've told you, it was inevitable."

I smile at him. "You're a good friend."

His cell phone rings. "Well, my dear, duty calls." With that he's out the door.

The week passes quickly. I have a lot of catching up to do after being out of the office. I'm glad to be busy; it helps keep me occupied until Friday. All I can think about, though, is seeing Jake again. We've been sending flirty texts all week. On Thursday I make a trip to Bloomie's after work to get some new lingerie. I find a black lacy push-up bra with matching panties. Then I stop by the grocery store to get the ingredients for my dessert. I decide to make a chocolate soufflé. I'll do most of the prep work beforehand, but for it to turn out right, I'll bake it once I'm there. I have trouble going to sleep, as I'm anxious about tomorrow. I hope Jake doesn't have a change of heart now that we're back to reality. He's a very private person; he said so himself.

Friday passes slowly, and I'm out the door at five o'clock sharp. I stop by my apartment and prep the soufflé. Then I slip into my new lingerie and a pair of black stilettos; I'm concealed only by a black trench coat. This is my surprise. It's actually rather unlike me, but Jake brings out my wild side. This time I do a shot for courage. I pack a small bag with some clothes and a toothbrush. Then I gather the dessert and head downstairs to hop into a cab. On the way over, I smile, thinking about Jake's reaction. It's been only a week, but it feels like a long time since I've seen him. Finally the cab pulls up to his place. I'm just about to knock when he opens the door.

"Hi," he says, giving me a warm smile.

"Hi." I smile back at him shyly. Then he pulls me into an embrace.

"Come on in," he says, taking my bags and placing them on the counter. "Open the small one first."

He pulls out the whipped cream. "What's this for? Did you make a pie?"

"No," I say, unbuttoning my coat. "I thought we'd have an appetizer first."

He looks at me, and I let the trench coat fall to the floor. A smile slowly spreads across his face. "God, Lexi, you are so sexy. Do you know how much you turn me on?" He grabs the whipped cream and walks over to me. "You are a dream come true," he whispers, as he opens the top and squeezes some into my mouth. He kisses me, and it tastes sweet from the whipped cream that's slowly dissolving on my tongue. "I've thought of nothing but you all week. I've missed you," he says.

"Show me how much."

He kisses me again, more deeply this time. After a while he says, "As hot as you look, I'm gonna need to take this off." He unhooks my bra and sprays the whipped cream over my breasts, slowly tantalizing me with his tongue. He lifts the can again, but I take it from him. "My turn," I say. Tonight I want to play the temptress. I pull his shirt over his head and unbutton his jeans. "Sit," I command, pushing him down on the couch. I straddle him and pull off his boxers, pouring the whipped cream on his stomach. I slowly lick it off, working my way down his glorious body. Then I take him in my mouth. I hear his intake of breath as he leans back and closes his eyes. I start out slowly, teasing him, and then I increase the pace and intensity, moving my head up and down, taking in as much of him as I can. "OK," he says, and attempts to sit up, but I ignore his protests. "Lexi, this is going to be over before we get started."

"We have all night." I keep going, and eventually he comes in my mouth. I swallow, looking up at him with a satisfied smile.

"You can bring me an appetizer anytime you want," he says breathlessly.

I laugh. "You haven't tasted my dessert yet."

"You're killing me."

"Actually I hope I didn't ruin your dinner," I reply, feeling a bit guilty.

"No, I was about to start the grill when you got here. Your timing is perfect."

We quickly dress, and then I ask him what he's making.

"Come. I'll show you," he says, leading me to the kitchen. He opens the fridge and takes things out. "We're having a gorgonzola-and-mixed-greens salad with my homemade raspberry vinaigrette, sautéed vegetables, herbed potatoes, and skirt steak."

"Well, you seem to be quite the chef. And here I thought you just grilled."

"I don't cook that often. I hope it's good."

"I'm sure it will be," I tell him. "Thank you for going to all this effort. What can I do to help?"

"Nothing. Just sit back and relax. Can I offer you a glass of wine?"

"Yes, please." Jake grabs a bottle from the fridge and pours me a glass. I really am touched that he went to all this trouble. "So how was your week?" I ask him.

"It was good. It's so different being in that office. They're much smaller, so there's less politics involved in terms of getting things done, but they also have fewer resources. I'll be going there quite a bit until things get more established."

"Oh? How often will you have to go?"

"I'm not sure yet," he says. "They need to build a bigger client base, which is where I come in. They don't have a lot of clients seeking out their services, so I'll be helping them find prospects. Once we start getting interest, I'll have to help them with their pitch strategy as well."

"You're obviously viewed as a very valuable resource if Hartman and Taylor has entrusted you with starting up the office."

"I guess. I know they're looking for someone to run the New Business group but haven't found anyone yet."

"Don't discount yourself. I'm sure they easily could find someone in this job market. They must value you highly if they're willing to fly you out there and put you up."

He smiles at me. "What about you? How was your week?"

"Pretty uneventful. I mostly played catch-up from being out of the office and so focused on the pitch. When do you think we'll hear back?"

"I hope by the end of the month."

"If we get it, at least it's another account for our San Francisco office," I tell him.

"That's true. They can use all the help they can get." He glances at the clock. "I'm going to put the steaks on."

"OK. I'll toss the salad."

"Great. Thanks."

Once it's prepared, I look in Jake's cabinets and get out plates and bowls. I manage to find the silverware and set the table. I join him on his deck and watch as he works.

"You're grilling the potatoes too?" I ask as he wraps them in foil.

"Yep. I coated them in fresh herbs and parmesan cheese. Now I'll cover them and grill them for about thirty minutes."

"Are you sure I can't help with anything?"

"Thanks, but I've got it covered."

I look around his yard and notice he has a table and chairs set up. "Do you want to eat outside?"

"Yeah, I figured we would."

"OK, I set the table, but I'll move everything out here."

"That was thoughtful. I'll help you."

We carry the dishes outside, and he grabs a citronella candle for the table. About forty-five minutes later, everything is ready. The food is delicious.

"I'm so impressed you made all this."

"You like it?" he asks me.

"I love it. Everything is perfect. Thank you for going to all this trouble."

"It really wasn't a big deal. I like to cook, but sometimes it's hard to do for just myself. I'm glad I have you now." He smiles at me.

"I'm glad too," I say, smiling back.

After dinner I help clear the table. "I'll wash the dishes," I say, but Jake shakes his head. "Come on. Please let me do something."

"You can get your dessert ready."

"Fine, but after that I'm helping you clean up." He watches as I prepare the soufflés. Once they're in the oven, I wash the dishes.

He tries to take one from me and says, "You're my guest."

"Jake, I don't want you to see me as a guest. Here, you can dry," I say, handing him a dishtowel.

The soufflés are done just as we're finishing up the dishes. I take them out of the oven and let them cool for a few minutes. "OK, they're ready," I tell him.

As we sit at the island, I watch anxiously for his reaction as he takes a bite.

"This is really good," he tells me.

"I'm glad you like it." We both finish, and he tells me he wants seconds. "Sorry. I didn't bring any more."

"Actually I had a different kind of dessert in mind."

"Oh, you can have as much of that as you like," I say, as he leads me toward the bedroom.

The next morning, I wake up from the sunlight streaming into the room. I open my eyes and find that Jake's side of the bed is empty. I walk downstairs, where I find him making pancakes.

"Wow, when you said you were cooking for me, I thought you just meant dinner."

He smiles at me. "I was up early. I hope you like pancakes."

"I love them."

We sit down at his breakfast bar and dig in.

"Do you have anything planned for today?" he asks.

"I'm going to get my hair cut." I haven't seen Marco, my hairdresser, in ages because I've been so busy with work. He'll probably reprimand me; he likes me to come in every six weeks.

"Where do you go?"

"To a salon that's actually a few blocks from here."

"What time is your appointment?"

"Eleven thirty."

"OK. I'll drive you," he says.

"Thanks. What are you up to today?"

"I have to do some grocery shopping, laundry, and run to the dry cleaner. My uncle is hosting a dinner tonight, and I don't have any clean suits."

"Oh, what kind of dinner?"

"He's having some of our top clients at his house. I'd invite you, but that would be a bit awkward considering he doesn't know we're dating."

"Don't worry. I understand."

"Did you make plans for tonight?" Jake asks me.

I didn't, but I don't want him to know I was waiting to see if we were going to do something. "I'll probably just have dinner with some girlfriends."

"OK. Can I stop by later?"

"Definitely." I look at my watch; it's ten after eleven. "I should get dressed."

"Do you have any clothes?" he says with a smirk.

"As a matter of fact, I came prepared." I head upstairs and quickly change. I come down, and he says, "I liked what you had on last night better."

"Then you'd better come over after your dinner."

"Believe me, I will."

Jake drives me to my appointment and gives me a tantalizing kiss goodbye. I can't wait to see him later.

I walk into the salon and head to the back to get my hair washed. I wait ten minutes before Marco is ready for me. Once I'm in his chair, he lectures me about how I haven't been in to see him. I apologize and tell him I've been busy, as I try to look chastised. But it's hard; I'm in such a good mood. "You seem different," he says. He narrows his eyes at me. "You've met someone." I nod and smile. "Tell me everything!" he exclaims. I give him the lowdown on Jake and our weekend in San Francisco. Sighing, he says, "Lexi, I'm so happy for you. Just enjoy it." He knows all about what happened with Ben.

"I'll try," I tell him.

"Try hard." He spins me around so I can see my hair. He did a nice job as usual. He left it long but lightened up my layers.

"Do you think I should color it?" I ask him.

"Don't you dare! You have a gorgeous, rich color most women would die for."

"OK, OK." I give him a light kiss on the cheek and head outside. I call Jill to see what she's up to tonight, and she says I should join her and Mel for drinks. "Sounds perfect," I tell her.

That night, over martinis, I reveal the news about Jake. Even though they don't know anyone we work with, I swear them to secrecy. I wonder if Jake will be mad I told them. I can understand keeping our relationship a secret from our coworkers but not my friends.

Just then I feel my phone buzzing. It's a text from Jake. "Read it," says Mel.

> *Jake: Stuck at this dinner. Would much rather be with you. What are you wearing?*

"Oh, write something witty," Jill says. If only they knew what I wore last night.

Me:	*Clothes. But I think you'll like what's underneath.*
Jake:	*Tell me.*
Me:	*You'll just have to find out.*
Jake:	*I look forward to it. I'll be over around eleven. Will you be home?*
Me:	*I'm out now, but I'll be home by then.*
Jake:	*Good. I can't wait to see you.*

Around ten forty-five I head home. Roland is at the front desk, and I tell him he can send Jake up when he arrives. I put him on my list of authorized visitors then head upstairs, contemplating what to wear. I have on an embellished, black, scoop-neck tank with merlot-colored skinny jeans that have a leather-type coating. I'm not wearing anything special underneath, which gives me an idea. I hear a knock ten minutes later. I open the door, and Jake smiles at me, looking all sexy in his suit.

"How was your night?" I ask him.

"Better now."

I invite him in and show him around.

"I like your apartment. It's very homey."

"Thanks, but you haven't seen the best part." I take him to my balcony, which faces east, giving me views of the lake and downtown. "Isn't it a great view?"

"Yes," he says, but he's staring right at me. "So tell me, what's underneath your clothes?" I motion for him to follow me into my bedroom. I slowly pull my tank top over my head then slide off my jeans. He smiles at my naked body.

"You know, you're the first guy I've brought back here."

"I'm honored. We'll have to christen each room."

And we do.

CHAPTER SIXTEEN

Over the next few weeks, Jake and I fall into a routine. On the rare occasion he's not traveling, we pretty much spend every night together. We usually sleep at his place, but once in a while, he'll stay at mine. He goes into work earlier than I do, so he often drops me off at my apartment before he heads into the office. Today I happen to have an early meeting, so he's offered to drive me. I can tell he's uncomfortable, and I assume he's nervous someone will see us walking in together.

"Why don't you drop me off down the block?" I suggest. "I can stop and get a coffee."

"There's a coffee shop in our lobby. That's ridiculous."

"Honestly it's fine."

"I don't want you having to walk."

"Jake, you do realize I walk to work every day, don't you?"

"OK," he relents.

"I'll just hop out at the corner when you get a red light."

"I'm sorry," he says, looking into my eyes.

"Jake, it's fine."

I give him a quick peck on the cheek and make my way to Starbucks. I watch as he drives off, and he gives me a wave. This is fine with me, but I can only take it for so long. I decide I need to bring up the status of our relationship with him. This is getting ridiculous. I'm looking forward to the day when we're out in the open, and I won't have to pull these kinds of shenanigans. It's just that things have been going so well that I don't want to rock the boat. I know it's a hot button with him. We don't get to see each other that often, so when we do, I like to keep the peace.

I head into my office and log in to my computer. I get an error message followed by a blue screen, which is usually a sign that I've lost whatever I was working on. Fortunately I didn't have any unsaved documents open—at least none I can recall. I check my BlackBerry for this morning's meeting details and head to the conference room. I'll deal with my computer later. I spend the entire morning in meetings and finally get back to my desk close to lunch. I try logging in again but get the same error message. I poke my head into Nicole's office.

"Hi. Are you able to get onto the network?"

"Yes."

"Great. It's probably just my computer then."

I call IT, and they work with me to troubleshoot the issue. The tech guy tells me there appears to be a problem with my hard drive, and he'll need to take my computer so he can investigate further.

"Can I get a loaner laptop?"

"Sure. I'll bring one up to you."

I'm very irritated. I'm super busy today, and this is my one free hour to get actual work done. It's funny how helpless I've become without technology. I feel like I can't do any work. What did people do back when there weren't computers or e-mail? They probably were more productive and had healthier relationships because people actually picked up the phone to communicate instead of hiding behind printed words. I hear a knock on my door and look up to see Randy from IT with my loaner.

"I should have your computer back to you by the end of the day."

"Thank you. I need to bring this one with me to meetings. I might not be back until after five. Should I drop it off somewhere?"

"Just leave it on your desk. I'll come get it."

"Thanks. I appreciate that."

It's nice when people go out of their way to be helpful. Why does it have to be an exception rather than the rule? Realizing I'm in a crabby mood, I tell myself to snap out of it. I think the situation with Jake this morning is nagging at me.

I spend the rest of the day in meetings and on conference calls. I get a text from Jake late in the afternoon.

Jake:	*You've been off IM. What time are you leaving?*
Me:	*Tech support has my computer. I'm not sure. Maybe seven?*
Jake:	*I'll drive you home. I have things to finish up, so I'll be here for a while.*
Me:	*Thanks. Where should I meet you? On a street corner?*
Jake:	*I wouldn't want anyone to get the wrong idea.*
Me:	*What are you implying, Hartman?*
Jake:	*Well, your skirt is rather short today.*
Me:	*My skirt is perfectly appropriate office attire. I'm insulted you would think otherwise.*
Jake:	*You're always very appropriate. It's just that it's been a distraction for me today.*
Me:	*Oh, perhaps I should wear it more often.*
Jake:	*Definitely.* ☺ *Let's head out together. I think it should be pretty quiet by then. If we run into someone, we'll make a game-time decision.*

I roll my eyes. Since when did this become a game we have to strategize? My cell phone rings, and I see it's my mom. We usually talk every few days.

"Hi, Mom. How are you?" She asks me how things are going with work. "They're good. I'm actually still here."

"Lexi, you've been working a lot of long hours. Make sure you don't overdo it." I assure her I'm fine; it's just a busy time, and this isn't the norm. "So how are things with you and Jake?" she asks.

I recently told my parents we're dating, but I haven't told them about Jake wanting to keep things quiet. They're so thrilled I'm finally seeing someone that I didn't want to bring it up. I'm not sure how they would take the news. It's not that I think it's a big deal; I just worry they'll interpret it the wrong way. I ask my mom about her current projects, and she fills me in on her latest client, a demanding divorcée. "She makes a decision but then keeps changing her mind, which sets back the project timeline. I keep warning her, and she agrees, but then when things are delayed, she throws a fit."

"It sounds like that could be why her marriage didn't last."

My mom laughs. "I suppose you're right. Well, I don't want to keep you from your work."

"Love you, Mom."

"Love you too."

I meet Jake in the lobby at seven. "Looks like we're all clear," I say in an authoritative voice. He gives me a funny look. "What do you want to do for dinner?" I ask, trying to lighten the mood.

"Let's pick something up and bring it back to my place."

I realize we haven't been out to dinner since our trip to San Francisco. "How about we eat out?"

Jake shrugs. "It's been a long day—another time."

"Will there be another time?"

"Yes, there will, just not tonight."

"OK, I'm fine with keeping this on the down-low, but do you have a plan?"

"No, I don't have a set timetable for when we'll go public," Jake says. "I told you, I do intend to tell people. Let's just wait until the timing is right."

When will that be? I wonder. *How will he decide when the timing is right?* I'm about to argue but decide to drop the subject for now. It's frustrating being at his mercy just because it's his issue, not mine. On the car ride home, I muse that this has become my life, a life of secrets.

We go to his place and decide to get takeout from Sushi Maki. The last time I ate there was when I ran into Jake, and Heather revealed I'd been engaged. That feels like ages ago.

"Fill me in on what I've missed at the office," he says as he unpacks our food.

"Nothing really. Nicole is dating someone new."

"Tell me something I don't already know."

"Actually I feel bad. I thought maybe things would work out with… What's his name?"

"Exactly."

"She seemed upset about it," I say. "Her birthday is coming up so I'm going to plan a little surprise party at work to lift her spirits."

"That's nice of you."

"Speaking of…your birthday is coming up. Am I allowed to take you to dinner?"

"Actually my parents are hosting a dinner for me at their condo on Sunday. I'd love for you to be there," he says.

Wow, he wants me to meet his parents. "OK." I smile at him. "I'd love to come."

"Good," he says, looking relieved.

"Are they having a lot of people over?"

"Just my immediate family. Aside from my mom and dad, Kate, her husband Adam, and Hailey will be there, and Nick and Danielle, his fiancée."

"I'm looking forward to meeting her. And I'm excited to see Hailey again."

"She'll be excited too. She asks about you a lot."

"Really?"

"Yes, really. Apparently you made quite the impression on her."

"Well, at least I have a good track record with your family so far," I joke.

"Don't worry. Everyone will love you."

As we're cleaning up after dinner, I realize Jake didn't answer me about taking him out for his birthday. And I can't help think he perfectly evaded the question.

The next day I'm knee-deep, working on a brief. I've been at it all morning, but it still needs work. Frustrated, I decide to take a break and come back to it. I'm about to check my e-mail when I receive a text message from Jake.

Jake: *How about lunch?*
Me: *Sure. Where do you want to meet?*
Jake: *Your place.*
Me: *Oh, that kind of lunch. I'm actually kind of hungry… and I mean for food.*

Jake:	*I'll make sure you're satisfied in every way.*
Me:	*You always do.*
Jake:	☺ *I'll be there at twelve fifteen.*
Me:	*You're on.*

I check my e-mail then try to get back to writing my brief, but now I'm distracted. I check my watch and see that it's only eleven. I sigh. What's the use? It'll just have to wait until after lunch.

At eleven fifty-five, I head out, excited about our secret rendezvous. When I get to my building, I go upstairs and quickly freshen up and brush my teeth. Jake knocks at exactly twelve fifteen.

"You're punctual as usual," I tell him.

"I tried my best not to be early," he replies, as he pulls me into an embrace.

"I have to be back for a meeting by one thirty."

"Don't worry. I'll have you back in time," he says, as he leads me into the bedroom. This is definitely a perk of living close to the office I hadn't anticipated. Twenty-five minutes later, we're sitting at my kitchen table having lunch. Jake picked up a grilled-chicken Caesar salad for me and a panini for himself.

"Thanks for getting lunch," I tell him.

"I told you not to worry about being hungry."

"That's not what I thought you meant."

"I told you I would satisfy you in every way."

"And you did."

He gives me a smug smile. Then he says, "So I have big news."

"What?"

"We won the pitch."

"Get out! Seriously?"

"Michael called shortly before I came over. Their fiscal starts next month, so we have a few weeks to staff up."

"Jake, that's amazing. Congrats!"

"Thanks, but don't forget that you played a huge part in helping us secure the win." His phone rings, but he silences the call.

"Do you need to take that?"

"No, it's just one of my Yale buddies. He got engaged recently and already wants to plan his bachelor party. That reminds me...I've been meaning to ask you, when would your wedding have been?"

"Labor Day weekend."

"Wow, that's coming up next month. Do you have anything planned?"

"No, to be honest I haven't really thought about it." This isn't exactly true. My friends have been bugging me about arranging another girls' night out, but I've been evasive. I guess I just want to avoid the whole thing.

"We should go somewhere," Jake says.

"I love that idea. Where should we go?"

"You leave the planning to me. Can you get the time off?"

I think for a minute. "It should be fine. We don't have work that Friday or Monday. We could leave Thursday night and come back the following weekend. I'd only have to take off four days. What about you?"

"I never take vacation. There's nothing pressing that I know of, so let's do it."

I'm beyond excited.

We walk back to the office, and Jake gets off the elevator first. I let him walk ahead of me, and Ross stops him a few feet away from my office. When I pass them, Jake gives me a casual "Hey, Lexi."

"Hi, Jake, Ross," I say then sit down at my desk. I resume my brief writing and find I'm much more focused now. Rihanna's "We Found Love" comes on the radio and takes me back to my first night with Jake in San Francisco. I turn up the volume and hum along as I type. I sense a presence; I look up and see Nicole watching me in the doorway.

"Sorry," I tell her. "Was the music too loud?"

She looks at me with narrowed eyes and says, "You had sex."

"What?"

"I said, 'You had sex.'"

"I heard what you said. How did you know?" I ask incredulously.

"You've been different these past few weeks. *Lighter* is the only word that comes to mind."

I wonder whether Jake is still outside my office talking to Ross, but I don't want Nicole following my gaze.

"You've been seeing someone," she says accusingly.

I feel myself turn a deep red; I've always been a terrible liar. "Yes, I have. I'm sorry I didn't say anything. I just didn't know where things would go."

"And?"

"Things are going really well."

"That's great! What's his name?"

"Nick," I say without missing a beat.

"What does he do?"

"He's an investment banker."

"Does he have any friends?"

I laugh. "I haven't met them yet, but I'll keep my eye open for you."

"Thanks." I think she's about to leave, but then she asks, "How's the sex?"

I pause for a moment, unaccustomed to divulging such personal information with people at work. But then again, Nicole is more of a friend than just a coworker. "Mind blowing," I finally answer.

"Lucky bitch," she says as she walks out of my office.

I'm just about done with my brief when my phone buzzes. It's a text from Jake.

> Jake: *Mind blowing, huh?*

So he *was* outside my door.

> Me: *Don't you know it's rude to eavesdrop on people's private conversations?*
> Jake: *You didn't answer the question.*
> Me: *I thought I did. You heard my answer.*
> Jake: *It was pretty loud and clear over lunch.*

I feel myself blush once again. I'm glad he's not here to see it. I choose to ignore him, but he responds anyway.

> Jake: *Nick. That's an interesting choice.*

Is he insecure about this? Seriously?

> Me: *It's the first name that came to mind. Don't read anything into it—although good looks definitely run in the family.*

I wait a few minutes. There's no response, so I change the subject.

> Me: *Thanks again for lunch today. And to go back to your initial question, it was very satisfying.*
> Jake: 😊
> Me: *Now please stop bugging me. I have work to do.*

Smiling, I return to my brief yet again. This time I finally finish it. I reread it once last time and decide it's perfect.

The next day I submit a vacation request, which Morgan approves. Now I just need to figure out where to tell people I'm going. Why does something as simple as taking a trip have to be so complicated? I send Jake an e-mail to let him know I got the days approved and to solicit his advice on where to say I'm going. He suggests saying I'm visiting friends in New York, which I easily can do. I just wish I didn't have to.

The rest of the week passes quickly, and tonight I'm meeting Jake's family. I fret about what to wear. I decide on a lilac sleeveless wrap dress with ruffle details at the bodice. It's soft and feminine. I pair it with silver espadrille wedge sandals. I brush out my hair and wonder whether I should pull it back. But then Jake calls to tell me he's five minutes away. I grab my Tiffany bracelet for good luck, along with Jake's birthday gift and the potted orchid I bought for his mom, then head to the lobby. I'm very nervous about meeting his family. With Ben it was easy because I happened to run into his parents during Mother's Day weekend while we were in college. It was still early on in our relationship, so there was no pressure. Now it's a formal event where I know Jake's parents will be judging whether I'm good enough for their son. I see Jake's car pull up. I take a deep breath and head outside. He comes around and opens the door for me.

"Hi. You look beautiful," he says, giving me a kiss on the cheek.

"Thanks. You look nice too." He's wearing a pinstripe button-down shirt and black pants. I notice he's wearing the same silver cuff links from my first day at Hartman & Taylor. "I like those cuff links. Were they a gift?" I figure this is better than overtly asking if they were from a girlfriend.

"As a matter of fact, they were. My mom gave them to me when I got the job at Hartman and Taylor."

I feel relieved. While I'm well aware he has a past, I prefer that he not wear it. "I wish I could have seen the house you grew up in," I tell him. Jake once told me his parents moved to a condo on Lake Shore Drive after he graduated from high school.

He parks in their building and grabs my hand as we ride the elevator up to their unit. "Nervous?" he asks me.

"A little," I admit.

"They'll love you. You're the first girl I've brought home in a long time. Believe me, they already think you walk on water."

Jake knocks on their door, and his mom answers. She has short, stylish, blond hair and is dressed in a nice blouse and pants. She regards me with the same icy-blue eyes as Jake. He gives her a warm hug then makes introductions. "Mom, this is Lexi. Lexi, this is my mom."

"Hi, Mrs. Hartman. It's so nice to meet you," I say, shaking her hand and offering her the orchid.

"What a thoughtful gesture. Thank you. Please call me Nancy. It's a pleasure to meet you. Jake's told us so much about you. Come on in."

She leads us into the kitchen, where everyone else is already gathered. "Lexi, good to see you again," says Kate. "This is my husband, Adam."

"Hi," I say, shaking his hand. Nick gives me a big hug and introduces me to Danielle. She's tall, with long, blond hair and warm brown eyes. I decide she's pretty in an approachable way.

She smiles at me and says, "I hear I have you to thank for Nick's creative proposal."

I smile back. "I may have given him some suggestions. I'd love to hear the story."

Just then Hailey bounds in. "Lexi!" she says, running up to me.

"Hi," I say, as I bend down to give her a hug.

"Will you come play with me?" she asks.

"Sure. I just need to finish talking to Danielle, and I'll be right in."

"OK," she says, as she runs back into the family room.

Danielle tells me the story of their engagement, and I tell Nick I'm impressed. I ask her to see her ring, and it's beautiful. They seem so happy together, and I can tell they're a nice couple.

"Come on. Let me give you a tour," Jake says.

The place is very well designed but feels lived in. "You have exquisite taste," I tell Nancy.

"Thank you," she says appreciatively.

I go into the family room and find Hailey coloring. "What are you making?" I ask her.

"A picture for the baby."

"That's very nice of you."

She nods. "Do you want to color?"

"Sure," I say, accepting a piece of paper and some crayons. I draw a rainbow with hearts and flowers. I write Hailey's name on it and tell her I made it for her.

"I love it!" she exclaims.

Jake's mom comes in and tells us dinner is ready. She's made Jake's favorite meal: Caprese salad, pesto pasta with sundried tomatoes and pine nuts, garlic bread, roasted red potatoes, and Chicken Vesuvio. "Everything is delicious," I tell her. I see where Jake gets his cooking skills.

Everyone chats easily over the meal. His family asks me a lot of questions but none about my time in New York. I'm guessing Jake told them about my situation. I wonder what his parents must think.

After dinner, Jake's mom suggests he open his gifts. I'm glad I thought to bring mine. She hands him a large package and says, "It's from your dad and me." Jake opens it to reveal a Fender acoustic guitar. "This is very generous," he says, giving them each a hug.

"Did you know Jake was in a band?" Kate asks me.

"Yes, he mentioned he sang backup."

"Do you guys ever play anymore?" Kate asks him.

"Nah. Once we started working, everyone got pretty busy. I miss it, though. I haven't owned one like this since high school. This is great," he says, strumming a few chords.

I hand him my wrapped box next. I didn't include a card; I'm saving it for his actual birthday. He opens it and sees the pair of Bulls tickets. He has an unreadable expression on his face.

"Don't worry. They're for you and Nick," I say quietly. "I already cleared the date with him."

"Isn't it awesome?" Nick exclaims.

"Thank you," he says, and kisses me in front of his entire family. I pull away, embarrassed. "This is perfect."

"I'm glad you like it. I know you've been to the skybox before, but I figured you've never sat courtside."

"They're courtside seats?" Jake says. "I didn't even look. That's awesome! How did you manage to score these?"

"Liv's fiancé, Jason, has a friend who works for Comcast Sports. I asked him to pull some strings."

I don't mention that I'm working on getting them into the locker room after the game. I'll leave that as a surprise for the day of. He opens the rest of the gifts, and then his mom calls us into the kitchen for cake. We sing "Happy Birthday," and Hailey helps him blow out the candles. We linger over dessert, and then I offer to help Nancy clean up the kitchen.

"Nonsense. I appreciate the offer, but you're my guest," she says. Now I know where Jake gets it from.

Kate announces they have to leave to get Hailey home for bed. She gives everyone a hug, and I wish her luck.

"Next time I see you, you'll be a big sister," I tell Hailey.

"Will you come visit me and the baby?"

"Yes, I definitely will."

Once they leave I hang out with Danielle and Nick. I really like them—they're both nice, down-to-earth people, and they're very easy to talk to. I don't know where Jake is; he was deep in conversation with his dad earlier. Suddenly he's by my side.

"Do you want to get going?" he asks me.

"I'm ready whenever you are." I thank his parents for dinner, and they both give me a warm hug.

"It was so great having you here," Nancy says. "Please come see us again soon."

"I will," I tell her.

Once we're in the car, Jake asks me what I thought. "Everyone was really nice," I tell him. "You have a great family."

"I do," he says.

"So are you going to play something for me later?"

"Maybe. Why?"

"I can't resist a guy who plays in a band. It's a huge turn-on."

A smile spreads across his face. "If I'd known that, I definitely would have forced a reunion." He pulls me toward him and kisses me. "Thank you for coming with me. It was nice having you spend time with my family. You know, I'd love to meet your family too."

"You already met my family. At the benefit, remember?"

"Yes, but that was different. We weren't dating then."

"That's true," I say, and change the subject.

I know he hasn't truly met them, but I'm not ready to take that step yet. My dad and Ben were very close. I think the breakup was hard on my father, and I don't want to introduce him to someone else until I know for certain he's the one. Jake definitely could be, but for some reason, I can't bring myself to think it.

CHAPTER SEVENTEEN

I stop by Simon's office Monday morning.

"So how was it?" he asks.

"I think it went well. Everyone was really nice."

"How did Jake like his gift?"

"I think he liked it once he realized I wasn't going."

"I'm sure that's not true."

"No, it is. He got a weird look until I told him the other ticket was for Nick."

"You need to give him time," Simon says. "It obviously took him a while before he was willing to move forward with your relationship. It's not going to happen overnight."

"I know. I just wonder how long it'll be before he comes around. I don't want to wait another six months before he's ready to go public."

"Patience, my dear. Just be happy you got to this point in your relationship."

"I know," I tell him. "I should be happy—and I am. I just wish I could share my happiness with others."

"Well, you can share it with me."

For now that has to be enough.

At ten thirty I head to Morgan's office for an account management status meeting. She wants to discuss where we see the greatest growth opportunities for our clients. I spent a good portion of last week mapping out my plan, which focuses on organic growth from Lumineux. However, I have an idea I've been toying with that would enable us to expand our beauty portfolio. I decide now is the time to bring it up. I listen as my peers give their updates, most of which also focus on trying to secure more revenue from existing clients. When it's my turn, I discuss how we can try to expand our scope into other areas of Lumineux's portfolio. We only have their skin care business, but they also sell a wide range of other personal care products. A different set of clients manages that business, but I think we can get Natalia to arrange an introduction.

"That's excellent, Lexi," Morgan says. "Why don't you put some time on my calendar so we can discuss your thoughts on how to best approach it?"

"I will, but I have one other idea. I think we should aim bigger than skin care. I think we should try to own beauty. A key staple would be landing a cosmetics account."

"I like your aspirations. That's been on the radar of our New Business team, but unfortunately there haven't been any promising leads."

"I may have one. When I worked at Aura, my client was always talking about the company's desire to launch a mass-market line. But there was a lot of dissonance among executives because they feared it would erode the equity of the brand. Initially they were going to use the Aura name to establish credibility. When I left, the idea seemed closer to fruition because they decided to keep it as a completely separate brand. I can call my client and see if there are any updates."

"Yes, you should definitely leverage your contact there. Do you want support from the New Business team?"

"Not yet. I don't want this to come off as a sales pitch. Let me have an initial conversation, and we can go from there."

Morgan pulls me aside after the meeting. "I was very impressed with your business plan. Keep up the good work."

When I get back to my office, I place a call to my former client at Aura. Fortunately he picks up the phone.

"Eric Mathews."

"Hi, Eric. It's Lexi Winters."

"Lexi, good to hear from you! How are things?"

"Very good. I moved back to Chicago. I'm with Hartman and Taylor now."

"I heard. They're lucky to have you."

I thank him and ask about his family. He updates me then asks what I'm working on. I tell him about Lumineux and the fragrance account we recently won.

"Still working on beauty, I see, although I'm not surprised. It suits you."

"Thanks. That's actually why I'm calling. I wanted to see what's happening with your foray into mass cosmetics."

"We got the green light last month," Eric says. "It's a go."

"Wow, that's exciting! Are you looking for an agency?"

"As a matter of fact, we are."

"I'd love to talk to you about the opportunity. Can I come out for a visit?"

"Your timing is impeccable. I'll be in Chicago after Labor Day for a vacation. I think I can manage to carve out some time to meet with you."

We put a date on the calendar, which works perfectly for me because I'll just be coming back from my trip with Jake. "Thanks, Eric. I'm looking forward to seeing you."

"You too, Lexi. See you soon."

After we hang up, I call Morgan to let her know about my meeting.

"Wow, you work fast. It sounds like a very viable lead. How do you plan to prepare for the meeting?"

"I'd like to keep it pretty informal," I tell her. "I know him well and don't want it to come off as though we're giving him a hard sell. I'll let him lead the discussion, and I'll have copies of our latest beauty work that we can reference, based on the direction it goes."

"I'm fine with that approach. Do you want anyone else in the meeting?"

"I don't think I want anyone from New Business, but Simon would be an asset."

"I trust your judgment," Morgan says. "Just let me know if you need any support."

"I definitely will."

Later that afternoon I stop by Simon's office.

"Lexi, twice in one day. To what do I owe this lovely visit?" I give him an update on my discussion with Eric. "That's wonderful news! I'd love to land a cosmetics account. It would really round out our portfolio and position us as beauty experts. With your experience we definitely have a strong shot if we're invited to pitch." I give him some background on Eric along with my thoughts on what we should share at the meeting. He says he'll board up samples of our best work and have the team develop a video montage with some of our spots.

Excited to share the news, I call Jake later that evening.

"How was your day?" he asks me.

"It was great. I shared my growth plan with Morgan."

"And?"

"And she is aligned with my approach and basically gave me cart blanche to pursue my cosmetics lead."

"Lexi, that's great! I'm so proud of you. Let me know if you need my help."

"Thanks," I tell him. "I want to meet with Eric first to feel him out. So how was your day?"

"It was good. I golfed with an old colleague today, and he may have a lead for an electronics account."

"That could be promising."

"We'll see if it pans out."

"Will the timing be OK with our trip?" I ask him.

"Yes, I'll make it work."

"Good, because I'm not letting you out of this vacation."

"I wouldn't dare try."

The next morning is filled with meetings. After lunch I decide I could use a mental break. I stop by Nicole's office to see if she wants to grab some coffee, but she's on a call. She gestures that I can come in.

"I'm looking forward to it too. See you later."

"Who was that?"

"Anthony. We're going out again tonight."

"Isn't that twice this week?"

"Yes, I really like him." I take this with a grain of salt. "We should go on a double date," she says excitedly.

"That would be fun."

"How about next weekend?" I tell her I'll have to check my schedule. "Don't you have it in your phone?" she asks.

I pretend to look at my calendar. "Next weekend isn't good."

"Just name the date."

Crap, I wasn't expecting her to pin me down. "Let me talk to Nick, and I'll get back to you."

"OK," Nicole says. "I'm dying to meet him. Do you have a picture at least?"

"I actually don't."

"Not even on Facebook?"

"We're not Facebook friends." She eyes me skeptically. I hate lying to her and feel very uncomfortable with where this conversation is going. "I have a thing about not friending guys I'm dating," I say lamely.

"Can't you just do a search so I can see what he looks like?"

"I will, just not right now. I've got to head to a meeting," I lie.

"You're the one who stopped by my office," she points out. I can't think of anything to say. "That's fine," she says coldly. "It's obvious you don't want me to meet him. I'm a little offended; I thought we were better friends than that."

"We are friends, but—"

She continues, "It's just that he's a big part of your life, and he seems to have ignited something in you. I want to meet the guy who has transformed you from the withdrawn girl I met a few months ago to the happy, carefree girl I see now."

Shit, what to do? Nicole is one of my closest friends at work and I've obviously offended her. Jake would kill me if I told her, but I don't want to risk our friendship. Can I trust Nicole not to tell anyone?

I close the door and pace around her office.

"OK, there is no Nick."

"What do you mean?"

"I'm actually dating someone at work. He doesn't want anyone to know. I'm sorry I lied to you."

Nicole looks at me with wide eyes. "Who is it? It's Ross, isn't it? I knew he had a thing for you!"

"It's not Ross. It's Jake."

"Jake, as in Jake Hartman?" I nod. She's momentarily speechless. "Wow, now that I never would have guessed. How'd it happen?"

"When we traveled to San Francisco for the pitch. I've had a thing for him for a long time. I just never thought he was interested in taking our relationship to that level." I really don't want to give her the details. "Look—now you know why I've been evasive. You know how private Jake is about his personal life. He would kill me if he knew I told you. You can't breathe a word of it to anyone."

"I won't, I swear. I just can't get over it!"

I look at my watch and realize I actually do have to be at a meeting. "I've got to go. We can talk more later."

Shit, what did I just do? I leave Nicole's office feeling very unsettled and fret about whether I should tell Jake. Even though Nicole was giving me the third degree, I don't think he'd understand. The secretive nature of our relationship is already an issue; I see no reason to bring unneeded stress. I convince myself that ignorance is bliss. Our trip can't come soon enough.

―•―

The week before we're slated to leave, I ask Jake where we're going.

"I want it to be a surprise," he says.

"Give me a hint so I know what to pack."

"Pack for warm weather."

"That's very vague."

"OK, we're going somewhere out of the country that has a beach."

"I was hoping that was the plan."

"I figured. I have a good memory, remember?"

"That's right. My ideal vacation." I smile at him. He really is so thoughtful.

Suddenly he looks concerned. "You have a passport, right?"

"Yes, I do."

"Good. I'm not letting you out of this trip either."

Like it's even an issue. I spend the next few days packing and getting things in order at work. Michelle is covering for me, and I know I'll be in good hands, but I'm a little stressed about being out of the country, especially when everyone at work thinks I'll be in New York. I call my cell phone company to add international coverage while we're away and to make sure there won't be issues with my e-mail account. They assure me everything will work just fine. We're leaving Friday morning. Jake has to be in San Francisco through Thursday, which works out because then I won't have to take Thursday as a half day. I don't know why I'm saving days; I haven't taken any vacation days at all this year. I guess it's a habit; at my old job, I was saving up for the wedding and honeymoon.

I work late on Thursday, tying up any loose ends. I e-mail Michelle the task list we discussed and tell her I'll be reachable if she needs me. I go home and make myself a quick dinner then pack my toiletries and carry-on. I'm ready to go. Jake is supposed to call me when he lands. The plan is that I'll sleep at his place, and we'll head to the airport together in the morning. I pace around my apartment, waiting for his call. Finally my phone rings, and he says he's on his way home in a taxi. I wait about twenty minutes then hop into a cab, already dreaming of palm trees and sandy beaches.

Jake's cab pulls up to the driveway of his building just as I arrive. My driver unloads my bags, and before I know what's happened, Jake pays for my fare.

"You didn't have to do that," I tell him.

He waves his hand in a dismissive gesture. "Get used to it. This trip is on me."

"You're too good to me," I say, wrapping my arms around him. "Now tell me where we're going."

"I wasn't planning on telling you until we got to the airport." I frown at him. "Just kidding. Come on in, and I'll show you." I can tell he's really excited. I follow him inside and take a seat on the couch. He brings his laptop over and says, "We're going to Aruba."

I gape at him. "Can you repeat that?"

"We're going to Aruba."

I throw my arms around him. "Oh, my God! I've never been there, but I've heard it's absolutely beautiful. I can't believe you booked us a trip to Aruba! I thought it was going to be Mexico."

"I wanted to give you your white sandy beaches."

I barely can contain my excitement. He pulls up the website for the Westin Resort & Casino, which is right on the beach. The grounds look spectacular, like a little piece of paradise, with a huge pool and endless palm trees. I have a thing for palm trees; as I'm from the Midwest, they signify a vacation.

"Thank you for planning all this," I say sincerely. "I'm looking forward to spending a full week with you."

"Me too."

"Now let me show you my appreciation," I tell him.

And I do.

I'm so excited that I barely can sleep that night. We have to be up super early for our flight, but I figure I can sleep on the plane. The alarm goes off, and I pop out of bed. Jake tries to snooze, but I throw the covers off and tell him to get ready. He looks at me sleepily and says, "At least we'll get to sleep in this week." By the time he gets out of the shower, I'm ready to go, suitcases in hand. The cab pulls up, and we're on our way to O'Hare. When Jake pulls out his phone to check his e-mail, I scold him.

"No work this week. You can check in twice a day, once in the morning and once in the evening."

"Deal. Same goes for you."

"OK."

We make it to the airport and check in for our flight. Of course Jake booked us in first-class. I give him a look, but he assures me he used miles and has plenty, given all his travel. We make it through security and grab breakfast before our flight. I stop by the newsstand to get extra snacks and reading material for the plane. Jake makes a face at my choice of *Us Weekly*, but I know he'll be reading it over my shoulder. We have about twenty-five minutes before we're supposed to board, so we go to the United Club. I've never been in there before; it's definitely a step up from waiting at the terminal.

"I feel like I have a glimpse into your lifestyle," I tell Jake. "I could get used to this."

He smiles at me. "Good."

Eventually we head to the gate and board our flight. I give a little knock on the outside of the plane before I get on. Once we're seated, Jake asks me why I did that.

"It's a superstition; I have to do it every time I travel. Do you have any travel quirks?"

"None that I can think of. Well, actually I like to be one of the first people to board the plane to make sure I can stow my bag, but now that I have status with United, it's not really an issue."

"Do you think the travel will let up anytime soon?"

He's quiet for a minute then says, "No, not anytime soon."

I sigh and snuggle up next to him. I'm used to it, but I still miss him when he's away.

After takeoff I read my magazine then close my eyes. I must have fallen asleep for most of the flight, because I'm woken by an announcement from the captain that we've started our descent. I look over at Jake, who's watching a movie on his laptop. He sees I'm up and takes off his headphones.

"Whatcha watching?" I ask him.

"The last season of *Entourage*. Great show. Have you seen it?"

"Yes. I saw all the episodes from that season. I won't tell you what happens. You can put it back on if you want."

"No, that's OK. I'd rather talk to you."

"Thanks again for planning this trip. It means a lot to me. And I'm excited to get to spend some quality time together."

"Me too," he says, taking my hand. "I'm sorry I've been away so much lately."

"I understand. I'm kind of used to it, but I love it when you're home. It feels lonely sleeping without you."

"I feel the same. I definitely sleep much better when you're lying next to me."

Jake kisses me softly on the forehead. The flight attendants come around to do their final checks. I look out the window as we descend, and it's nothing but blue skies. I usually hate landings, but the wheels touch the ground almost effortlessly, and I let out a sigh of relief. As we're taxiing to our gate, the captain welcomes us to Aruba. I can't believe we're here!

Jake and I breeze through customs then collect our bags. We find the exit for the shuttle that will take us to our hotel. We walk outside, and I'm struck by the heat and endless rows of palm trees. "This is what my heaven looks like," I say, and sigh contentedly as we board the bus.

When we arrive at the hotel, I feel the photos didn't do it justice. We walk into a spacious lobby that's bright and airy, and flanked with huge pillars, high ceilings, and displays of various tropical flowers. I look around while Jake checks us in. "You like?" he asks, coming up behind me.

"Yes! It's perfect," I say, turning around and wrapping my arms around him.

The bellhop takes our bags and shows us to our room. Jake has booked us an ocean suite with two private balconies that offer spectacular views of the pool and ocean. "This is amazing," I say as I look around, "although a regular room would have been just fine."

"If it makes you feel better, I used points. But I like doing nice things for you. I know you don't expect it, but I want to give you anything I can."

"Thank you. I just wish I could return the favor."

"Your being with me is all I need."

"You really are one of the good ones," I tell him. "Now let's test out this heavenly bed."

Afterward I change into my swimsuit then step onto the balcony and look out at the ocean. Already I feel more relaxed. Joining me, Jake says,

"Let's go check out the hotel." We head downstairs and find the pool. It's very spacious, with water features and hot tubs that spill into the main pool. It's also right next to the beach, which is dotted with grassy umbrellas. We walk over to the sand, and I take off my shoes. I thought it was just the pictures, but the water really is turquoise. Jake and I take a walk down the beach, and I bask in the sensation of the water lapping at my feet.

He picks me up and says, "Do you want to get wet?"

"Don't you dare! I don't like swimming in the ocean."

"Really? Why not?"

"I don't like the salt water," I confess. "I'll go in up to my knees, but that's about it."

"OK. I won't throw you in. But I thought you liked snorkeling."

"I do—the goggles help. I'm definitely up for an outing."

We talk about what we want to do then head to the concierge to get dinner suggestions and to book our activities for the week. We know we want to relax at the hotel tomorrow then do a day of snorkeling, some sightseeing, and a day of shopping in town. Beyond that, we're open to suggestions. The concierge makes some recommendations, and we decide to do a jeep tour because it's a great way to explore the island. We also make arrangements to visit Arikok National Park, a nature preserve with historical sites of the island, including underground caves and sand dunes; Bubali Bird Sanctuary; and Gold Mine Ranch, which offers horseback-riding excursions. For beaches outside of the hotel, she suggests Baby Beach, which sounds good to me because the waters are shallow, and she says we can go a long distance and still touch the bottom. I'm a bit concerned that our vacation will be too action packed, so Jake and I decide to leave a few days open toward the end of the week. As it gets closer, we can decide whether we want to do more sightseeing or just hang out at the beach. The concierge prints our itinerary and hands it to us.

"Are you happy with everything we've picked out?" Jake asks me.

"Yes, everything is perfect," I say, pulling him in for a kiss.

And for the first time in a long while, everything does feel perfect.

CHAPTER EIGHTEEN

The next few days pass quickly. I love all the tours we've taken, but I'm looking forward to spending the day walking around Oranjestad, the island's capital. Sometimes I think you get the best feel for a place just by exploring on your own. We take a cab to the downtown area; our driver is very friendly and gives us a history of the island. He drops us off in the heart of town, and we make arrangements for him to pick us up later. As I look around, I'm struck by the rows of shops with Dutch Caribbean facades painted in bright colors. They're very charming. We walk for a while and explore the shops. I make a few duty-free purchases, and then I go on a quest to find souvenirs for Hailey, Molly, and Charlie. Jake and I hit an outdoor market, and we walk through the rows of vendors as I look for the perfect gift for his niece.

"What do you think Hailey will like?" I ask him.

"I don't know. Jewelry?"

"I don't know if they'll have anything in her size, but we can look." Then I stumble upon a wooden puppet of a parrot that's painted in pinks and reds. "What about this? Do you think she'll like it?"

"Yes. She has a small hand-puppet collection but nothing like this."

I bargain with the vendor and buy it. I end up getting a ceramic painted lizard for Charlie—he's now into reptiles. The vendor tries to convince me to buy a sterling silver bracelet, but I shake my head.

"Come on. I'll buy it for you," says Jake. "You should have something to commemorate the trip."

"I already have a silver bracelet I wear a lot," I say, holding up my wrist so he can see my Tiffany bracelet. "I guess I could get a ring or a pair of earrings." I don't wear rings that often, but I find one I like. Jake insists on buying it for me. I don't protest; I think it costs less than ten dollars. For Molly I buy a bracelet that's silver with turquoise beads.

We're both getting hungry so we decide to stop for lunch. There's a plethora of cafés, bars, and restaurants. We stop to look at menus then ask a local for her recommendation. She points out a café up the street, where we go and request a table outdoors.

"This really is paradise," I tell Jake. "I haven't taken this kind of vacation in ages."

"Well, you deserve it. I'm so glad we were able to get away."

"Me too, and I'm impressed you really haven't been working that much."

"I have—I just do it when you're sleeping," he jokes. "But seriously, I didn't realize how much I was always on until we got here. Things have been so busy that I'm constantly working, and it feels good to get a mental break. So," he says, changing the subject, "what's your favorite place you've traveled to?"

"I'd have to say London. I studied there the summer before my senior year of college. I loved the energy of the city and the culture. I'm so glad I got the experience of living abroad. Plus I got to travel around Europe afterward."

"I like London too. I traveled through Europe after I graduated, and it was definitely one of my favorite cities."

"Where else did you go?" I ask him.

"Spain, France, and Italy. Rome was my favorite—I loved the mix of old and new. It was amazing to walk down a modern street and see ancient ruins and know the past is right there with you."

"I loved Rome too," I tell him, "although I never made it to France. I'd love to visit Paris. It seems like such a romantic city. I was actually supposed to have a photo shoot there, but it got canceled."

"Paris is nice. We'll have to get there someday."

I smile at him. "I'm going to hold you to it."

After we eat we stroll through the shops some more. I'm surprised at all the prestigious and upscale stores that sell everything from electronics to jewelry. I look at my watch and see we have ten minutes before we're scheduled to meet our cab driver. We head back to our designated spot, and there he is, waiting for us.

"How was your day?" the driver asks as he opens my door.

"It was great. This is a beautiful island." He beams at me; I can tell he's very proud. Jake and I are both quiet on the drive back, each lost in our own thoughts.

The next morning I tell Jake I'm going to get us coffee. Instead I stop by the concierge and look into tee times. Jake is an avid golfer, and the courses here are breathtaking. I know he'll protest if I tell him what I'm doing, so I decide to surprise him. The concierge books us eighteen holes for Friday on the grounds of a five-star hotel. He's done so much for me; I want to do something for him in return. I stop by the coffee bar afterward so as not to blow my cover. Then I head back upstairs and pack a bag. We're going snorkeling today; Jake and I have been many times before separately, so I'm excited we'll get to share the experience. He's actually gone scuba diving, something I've never tried, so he booked the snorkel trip instead. Once we're ready, we head down to the lobby to wait for the tour bus. It takes us to Baby Beach, a beautiful expanse of white powdery sand that opens into a calm lagoon. We put on our snorkel gear and head into the water. Then we walk until we reach the area where the bay opens out to the sea and find beautiful tropical fish and colorful coral. The water is so calm and clear that I wish I thought to buy an underwater camera. When I surface I'm able to make out sailboats in the distance—it's truly picturesque. We snorkel for the next hour or so then take a break. We head back to the beach and stretch out on our towels, letting our wet bathing suits soak up the hot sun. A young couple comes over and puts their stuff down by ours. I give the girl a friendly smile, and she smiles back.

"Hi. I'm Lexi, and this is Jake."

"Vanessa, and that guy in the water over there is my husband, Seth."

"Nice to meet you. Where are you two from?"

"Philly. We're here on our honeymoon."

"Congrats!"

"What about you guys?"

"Just a vacation. We're here from Chicago."

"Oh, I love Chicago. Seth has family there."

"Whereabouts?"

"His cousin lives in Lincoln Park," Vanessa says, "and his uncle lives in some suburb. I can't remember which one."

"Jake lives in Lincoln Park."

Seth sees us talking and makes his way over. "Seth, this is Lexi and Jake. They're here from Chicago."

"Nice to meet you."

Seth and Jake engage in a conversation, and I spend the rest of the afternoon chatting with Vanessa. We all grab lunch together then head back into the water. Our tour leader gives us the signal that it's time to wrap things up. We go back to the beach to dry off and pack up our things. Then we make plans to have dinner with Seth and Vanessa that evening. We really hit it off and thought it would be fun to dine together. Now that I think about it, Jake and I never have been on a double date before. They're dropped off first, so Jake and Seth exchange numbers to firm up our dinner plans.

We don't get back to our hotel until close to four. We're both hungry, so we have a light snack by the pool.

"What do you think we should do tomorrow?" Jake asks me.

"Actually I have a surprise for you."

"You do? What is it?"

"You'll have to wait until tomorrow."

"I hate surprises," he says. "Just tell me now."

"Really? Why do you hate them?"

"I just don't like being caught off guard."

"Well, this is a good surprise," I tell him. "But since you hate them, I will tell you I booked you eighteen holes."

Jake looks excited. "But what about you? You don't golf."

"I'm driving the golf cart! I can't wait. I've always wanted to drive one."

He laughs at me. "Thank you. Are you sure you won't be bored?"

"Trust me, being here with you and this view, I could never be bored. Besides, you're always doing nice things for me, so I wanted to do something nice for you. Now let's go upstairs, and I'll do something else that's nice for you."

"Who am I to say no to that?"

Jake and I spend the next hour in bed, then shower and get ready for dinner. I put on a printed tank dress and pair it with braided black gladiator sandals. My hair is naturally wavy, and I let it air dry—there's no use straightening it in this humidity. I add just a touch of makeup to enhance my tan.

Jake comes out of the bathroom after his shower and looks me over approvingly. "You look very pretty in that dress."

"And you're so hot in that towel—but even more so if I take it off."

He swats my hand away. "We'll be late for dinner. We have people to see."

"OK," I say, pouting at him.

"I'm glad I have that effect on you."

"Jake, you have that effect on me like no one ever has. I'm always ready for you."

"Really?" he says, walking toward me.

"See for yourself." He grabs his phone. "What are you doing?"

"Texting Seth that we're running a few minutes late for dinner."

I smile at him—a victorious smile.

Twenty minutes later we're ready. Seth and Vanessa are staying at a hotel a few miles away, so we're meeting them at the restaurant. The maître d' leads us to a spectacular patio draped beneath a pergola that's dotted with beautiful greenery and tiny twinkling lights. I love eating outdoors, and the views here don't disappoint. Seth and Vanessa are waiting for us at the table.

When we apologize for being late, Vanessa gives me a knowing look. "We're the newlyweds," she says. "We should be the ones running late."

We all laugh as the waiter comes to our table. We order a round of drinks and a few appetizers. I ask Vanessa about her wedding, and she's more than happy to provide all the details. Jake turns to Seth, and from the pieces of conversation I overhear, I assume they're talking about work. After we order our second round of drinks, Vanessa says, "I've brought Table Topics. Wanna play?"

"What's Table Topics?" I ask.

"It's a game of conversation starters. Seth and I figured we'd be on our own all week, so we brought it to keep us entertained."

"OK, that sounds fun. How does it work?"

"We each take turns picking a question, and everyone has to answer," she says. "You go first."

I reach in and pull out a card. "If you could have any talent, what would it be? Hmm, I guess I'd want to be a singer and star on Broadway."

"What about touring?" Vanessa asks. "Would you want to be a pop star?"

"No, but I'd love to be in a musical like *Phantom of the Opera*. The idea of constantly being on the road and stalked by paparazzi doesn't appeal to me. What about you?"

"I'd love to be able to act," she says. "My dream job would be to star in a sitcom like *Friends*."

"Why not the movies?" asks Seth.

"I'd do movies, but TV seems like it would be more fun and less pressure. Plus it's a steadier job."

"If I could have any talent," Seth says, "I'd be a martial arts master. I'd love to be able to kick ass like Bruce Lee." We all laugh.

"Last but not least," Vanessa says to Jake.

"I'd be a mind reader." Jake looks at me and says, "You women are so confusing. I'd love to see what goes on in that head of yours."

"All you have to do is ask," I tell him.

Vanessa goes next. "If money and skill were no object, what would be your dream job? I'd be an artist and open my own gallery. I love painting, but I'm not very good at it. There's something calming about expressing your thoughts on canvas."

"I'd be a nature photographer. I'd love to capture animals in the wilderness," says Seth.

"You're on your own with that," teases Vanessa. She looks at me, indicating it's my turn.

"I'd work for the Make-A-Wish Foundation. I volunteer there once a month, but I'd love to make it a full-time job."

"Now you're making me feel bad," says Vanessa. "I'd like to do charity work too. I'll donate some of the proceeds from my auctions to the foundation."

"That sounds great. I'll hold you to it."

"Looks like I'm last again," says Jake.

"You can go first next," Vanessa tells him.

"OK. I'd be a scientist and find a cure for cancer."

"Now I really don't want to play with you guys anymore," says Vanessa. "How about something less serious? I'm going to ask a question that isn't in the box. Where's one place you'd like to do it but haven't? Jake, you're up first."

"Well, you're not giving me much time to think."

"Don't overthink it. Just say the first thing that comes to mind."

"OK, a hot tub." Then he turns and looks at me, waiting for my answer. I meet his gaze. "Your desk at work, in the middle of the afternoon." Jake smiles and raises his eyebrows at me.

"Looks like we're saved," says Vanessa, as the waiter comes with our food.

We take a break from the game to eat; everything is delicious. Then we decide to head to the casino at our hotel after dinner; Jake and I haven't been yet. We're all too stuffed to order dessert, so we request the check. "One last question before we go," says Vanessa, as she hands the box to Jake.

He grabs a card and reads it aloud. "What's the one quality you love most about your partner? I guess I'd say I love how strong a person Lexi is. She's had some big setbacks in her life, but she still has an optimistic outlook. Most people would become jaded, but she embraces those experiences and uses them as opportunities to help others. And she has an amazing ability to connect with people wherever she goes. She always seems to find common ground and makes friends very easily, even with some whom I consider difficult personalities. I guess that was two. I'm making up for being last."

I smile at Jake. I've never really thought of myself as a strong person. I by no means view myself as fragile and definitely would say I'm assertive, but I usually view strong personalities as being aggressive types, which I'm definitely not. It's interesting to see Jake's perspective of me. With my aunt passing away and Ben cheating on me, I could have become bitter, but I always try to find the silver lining. In fact, my mom always tells me I'm an eternal optimist. I half listen as Vanessa and Seth give their answers; I'm trying to think of what to say about Jake. There are so many things that it's hard to choose just one.

When it's my turn, I say, "His integrity. Jake always wants to do right by people and is upfront and honest. He never would lie or cheat to get his way—he believes hard work gets rewarded, and he's one of the hardest-working people I know. He works for the family business, so he easily could use that to his advantage. But in fact it's the opposite. He works twice as hard to make sure he's viewed as successful on his own accord. I respect that."

"No wonder you guys are together. You're both perfect," Vanessa says, rolling her eyes.

"At least Seth will admit you're together," I whisper to her as we're walking out. "Jake wants to keep our relationship a secret."

"Thank God there's a flaw. You two were starting to make me feel inadequate. I guess we can still be friends," she says, linking her arm through mine.

The four of us head to the casino. Jake wants to play blackjack, but it intimidates me, so I decide to play the slots. He tells me to meet him at the tables when I'm done. Vanessa and I play, and I end up winning two hundred dollars, which is major in my book. I walk over to Jake, excited to tell him about my winnings. He's at a table with a fifty-dollar minimum. It would give me a coronary to spend that much on one hand, but Jake doesn't seem to think it's a big deal. When I ask him how he's doing, he says he and Seth are each down a few hundred dollars. I'm ready to call it quits, but Jake tells me he wants to try to win some of it back. "Stay with me," he says. "You're my good luck charm."

Apparently I am, because he ends up coming out seventy-five dollars ahead. I look at my watch; it's 1:00 a.m. "I'm tired," I tell Jake. "Let's go upstairs."

We say good night to Seth and Vanessa and promise to keep in touch. When we get to our room, I rummage through my suitcase.

"What are you doing?" Jake asks. "I thought you were tired."

"I am, but I thought we'd go for a dip in the hot tub before bed," I say innocently, as I pull out a swimsuit.

Jake gives me a slow, sexy smile and takes the swimsuit from my hands. "I don't think you'll need this."

I take his hand and say, "Come on. Let's go make your fantasy a reality."

When the phone rings the next morning, I'm disoriented. I look at the clock and realize it's our seven o'clock wake-up call. I roll over, and Jake is still fast asleep. He looks so cute and relaxed. I gently nudge him and say, "Wake up."

He opens his eyes and looks at me. "I was in the middle of a great dream, but this is nice too," he says, reaching for me.

"No time. We have golf today, remember?"

"How could I forget?"

Jake's tee time is in an hour, so we quickly dress. I tell him he looks nice in his golf shirt and khaki shorts.

"You're in a good mood," he comments.

"I'm really looking forward to driving the golf cart."

We grab a light breakfast of coffee and bagels, and then we're on our way. We take a cab to a resort a few miles up the road. I would have booked the golf course at our hotel, but I did some research online, and this one is supposed to be the best. When we arrive, Jake rents clubs and shoes.

Fortunately it's just the two of us in our group. "Good. I have you all to myself," I tell him.

Jake hands me the keys to the golf cart, and I clap my hands in delight. "You're like a teenager out for your first drive," he says.

I steer us to the first hole, and Jake hops out. I watch as he takes a few practice strokes, and then he tees off and hits the ball straight down the fairway. I don't watch golf that often, but I can tell it's a good shot. I keep up with the cart after each stroke and notice most holes are on par.

"Are you sure you're not bored?" he asks me.

"Do I look bored? I get to watch you. Plus we're surrounded by breathtaking views. Do you golf often?"

"I do in the spring and summer, and I try to hit the range in the fall and winter so when I entertain clients I can play respectably. Believe it or not, I do a lot of business on the golf course."

"I believe it. What's your handicap?"

"Four."

"Is that good?"

"It's not bad," he says. "The higher the number, the poorer the player is. Here, you wanna take a swing?"

"OK. I'm used to playing tennis. We'll see how it goes."

Jake shows me the correct stance and helps me practice my swing a few times. I hit the ball and ground it about twenty feet.

"Not bad for your first time. You can putt my next shot."

I do much better at the putting. "I can see how this can get addictive. I actually play a mean game of mini golf."

He raises his eyebrows. "Really?"

"Well, I haven't played in years, but I used to be pretty good," I say as I sink in a shot. I give him a satisfied smile.

"Beginner's luck."

Finally we make it to the eighteenth hole. "You know," says Jake, "I've never done it on a golf course."

"Too bad, Hartman. You used up your wish last night."

"Yes, the hot tub. Well worth it," he says, giving me a mischievous grin. I blush at the memory; I did put on quite a performance, given it was his fantasy. After the game we head back to our hotel for lunch. "Thanks for today," Jake says, wrapping me in an embrace.

"Thanks for letting me do something special for you, although I didn't give you much of a choice. I can't believe tomorrow is our last day here."

"I know. I'm not ready to go back to reality. What do you want to do?"

"How about we spend the day by the pool? We've been running around, so it'll be nice to sleep in and relax."

"I agree. I'll book us a cabana."

"Sounds perfect."

Tonight we return to Oranjestad for dinner. We found a great restaurant when we were in town shopping the other day. It's in an old-style plaza shopping center that features a nightly waterworks show set to music. We dine al fresco, and I love watching the eclectic mix of people walking by. Everyone seems happy and carefree.

"What are you thinking about?" Jake asks, breaking my reverie.

"Just that it's so relaxed here. I'm not looking forward to the stress of coming home."

"I know," he says, taking my hand. "It's been an amazing week. I wasn't sure how we'd travel together, but it worked out very well."

"Yes, we're very compatible."

It's funny that we've been dating for a while but don't get to spend that much time together. Our longest stretch has been just a few days. The waiter comes by with our drinks. I ordered their signature cocktail, which is fruity and delicious.

"Here, try this," I say, giving Jake my straw.

He takes a sip and makes a face. "Too fruity for me."

"You're just saying that because it's a girly drink."

"Guilty. It's not that bad." We place our order, and I ask Jake what his travel schedule will be like when we return to Chicago. "I have to go to San Francisco on Monday."

"I figured as much. When will you be back?"

"Thursday."

"OK, let's have dinner that night."

"I'll have to check my schedule. I may have a date with Ashley."

I hit him on the arm. "How did you meet her anyway?"

"Through Nick. Believe it or not, she's actually quite smart. She's the head of human resources for a consulting company."

"Really? I never would have guessed. She doesn't strike me as a people person. She wasn't that friendly when we met."

"I'm sure she saw you as a threat," he says.

"I find that hard to believe."

"Lexi, you're way more attractive than her."

"You're just saying that because you have to."

"I'm not. Yes, Ashley's pretty, but you're much more my type."

"And you're my type," I say, pulling him in for a kiss.

The waiter arrives with our food, and Jake says his entrée is the best fish he's ever had. He makes me take a bite, and I have to say it's pretty good. We take a stroll after dinner to kill some time before the water show starts. A few minutes beforehand, we find a spot in front of the fountain. It's a really nice show and reminds me of something you'd see in Vegas. Jake puts his arm around me, and we stand there watching the water rise and fall in time to the music. The show lasts about ten minutes.

"Do you want to hit the clubs or head back to the hotel?" Jake inquires.

"The clubs would be fun, but I want to head back and make some fun of our own."

"I was hoping you'd say that. I was thinking the same thing."

"As I said earlier, we're compatible in every way."

He gives me a slow, sexy smile. I grab the back of his head and pull him in for a kiss, which he returns in earnest. As we stand in the middle of downtown, I can't help think how nice it is to kiss him without a care as to who sees us.

It's the Saturday night of what would have been my wedding; it's also the last night of our trip. I've tried to act normal, but I think Jake can sense I've been in a pensive mood. A million different emotions are running through my head. On the one hand, I never thought I'd be in another committed relationship and have come as far as I have, but on the other, I still feel like I'm starting over instead of embarking on my next chapter. Ben and I used to joke about trying to start a family on our honeymoon. That just feels so off from where I am now. I look over at Jake and realize how lucky I am to have met him.

As I get ready for dinner, I make a concerted effort to snap out of my dark mood. Jake won't tell me where we're going. "I'm ready," I say as I step out of the bathroom.

He gives a low whistle then cradles my face in his hands. "You look beautiful, as usual. Now let's go," he says, taking my hand.

He surprises me with dinner on the beach at sunset. It's a beautiful night, and we have a secluded table right by the water. The waiter brings us a bottle of champagne.

"What's this for?" I ask Jake.

"I thought we'd celebrate. I know tonight was supposed to be a momentous day in your life, so I want it to be special. I'm sure it's been looming over your head, and I hope after today you can be a step closer toward putting the past behind you."

"You're very thoughtful. Thank you for tonight—and all of this," I tell him. "This trip was exactly what I needed. You're exactly what I needed."

Jake smiles. "How are you doing, honestly?"

"I'm fine." He looks unconvinced. "Really, I'm fine."

"You know," Jake says, "you're pretty much an open book when it comes to your emotions. That's one of the things I love about you. There's no pretense. But when it comes to your relationship with Ben, you're very closed off. I want to know what you're thinking, but I don't want to pry. I want you to know you can talk to me."

I study his earnest face. "Jake, it's just not something I like to talk about. I've spent a long time trying to get over what happened and move on with my life. I will tell you that a lot of the pain is gone, and you're a big part of that, but I still harbor some resentment. I think it'll go away with time, but it's a hard thing to forgive. When I think back to my frame of mind nine months ago, I never would have thought it possible for me to be where I am today. You're an amazing man, and I'm so lucky to have found you. Of course I was initially attracted to you because of your looks," I say jokingly, "but now I know there's so much more. You're so generous and have such a big heart. You're charismatic and hardworking and don't have an entitled attitude even though you easily could. You always see the best in people, even when they don't see it in themselves. But most of all, you make me feel truly special."

"Lexi, you *are* special. You're the most incredible woman I've ever met. I've had lots of girlfriends, but no one's ever gotten under my skin like you have. You're warm, caring and selfless. You're always looking out for everyone else; it's about time you have someone looking out for you. I want to do that for you, if you'll let me. I know you're scared of getting hurt again, but I promise you I'll never hurt you."

"That means a lot to me," I tell him. "And I know you'd never intentionally hurt me, but sometimes things happen."

"Let me make this clear. I've never cheated on anyone, and I won't cheat on you. I don't know what the dynamic was with you and Ben, but in my opinion, people cheat when they aren't totally fulfilled in their relationship. It's like a subconscious way of trying to fill a void. You said you and Ben hadn't seen each other a lot because you were on different schedules, so maybe you weren't connecting…I don't know. I can assure you I'm completely satisfied in our relationship, in every way possible."

I smile at him. "Me too. You know, I've dissected my relationship with Ben so many times, trying to figure out what went wrong, and I really can't think of anything. That's what kills me. I was obviously very fulfilled in our relationship, but I guess it wasn't enough for him."

"Whatever his reasons," Jake says, "he went about it the wrong way. Sometimes two people just don't work together, but that doesn't mean there's anything wrong. It just means you need to keep looking until it's right." He reaches across the table for my hand. "I know I've found what's right for me. Even though we've only been together for a few months, I know I'm completely in love with you."

I stare at him in shock. I knew he cared about me, but I didn't know he felt this way. I don't know what to say. "Jake, you know I care for you very deeply. This all has just happened so fast. Can you give me some time?"

"That I can do. You're worth the wait," he says.

I move over and sit on his lap. Then I cradle his face in my hands and kiss him. Instead of going back to my seat, I stay on his lap and admire the view of the sun setting over the ocean. When the waiter comes, I ask him to take our picture. He takes one, and then I zoom the camera in and ask him to take another. I want one with the view as well as close-up of us. Both pictures turn out great, and I make a mental note to have them framed for Jake as a thank-you for the trip.

After the bill comes, we decide to take a walk on the beach. We stroll down the sand, hand in hand. I'm miles away from where I thought I'd be, but I decide I wouldn't want to be anywhere else.

We get back to the hotel and pack. I've always hated this part of a trip—it's so depressing. Jake just throws all his clothes into his suitcase.

"Aren't you going to fold anything?"

"Why bother? I'm going to wash it or take it to the dry cleaner anyway."

I wish I could do the same, but the orderly part of me resists. We get in bed early, and for once Jake keeps his distance. Although it's been an emotionally draining day, I have trouble falling asleep. I toss and turn, trying to get comfortable, and finally settle on my side. Jake wraps his arms around me from behind, enveloping me in a big hug. Finally I feel myself relax.

After a few minutes, he says, "I've been meaning to ask—what was that comment you made to Vanessa the other night about not believing in soul mates?"

"You were listening? I thought you were talking to Seth."

"I was, but I'm a great multi-tasker."

"She told me that when she met Seth, she knew he was her soul mate. She wanted to know if it's something I believe in."

"And you don't?"

"I don't know. I used to, I guess."

"Do you think Ben was your soul mate?" he asks quietly.

"Maybe. We met when we were in college, so it's hard to say. I'd like to believe there's someone out there for everyone, but I don't know if I believe there's just one perfect person. Sometimes I think there are a lot of people you could be happy with, and the one you find is just a case of good timing. If there is such a thing as a soul mate, how do you ever really know if that's the person you end up with?"

"I don't know," Jake says. "I guess you just find each other—like how you and I kept running into each other before we got together. Can you honestly tell me you bumped into anyone else at work like we did?"

"No, but that could just be coincidence."

"Maybe, but perhaps it was the universe's way of bringing us together. For so long I tried to bury my feelings for you, but with each chance encounter, I thought maybe larger forces were working to bring us together, and maybe I wasn't supposed to be fighting anymore."

I'm quiet for a minute. I'm surprised Jake feels this way. I thought only romantics like me believe in fate—although now I'm somewhat jaded. I used to believe in the idea of soul mates, but I thought I'd met mine, and I worried that was it for me. Now I'm starting to wonder whether Ben was a means to an end.

"Whatever the forces that brought us together, I'm glad they did," I say, turning to face him.

I fall asleep in Jake's arms. I dream I'm lost in the woods, searching for a way out, but I keep ending up in the same place I started.

CHAPTER NINETEEN

I'm awake before our wake-up call; I guess it's the anticipation of leaving. I have a thing about needing to be on time to the airport. I quietly creep out of bed and go the bathroom, where I wash my face and brush my teeth. As I'm finishing I hear the phone ring. I run to pick it up so Jake doesn't have to be bothered; the phone is on my side of the bed. Although I swear he can sleep through anything.

"Wake up," I say, as I gently nudge him. I let him lie there for a few more minutes while I pack my toiletries. It's ironic that I probably would have been performing this same task if things had turned out differently with Ben, although I'd be packing for my honeymoon. Thinking about my wedding used to make me very depressed, but being here with Jake has changed my outlook. *He* has changed my outlook. I glance at the clock and see it's already seven forty-five. I walk over to Jake's side of the bed and throw the covers back.

"Time to get up."

"OK, OK," he says grouchily. Neither of us is a morning person. "I'm going to take a quick shower."

While he's showering I get dressed then walk out on the balcony, taking in the view one last time. I stare out at the vast ocean, reflecting on the trip and how it's brought Jake and me closer. I hear the sliding door, and Jake comes out to join me.

"What are you thinking about out here all by yourself?"

"That this trip was the perfect answer to this weekend. I honestly have been dreading it for so long; I feel like a weight has been lifted."

"Good. That was the whole point. I had an amazing time."

"Me too. I wish we didn't have to leave."

"We'll come back," he says, taking my hand.

We gather up our luggage, and I take one last look around before closing the door behind me.

It's hard to go back to work on Monday. I walk into the office and am just getting settled when Michelle pops her head in.

"Welcome back! How was the Hamptons?"

"Great! Very relaxing."

"It looks like it. You're nice and tan."

"We went to the beach a lot."

"I'm so jealous. I've always wanted to go there."

"If you ever do, let me know, I can give you lots of recommendations. Did I miss anything here?"

"Not too much," Michelle says. "I put a status meeting on your calendar for later this morning. I figured I'd give you a chance to get settled before I bombarded you."

"Thanks. I appreciate that."

"Well, I know you have a lot of catching up to do, so I won't keep you. I just wanted to say hi."

"Thanks," I tell her. "Maybe we can grab lunch later this week once I'm caught up."

"Yes. Let's do that."

I boot up my computer and check my voice mail while I'm waiting. I have a message from Eric that Aura is still working through some logistics for the mass cosmetics line. He feels it's too early to meet and suggests we postpone until he can give me more concrete information. I call him, but he doesn't answer, so I decide to send him an e-mail instead. I thank him for his message and tell him we're eager to help and ask him to let me know once things are more solidified. Then I send Morgan an update and assure her I'll be diligent about following up while the lead is still hot. I'm really disappointed because I was excited about the opportunity. My vacation glow is fading fast. I shoot Jake a quick text that I miss him already. Four days seems like a long time to be away from each other, and I'm looking forward to Thursday night.

I hear a knock on my door and look up to find Michelle. It's ten thirty already. We chat more about my trip, and then I thank her for handling things while I was away. I hate having to lie to people about where I was and who I was with. It's a good thing I've been to the Hamptons many times before—it's very easy to fake it. I listen and take notes as she gives an update. She informs me Natalia has scheduled a working meeting with all the agency partners on Thursday followed by a dinner. This isn't a good start to my day. After she leaves, I text Jake that I now have a client dinner on Thursday, but we can see each other afterward. I don't hear from him for a while, but then I get a text shortly before five. It says he's had a busy day, but he misses me too. He had to push his flight on Thursday because he has a late-afternoon meeting, so we'll get together on Friday. I'm bummed, but it's just one more day; I can handle that.

I spend the evening unpacking and doing laundry. Once my suitcase is emptied, I realize I can't find my Tiffany bracelet. For a minute I panic, thinking I left it at the hotel. I try to remember the last time I wore it. I close my eyes and recall having it on the last night of our trip, when Jake surprised me with dinner on the beach. I call the hotel and leave my contact information with the front desk in case it turns up. I go through my suitcase again, which proves fruitless. Jake calls me shortly before I'm about to get in bed.

"Hi, babe. How was your day?" he asks me.

"It was OK. Luckily nothing too pressing happened while I was away—although I did get a message from Eric at Aura saying that he needs to push our meeting. What about you?"

"Funny you should mention that. I just learned of a potential opportunity for a prestige cosmetics client."

"Oh, but what about Aura?"

"I'm not ruling it out, but I'd like to keep our options open. Given your background, I was hoping you could help me with the initial call to see if it's the right opportunity."

I'm a bit torn. I really was hoping the Aura lead would come to fruition, but Jake is right that we can't rely on it and let it prevent us from other potential opportunities. "OK, I'd be happy to help. When's the call?"

"Friday at noon."

"I'll put it on my calendar. Do you have anything you can send me in advance?"

"No. Just come by my office about five minutes beforehand, and I'll fill you in."

We talk for another twenty minutes then say good night. "Looking forward to Friday," I tell him.

"Me too, Lexi. Me too."

On Wednesday morning I pass Nicole's office and notice her door is ajar. I peek in and see she's on the phone. I go to my office and send her an IM.

> Me: Welcome back! Where have you been?
> Nicole: An unbearable client off site for the past two days. How was your trip?
> Me: Incredible! Can you grab lunch with me later?
> Nicole: Yes. Let's do it!
> Me: Great. I'm in meetings all morning, but I'll be done by noon.

My meetings run longer than I expected, but I'm back at my desk by twelve fifteen. Nicole is waiting for me.

"Hi," she says. "You look nice and tan."

"Thanks. Spending a week in the sun will do it. Where do you want to go?"

"Somewhere we can talk."

I catch her meaning. She knows I went to Aruba with Jake. "There's a great sandwich place by my apartment," I tell her. "It's a fifteen-minute walk from here."

"I'm not walking in these shoes."

"Did I mention each order comes with a freshly baked cookie?"

"Sold. We'll cab it." On the way she immediately quizzes me about my trip. "So how was it traveling with Jake?"

"It was amazing. I was a little nervous considering we hadn't spent that long of a stretch of time together, but we're very compatible. We hung out at the beach, did a lot of sightseeing, and just relaxed. It was so nice being in public like a normal couple."

"I'm so jealous," Nicole says. "When people find out you two are dating, they're going to freak out. Jake is the illicit guy everyone wants to date but knows they don't have a chance with. If it can't be me, you're the next best thing."

I laugh and say, "You seem to have no problem with your choice of suitors."

When it's our turn in line we order lunch and Nicole asks for fruit instead of the cookie.

"You're making me feel guilty," I tell her.

"I'm on a new diet," she informs me.

I eye her well-toned body. "Like you need to be on a diet."

"I have to stay this way somehow," she says with a laugh.

Once we sit down I decide to bring up something that's been on my mind. "That day I told you Jake and I were dating, you made a comment about how I was withdrawn when I started working here. You were right about that, you know." Nicole looks at me, waiting for me to go on. "The reason I moved back to Chicago was because I'd just broken things off with my fiancé. I caught him with a friend of mine."

Nicole nods. "I figured as much but didn't realize the engagement part."

"How did you know?"

"Lexi, it doesn't take a rocket scientist to figure it out. You told me you weren't dating anyone, but then you never were interested in getting set up or going on dates. Most single girls our age are obsessed with finding a guy. You were the opposite. You seemed plenty interested in asking me about my love life, but you never shared anything about yours. I figured some guy must have done a number on you." Nicole is more perceptive than I thought. "So this friend, were you close with her?"

"Not really. We were just friendly at work."

"Well, that's good. At least you didn't lose two people."

"True, although she also lost out. I heard she was fired."

"Because of you?"

"Not directly. I think there were other issues, but it didn't help that I was very close with her boss."

"That's karma for you. Anyway, you and I actually have a lot in common. I was engaged once too."

I practically choke on my salad. "You were engaged?"

"Yes," Nicole says, "to my high school sweetheart. He proposed to me right out of college, but I started having second thoughts shortly after. I just felt like I never really got to experience dating. He was the only person I'd been with, and I wondered what else was out there. I loved him but almost more out of habit than a deep, passionate love. So I broke things off. That was well before I started working here, so no one knows."

"Wow. I'm proud of you. A lot of people wouldn't have had the courage to end things."

"I trusted my instincts. Now you know why I'm a serial dater. I have to make up for lost time." I laugh and ask her if she feels like she's ready to settle down yet. "I'm open to it. At first I just wanted to go for quantity and see what was out there. Now I'm definitely being pickier. If I happen to meet the right guy, I'm not opposed to being in a serious relationship."

"I can't get over that we both broke off our engagements, although at least yours was by choice."

"Well, just look at you now," she says. "So does Jake know you told me?"

"No, he'd freak out. And there's nothing he can do about it, so I figure why worry him." Nicole nods as she takes a bite of my cookie. "Hey, get your own," I say, as I jokingly slap her hand away.

On the cab ride back to the office, I muse that I've always thought of myself as a truthful person, but lately it seems I'm always lying to somebody.

At a quarter to noon on Friday, I run downstairs to pick up lunch for Jake and me. I didn't ask him if it was a lunch meeting, but he's always so busy that I doubt he had time to grab anything. At five of, I poke my head into his office.

"Hi," I say, doing my best to sound nonchalant given there are people nearby.

"Hi, Lexi. Good to see you. Come on in, and close the door."

"I wasn't sure if you had time to pick up lunch, so I got you something," I say, handing him a sandwich.

"That was sweet of you. Thanks. Now come here," he says, and wraps his arms around me, pulling me into a deep embrace. Then he walks over to his phone and buzzes Joann. "Hi. Lexi and I are about to jump on a call with a prospective client. We aren't to be disturbed for the next hour."

"Got it, Mr. Hartman."

"Thanks, and hold all calls." He hangs up and dials another number on speakerphone.

"Aren't you going to give me an overview?"

"I don't think you'll need one. You'll catch on pretty quickly." He turns the volume down, and then I hear a recording. I look at him, confused.

"That's my voice mail greeting."

"It is."

I stare at him for a minute and then glance around his office; his desk is neater than usual. He typically has stacks of file folders heaped all over it, but they're gone.

"You cleaned up," I comment.

"I did." He smiles at me. Then he stands up, walks over to my chair, and takes my hand, pulling me up. "You made *my* fantasy come true. I thought I'd return the favor."

I'm momentarily speechless. "Are you sure about this? What if someone walks in?"

"No one will," he says but locks the door to be certain. "And you don't have to worry about anyone hearing us—these are pretty thick walls." I trust he's right; he of all people wouldn't want us to get caught. Then he says in a low voice, "You should be very glad about that, given the things I have planned for you."

Whoa. He kisses me in earnest and swiftly undoes each button on my blouse. "It's too bad this isn't a video conference call," I tell him.

Jake laughs. "We'll add it to the list."

His lips find mine again, and he lays me down on the desk then straddles me. I'm a little tense at first, but as soon as he kisses my neck, I lose myself in the moment. He knows just the right way to touch me to leave me burning with desire. Then he takes his necktie and places it over my eyes, like a blindfold. "This will add to the anticipation," he whispers in my ear. Jake does things to me I've never before experienced. It makes me wonder whether he read *Fifty Shades* after all. And if it's possible, the reality is better than my darkest fantasy.

Afterward we sit up, and I attempt to smooth out my clothes.

"Well, that was an unexpected surprise," I tell him. "And a very good one, I might add. You've been holding out on me." He gives me a smug smile. I rummage through my bag until I find a hairbrush. "It's a good thing I always keep an extra in my purse," I tell him. "I must look like a mess."

"You look very sexy."

"As do you," I say, working my fingers through his mussed-up hair. Then I look over at his desk and say, "I hope you have Windex."

He laughs a deep laugh. "I'm starving. Let's eat." I pull out the sandwiches and hand him his. "What did you get me?" he asks.

"Turkey with avocado, lettuce, and mustard. No mayo or tomato."

"You know me well. Thank you."

After we eat I give him a big kiss and say, "You sure know how to make a girl's dream come true. I hope you'll think of me now whenever you're at your desk."

"Lexi, you're always on my mind."

I give him a smile and sashay out of his office. Then I text him later that afternoon.

Me: *Thank you for lunch. You sure satisfied my appetite.*

Jake: *I'd say the pleasure was all mine, but clearly that wasn't the case.*

Me: 😃

Over the next few weeks, Jake and I fall back into our usual routine. He's traveling frequently, and we only see each other on the weekends. I'm starting to feel like we're in a long-distance relationship. It's a good thing I have work to keep my mind occupied. It's Friday, and I'm about to head into a meeting when my cell phone rings; it's Molly's mom, Rachelle. I haven't spoken to her in a few weeks, so I take the call.

"Hi, Rachelle. I've been thinking about you. How are things?"

"Good actually. I wanted to let you know we've been doing some experimental treatments, and Molly has been responding very positively. Things are finally turning around," she whispers.

"That's so wonderful to hear. Congrats!"

"Molly has been asking to see you," Rachelle says.

"I'd love to see her too. When's a good time?"

"Are you free Sunday? You could come over in the afternoon."

"Sunday's perfect," I tell her. "See you then."

We hang up, and a sense of relief washes over me. I know I should be cautiously optimistic, but I revel in the thought that Molly may make a full recovery.

That night, over dinner, I tell Jake the news. "That's fantastic," he says. "I know you two have a special bond."

"We do. I'm going to see her on Sunday."

"I'd like to meet her," Jake says.

"Really? You want to hang out with a four year-old?"

"Yes, she's obviously important to you. I have an idea. Do you think she'd mind if we brought Hailey? We can make it a play date."

"I love that idea, but I'd have to ask." I call Rachelle back, and she says it's fine to bring Jake and Hailey as long as neither of them is sick. "We're on!" I tell him. This will be interesting.

On Sunday Jake and I pick up Hailey and tell her about Molly. I explain to her that Molly was sick and had to take medicine that made her hair fall out, so it might look funny. I also reassure her Molly is much better and is very excited about our visit. I'm a little nervous about how things will go, but I think it'll be fun for the girls to get together. When we pull up to the house, Molly is waiting for us at the door, wearing a long blond wig. She jumps up and down when she sees us and runs out to give me a big hug. I make introductions, and Rachelle invites us in. I see that Molly is wearing the Wonder Woman costume I gave her.

"I like your costume," says Hailey.

"Thanks. I'm Wonder Woman—she's a superhero. Lexi got this for me. Do you want to dress up too?" Hailey nods. "Come with me to my room," Molly says as she takes Hailey by the hand. Jake and I follow them upstairs, but Molly informs us adults are not allowed.

"Oh, OK," I say. "We'll be downstairs if you need something."

Jake and I head into the kitchen, and I tell Rachelle we've been kicked out already. "I think this is working out just fine," she jokes. She offers us something to drink, and Jake and I accept a glass of lemonade. Rachelle is very interested in learning about Jake. I told her I was dating someone at work, but I haven't disclosed many details. She asks him what he does and how we met. It's funny—I've never had to share the story before. I look at Jake with an amused expression, letting him take the lead.

"Well, I first met Lexi when she interviewed for a position on our Lumineux account. It was an account I'd just brought into the agency, so I wanted to make sure we hired the right person. I was very intrigued by her, and we immediately established a good rapport. After that we kept running into each other outside of work. And with each encounter, I was pulled in further. At first I suppressed my feelings because I was hesitant about dating someone at the office. But then I figured maybe things were meant to be. She's unlike anyone I've ever known."

"That's so romantic," Rachelle says. I'm about to ask her how she met her husband, but we're interrupted by the return of Hailey and Molly.

"Let's go play in the basement," Molly says, motioning for Jake and me to follow.

"Duty calls," I joke to Rachelle.

We go downstairs, and it's every little girl's dream. Bright flowers in various sizes adorn the yellow walls, except for one, which is finished with chalkboard paint and displays drawings. Benches with colorful bins full of toys line one wall. There's a princess ball pit in one corner and a trampoline in the other. In the center of the room is a princess castle, complete with a canopy. Then, around the bend, is another room with a kid-size table and chairs set up on colorful tiles; it appears to be an art area. Flower hooks hold a clothesline, which displays Emma and Molly's masterpieces.

"I love it down here," I tell Molly.

"Me too!" exclaims Hailey. "Can we have a tea party?"

Molly nods as she retrieves her princess tea set from one of the bins. "We can have tea at the table," she informs us. She instructs each of us where to sit. "Do you want to dress up in something else?" she asks Hailey, who nods and follows her to the dress-up bin. They choose new costumes, and Molly asks Jake if he wants to dress up too.

"Sure. Do you have anything that will fit me?"

She studies him and says, "Here, you can wear this," as she hands him a tiara.

I do my best to stifle a laugh. Jake is a good sport and plays along. He places the tiara on his head, but it keeps falling off. "I think it's too small," he tells Molly.

"That's because you need bobby pins." She opens a drawer and hands me some. "Here, Lexi. You pin these on Jake." I put the bobby pins in his hair, which do the trick to secure the tiara. "You need something else," Molly informs him, and produces a hot-pink feather boa.

He puts it on, and I take out my phone and snap a picture of him. "Blackmail," I whisper. Then I turn to Molly and ask, "What about me? Do you have anything I can wear to the tea party?"

She looks in her dress-up bin and pulls out some necklaces and a scarf. She gives each of us a necklace, including Jake, and hands the scarf to me.

I tie it around my head. "Now we are ready for tea," she says. She pours each of us a cup, and I pretend to drink mine.

"Wait, we didn't put the sugar in yet!" Hailey admonishes us.

"Sorry. I thought it tasted a little funny. Please pass the sugar." I put in two spoonfuls, and Jake does the same.

"Mmm. This is the best tea I've ever had," he tells the girls. "Are there any cookies?"

"We forgot the cookies!" says Molly.

"Let's go bake some," says Hailey.

They go over to the play kitchen to whip up a batch. As I watch them work, I'm amused by their conversation. Then Molly tells Hailey about her Make-A-Wish commercial. I smile at the memory of it. The experience lifted her spirits and Rachelle told me it ignited her passion for acting. She belongs in front of the camera.

What are you smiling about?" Jake asks.

"Nothing. I'm just glad we did this," I say. "Thanks for coming with me and suggesting we bring Hailey. The girls are having a great time together."

"I'm glad it worked out. So what are you planning to do with that picture?"

"I haven't decided. Just know that if you ever cross me, I won't only post it on Facebook, but I'll also make copies and hang them around the office."

"You wouldn't dare!"

"Oh, but I would."

"Well then, I'll just have to find something to hang over your head."

"Go ahead and try."

"Believe me, I know all your weaknesses," he says with a dark expression. I feel my cheeks redden. The girls come back with the cookies. "They're ready. Which one do you want?" Molly asks. I choose one with chocolate frosting and sprinkles. Jake asks if he can have two.

"Did you eat all of your lunch?" Molly asks him.

"Yes, I did."

"OK, you can have two."

I look at my watch and see that it's after five. "Girls, unfortunately we're going to have to wrap things up soon." This is met with a lot of groans and protest. "I know you're having lots of fun playing together, but it's almost dinnertime."

"You can stay here," Molly offers.

"We'd love to, but your mom said you're going out to eat with your grandma. Another time." I let them play a few minutes longer, and then we all head upstairs.

I tell Rachelle the girls had a great time playing together. "I'm so glad. Molly doesn't have that many play dates. She usually tags along with whomever Emma is playing with. You're all welcome to come over anytime."

"Thanks," I tell her. "We should definitely do this again."

She gives Jake a hug and says, "It was so nice meeting you. Lexi is very special to our family, and I'm glad we finally got to meet the one responsible for her happiness."

"She's a special girl," Jake says, smiling at me. "And Lexi always speaks so fondly of Molly that I wanted to meet her." I realize I forgot to give Molly her gift from our trip to Aruba. "I'll be right back," I tell everyone. I get my purse and come back with the wrapped package.

"This is a little something I got you when I was on vacation." Molly takes the package from me and says, "Can I open it now?"

"Sure."

She rips open the paper and sees the bracelet. She puts it on and admires her wrist. "Thank you so much. I love it!"

"I'm glad. Thank you for inviting us today."

"Yes," says Hailey. "Thanks for having me over to play," she tells Molly as she gives her a hug.

"Wait, let me get a picture," I say, wanting to capture the moment. I text Rachelle the photo, and we head out.

Hailey is very talkative on the drive home. Jake calls Kate to let her know we're on our way. It's hard to pay attention to their conversation because

Hailey is gushing about Molly's basement. After he hangs up, he tells me Kate invited us to stay for dinner.

"I told her I had to check with you first," he says.

"That's fine."

"Are you sure? We've been out in the burbs all day."

"Honestly I don't mind." He calls Kate back to tell her we're on.

"She probably just wants us to be a diversion so she can rest," I joke.

"Probably, although she has Adam."

"That's my point. She has to take care of *two* children."

"Women," he says, and rolls his eyes.

CHAPTER TWENTY

That night, on the drive home from Kate's, Jake says, "So your birthday's next week." My birthday is this coming Thursday. He hasn't mentioned anything about it until now, and I didn't know if I should bring it up.

"I wasn't sure you remembered."

"Of course I remembered. We talked about it when we were in San Francisco."

"Well, that was a long time ago. Plus we didn't *really* talk about it. You just looked at my license, and if I recall, there was a lot of wine involved."

"Trust me, I have a very good memory. Is there anything special you want?"

"It's thoughtful of you to ask, but I really don't need anything. My only wish is to spend my birthday with you."

Jake's face falls, and he says, "I'll be in San Francisco through Friday. But we'll definitely celebrate on Saturday."

"OK," I say, pouting.

"I'm sorry, Lex."

I really shouldn't be upset, but in my family, we've always made a big deal about our birthdays. I know Jake and I will celebrate on Saturday, but it's just not the same.

On Monday Liv invites me over for dinner. "What are you going to do for your birthday?" she asks.

"I don't know. I took the day off weeks ago, thinking maybe Jake and I would do something, but he'll be in San Fran. We're going out Saturday night."

"Out? As in to a restaurant?"

"I assume. But now that you mention it, he just said we'd celebrate that night." I give an inward sigh.

"How are things going?"

"Good, although I think he's upset I haven't introduced him to my family. He's made comments about it here and there, and he seems more distant lately, but maybe I'm reading into things. He's been really busy, so I could be taking it the wrong way."

"So when are you going to have him meet your family?" Liv asks.

"I don't know. I don't have a set timeline. My dad once said he doesn't feel the need to meet anyone I'm dating unless we plan on getting married."

"Lexi, that was a long time ago. Wasn't that before you met Ben?"

"Yes, but given how that turned out, I'm in no rush."

"So do you think he's the one?"

"I'd like to think so," I tell her. "But I thought Ben was the one. How do you ever know really?"

"When you know, you know."

"But you didn't know with Jason."

"Not right away, but once I decided I liked him, I knew."

"Really? You never told me that."

"I knew he was different from anyone I've ever dated," she says. "I found myself thinking about him all the time—what he'd think or do in different situations—when he wasn't there, and I realized he was the guy I wanted to be with. He loves me for who I am, and I feel like he really gets me. And I never have to worry about what's he's thinking because he's always honest with me."

"Sounds like me and Jake."

"That's my point. You're really into him, but you're so scared of getting hurt again that you won't let him in fully." Liv can read me like a book. "Does he make you happy?"

"Yes."

"Then tell him."

"I will, when I'm ready."

"Now where have I heard that before?"

After my conversation with Liv, I have a hard time falling asleep. I know I should open up to Jake, and I feel like I have in many ways. But I'm just not ready to give myself completely. To be honest, I'm not even sure what's holding me back at this point; it's something I can't quite articulate. I'm worried Jake is losing patience with me because he's seemed different these past few weeks. Granted, I've only noticed small, subtle changes, but they're there. I just hope he thinks I'm worth the wait.

Simon stops by my office the next morning. "Why so glum?" he asks.

"I didn't know I was."

"Birthday getting you down?"

"No, I actually enjoy my birthday. It's the one day a year I hear from all the people I care about."

"And some people you don't," he teases.

"That too."

"What are you doing on Thursday?" he asks.

"I took the day off, but I don't have anything special planned. I'll probably sleep in and go shopping."

"Well, at least let me take you out for a drink."

"OK," I tell him. "That would be nice."

"I hope you don't mind meeting on the earlier side. I have a client obligation after work."

"How early?"

"How about eleven in the bar at the Sofitel?"

"That sounds perfect. You know I love it there."

"I know, and it's not too early for a Bloody Mary."

"Deal. Thanks."

"See you then."

After he leaves, my thoughts turn to Ben. I wonder whether he'll call me—he always made a big deal about my birthday. I still haven't returned any of his calls. I probably should, but I think it's best to cut ties completely. I've always felt it's never a good idea to remain friends after a breakup; it always ends in heartache.

I wake up Thursday morning to a text from Jake.

> *Happy birthday to my beautiful girl. Wish I could be there with you to celebrate.*

I smile and roll out of bed. It's 8:00 a.m.; he's on Pacific time and won't be up yet. I go for a leisurely run along the lakefront then shower and get dressed. I decide to wear a black shirtdress that has gold buttons down the front, a sash at the waist, and a pleated skirt that gives it a feminine shape. I pair it with sleek, purple pumps that have a gold cap at the toe, along with gold bangle bracelets. Once I'm dressed I eat a light breakfast. If I'll be drinking, it's best to not do so on an empty stomach. I check my phone, and already I have a bunch of messages. They definitely lighten my mood, although I'm still bummed Jake isn't here. I tell myself it's just one day, and I'll see him this weekend.

I walk to the Sofitel and scan the lobby. I don't see Simon, so I take a seat on one of the couches.

A woman from the reception desk approaches me. "Are you Lexi?"

"Yes," I tell her, slightly puzzled.

"This is for you," she says, handing me an envelope. It's written in Simon's handwriting.

> *Lexi, I have a surprise for you. Come to room 714.*

Inside the envelope I see a room key. Curious as to what he has up his sleeve, I head upstairs and let myself into a luxurious suite. "Hello?" I call out as I walk in. I make my way through the modernly furnished rooms, taking in the panoramic views offered by the floor-to-ceiling windows. I look around and see there's a room service tray in the dining room, and the table is set for two. Is he surprising me with lunch? "Simon, where are you?" I finally open the door to the master suite and find two massage tables set up.

"I thought you could use some relaxation on your birthday," says a voice from behind me. I turn around, and Jake is standing there. I'm momentarily speechless.

"What are you doing here?" I manage.

"You told me you wanted to be with me on your birthday. So I took an earlier flight home."

"I can't believe you're here," I say, realizing he's constantly coming through for me. Suddenly I'm overwhelmed and feel tears well in my eyes. Fortunately Jake doesn't notice because he has me enveloped in a big hug. "I can't believe you did this for me."

He looks into my eyes. "Sometimes wishes do come true." In response I smile and kiss him earnestly. "We have an hour until our couples' massage," he says.

"I can think of a great way to spend it," I reply, leading him toward the bed.

After our massages, Jake asks me what I want to do. "I don't know. I'd planned on going shopping."

"OK. Let's go shopping."

"Really?"

"Really. Who are we going to run into on a Thursday afternoon? Just tell me where you want to go."

"I don't care where we go, as long as we're together."

"How about we head up Michigan Avenue since it's a few blocks from here? But before that, I thought we'd have lunch."

Jake takes my hand and leads me to the dining room. He removes the covers from the plates and reveals my favorite foods: a Wildfire chopped salad, stuffed mushrooms and rigatoni alla vodka from Carmine's, and a slice of Portillo's chocolate cake for dessert. I'm overwhelmed by his thoughtfulness.

"When did you get all this?"

"I have my ways."

"Thank you. You spoil me."

We eat lunch then spend the afternoon shopping on Michigan Avenue. I take Jake's hand as we stroll and bask in being able to act like a normal couple here at home. "Aren't you going to buy anything?" he asks me.

"I don't know. I was just enjoying your company."

"Well, you have to get something."

"Fine. Let's look at the shoe department at Bloomingdale's."

Once we're there, I find a pair of tall black motorcycle boots that I love. I model them for Jake and he approves. "There," I say with a smile. "I've bought something."

"Good. Now let's go back to the hotel so I can give you your gift."

"Jake, you're here, which is a gift in itself. Plus you already got me a night at the suite and the massage."

"I know—this was just a small thing I wanted to do."

On the way out, we pass through the men's department, and a striped blue tie catches my eye. "This would look great on you," I say, holding it up to Jake. "It brings out the blue in your eyes. Let me buy it for you." He's about to protest, but I cut him off. "Please, you never let me buy you anything. It would make me happy."

He regards me for a moment then agrees. "If it'll make you happy, how can I say no?"

When we get back to our room, Jake produces a small, wrapped present. My heart momentarily stops beating, but I realize it's a ridiculous thought. I unwrap the paper to reveal a blue Tiffany box. I open it and see a heart charm bracelet, just like the one I lost. "This is perfect! I've been so upset because I lost mine."

"It *is* yours. I'm sorry I took it, but I wanted to have it engraved as a surprise. I know it's special to you." I hold it up and see a big cursive "L" on the charm. There's also a second heart with a "J" engraved on it. "Turn it over," Jake says. I look, and the inscription reads, "You have my heart." I'm so touched.

"I absolutely love it. Now I can always have you close to me," I say, studying the charm. I don't say it out loud, but what am I going to say if people ask me about it? It's an interesting gesture for someone who wants to keep our relationship private. I guess I won't wear it to work for now. "So where are we going for dinner?"

"How do you feel about French food?"

"I like it."

"Good, because I saw a really cool French restaurant here at the hotel."

For a moment disappointment courses through me, but I quickly push it aside. I've heard it's a very cool, modern restaurant, but I know he has an ulterior motive; he doesn't want to risk anyone spotting us. I assume mostly tourists eat there.

We freshen up then head downstairs. "Welcome to Café des Architectes," the hostess says.

"Hi. Reservation under 'Hartman,'" Jake tells her.

She glances at her computer screen and says, "Ah, right this way."

I look around as she leads us to our table. The dining room is very chic, with long red banquettes, sleek red-and-black chairs, and glass-topped tables framed with a mirrored border that reflects the nightlife from outside. Large artistic pendant lights hang from the ceiling, and decorative black-and-white vases filled with fresh flowers adorn the room. We look at the menu, and I decide to order a martini. They have a nice selection of cheeses, so we agree on a flight to start. After we put in our drink and appetizer order, Jake asks me what my favorite birthday memory is. "And you can't say today."

"Hmm, I guess it's my sweet sixteen. My parents threw a huge party at our house. They set up a tent in the yard and even brought in a sand volleyball court. They invited all my friends, and we had a huge barbecue followed by a bonfire, complete with s'mores. But my favorite part was at the end of the night. I was helping my parents clean up, and my dad asked me to take the garbage out to the garage. I opened the door and saw a shiny, red Jeep with a big bow on it."

"I knew sweet sixteens were a big deal, but I've never heard a story quite like that."

"What about you?" I ask him. "Were birthdays big at your house?"

"Not really. My mom made our favorite meals, and she'd let us eat dessert before dinner."

"That's a big deal when you're a kid."

"I guess," he says. "Speaking of, how about we order you a birthday dessert?"

"I would, but I feel so full. Not to mention I had the Portillo's cake earlier."

"Come on. You have to have dessert on your birthday."

"Fine," I relent. "You choose something. I'll be right back." I go to the washroom, and when I come back, Liv and Jason are seated at our table. "What are you doing here?" I ask in surprise.

"I invited them for dessert," Jake says, as the waitress approaches our table with a small cake complete with a candle. They all sing to me, and Jake tells me to make a wish. "I will," I say, "but it already came true."

After we finish dessert we head to the bar for drinks. We end up hanging out until well past 2:00 a.m. Normally I'd be exhausted, but I've been running on adrenaline. I've had way too many martinis, and for once I think Jake is drunk too. He's not usually one for PDAs, but he pulls me onto his lap and kisses me in front of Liv and Jason. "I think that's our cue," Liv says. I laugh and give her a hug.

"Thank you so much for coming out," I tell her and Jason.

"Thanks for inviting us," she says to Jake.

Once they leave I turn to Jake. "Thank you for inviting Liv and Jason. It was the perfect end to a perfect day."

"The night's not over yet," he says with a heated expression.

"Aren't you exhausted?"

"For you? Never."

Later that night, Jake and I are lying in bed, and I turn to him and say, "This is the best birthday I've ever had. Thank you."

"You're welcome," he replies, smiling. "That's a big compliment considering your sweet-sixteen story."

"That was different. Everything you planned today had a lot of thought behind it."

"That's because I love you."

This is the first time he's said it since the trip. I want to respond, but I can't bring myself to say the words.

On Monday morning, Simon stops by my office. "How was your big birthday weekend?"

"It was good. You were very convincing."

"I'm glad, but I still owe you a birthday drink."

"I won't turn you down," I tell him. "Do you want to go out one night this week?"

"Actually I had something else in mind. You've been bugging me about meeting Lance, so I'm having a small dinner party."

"Oh?"

"Are you and Jake free the Saturday night prior to Halloween weekend?"

"I'm sure we are, but let me check with him. I take it no one else from work will be there?"

"Would I ask you if I were inviting anyone else? Besides, you're one of the few people I deem worthy to associate with outside of the office."

"I guess I should be honored. Will it have a Halloween theme?"

"Yes. You'll need to come dressed as your favorite couple."

"I wouldn't have pegged you as being into the Halloween spirit."

"I'm not," Simon says, "but Lance is. I do it for him."

"How noble of you."

"OK, enough chitchat. I have work to do."

"You're the one who stopped by my office. I'll talk to Jake and let you know."

Jake is in San Francisco, but we talk later that evening. "Simon stopped by today to invite us to a dinner party the Saturday before Halloween weekend." Jake is quiet, so I add, "We'd be the only ones from work there."

"Do you want to go?"

"Yes. I'd love to meet Lance."

"OK. We'll go then."

"It's a costume party. We have to go as our favorite couple." More silence. "I take it you're not into Halloween?"

"How'd you guess?"

"Come on," I tell him. "It'll be fun."

"Fine. Think up some costume ideas, but I get the final say."

That night, while I'm lying in bed, I brainstorm some options. I immediately dismiss all the thoughts that pop into my head; I don't want to go for the obvious. Hoping something will come to me, I decide to sleep on it.

The next day I'm in a meeting when my cell phone rings. It's Eric, so I excuse myself to take his call. "Hi, Eric. How are you?"

"Great, Lexi. I wanted to let you know that our senior management has approved our mass cosmetics line. Of course they want to get in market early next year, so we need to move into high gear. How soon can you meet with me?"

"I can be on a plane tomorrow."

"That's great to hear," he says, "but I'll come to you."

"Just name the time."

"How about Friday at ten thirty?"

"That'll work fine."

I give him our address and tell him I look forward to seeing him. Then I e-mail Simon and Morgan that it's show time.

On Friday at ten fifteen, I receive a call from reception announcing Eric's arrival. I go to greet him and spot him before he sees me. I take in his familiar features and reflect that it's weird to have a part of my past standing here in the lobby.

"Lexi, it's so good to see you!" he says, giving me a hug.

"You too. You look great."

"Thanks. I've lost ten pounds."

"I can tell. I remembered how much you love deep dish, so I was going to offer to take you out for pizza, but maybe you'd prefer somewhere else."

"I'd love to join you for lunch," he says, "but I've tacked on other business, given I made the trip out. Another time if that's OK."

"No problem."

I lead him to the conference room where Simon is waiting. I make introductions, and then Simon gives Eric a brief overview of his background. "So tell me about this new line," I say, prompting Eric to take the lead.

He gives us an overview of the brand, its positioning, and their distribution strategy. Based on what he's disclosed, I cue Simon on which work to share. It's a very good discussion, and Eric seems to be jibing with Simon. "Are you going to put out a request for proposal?" I ask Eric.

"I've thought about it," he says, "but to be honest, I think an RFP would be a waste of time. We're very happy with The Studio, but we can't use them because we need to have a separation of responsibilities between the brands. I like what I've seen here, and I have the utmost confidence that you know the business. I'd like to give you an initial project, and if things go well, we can look into a more permanent arrangement."

"We'd welcome the opportunity," I tell him. "Are you prepared now to talk about what the project entails?"

"Yes. I've brought a brief for the first project, but I still need to work through our long-term expectations. As I mentioned on the phone, this all has happened so quickly."

I can't believe he's already prepared a brief. He walks us through it, and Simon and I ask a lot of questions. Once we have a good sense of our deliverables, I tell Eric I'll get him an estimate. "Sounds great. Thanks, Lexi. I look forward to working with you again." He turns to Simon and says, "There's some beautiful work here. I'm excited to see where we can go."

Simon and I walk him to the elevators, and when he leaves, Simon picks me up and twirls me around.

"I think you've just landed us our first cosmetics assignment!"

"I believe I have, with your help of course."

I go to Morgan's office to share the news.

"Congratulations!" she exclaims. "That's wonderful news! I'm very impressed with how you sensed an opportunity and figured out the right way to navigate it. I've seen great things from you since you started here. I also called Natalia to get some informal feedback, and she had nothing but positive things to say. I'd like to elevate your role, Lexi. If this Aura opportunity comes to fruition and becomes a retainer piece of business, my plan is to promote you to vice president and have you oversee all our beauty accounts."

"Wow. I'd be thrilled to take on the challenge," I tell her. "I appreciate your confidence in me."

"Well, you've earned it. I realize it may not happen for a few months, so I've put in a request for a spot bonus. I'll let you know once it goes through."

"Thank you, Morgan. I really appreciate it."

"Thank *you*. Now go out and celebrate."

I leave her office feeling elated. I get back to my desk, and I'm about to call Jake when I see that he texted me.

> *Looking forward to seeing you tonight. Let's have dinner at your place. There's something I want to run past you.*

I debate about sharing my news but decide I'd rather do it in person.

> *Sounds good. I have something to discuss with you too. See you later.*

Jake comes over a little after seven with Chinese takeout.

"Hi," I say giddily.

"Hi. You're in a good mood. I hope it's because you're excited to see me."

"I'm always excited to see you," I say, leaning in to kiss him. "Come on in." I hum as I take out the cartons and set them on the counter.

Jake looks at me suspiciously. "OK, what's the deal?"

"I do have news, but isn't there something you wanted to run past me?"

"Yes, but you go first. I'm curious to know what's inspired this mood of yours."

"OK, Eric basically handed us a cosmetics project without even soliciting an RFP."

"Lexi, that's amazing! You recognized the opportunity and obviously went about it the right way. He must have a lot of confidence in you, considering he doesn't have any other ties to the agency."

"Thanks," I say, pleased that he's excited.

Then he adds, "I think it's safe to assume we're a shoo-in for the rest of their business."

"I hope. He's looking at this as a test, but I can't imagine it won't go well."

"We have to celebrate."

"Wait, there's more. When I told Morgan the news, she said that if the business comes through, she wants to promote me to VP!"

Jake looks at me with a funny expression. I know he's not jealous of my success, so I can't read why he doesn't seem happy about it. He quickly changes his expression into one of pride and engulfs me in a hug. "Lexi, I'm so proud of you. It's so well deserved, and I'm glad you're getting the recognition you've earned."

"Thanks," I say, smiling into his shoulder. "Now let's celebrate."

"Do you have any champagne?"

"I don't think so."

"I'll go buy a bottle," he says.

"Jake, that's ridiculous. I have wine in the fridge. A toast is a toast."

He agrees and retrieves two wineglasses from my cabinet. He pours us each a glass and says, "To a promising future."

"Cheers to that," I say.

I wake up later that night and discover Jake isn't in bed. I get up and find him lying on the couch watching TV.

"Sorry. Did the noise wake you?"

"No, what are you doing up?"

"I don't know. I couldn't sleep."

"Come back to bed."

"I'll be there in a few minutes," he says.

"Is everything OK?"

He sees my worried expression and says, "Everything's fine. I just have a lot going on at work."

I get back in bed, but now I have trouble falling asleep.

The next morning, I wake up before Jake, so I go out and get us bagels. I leave him a note, but he's still sleeping when I get home. I wonder how long he was up last night; he's usually an earlier riser than me. Finally he emerges at close to eleven.

"Bad night?"

"I guess so."

"I got us breakfast, or should I say brunch?"

"Thanks. That was nice of you." As I'm toasting the bagels, he says he came up with an idea last night. "How do you feel about planning a long weekend in San Francisco?"

"I'd love it. We haven't been there together since the pitch."

"That's what I was thinking."

"Although it'll be hard to top that weekend."

"I'm up for the challenge."

I laugh. "Actually I'll agree to it on one condition: We have to go to Napa."

"I know I promised you we'd do Napa, but I didn't get to show you around the city last time you were there. It might be hard to do both if you only come for the weekend, unless you want to extend the trip."

"Things are so busy—let's start with a long weekend. Then I'll have a good excuse to come back. We can look into taking a longer trip after the holidays."

"I was thinking sooner than that," he says.

"Things are a bit crazy with work between now and the end of the year. It would be hard to find time to get away."

Jake looks disappointed. "You'd just need to take a Friday off. Surely you can find one between now and the end of the year." I hesitate, and he adds, "All I'm asking is for one weekend, just you and me."

I want to tell him it's always just the two of us, but instead I say, "I'll check my schedule." He seems satisfied with that. I decide to change the subject. "I've narrowed it down to two options for our Halloween costumes. I want you to be the deciding vote."

"What are your ideas?"

"Danny and Sandy from *Grease* or Ken and Barbie."

"Ken and Barbie is something different, but what would we wear?"

"I looked online. I can order a retro Barbie shirt and pair it with a mini skirt and a blond wig. You wouldn't have much of a costume. We can order you a Polo-type shirt and have 'Ken' monogrammed on it. You can wear it with khakis or jeans and part your hair to the side."

"A costume that isn't really a costume—I'm sold. And I like the idea of you in a mini skirt."

I smile at him. "Barbie and Ken it is."

On Monday, Jake texts me to see if we can set a date for my visit to San Francisco. Clearly it's important to him, so I pick a date. I call him, and he answers right away.

"I checked my schedule," I say. "How about the first weekend in November? It's before your sister's due date, and it really seems to be the only weekend that'll work."

"I'll book your ticket today. I'm really looking forward to spending some quality time with just the two of us away from the office."

I tell him I am as well, but in the back of my mind, I can't help wonder what the urgency is. At least a weekend getaway will give me the chance to talk to him about why he's been acting off recently. I tried bringing it up during our past few conversations, but he brushed off my attempts then resumed acting normal. This time I plan to pin him down. He will talk to me, whether or not he likes it.

———•◆•———

Work is really busy now that the holidays are approaching. Natalia and Paul basically will be unavailable come December, so we're trying to cram two months' worth of work into one. Simon stops by my office and asks if Jake and I have decided on our costumes.

"Yes, but it's a surprise."

"It'd better be good," he says. "There's a prize for best costume."

"Oh, it's good. Are you expecting a big turnout?"

"We'll have around twenty people. I wanted to keep it small, but it's Lance's favorite holiday."

"I'm really looking forward to meeting him."

"And he you. So what are your plans for the holidays?"

"I'm not sure. I haven't broached the subject with Jake yet. You?"

"We're going to Vermont to visit Lance's family. We do Thanksgiving with mine and Christmas with his."

"It's nice that you've split it up that way. I'm sure having a set plan avoids a lot of family drama."

"Oh, there's still drama," he says, "but it definitely helps."

I look at my watch. "I've got to go to a status meeting," I tell him." See you this weekend."

"See you."

It's the Saturday of Simon's Halloween party. I spend the afternoon in the suburbs trick-or-treating with Charlie, Scott, and Jules. I've never been that into Halloween, but there's something endearing about watching kids experience the magic of dressing up and getting excited over each piece of candy. I don't get back to my apartment until after six. Jake is coming by in an hour so we can get dressed then head to Simon's. I take a quick shower, dry my hair, and put on my costume sans the wig. I also eat a light snack. I know Simon will have tons of food there, but I never like to walk into a party hungry. Jake knocks on my door around seven. He's already dressed, with his hair parted to the side, like I suggested.

"I like your hair like that," I tell him.

"Thanks. I actually may consider wearing it this way for a change."

When I put on my wig and apply a fresh coat of hot-pink lipstick, Jake makes a face. "What? It's part of my character. Are you ready to go?"

"I'm ready."

I grab the bottle of Johnnie Walker Black I picked up earlier, and we're out the door.

Simon and Lance live in a contemporary townhouse in Lakeview. We walk in, and the place is decked out with Halloween decor—all done tastefully of course. I almost don't recognize Simon—he is supposed to be Belle and is wearing a beautiful yellow ball gown and a brown wig that's styled in an elegant updo.

"Seriously, how is it that you're prettier than me?" I say as I kiss him hello. "Who did your makeup?"

"I did."

"Nice job. You can give me some tips."

Lance comes over dressed as the Beast. He's wearing a gold vest with a white blouse beneath it, a royal blue jacket with gold trim, and navy pants. He dons a shaggy brown wig and is wearing makeup that has transformed his nose and mouth to complete his look. Even with his costume I can tell he's very distinguished looking. He's tall, with broad shoulders, tan skin, and warm hazel eyes that crinkle at the corners. He looks to be in his midforties. He and Jake shake hands, and then Simon introduces us.

"Lexi, this is Lance. Lance, this is Lexi Winters."

"Lexi, it's so nice to finally meet you. Simon has told me a lot about you."

"Likewise. Thank you so much for having us." I offer him the bottle of Scotch.

"Thank you," Lance says. "That was very thoughtful. Scotch is my favorite."

"Simon told me." I see them exchange a smile, and I find myself smiling too. It's nice to see Simon outside of a work setting looking relaxed. He's always so high-strung at the office. "Simon told me you take this holiday very seriously. He wasn't kidding. If I'd known, I would have put a bit more effort into my costume."

"I love the Ken and Barbie idea," he says. "Very original."

"Thanks, although you guys look as though you had professional stylists dress you."

"That's because we did," says Lance. I don't know whether he's kidding. "My friend Lanie works for Disney. She got us the costumes and provided us with makeup tips."

"Simon, you've been holding out of me," I say. "I didn't know you had a Disney connection."

"It hasn't come up. Are you a Disney fan?"

"Yes, Disney World was my favorite place on earth as a kid, although I haven't been in years."

"You'll have to take her—I don't do Disney," Simon tells Jake.

"We'll add it to the list," Jake tells me.

"There's a list?" asks Simon.

"A short one," he says. "So far it's San Francisco, Napa, Paris, and now Disney."

Lance is a business consultant and often travels to San Francisco as well, so he and Jake engage in a conversation.

I look around and ask Simon if he did all the decorating.

"Yes, but Lance and I made a lot of the decisions together."

"Your taste is immaculate, though I expected nothing less."

He waves his hand in a dismissive gesture. Lance turns his attention back to me and asks, "Would you like a tour?"

"I'd love one."

We follow Lance as he shows us around their three-level home. He tells us little tidbits about how they chose various things and strikes me as very warm and self-deprecating. I like him immediately. We make our way back to the kitchen, and he tells us to help ourselves to food.

"Did you make all this?" I inquire.

"God, no," Lance says. "We had it catered."

Jake goes to get us drinks, and Simon introduces me to some of his friends. It's an eclectic mix of people. I look around at everyone's costumes. There's Sonny and Cher, Popeye and Olive Oyl, Bert and Ernie, and Mr. Incredible and Elastigirl. Then I spy a Danny and Sandy walking in. I'm glad Jake and I chose Ken and Barbie. At least this way, we're original. Simon introduces me to Sandy, whose real name is Gabrielle. She and Simon worked together years ago and still keep in touch.

"She's the old you," he informs me. I look at him, confused. "You know, my former work wife."

"Oh." I smile at him. "Then Gabrielle and I have lots to discuss."

"I'll leave you to it."

Gabrielle and I spend the next hour sharing Simon stories. She's actually a lot like me; I guess Simon has a type. Jake comes over, and I introduce him to Gabrielle. He makes polite small talk but seems distracted. I feel bad that I haven't spent a lot of time with him, so I excuse myself and ask Jake if he's having a good time.

"Yes," he says unconvincingly.

"You won't win any awards for your acting."

He smiles and says, "It's not really my kind of crowd. I'm actually tired and was thinking of going soon." I look at my watch and see it's not even midnight. I think he senses I'm not ready to leave. "You can stay and meet me at my place."

"Are you sure?"

"I offered."

"I know. It's just that I've never met Lance before, and I hardly get to spend time with Simon outside of work."

"Do you have a spare key with you?" Jake asks.

"Yes."

"OK. Stay and have a good time. I'll see you later."

He quickly brushes my lips then says his good-byes to Simon and Lance. After he leaves I ask Simon if Jake seems different.

"Not that I've noticed, but I rarely see him these days."

"I can't explain it, but he seems distracted. He said he's busy with work, but I'm starting to worry."

"Lexi, you have nothing to worry about," Simon says. "Jake is enamored with you. Always has been, always will be."

"I hope so."

I stay for another hour then call it a night. I thank Simon and Lance for having me and tell Lance I'm so happy we finally had a chance to meet. I take a cab to Jake's and quietly let myself in. I get ready for bed then climb in beside him.

"What time is it?" he mumbles.

"Almost two. Sorry to wake you."

He falls back asleep minutes later. I snuggle up next to him and feel his chest rise and fall with each breath. Even though we're so close, I feel like he's miles away.

CHAPTER TWENTY-ONE

THE following Friday I get a Facebook message from Vanessa. We've exchanged a handful of e-mails since our vacation in Aruba, but I haven't heard from her in a while. She tells me she and Seth just bought a house in the suburbs, and she's pregnant. It's still early, and she's not telling anyone yet, but she knows her secret is safe with me. She goes on to ask how I'm doing and whether Jake has told people we're dating yet. As with my other e-mails, my response will remain the same. I've really tried to be patient with Jake, but it's starting to get to me. I write her back that I'm thrilled for her and ask her to keep me posted on her pregnancy. I also ask her about the house, how she's feeling, and how Seth is doing, and send him my best. As happy as I am for her, I'm slightly resentful that she's moving forward while I seem to be standing still.

I don't have plans to see Jake until the next afternoon; he had to meet a client for cocktails last night so he took a flight in this morning. The timing worked in my favor because this morning I'm going wedding-dress shopping with Liv and her mom. I'm accompanying them to two places in the city, and then they're heading to the suburbs on their own. Liv's mom picks us up at nine thirty.

"Hi, Marianne," I say as I climb into the backseat.

"Hi, Lexi. How are you?"

"I'm doing great. I'm really looking forward to seeing Liv try on dresses."

"I know. Isn't it wonderful?"

I've always had a close relationship with Liv's mom. Liv and I practically lived at each other's houses while we were growing up. We get to the first bridal shop, and Liv is greeted by a young salesgirl with numerous piercings who looks like she's right out of college. Liv gives me a look as if to say, "Is she really the one who's going to be helping me?" The girl informs us Liv will be meeting with Bonnie and pages her. "Thank God," she mouths to me.

A saleswoman who looks much more the part comes over and introduces herself as Bonnie. She asks Liv to describe what she's looking for. She listens then tells Liv she'll bring out some options, but she should look around to see if anything else catches her eye. The three of us comb through the racks, and Liv pulls out dresses. She holds one up and asks me my opinion.

"Honestly I think you need to try them all on. I didn't love my dress on the hanger, but once I put it on, I knew it was the one."

"God, Lexi, are you OK doing this? I've been so wrapped up in my wedding plans that I didn't think about how it would make you feel."

"Liv, I appreciate your concern, but nothing would make me happier than seeing you in your wedding dress. This isn't about me. We're here to celebrate you and your special day."

"Thanks," she says, giving me a hug. "I couldn't imagine doing this without you."

As we're waiting, Liv's mom puts a reassuring arm around my shoulder. "Liv is lucky to have a friend like you," she tells me. I know it's supposed to make me feel better, but I fight the urge to cry. Bonnie comes back with an armful of dresses and shows Liv to a room. Marianne and I wait outside while Liv tries them on.

She comes out to model the first dress. It's a strapless A-line gown with beaded details along the waistband. "What do you think?"

I let Marianne speak first. "It's beautiful, honey. Simple, elegant, and it doesn't overwhelm you."

Liv looks to me. "I agree. It's a beautiful dress. I don't know if it's the one, but you should put it in the 'yes' pile."

She does a little twirl then goes to try on her next one. Marianne and I rule out the next two, and she throws the next dress over the door. "This one wasn't even worth showing you," she says.

She takes a while before she comes out with the next dress. "Liv, are you OK?" Marianne calls out.

Liv opens the door and emerges with a small smile. As she stands in front of us, tingles race up and down my spine. I look at Marianne, whose eyes are watering as she whispers, "That's it." I nod my agreement. The dress is white satin with intricate flower beading along the bodice. The dress puckers on each side at the waist, forming an upside-down V-shaped band; then the beading continues to cascade in a slightly off-center line down the front. Bonnie brings Liv a beaded tiara and veil so she can get the full effect.

She studies herself in the mirror. "What do you think?" she asks me.

"I absolutely love it. I got the chills when you came out wearing it."

She nods. "I think I'm done."

Marianne laughs. "We'll put it at the top of our list, but I'd like to keep our other appointments just to be sure."

Liv thanks Bonnie for her help and has her write up the details so she can find the dress when she comes back.

As we're heading to the car, Liv says, "Mom, I'll try on other dresses, but that's the one I want."

"I know. Let's just be sure. It's a big decision."

We get to the next bridal salon, and Liv tries on dresses, but I can see her heart's not in it. I think Marianne senses it too, so she suggests we look at bridesmaid dresses.

"That's a great idea," Liv says. "Lexi is already here."

The saleswoman brings out a catalog. "This will give me a sense of what you like. Then I can bring out some options." Liv and I look through the book; she's leaning toward a strapless tea-length dress with a sash at the waist.

"What do you think?" she asks me.

"I love the style and think it'll look flattering on everyone."

The saleswoman returns with a few samples for me to try on. Liv and I both agree on the same dress, so Liv asks to see the color options. She studies them and says, "I can't decide if I like the deep purple or chocolate brown."

"Why don't you take them with you to the florist? They might be able to help you decide which color scheme you like best," I suggest.

"That's a great idea. Can I take swatches of them both?" she asks the saleswoman. She nods and asks that Liv bring them back when she's done.

"I'm exhausted," Liv says as we get into the car.

"Do you want to go to the other appointments?" Marianne asks her.

"Yes. We may as well as long as we have them. I'm only going to do this once, so I want to enjoy it." She eyes me in the backseat and mouths, "Sorry." I shake my head, implying it's nothing to worry about.

I'm in a wistful mood on the ride home. The experience has brought up feelings I've been trying to bury. I do my best to push them aside, but today's events—coupled with Jake's mood swings—have left me in a dark mood.

"Where should we drop you off?" Liv asks me.

I realize I haven't checked my phone and see that Jake texted me to say he's on his way home from the airport. I have them drop me off at his place; I'm about to let myself in when he opens the door.

"Hi," he says, and gives me a big hug. "Who was that?" he asks, motioning to Marianne's car.

"Liv and her mom. I went wedding-dress shopping with them this morning."

"How was it? Did she find something?"

"I think so. They're going to a few other places, just to be sure, but I think she found the one. She was more interested in having me try on bridesmaid dresses at the next appointment, so I think it's safe to say she's in love with that dress."

He laughs. "How were the bridesmaid dresses?"

"Not bad. I don't know that I'd wear it again, but it's a pretty dress, and at least it's flattering."

"I can't imagine anything not looking flattering on you," Jake says, eyeing me. I laugh and playfully brush off his attempts to get close. "What's wrong?" he asks.

"Nothing. I'm just not in the mood." I think this is the first time I've ever turned Jake down, but he doesn't press the issue further.

"Here. Come with me upstairs while I unpack." As he's putting his things away, I tell him the news about Seth and Vanessa. "Wow. I can't believe she's pregnant so fast. Were they trying?"

"I didn't ask her that," I say in a slightly irritated tone.

"Well, please tell them I say congratulations." Jake changes the subject and asks me what I want to do for dinner.

"I'd like to go out somewhere," I tell him. He asks me what I have in mind. "I don't know. It just would be nice to go on a date like normal people."

He studies me for a moment then says, "OK. Let's go out. I know this great Italian place in Logan Square. I don't think we'll run into anyone there."

I'm about to make a sarcastic reply, but I hold my tongue. At least we're going out. "I have to run some errands. What time should I be ready?"

"How about I pick you up at seven thirty?"

"That's fine."

"Wait—I'll drive you home."

"No, that's OK. I have to make a couple of stops along the way. See you later," I say, giving him a quick peck on the cheek.

I really don't have errands to run, but I need some space. I go home and head to the gym, thinking a workout will lift my spirits. Afterward I get ready for a rare night out, and I'm downstairs by seven twenty-five. Jake is out front already and opens the car door for me.

"You look great," he says, kissing my cheek.

"Thanks. You look nice too."

On the drive over, I ask him how he knows about the restaurant. "I've been there a few times, but it's been a while since I've been back. It's kind of a neighborhood gem."

When we arrive, he says, "I made a reservation under 'Hartman.'" Then he drops me off and looks for parking. I check in, and the hostess tells me it'll be about fifteen minutes before our table is ready. I look around and like the restaurant's rustic charm. It has exposed brick walls lined with artwork of the Italian countryside. Wooden beams run along the ceiling, which has amber pendant light fixtures hanging over each table. The doorway to the kitchen looks like an old archway, and a long wooden shelf filled with wine bottles stands above it. Jake walks in, and we find two open seats at the bar. I see him looking around, making sure we don't know anyone here. I find it irritating. The bartender comes to take our drink order, and shortly after our table is ready. All the tables are packed closely together, but fortunately ours is next to the window. I study the menu and decide on Chicken Vesuvio.

"Do you want to split an appetizer?" Jake asks.

"Sure. What do you want?"

"You know I'll eat anything. You choose."

"OK, let's do the bruschetta."

"Done. Now, are you going to tell me what's bothering you?"

I didn't realize he'd noticed. "It's nothing," I say hesitantly. I don't feel like getting into a fight.

"Lexi, it's obviously something. You've been pissed off all afternoon. The least you can do is tell me what's wrong."

"Fine," I say with a sigh. "I'm getting really sick of having to hide our relationship. I want to be able to go out to a restaurant with you on a Saturday night without you looking over your shoulder or having to drive to some remote neighborhood where we won't run into anyone. I want to be able to arrive at work without having to be dropped off down the block. I want to go out to a movie with you or grab coffee. I want us to be out in the open like any other normal couple. Is that too much to ask?"

"I understand your frustration," Jake says, "but we're out in the open in every way that matters to me. I've introduced you to my friends and family, which isn't something I take lightly. I've let you into my personal life, and work…well, that's just business."

"It's not just business to me. I feel like you're hiding from our relationship."

"You should be one to talk."

"What do you mean?" I ask him.

"Have you talked to Ben yet?"

"No. What does he have to do with this?"

"Just let me finish," Jake says. "Why haven't you talked to him?"

"I've told you before—I don't have anything to say to him."

"Well, like it or not, he's a part of your past. And I feel like your avoiding what happened is preventing you from being able to move forward...with me. Do you realize you've dodged all my attempts at getting to know your family?" He pauses then says, "Give me your phone."

Shit, I know what's coming. Silently I hand it to him. He scrolls through my pictures until he lands on the one of Ben and me. "You still haven't deleted this," he says.

What can I say? I stare at him and know he's right. A part of me is still hanging on to the past. "I didn't realize you felt that way," I tell him.

"Well, I do."

"If it's important to you, I'll talk to him."

"Lexi, you should want to do it for yourself, not for me."

Feeling bad for being a total bitch, I try to lighten the mood. It takes a little while, but by the time dinner arrives, I feel like Jake has thawed. The food is delicious.

"Here, taste mine," I say, offering my fork to him.

He takes a bite and agrees. "Want to try mine?" He ordered a seafood pasta.

"No, thanks. Too fishy for me." After dinner we go for a walk. The restaurant is in a very cute neighborhood. "How did you find this place?" I ask him.

"A client of mine recommended it."

"We'll have to come back."

I lace my fingers through his as we walk. It's a chilly November evening, and I wish I'd thought to bring my gloves. As we're walking, a light snow begins to fall, the first of the season. I notice some houses have Christmas decorations. "I love this time of year," I comment to Jake. "This is the reason I live here. As much as I hate the cold, I couldn't imagine living somewhere

where there isn't snow for the holidays. When I was younger, we used to travel to Florida during winter break. Everyone had their decorations up, but it just wasn't the same." I look at Jake, but his expression is unreadable.

We walk in silence, and after a few minutes, he says, "Lexi, know I'm trying. I want nothing more than to show you off to the world. I do intend to go public with our relationship—I'm just waiting for the right time to tell my uncle. He was very disappointed in me when the scandal with Jessica broke, and it's taken me a long time to earn back his trust."

"Oh, you didn't tell me that."

"I told you he was supportive, which he was, but I can tell he thought I was being young and foolish. He's been grooming me so I have a future with the company. I just need to be careful about how I navigate this."

"I understand, but isn't this a different situation? You weren't in a committed relationship like we are."

"I know. I just want him to take me seriously." We walk back to the car, and we're both quiet on the drive home. "Do you want to stay at my place tonight?" Jake asks. "I doubt I'll find parking by you."

"That's fine."

"You know," he comments, "you should think about bringing some stuff over aside from just a toothbrush."

The thought has occurred to me, but I've been hesitant about leaving my belongings at his place. On some subconscious level, it feels like a permanent arrangement. I swallow the lump that's formed in my throat and say, "I will."

As we're lying in bed I think about what Jake said, and I know he's right. I do need to deal with my past so I can move forward with the present. I've been holding back from him, afraid to give myself fully. As much as I've moved on, I'm still scared of getting hurt again. I never wanted to open myself up to that kind of vulnerability again. But then I met Jake, and he's given me a reason to question that decision. Giving all of yourself to another person takes a lot of courage. I know Jake thinks I'm strong, but when I look deep within myself, I still feel fragile. The heart is one of the most powerful muscles in the body, so why do I feel the need to protect it?

On Sunday afternoon, I get up the nerve to call Ben. Thankfully I get his voice mail. I leave him a message that I'm ready to talk.

On Monday Jake stops by my office, looking very serious.

"What's up?"

"I need to talk to you about something. Can we have dinner tonight?"

"Sure. Is everything OK?"

"Yeah, everything's fine. Meet me at five thirty, and I'll drive you home."

"OK, see you later."

I'm distracted the rest of the afternoon. What could he want to talk to me about? I briefly wonder whether he's going to ask me to move in with him, but considering he won't tell people we're dating, that would be a bit extreme. I make it through the rest of the day and walk the few blocks to our designated meeting spot. He's on the phone the entire drive back, so I can't ask him what this is about. Miraculously he finds a parking spot in front of my building. We walk in, and I ask him if he wants to order in or go out. I don't know if he answers because I'm suddenly paralyzed. There, sitting on a chair in my lobby, is Ben. He stands up when he sees me.

"Hi, Lexi," he says quietly.

When I manage to find my voice, I say, "What are you doing here?"

"You said you were ready to talk. I wanted to do it in person."

It takes me a minute to regain my composure. I look uncomfortably at Jake, and I can tell he knows who Ben is. My manners take over, and I make introductions. "Ben, this is Jake. Jake, this is Ben."

"Hey," says Ben.

Jake gives him a curt nod. He turns to me and says, "Well, you two have a lot to talk about. Call me later."

"I will," I say to his retreating back.

After he walks away, Ben says, "It's good to see you. I've missed you." I don't say anything. "Can we go somewhere and talk?"

"Fine. There's a coffee shop around the corner." No way am I bringing him up to my apartment.

We walk there in silence. The place is busy, but a few tables are open. "Sit down. I'll get us some coffee. Do you want your usual?" I nod. It's weird that he knows me so well, yet now he's like a perfect stranger. I sit, still reeling from the fact that he's here. As he's standing in line, I study him. He looks exactly the same, and I'm slightly resentful he doesn't show any signs of suffering. He returns with our coffee.

"So how have you been?"

"I'm fine."

"Was that your boyfriend?"

"Yes," I tell him. "I've moved on. You should too." Maybe he already has. I look at him expectantly. He seems nervous.

"Why didn't you return any of my calls? Why wouldn't you talk to me?"

"What's there to say? I thought I was going to spend the rest of my life with you, and the minute I leave town, you're sleeping with someone else. Clearly I wasn't enough for you. And I guess I never wanted to know why."

"Is that what you think?"

"Yes. What am I supposed to think?"

"Lexi, you were enough for me…*are* enough for me. I just got freaked out with the pressure of the wedding. And I was working long hours, and you were traveling a lot. It was a stressful time. I didn't intend for any of it to happen. I stopped by your office that day you called and said you left a file at work. Claire happened to be in the lobby. I remembered her from your holiday party. She struck up a conversation, and one thing led to another."

"How exactly does one thing lead to another?"

"I don't know," he says. "She was flirting me with me, and I could tell she was interested. I was flattered, so I flirted back, thinking it was harmless. I mentioned you were out of town, and she asked me if I wanted company. I said no but felt kind of bad for giving her the wrong impression. She seemed to understand and asked me to have a drink with her. I figured I owed her that much. One drink turned into many. Look, I screwed up. You don't think I know that? I jeopardized my future with the one person who mattered most. Lexi, I want to be with you. Since you've been gone, you're all I can think about. I can't imagine being with anyone else. I still love you."

I digest this news. "Ben, part of me will always love you too. But I could never trust you. I'd always be questioning your whereabouts and intentions. And as much as you say it wasn't about me, something was missing for you if you needed to seek something outside of our relationship. That's not something I can get past."

He looks at me sadly. "I'm so sorry, Lexi."

"So am I."

"Does this new guy make you happy?"

"Yes, he does."

"Good. That's all I want for you—to be happy."

"I hope you'll be happy too."

I honestly mean it. And with those words, I'm finally able to let go of the anger I've been carrying around for so long. Now I understand what Jake meant. It was always there, even if I couldn't see it. I have nothing left to say, so I stand up. Outside, Ben gives me a big hug. He tries to kiss me, but I turn my head. He gets into a cab, and I watch as he drives away, knowing it will probably be the last time I'll ever see him. Tears sting my eyes as the reality sinks in that I'll never speak to him again. He was such an important part of my life for so long, and now that chapter is finally closed. I take a deep, cathartic breath. Then I pull out my phone and scroll until I find the picture of the two of us. "Good-bye," I whisper, then hit "delete" and head straight to Jake's place.

I knock on the door, and he opens it, surprised to see me. "Can I come in?"

"Of course."

He looks distraught and makes no move to touch me. I sit down on the couch. "I'm sorry. I didn't know he was coming, and it caught me off guard."

"I understand. How'd things go?"

"Good, actually. You were right. I should have spoken to him a long time ago. We definitely had unfinished business." Jake rakes a hand through his hair but doesn't say anything. It's weird to see him acting so subdued. "He was my everything for so long. It was wrong of me to try to avoid dealing with the situation. I guess I thought if I avoided it, the hurt and humiliation would go away. And now that I've seen him, it actually has."

"Lexi, that's understandable. You guys have a history." He pauses and says, "I can't compete with that."

I see the anguish and fear in his eyes, and then it hits me. He thinks I'm going to go back to Ben. I feel terrible knowing I've caused him pain, this man who helped me overcome mine. The protective strings around my heart slowly unravel, revealing my scars, newly healed. Though they will always be there, I now realize the extent of my strength, because I am capable of love again. I just need to let it in. "Jake, yes, we have a history. But you're my future. I'm sorry I haven't been able to make my feelings clear to you. I've been so scared of getting hurt again that I haven't fully let you in, although I'm sure you know that. When I called things off with Ben, I never thought I'd be able to feel that way about someone again. But then you came along, and you changed all that. You brought color back into my life. You make me so happy—happier than I ever thought possible. I'm a better person when I'm with you. I want to be with *you*, not Ben, and not anyone else." I touch his face and say, "I'm so completely in love with you." He smiles for the first time all night. I stare into his eyes and feel my own well up with tears. For once I let them fall. He tenderly wipes them away and pulls me in close. "I'm yours," I whisper. "I'm giving you all of me. Just don't ever do anything to break my trust."

He gets a funny look and says, "Lexi, I—"

"Shh. No more talking." And I cover his lips with mine.

The next morning the alarm goes off, but Jake is already out of bed. I look at him sleepily and mumble, "Why are you up so early?"

"I was having trouble sleeping. But I liked watching you."

I sit up and ask, "Is something bothering you?" After last night I would have expected him to not have a care in the world. He shakes his head. "That reminds me. Didn't you have something you wanted to discuss with me?"

He looks at me for a moment and says, "It was nothing important. Being here with you is all that matters."

"Then come back to bed."

He crawls into bed next to me and playfully avoids my kisses. "We'll be late for work," he admonishes.

"I love you, Jake Hartman, but stop worrying so much."

"I love hearing you say those words. Say them again."

"I love you, Jake Hartman."

And for the first time in as long as I've known him, Jake is late for work.

CHAPTER TWENTY-TWO

My relationship with Jake is stronger than ever. Whatever weirdness I felt between us seems to have subsided. Maybe it was all in my head. We fall back into our routine. He's still traveling a lot, but we call and text every day. It's the Thursday before I'm scheduled to leave for my weekend with him in San Francisco. Around three my office line rings. I see that it's Jake. He never calls me at work. I close the door and say, "Hi. Is everything all right?"

"Everything's fine. I just wanted to let you know my sister is in labor."

"Oh, that's so exciting!"

"I know, but the timing couldn't be worse. You were supposed to come visit; Adam is at work; my dad and I are both out of town."

"Well, I'm sure Adam will make it to the hospital in time. Is she waiting for him to drive her?"

"No, luckily she's with my mom. She'll take Kate and Hailey to the hospital, and then she'll bring Hailey home once Adam gets there."

"So your mom won't be able to be there for the delivery?"

"No, she always planned to watch Hailey, so she knew that going in."

"I can watch Hailey."

"It's nice of you to offer, but don't you have work to do?"

"Yes, but I don't have any more meetings. And I can take my laptop with me."

"OK, but how will you get there?"

"Did Adam leave yet?"

"I'm sure he's long gone."

"OK, what if I take the train?"

"How would you get to the hospital from the train station?"

"I can take a cab."

"Lexi, I appreciate your wanting to help, but it's just too complicated."

"What's complicated about it?"

He hesitates. "Let me call my mom and run it past her." We hang up, and he calls back a few minutes later. "You made my mom's day. As long as it's not too much trouble, she'd love to take you up on your offer."

"Great. Give me her cell phone number."

I jot it down, and Jake tells me he's going to try to get a flight home tonight. "Thanks for doing this, Lexi. It means a lot to me and my family."

"I'm glad I can help. And I get to spend time with Hailey. It's a win-win. I am bummed I won't get to visit you in San Francisco this weekend, but at least we'll get to spend time together here."

"I know. I was really looking forward to it too." He sounds disappointed.

"I promise I'll come out another time. Call me when you land."

"OK. Love you."

"Love you too."

I look up the train schedule online. If I leave now, I probably can make the three forty-five. I quickly send my team an e-mail then dash out of the office. I decide I'm better off walking to the station than trying to get a cab. It was a good move because I make it with a few minutes to spare. Then I call Jake's mom to let her know I'll be at the hospital around five.

"Great news: Adam just got here," she says.

"That was quick."

"I know. I don't want to know how fast he was driving. What time does your train arrive? Hailey and I will pick you up."

I give her the details, and she profusely thanks me. I tell her I'm happy to do it. When I get off the train, I spot Jake's mom and Hailey, who's waving furiously at me from the backseat. I get in, and she excitedly tells me she's going to be a big sister. "I know. That's so exciting!" I turn to Nancy and say, "If you want, you can drive to the hospital, and I can take Hailey back to Kate's house."

273

"That's what I was thinking too. My car has a GPS you can use to get there."

She pulls up to the entrance and says she'll call with an update. I'm a bit nervous about driving her car, so I'm extra cautious. Hailey is chatting away in the backseat, and for the first time, I have a glimpse into what it must be like to be a parent. With the help of the GPS, I find my way back to Kate's house. It's just about six o'clock when we arrive.

"Are you hungry?" I ask Hailey. I realize I don't know whether she's eaten or what her bedtime is.

"Yes," she tells me.

I look in the cabinets and find a box of macaroni and cheese. "How's this?" I ask her.

She nods her approval then draws at the table while I get dinner ready. I'm hungry too, so we share the box. Hailey seems to think this is very funny. After dinner we play a few rounds of Candy Land and Chutes and Ladders. I ask her what her bedtime is, and she tells me seven thirty. That's one thing I love about kids—they're usually honest. Around seven fifteen, we head upstairs. Hailey helps me find her pajamas, and then I read her a few books.

We're about to go to the bathroom to brush her teeth when the phone rings. I answer, and it's Nancy, calling to check in. "Lexi, I'm so sorry I didn't give you any information about Hailey's schedule. My mind is obviously elsewhere." I tell her not to worry; I have things under control. Then I put Hailey on so she can say good night. I ask Nancy how the labor's going, and she says Kate is dilated to seven. She expects it'll still be a while and asks if I mind staying.

"No problem," I tell her. "I can stay as long as you need me."

Once Hailey is in bed, I finish up some work and e-mail my team that I'll be working from home tomorrow. At this rate I have no clue how long I'll be here. Once I'm done, I turn on the TV and watch a *Law & Order* rerun. A little after nine, my cell phone rings. It's Jake, and he's landed. He's on his way over to Kate's. At nine thirty Nancy calls to inform me Kate had a girl, Lily Grace.

"That's wonderful. Congratulations!"

"I can't thank you enough for making it possible for me to be here," she says. "I'm so happy Jake found you. We all are."

I thank her and hang up the phone, reflecting that he has a very nice family. Jake arrives a short while later, and I give him the news.

"Wow, another girl. I'm sure Hailey will be thrilled. I'm not sure about Adam. I know he really wanted a boy."

"I'm sure he'll be happy to have a healthy child," I tell him.

"I know, but every dad wants a son. Now come here. I've missed you." He wraps his arms around me and kisses me hungrily. Then his hands caress my body over my clothes.

"Jake," I say in a warning tone.

"What?"

"Here? At your sister's house?"

"Why not?" he says, still kissing me.

"What if Hailey wakes up?"

"She's sleeping."

"What if your mom walks in?"

"She said she'd text me when she was leaving."

"Where would we do it?"

"Right here, on the couch."

"I don't want to ruin their couch."

"I don't think we'll ruin it."

"You know what I mean." He walks over and grabs a T-shirt from his bag and lays it on the couch. "Satisfied?" My mind says no, but my body betrays me. Jake knows I never can resist him. "That's enough talking," he says.

We're snuggling on the couch when Nancy comes in around eleven fifteen. She gives each of us a big hug and shows us photos of Lily on her cell phone.

"You two must be exhausted. Do you want to stay here in the spare bedroom?"

"That's OK," Jake tells her. "I'm two hours behind, remember? I'll drive Lexi home."

I try to stay up on the ride home, but I find it hard to keep my eyes open. I feel Jake nudge me, and I see we're in his garage. "Do you want me to carry you in?" he jokes. I shake my head. When we get upstairs, I throw on one of his T-shirts and crawl into bed. "Good night," he says as he tucks me in bed, kissing my forehead.

"'Night," I say and fall asleep immediately.

The next day, Jake and I work out of his house. It's a good thing I don't have that busy of a schedule. It's nice being home with him, especially since I barely get to see him during the week anymore. When it reaches noon, Jake asks if I want to go out and grab lunch. "Yes, I'd love to!" We walk to a restaurant around the corner from his place. It's so nice to be out with him in public.

"You're in a good mood," he comments.

"I'm just happy to be out with you." He nods but doesn't say anything. "So when can we see the baby?" I ask.

"Well, I'm going to the game with the guys tomorrow, remember?"

"That's right."

"It starts early afternoon, and we'll probably go out after. I think Kate gets discharged on Sunday. We can go then."

"So soon? You think she'll be OK with having us over right when she comes home?"

"I'll call her to make sure, but I can't imagine she'd have an issue if we stopped by for a little while." He calls her, and Kate assures him it's fine.

"Good. I can't wait to meet the baby."

The next day, I head out to buy a gift for Lily and a little something for Hailey. I love shopping for babies—we don't have any in my family, so I rarely get the chance. I recruit Liv to come with me. We look at all the little clothes, and I find it hard to believe someone could fit into something so tiny. I find an adorable Splendid outfit and hold it up for Liv. "Can you believe this?" I say. "This is something I would wear." After I make my purchase, we head out to lunch.

"What's the latest with the wedding planning?" I ask Liv.

"I finally made an appointment to meet with the florist. Will you come with me?"

"Of course! I'd love to."

"Good. I really value your opinion. Also, there's something I've been meaning to ask you." She pulls a wrapped gift out of her bag. "Here, read the card first." It's a card about friendship; at the bottom, it asks me to be her maid of honor.

"Oh, Liv, of course I will!" I give her a big hug. "You didn't have to get me anything, though." I unwrap the paper to find a box of really cute monogrammed note cards. "Thank you. That was very thoughtful. How many bridesmaids are you going to have?"

"Five. You, my cousin Madelyn, Jill, Melanie, and Jason's sister." We talk about the wedding planning over lunch. I tell her to e-mail me the dates she's free for her bridal shower. "Already?" she asks.

"Yes, you don't know how hard it is to coordinate schedules. Plus I'm sure you'll have other showers, so we've got to get on it now."

"I'm lucky I have you. You're so organized."

"I can't believe my best friend is getting married!"

"I know," she says smiling.

After lunch I go to a bookstore to pick up something extra for Hailey. I come home and wrap the gifts then head to the gym. Around five Jake calls to check in. "How was your day?"

"Great. I got gifts for Lily and Hailey. How's the game?"

"Awesome! Shit, I didn't think of getting anything for them."

I laugh; he's such a guy. "They can be from you too."

"Thanks. Let me know how much I owe you."

"Nothing," I tell him. "You never let me pay for anything."

"Don't worry. I'll get it out of you one way or another," he says in a low voice.

"I look forward to it," I tell him.

"We're going out for a few drinks. Can I come by after?"

"Sure," I say. "See you later."

On Sunday afternoon, Jake and I head back to the burbs. When we walk into Kate and Adam's house, Hailey runs over and gives me a big hug. "Lexi, come meet baby Lily," she says.

"I'd love to, but first I have something for you." When I hand her the wrapped gift, she squeals with delight and rips off the paper. I got her a "big sister" book and a talking baby doll. "You'll have to feed and change your doll, just like Lily," I tell her.

"I love it!" she says. Then she looks at the book. "Will you read it to me?"

"Sure, I'd be happy to."

As I read the book to her, Jake goes to find Kate. After I finish I say, "Let's go find your mom."

Kate is upstairs in the nursery. I congratulate her and tell her she looks fabulous, which she does.

"Do you want to hold Lily?" she asks.

"Yes! It's been ages since I've held a newborn." I sit in the glider, and Kate hands her to me. I stare at her tiny features. "She's beautiful."

"Thanks," Kate says, beaming.

The phone rings, and Adam yells, "It's the night nurse."

"I've got to take that," she says. "I'll be right back."

Hailey is calling for Jake, so he goes off to find her, leaving me alone with Lily. I talk softly to her, telling her what a lucky baby she is. "Your Aunt Lexi is going to spoil you," I say. I look up and see Jake staring at me from the doorway. "She's precious, isn't she?" I ask him.

"Yes, she is," he agrees.

"Do you want to hold her?"

"In a few minutes. You look pretty comfortable."

"Good," I say, looking at Lily. "I want more time with you." I redo her swaddle and rock her until she falls asleep in my arms.

I look up at Jake. "How many kids do you want?" he asks.

"I don't know…two, maybe three."

"I can deal with that."

He smiles at me, and I smile at him in return. A warm glow spreads inside me. I recognize the feeling even though it's been absent for a long time. It's contentment.

———•◦•———

It's getting close to Thanksgiving, and I decide it's time for Jake to officially meet my family. I broach the topic about him joining us for dinner, and he readily agrees.

"Are you sure your family won't mind?"

"They'll be fine. They've gotten the chance to get to know you. I'd like to do the same with your family."

"OK," I say, smiling at him.

I can't help wonder if he has an ulterior motive. I've never asked, but I have a suspicion his family gets together with Bill. I've just handed him a solution to what would have been a difficult situation to navigate. As frustrated as I am that he hasn't come clean to Bill, I decide not to let it get to me. It took me a while before I was ready to deal with Ben. I did it on my own time and when I was ready, even though it did require a push from Jake. I decide I'll let him talk to Bill on his own timeline, not mine. I owe him that at least. But since I know how cathartic it was for me, I want him to experience the same.

I thought the weeks before Thanksgiving would be slow, but in fact it's the opposite; I feel like I'm busier than ever. I guess our clients want to cram in as much as possible before people start taking time off. When the week of Thanksgiving arrives, I feel thankful to have a few days off. Given it's a shortened workweek, Jake isn't traveling. We decide to make our own Thanksgiving dinner on Wednesday night. That's when I tell Jake I can't cook a turkey.

"I wasn't expecting you to. It was more the gesture of celebrating everything we're thankful for, just the two of us. We'll have turkey tomorrow."

"OK. I can make us turkey sandwiches so we're somewhat in the spirit." Over dinner Jake insists we each share what we're thankful for. "You go first," I tell him.

"I'm thankful that I have my health and a supportive family. I'm thankful that I'm able to do what I love and that I've turned it into a successful career. But most of all, I'm thankful for you. I didn't know what I was missing until we met. My life was focused on work and winning the next big account. But now that we're together, I know there's so much more, and I couldn't imagine having all this without you to share it with."

"Well, you basically covered everything I was going to say," I tell him. "I'll add that I'm thankful for hope. Hope is what brought me through my dark period last year—the hope that there was someone else out there for me and that my world wasn't ending. Then I met you, and you continued to give me hope. I was able to rise above my heartache to see that my heart ached because I was with the wrong person. That ache is gone, not because I've gotten over Ben but because my heart is whole now that I've found its other half."

"It's definitely a good thing I went first," Jake says. "There's no way I can top that. That's the best thing anyone has ever said to me."

He pulls me in for a kiss, and our dinner is all but forgotten.

The next morning I prepare my apple cobbler. I decide to bring two to make sure there's enough—it's usually one of the meal's highlights. Jake watches as I work, and I tell him he can help peel the apples. That's my least favorite part. I show him how to do it, and he catches on quickly.

"I want to pick up something for your parents," he says. "What kind of flowers does your mom like?"

"Her favorite is roses."

"Easy enough. What about your dad? What does he like?"

"It's sweet of you to want to bring him something. He's not a smoker, but once in a while, he enjoys a good cigar."

Jake peels as I work, and then he says, "Do you mind if I head out to get some things?"

"Trying to get out of your apple duties, huh?"

"I peeled most of them."

"OK, you're off the hook. Just be back here and ready to go by three."

"Sounds good. See you in a bit."

I finish making the cobbler then jump into the shower. I'm actually really looking forward to Jake meeting my family. It's strange that we've been together so long and he's never met them aside from at the benefit, which technically doesn't count. I guess I've been hesitant about introducing him to the people who matter most and who have been so protective of me. I think Jake realizes the symbolism of the gesture.

At five to three, Jake knocks on my door. He helps me carry the cobblers down to the car. After he arranges them on the floor of the backseat, he opens my car door for me, as usual. I admire how cute he looks. He's wearing a white button-down shirt under a charcoal-gray striped V-neck sweater and black pants.

"You look nice," I tell him.

"Thanks. So do you."

On the drive over, he doesn't seem nervous and chats easily with me. I see he's picked up a bouquet of pink roses for my mom and a box of Cuban cigars for my dad.

"Where did you get those on such short notice?"

"I keep a stash on hand for bachelor parties, when the guys are over, that sort of thing. So, remind me, who will be there?"

"My parents; Jules; Scott; Charlie; Tara and possibly some new guy of hers; Scott's parents, Barbara and Larry; my Aunt Sandra and Uncle Barry, and their son Doug."

"Sandra is your dad's sister?"

"Yes, his younger sister. And then on my mom's side, my Uncle Steve, who was married to my Aunt Lynne, and his three sons, Jonathan, Andrew and Ryan. But they're not coming until later. They usually eat dinner with his side of the family, but they always stop by for dessert."

"It's really nice that you still get together with them. Are you close with your cousins?"

"Yes, Jonathan and Andrew are like the older brothers I never had. I'm the closest with Ryan because he's my age. They're all very protective of me."

"I can handle them."

"OK, you've been warned."

When Jake pulls up, there are already a few cars on the driveway. We walk in, and the house is filled with the wonderful aroma of cooking. Jake shakes hands with my dad, and my mom gives him a hug. He offers her the flowers and my dad the cigars, which he gladly accepts. I introduce him to my aunt, uncle, and my cousin Doug, who's a senior at Indiana University. He and Jake become engrossed in a conversation, so I go help my mom in the kitchen. Periodically I check on Jake, but he seems to be holding his own. Barbara, Larry, Jules, Scott, and Charlie arrive, and I excuse myself to make introductions. Charlie is very excited to meet Jake and tells him everything he knows about sharks. Jake listens intently then asks him if he likes sports, and Charlie enthusiastically nods.

"Lexi told me there's a basketball net in the basement. Wanna go play?"

"Yeah!"

"You're a gem," jokes Jules as she helps herself to a glass of wine.

The boys go downstairs, and Jules and I help my mom put out the rest of the food. Just as we're about done, Tara arrives.

"Nice timing," I tell her.

"Sorry. I got a ride from Jordan, and she was late."

"Where's your friend?" asks Jules.

"He's not coming," she replies crossly. None of us go there. Tara is always having some kind of relationship drama. "Where's Jake?" she asks me.

"Downstairs with Charlie. Come on. I'll introduce you." We head to the basement, and all the boys are playing a serious game of H-O-R-S-E. "Jake, I want you to meet my sister, Tara."

"Hi," he says, offering her a hug. "I've heard a lot about you."

"Same here. All terrible things of course," she teases him.

"I don't doubt it. Wow, you guys have such a strong resemblance."

"You think so?" Tara says.

"Aside from the hair, yes."

Tara's hair is lighter than mine, with rich caramel highlights. Whereas mine is long, she wears hers in a stylish bob.

"I'm the older and wiser one," I tell him.

"You've definitely got the older thing going for you," Tara replies. Then she turns her attention back to Jake. "So you and Lexi work together. How's that going?"

"We actually don't see each other that much at work. I travel a lot to our office in California."

"So it's working out well," I say jokingly.

"What about you?" Jake asks her. "How do you like working with your mom?"

"I really enjoy it. My mom is a brilliant designer, and I'm learning a lot from her. I'm still finishing up getting my degree, so I only do it part-time."

"So it's working out well," I say again. Tara gives me a look. "What? I thought I was being funny." We're interrupted by my mom calling everyone to dinner.

We'll be sitting in two separate rooms. Even though I'm a grown adult, I'm usually at the kids' table in the kitchen. It appears that Jake has influence because he and I have graduated to the dining room. We're sitting with my parents, Barbara, Larry, Aunt Sandra, Uncle Larry, and Doug. He's in by default. They all ask Jake a lot of questions.

"Give him a chance to eat," I joke.

"I'm fine," he tells me.

To give Jake a break, I ask Doug about his job prospects. When there's a pause in the conversation, Jake turns to my mom and says, "Everything is delicious. I can see where Lexi gets her cooking skills."

"I don't know about her cooking, but wait until you taste her cobbler," she tells him.

"I'm very much looking forward to it. I actually helped her make it."

"Really?" asks my aunt.

"Well, I peeled the apples, but I consider that participating in the process."

Everyone laughs. After the meal I help my mom clear the table, and Jake heads into the family room with the men to watch football. I'm glad he seems to be fitting in, though I wasn't that worried. I was most concerned about my dad. He seems to like Jake, but I sense a hesitation. I pull him aside and ask him what he thinks.

"He seems like a nice young man. He has a good head on his shoulders, and he treats you well. And he obviously makes you happy. I haven't seen you glow like this in a long time."

"Thanks, Dad. He does make me happy."

"That's all I want for you," he says. "I just don't want to see you get hurt like you were with Ben."

"I know, and I really hope this works out. I actually think he and I are a better match. Our relationship is built on common interests and ambitions versus just a shared history."

My dad considers this and says, "Just follow your heart, and the rest will work itself out."

There's a knock at the door, and in walks my Uncle Steve with Ryan. Tara rushes over to hug them.

"Where are Jonathan and Andrew?" she asks.

My uncle shrugs apologetically. "They decided now that they're both engaged they had to split time between the two families. I'm afraid it's just the two of us."

"We're happy to have you," my mom says, giving Steve a warm hug.

I find Jake and bring him over. "Uncle Steve, Ryan, this is my boyfriend, Jake." They all shake hands, and I tell Jake he's lucky to have escaped the line of questioning from Jonathan. "He's a tough negotiator, and he'd have drilled you."

"I can stand in for him," Ryan jokes.

"On that note I think it's time for dessert," my dad says.

We all head into the kitchen, and Ryan holds me back. I motion for Jake to go ahead. "Lookin' good, cuz."

"Thanks, you too."

"I just wanted to see how things are going with the new guy."

"Really good. I guess he's not so new anymore. I just hadn't introduced him to anyone yet. You know I'm kind of cautious these days."

"I know. You were in a very different place last Thanksgiving. I'm glad to see you happy again."

"I am happy."

"I could tell from your e-mails. Just let Jake know that if he screws things up, I'll kick his ass."

I laugh. "Why don't you tell him yourself?"

We head into the kitchen, and Ryan makes his way over to Jake. I decide to let Jake handle Ryan on his own. I fill my plate then head to the dining room and sit next to my Uncle Steve. He asks how my job is going, and I tell him about the cosmetics project and my work for the Make-A-Wish Foundation.

"That's my Lexi, always trying to save the world."

"Just one kid at a time," I tell him.

"You've always had a big heart. I'm glad you have someone to share it with," he says, nodding toward Jake.

"I hope I will after tonight. It looks like Ryan is giving him the third degree." I meet Jake's eye, and he gives me a reassuring smile. He and Ryan then head downstairs.

"We're going to shoot a game of pool," Jake tells me.

"Have fun."

I'm glad to see them getting along so well.

I help my mom clear the table and wash some of the dishes. "Thanks, Lexi. I appreciate the help, but you go enjoy yourself."

"Are you sure?"

"Yes, Dad and I will take care of it when everyone leaves."

I head to the basement and find Jake and Ryan engaged in an intense game of pool. "Who's winning?" I ask them.

"Jake," Ryan says in a mock bitter tone. "You didn't tell me he was a good pool player."

"I didn't know, but it doesn't surprise me. Jake is good at everything," I say, rolling my eyes. He smiles at me and holds my gaze as he sinks a ball into the pocket. "Show-off."

"Do you want to take my next shot?" Jake asks.

"Do you want to win?"

"Yes, but you can help even things up a bit for poor Ryan here."

"OK." I take the next shot and sink it in. Jake looks at me with a surprised expression. "What? You think I grew up with a pool table and don't know how to play?"

"You asked me if I wanted to win. I thought that meant you would put me behind."

"On the contrary," I tell him as I sink the next shot.

"I may as well leave," Ryan jokes. "Lexi is a hell of a pool player."

"Well, it looks like I still have more to learn about you too," Jake says.

"You two carry on. I'm going upstairs to find Charlie," I say.

I head upstairs and find him playing a game with Larry. "Can I join?"

"Sure, Auntie Lex. You can be on my team."

"OK, what are we playing?"

"Go Fish."

Jules comes over a short while later and informs Charlie it's time to go. I give him a big hug and tell him I'll see him soon.

"Wait!" he says. "I have to say good-bye to Jake."

"Oh, I'll go get him." I go downstairs and tell Jake that Charlie wants to say good-bye.

"I'll be right up. We're just about done with our game anyway." Jake comes upstairs and gives Charlie a big high five. "Thanks for playing basketball with me," Jake says. "Let's play again sometime."

"OK, you can come over with my Auntie Lex."

I look at Jake and ask, "Are you ready to go?"

"Whenever you are."

We say our good-byes, and Jake thanks my parents for having him.

"It was a real pleasure," my mom tells him.

On the ride home, Jake says, "You look happy."

"That's because I am. I think everyone really liked you." Out of the corner of my eye, I see him smile.

"And this surprised you?"

"Of course not. It was just nice having you there."

"Thank you for inviting me. I know how protective you are of your family."

"Jake, I know you've been wanting to meet them, and I've really wanted to introduce you. My parents were so disappointed when things didn't work out with Ben that I've just been cautious about introducing them to someone unless I knew for certain where it was headed. My dad once told me he didn't need to meet anyone unless I knew the guy was the one for me." I let the words hang there for a minute.

Jake takes my hand and brings it to his lips. "Lexi, I've known you were 'the one' for a while. I was just waiting for you to catch up."

I smile back at him as I let the words sink in. We drive home in comfortable silence, each of us lost in our thoughts. Now that Jake officially has met my family, I feel like the last piece of the puzzle finally has fallen into place. Well, almost the last. Now Jake just needs to tell his uncle about us. Why do I have a nagging feeling that's easier said than done?

CHAPTER TWENTY-THREE

After Thanksgiving the office is abuzz with news of the holiday party. Everyone is trying to guess this year's theme and where the after party will be. Apparently they always pick a hot, trendy place. As excited as I am about my first Hartman & Taylor holiday party, my attention is focused on preparing for a presentation to Aura's senior management at the beginning of next week. We're sharing our ideas for the name of the cosmetics line, our campaign idea, and promotional launch strategies. This is our chance to nail the account, so everything has to be exactly right. I meet with Simon to review the work. It took a bit of coaching, but I'm really happy with the end result. Simon and I are flying to Boston on Friday to meet with Eric, who wants to review everything one final time and prepare a joint presentation. His reputation is on the line because it was his sole decision to bring us in and not put out an RFP. As such, he has a vested interest in making sure we look good so he looks good. The meeting is on Monday, so I expect we'll be working the whole weekend. I tell Jake not to bother coming home from San Francisco, and I'll see him the following Friday.

"Actually I have good news," he says. "I don't have to go back to San Francisco until January. We just wrapped up a pitch, and with the holidays coming, things are quieting down."

"Jake, that's awesome. I'm looking forward to finally being in the same city as you for an extended time. Although it figures that when you're coming home, I'm leaving."

On Friday, Simon and I head to Boston to meet up with Eric. He and I have a very good working relationship, but it's a grueling weekend. Eric wants to make the presentation very corporate, whereas Simon and I are used to telling a story that leads up to the big reveal. We end up compromising and decide Eric will do a lot of the upfront introduction. Simon tells him he can weave in as many charts and as much data as he wants as long as he has free reign over the creative portion. Eric agrees, so Simon and I focus on perfecting our story. Once it's in a good place, we review it with Eric on Sunday night. He has a few suggestions, and then he shares his portion of the deck with us. All the content is locked, but it takes me a while to format the deck so it all looks the same and has a unified voice.

Simon and I don't get back to our hotel until after ten. "We're ready," he assures me before we part ways. I know we're ready; I just hope Aura likes the campaign. I have a lot riding on this too.

We start at 8:00 a.m. sharp the next morning. We have ninety minutes to present our work followed by a half-hour Q&A session. I was expecting the meeting to be more of a discussion, but it's very formal, and the executives don't engage in any kind of dialogue about the work as Simon is presenting. I can't read the room, and I really wish Jake were here. The CEO is present, and I feel out of my element. It's really Eric's meeting, and he does a good job setting the stage for why our work is the right approach. Simon is very dynamic, and I interject a comment here and there, but it's his show. When it comes time for the Q&A, most of the questions are about our fee. I share our approach and discuss how we'd structure the team. They thank us for our time, and then the meeting is over. Eric walks us to the elevators and tells me he'll be in touch.

"How do you think it went?" I ask Simon.

"Swimmingly."

"Seriously?"

"Your guess is as good as mine. It was a tough crowd."

"I know," I tell him. "It's like they all had poker faces. I don't get it. This wasn't a pitch, so why couldn't they engage in more of a discussion and give us feedback?"

"It is a pitch, in a way. We're just pitching against ourselves."

"Well, in that case, I hope we win."

We head to the airport, and my cell phone rings while we're at the gate. "It's Eric," I tell Simon. I take a deep breath and answer. "Hi, Eric. I hope you're calling with good news."

He's silent for a minute then says, "They loved it. They're buying your first idea—as is."

Oh, my God. He fills me in on the conversation after we left the room, and I hang up, stunned.

"What? The suspense is killing me."

"They're buying our first idea. They want to put us on retainer immediately."

Simon smiles at me. "I guess I'm looking at Hartman and Taylor's next vice president."

On Tuesday morning a company-wide e-mail goes out with news of our cosmetics win. The agency is throwing a special happy hour to celebrate. I haven't seen Jake yet, so he and I plan to go down for a few drinks then meet up and have a celebratory dinner. At five I head downstairs with Nicole and hang out with her and Courtney for a while. I work the room, talking with my creative team then Simon.

"How are things going?" he asks me.

"Good, really good. I'm still on a high. What about you?"

"Same here. Winning never gets old."

"Cheers to that," I say as we clink glasses.

"I'm glad we got to work on this project together. I feel like I hardly see you anymore. Just because you're practically married, you can still stop by and see me from time to time," he says a bit haughtily.

"I'm sorry. I haven't been intentionally neglecting you. And who said anything about marriage?"

"You don't have to. I can see the writing on the wall. Haven't you two discussed it?"

"Not in so many words," I tell him. "Maybe he doesn't want to bring it up because of what happened with Ben."

"Do you still believe in marriage?"

"Yes, absolutely."

"Do you want to be married to Jake?"

I glance over to where I see Jake standing and say, "Yes, without a doubt. I've been thinking about it a lot lately, and it's absolutely what I want. I've been hoping he'll bring up the subject, but he hasn't, and it's not going to come from me."

Never in a million years would I have thought I'd be ready to commit my life to someone less than a year after my previous engagement. In a way I think Jake is more right for me than Ben ever was. I loved Ben and think we would have had a great marriage, but as I told my dad, a lot of our relationship was based on a shared history. With Jake everything we built was from the ground up, and we formed such a strong bond in a short time. He always encourages me to share my feelings and is very open with me. I feel I can tell him anything. He probably knows me better than I know myself. If Ben hadn't cheated and I had to go back and choose again, I'd choose Jake.

Our eyes meet across the room, and he gives me a slow, sexy smile. I don't think there ever will come a day when I don't find him utterly attractive. He's finishing up his conversation, so I make my way over to where he's standing. We have a rare moment alone together.

"Hi, Mr. Hartman. How's it going?" I ask coyly.

"Good, Ms. Winters."

"Any big plans for this evening?"

"As a matter of fact, I have a hot dinner date," he says.

"Really? I hadn't heard you were seeing anyone."

"Oh, yes. It's quite serious."

"Really? I happen to be seeing someone too."

"Oh, what's he like?"

"Smart, successful, and extremely sexy."

"Lucky girl."

"I am," I say, touching him lightly on the arm.

"And I'd say he's one lucky guy. You're looking mighty fine these days," he says, eyeing my dress.

"Jake," I admonish, "don't you know it's inappropriate to leer at a co-worker?"

He leans in closely and says, "If you think that's inappropriate, wait until I get my hands on you later. It's taking all my willpower not to do inappropriate things to you right here, right now."

The color rises in my face as I whisper in his ear, "The more inappropriate, the better."

He smiles at me, and I glance over at the bar and see Michelle watching us. I motion for her to come over. "What are you guys talking about so intently?" she asks.

"Lexi was just telling me about her boyfriend."

"I've heard a lot about this mystery boyfriend. I'm dying to meet him." Michelle looks at us closely and says, "If I didn't know any better, I'd say you two were dating." I see Jake looking uneasy.

"What makes you say that?" I ask, trying to laugh it off.

"I don't know. You two just seem very comfortable with each other."

I try to think of a reply, but Jake jumps in. "No, we're definitely not dating. Just good friends. You obviously would have heard about it if we were together. And besides, Lexi is far from the type of girl I typically date."

I open my mouth to say something but then close it. I'm rendered momentarily speechless. I'm so furious that I need to leave this situation before I say something I'll regret. I look at my watch. "Well, I should be going. I don't want to keep my date waiting. See you, Michelle, Jake," I say, giving him a curt nod. I storm out of the bar. It's one thing not to tell people about us, but it's another to blatantly lie about it.

I head home, stewing, and think of what I plan to say to Jake. Twenty minutes later, I hear a knock. It's interesting that he didn't use his key. I open the door and motion for Jake to come inside. He knows I'm pissed. I don't say a word; I'm too angry to speak.

"Look, she totally caught me off guard," he says, trying to placate me. "I didn't know what to say."

"Well, you didn't have to lie about it. You keep saying you plan to come clean about us. You had your chance, and you chose not to act on it."

"With Michelle? You think she's going to be the first to know?"

"Well, no, but you haven't told anyone else now, have you? I'm beginning to think you never had any intention of going public about us." Suddenly I feel like a naïve mistress who keeps believing her lover when he tells her he's going to leave his wife. In the end, though, he never does. "Are you ashamed of me?" I ask quietly.

"God, no! Why would you think that?"

"What do you expect me to think? I could understand you not wanting to tell anyone in the beginning, but I don't understand what the issue is anymore."

"I thought it would be best for us…and for you."

"Don't make this about me, this is your issue, not mine."

"I just—" Suddenly his cell phone rings. He looks at it and silences the call. "Lexi, I don't want you to have to take the fallout."

"I'm OK with it. I don't care if people know." He looks skeptical. "Look, Jake, I love you. But I can't do this anymore. I'm tired of worrying about who might see us when we're in public together, and I'm tired of worrying about letting something slip with my friends at work. I can't share things with them like a normal person. I'm sick of keeping secrets. And I shouldn't have to." I'm interrupted by his cell phone ringing again.

He looks at it and says, "It's my uncle again."

"It sounds urgent. You should take it."

"I'll just be a minute." I wait while he finishes his conversation. "Hi. Sorry. I was in the middle of something. What? You said it wouldn't be until at least after the holidays." He walks into the other room; he seems panicked. A few minutes later, he comes out of my bedroom and tells me, "I have to deal with something. This conversation isn't over. I'll call you later." With that he walks out the door.

I'm stunned. Did he seriously just leave in the middle of our conversation to take care of something for his uncle? I'm pissed all over again. I pace around my apartment for a while, too antsy to do anything. Eventually I make myself dinner even though I'm not hungry. I shower and see that it's almost nine, and I still haven't heard from Jake, so I decide to go to bed.

He calls a half hour later, but I ignore it, and then I turn off my phone. Let him worry. I'll deal with him tomorrow.

I toss and turn all night, unable to sleep. When my alarm goes off, I feel groggy. I accidentally fall back asleep, and when I wake up, it's eight fifteen. Crap. I hate being late. I check my phone and see I have two missed calls from Jake. I figure we'll talk things over tonight; it's best not to get into this kind of conversation before work, and I don't want to be rushed. Sometimes I'm better at expressing my feelings by writing things down. I'm about to e-mail him my thoughts when I see an invitation for a mandatory meeting at nine—shit, the one morning I'm running late. I do a quick body shower then rush out the door. My cell phone rings, and it's Jake again. I hit "ignore."

Just as the meeting is about to start, I arrive. It's a packed house. Jake is up front, looking very uncomfortable. Our eyes meet, and I look away. Bill is there, which is unusual. I wonder if we had a major new business win—or loss. Perhaps he's here to share the news of our cosmetics victory, but it's a small project that doesn't seem to warrant his presence.

Everyone quiets down as Bill starts speaking. "Thank you all for coming on such short notice," he says. "I have some exciting news to share with you. Over the past year, Hartman and Taylor has been on a hot streak. And I just got a call this morning from *Advertising Age* that we've been named agency of the year." The room erupts with cheers and claps. I now see there are bottles of champagne on the credenza behind him.

"Let's have a toast!" someone shouts.

"We will, but there's one more thing we have to celebrate. Much of our success is a result of the hard work of this man standing next to me," he says, as he clasps Jake's shoulder. "Now that our office is in a good place, we need his talents where they'll be most useful. I'm pleased to announce the promotion of Jake Hartman to president of Hartman and Taylor, San Francisco." There's a thunderous round of applause. I stand there stock-still, unable to look at him. Bill continues, "Although we'll miss him, he's already made such progress in helping the office get off the ground. It just made sense to have him based there permanently."

I feel as though the bottom has just dropped out from under me. I finally meet Jake's gaze, and he's looking at me with a pleading expression. I break eye contact and can think of nothing but my escape. Thank God I was late for the meeting and grabbed a spot by the door so I can make an early exit. Jake is held up by people congratulating him, so I run back to my office and grab my purse and coat. I make a beeline for the elevator and press the "down" button insistently, willing it to come. The doors open, and I head inside to safety.

"Lexi, wait!" Jake calls as he hastily makes his way toward the elevator. I quickly push the "lobby" button. Our eyes meet as the doors close, but it's difficult for me to read his expression through my haze of tears.

I run outside and let the crisp, cold air fill my lungs. A light snow has begun to fall, and I realize I'm still wearing my heels. I don't bother changing into my boots because I want to get a head start before Jake chases after me. I try not to think as I walk, instead focusing on putting one foot in front of the other. It's all I can do to make it home. A biting wind stings my face, but I hardly feel it; I'm numb down to my core. When I get to the lobby, I give Roland strict instructions that he isn't to let Jake or anyone else up to my apartment. He sees my face and nods his understanding, not saying a word. I walk into my apartment and close all the blinds, relishing in the darkness and trying to shut out the world. I send a quick e-mail to my team, letting them know I went home sick. Then I turn off my ringer and lie in bed for I don't know how long. It could be minutes, hours. I feel such a complete sense of betrayal. How could Jake do this to me? I've felt this way once before and vowed to never let it happen again. I'm so angry with myself for giving in. I tried to protect myself; I really did. I kept Jake at an arm's distance for so long, but he was very convincing. I really thought it was different this time. He knew how much I valued the truth above all else, so in a way, his betrayal is worse than what happened with Ben. I'm awoken from my reverie by a recording on my answering machine. I should have turned that off too. It's Roland calling to tell me Jake's here. I pick up mid-message and say, "I don't want to see him."

"I've told him that, but he won't leave. He said he'll wait."

"Well, tell him he'll be waiting a long time, because I'm not coming down!" I angrily stab at the "off" button and slam the phone back into its cradle. I'm overcome with emotion and sob into my pillow; eventually I fall asleep from exhaustion.

I hear someone stirring, so I open my eyes. I see that it's dark outside. I bolt upright, fearing Roland decided to let Jake in.

"It's only me," says Liv. "I came to check on you."

"How did you know?" I ask her.

"Simon called me." I nod. "Oh, Lexi," she says, enveloping me in a hug, which just brings on a fresh wave of tears. "Do you want to talk about it?"

I shake my head. "I just don't understand how this happened…again."

"What do you mean by 'again'?"

"I opened my heart to someone," I tell her, "only to have it shattered to pieces. I know I was able to do it before, but I don't think I can get past another heartbreak," I sob. It feels like someone took a knife to my chest, slicing open my scars, revealing my deepest fears. And all that remains is emptiness. When I reflect on the progress I've made rebuilding my life over the past year, I now realize it was all a facade. All it took was one simple blow to have it come undone. Suddenly I feel panicked, and all the feelings I had when I found Ben with Claire crash down on me.

"Lexi, take a deep breath. I'm going to get you a glass of water." She comes back and makes me take a sip. I shakily accept the glass to placate her. "So you had no clue?" she says.

"Absolutely none. I found out just like everyone else. I was blindsided. How could he make a decision like this without talking to me first?"

"I'm sure he has an explanation for what happened. I know he loves you, and I can't imagine he'd do something like this intentionally. It doesn't make sense."

"I know, but he did."

"You have to talk to him."

"I know, and I will."

"Lexi, I mean it. For a long time you tried to hide from dealing with the fallout from Ben. And look where that got you. You need to deal with this."

"I will, I promise. I just need some time to absorb it."

"OK. Have you eaten anything?" I shake my head. "I brought Ben and Jerry's Chocolate Fudge Brownie ice cream," she says, trying to tempt me.

"Thanks. I'll have some later." I can tell she's worried; I never turn down Ben and Jerry's.

"Do you want me to stay?" Liv asks.

"No, that's OK. I'd rather be alone."

Instead of leaving, she crawls into bed next to me. I'm happy to have the company.

I stay home the next two days, not leaving my apartment. I call into work and say I have a bad virus, which in a sense, I do. I can't eat; I can hardly sleep; and I feel terrible. I look terrible too—my eyes are red rimmed and puffy from crying, and my hair is a limp mess. I haven't had the energy to shower; I haven't had the energy to do much at all. My phone rings, but I don't bother to answer it. I haven't checked my phone or listened to any of my messages since the announcement about Jake's promotion. I don't feel like talking to anyone. I scroll through my call log and see I have seventeen missed calls from Jake, three from Simon, and one from my mom.

I take a deep breath and call my voice mail, which informs me my mailbox is full, and I should erase all unneeded messages. The first one is from Jake on Monday night, after our fight. "Lexi, I really need to talk to you. Please call me as soon as you get this." The next one says pretty much the same thing. Then there's one from Tuesday morning, the day of the announcement. "Lexi, it's urgent. Please call me." The rest are his apologizing and begging me to call him back. In his last message, he sounds like he's crying. "These past few days have been unbearable. I feel lost without you. I love you so much. Please talk to me." I realize I've never seen Jake so vulnerable before; I've always thought of him as the strong one. If it's possible, my heart breaks even more. Then I check my answering machine, and I have a couple messages from the front desk. I call downstairs, and Roland seems happy to hear from me.

"Miss Lexi, I was concerned about you. You have a bunch of deliveries. Should I send them up?"

"What are they?"

"They appear to be flowers."

"No, I don't want them. Feel free to give them to other residents or throw them out." Flowers aren't going to cut it. I won't accept any kind of gift as a peace offering.

Finally, on Thursday, I decide I'm ready to talk to Jake. Unlike with Ben, I need to know what happened. I assume Jake is at the office, so I send him a text message.

> Me: *I'm ready to talk. Let me know if you can stop by on your way home.*

I get an immediate response.

> Jake: *I'll be there in twenty minutes.*

I take a look in the bathroom mirror and attempt to do something with my lifeless hair. I decide it's hopeless, so I throw on a black, cable knit hat and go downstairs. I wait out front so I won't have to bring him up to my apartment. I don't trust myself alone with him and need to stay strong. I watch him as he approaches. He looks terrible. He's usually so clean-cut, but he looks like he hasn't shaved in days, and he has dark circles under his eyes.

"Hi," he says quietly, studying my face.

"Hi. Let's take a walk."

We find a bench, and I sit down. Jake sits next to me and takes my hand. "Lexi, I'm so sorry. I didn't mean for you to find out this way. I tried telling you on so many occasions, but something always seemed to come up. That night Ben showed up, I intended to discuss it with you. I had a big dinner planned, and I was going to ask you to come with me. And even before that, I planned on telling you, but then you shared the news of your pending promotion, and I didn't want to do anything to jeopardize your career. I knew you wouldn't be able to start up a new account if you moved with me. So I was waiting for the right time, and I hoped that once you were established in your new role, it might be a possibility for you to transfer. Things weren't supposed to happen for another few months at least. But then Bill called and said there were some political issues going on, so they want me there right away. I tried calling you before the announcement, but you were mad at me and didn't pick up your phone. The last thing I ever wanted to do was hurt you. I love you so much, and it kills me knowing that I did." He looks at me, waiting for me to say something.

I'm quiet for a minute, taking in his words. "You say you love me, but you don't."

"What are you talking about? Lexi, you're the love of my life."

"No," I say with more force than intended. "You may think you're in love with me, but you aren't. When you love someone, you want to shout it from the rooftops, not hide it. When you love someone, you treat her as a partner, an equal. You don't go making life-altering decisions like deciding to move halfway across the country without discussing it. Yes, you were going to tell me, but that implies you already made the decision. When you love someone, you don't lie."

Jake cuts me off. "Lexi, I've never lied to you."

"You omitted the truth. That's the same thing as lying. What makes it worse is it sounds like you've known about this for a long time. I know you were scared, but if you had asked me to move with you, I would have said yes." He looks at me, and I can see there's hope in his eyes. "Jake, I love you, but I can't be with you. Not after this."

"Please don't throw what we have away," he pleads. "You once said we were perfect together. We still can be."

"Jake, there's no such thing as perfection."

"Look, I know I should have told you sooner, discussed it with you. But it's not like I wasn't planning on telling you. Believe me, I was."

"Just like you were going to tell Bill about us? The fact is that you didn't, in either case. Do you know how it felt, sitting in that conference room with all those people and learning that you'd be moving to a new role in a new city—without me? I never should have found out that way. You, of all people, should know how important honesty is with me."

"I know that. I don't know how to apologize enough. Tell me what I have to do to make it up to you."

I look at him sadly. "There's nothing you can do. I've felt this certain once before, and that was when I caught Ben cheating on me."

"Please don't compare me to Ben. I'm nothing like him."

"You're right," I say, "although you have one thing in common: You both broke my heart. And it hurts that much worse the second time around." He looks so pained as I say the words. I stand up, and he stands too. Then I give him a long kiss on the lips. "Good-bye, Jake." He stands there looking shocked.

"Lexi, wait." He takes my hand, but I pull away. "Please," he begs. I turn and walk back toward my building, away from our past and toward an uncertain future. "This isn't over," he yells after me.

But in my mind it is. I will myself not to look back, but I can't help it. I turn around, and he's standing there, with his hands in his pockets, staring at me with a look of despair. I thought I couldn't shed any more tears, but they relentlessly fall.

CHAPTER TWENTY-FOUR

Later that evening I get a call from Simon. He seems surprised when I pick up the phone. "Lexi, thank God! I haven't heard from you in days and was getting worried. I had visions of finding you passed out in a drunken stupor with Katy Perry's 'Wide Awake' playing on repeat."

I manage a small smile. "I'm here, sober as can be."

"We've got to do something about that. But seriously, are you OK?"

"No, but I will be. I know the drill. I've done this before."

He sighs. "So you had no clue?"

"None. Did you know?"

"No, I honestly didn't. I thought Jake was a shoo-in to run our office one day. Maybe this is a starting point for that. Have you talked to him?"

"Earlier today. He apologized profusely and said he was going to tell me, but I told him what he did was unforgiveable."

"Is it?"

"Why would you even ask me that?"

"Look," Simon says, "I know you're hurting right now, but do you honestly think he wouldn't have told you?"

I think back to the times Jake said he wanted to discuss something with me. It's true that things came up, but there were plenty of other opportunities; he just chose not to act on them. I feel so betrayed. "It would be hard for me to move past this," I tell Simon.

"I understand, but you and Jake are so good together. A match like yours doesn't come around often. Are you sure you want to give up so easily?"

I've been pondering this very question for the past few days. I know I said I don't believe in soul mates, but I do. I just didn't want to admit that

I was wrong when I thought I'd found mine in Ben. I know that now. Can I give up on the one person I'm meant to be with?

"Simon, I know it may not seem like what Jake did was as bad as what Ben did, but he of all people knows how much I value honesty. He's broken my trust, and that's hard to repair. So I'm not saying never—just no to right now."

"That's fair," he says. "Do you want to meet up for a drink?"

"No, I'm not up to going out."

"Well, you'd better get ready because tomorrow is the holiday party."

"I'm not going."

"Lexi, you have to."

"I don't have to do anything," I say flatly.

"Let me rephrase that. I think you should go. It's the agency's event of the year, and you shouldn't miss out on account of Jake."

"I'm not ready to face everyone."

"First of all, no one else knows aside from Nicole and me. And second, you have to go back to work sometime—like Monday for instance."

"I need the weekend to regroup," I tell him.

"OK, I wanted it to be a surprise, but they usually announce senior-level promotions at the party. You've worked so hard—you should be there when your name is called."

I consider this for a moment. "All right, I'll go. But I'm leaving right after the show."

"Deal. I'll escort you there personally so you don't have to go alone."

"Thanks, Simon. You're a good friend."

The next morning Simon knocks on my door at 8:00 a.m. sharp. "I've brought reinforcements," he says. He hands me a cup of coffee then opens the door. He's brought my hairdresser, Marco.

"Marco, it's good to see you!" He gives me a sympathetic smile and envelops me in a hug. Tears prick my eyelids, so I quickly pull away. "What are you doing here?" I ask.

He studies my limp hair and says, "Simon thought you could use my services." I look at Simon questioningly.

"Well, if you're going to see Jake, you may as well look good."

"Simon, I said I'd go, but I don't plan to see or talk to Jake. I agreed to this because there'll be hundreds of people there, so he'll be easy to avoid. I'm making my appearance to put in some face time, and then I'm leaving."

"Fine, but should you happen to run into him, let him know what he's missing."

Marco jumps in. "Why don't you go wash your hair, and I'll blow you out."

"OK. I'll be right back."

This is probably Simon's diplomatic way of telling me I need to take a shower. I let the warm water wash over me and close my eyes, feeling its soothing effects, wishing it also could wash away my sorrow. I quickly shampoo and condition my hair then throw on a robe and take a seat at the kitchen table, where Marco has set up shop. As he works on my hair, I decide there's something therapeutic about it.

"How should we style it?" he asks.

"Honestly I don't care. Do whatever you want."

"Well, what are you wearing?"

"I haven't given it much thought."

"Come," Simon says, taking my hand. He opens my closet and rifles through my clothes. "What about a dress?"

"Fine. I'll wear that black one." It suits my mood.

"Let me see it," says Marco. Simon pulls it out of the closet and lays it on the bed. It's a short, fitted, A-line dress with flowing, sheer chiffon sleeves; it has sort of a vintage look to it. "I love it," says Marco. "We'll do a retro look for your hair."

"Fine," I say.

Honestly I don't really care, but I don't want to be rude. For the next twenty minutes, Marco fusses over my hair then holds up a mirror. He's done a deep side part with very soft, loose curls. "It's beautiful," I say, and give him a smile that doesn't quite reach my eyes. I go to grab my wallet from my purse, but he shoos my hand away.

"This one's on me," he says. Normally I'd protest, but I don't have the energy.

"Thank you," I reply as he envelops me in a big hug.

"Go finish getting ready, and let me see how you look."

I go to the bathroom and apply my makeup, trying my best to cover up the dark circles under my eyes. I slip on the dress and look at myself in the mirror. It's funny how I look the same, but everything is different. I want to put my pajamas back on and crawl into bed. I'm really not ready to face everyone; I've never been a good liar, and it'll be hard to put on a brave face.

Simon must sense my hesitation because he comes in. "You look breathtaking," he says. "But you need some jewelry." I nod toward my box on the dresser. He goes through it and produces a delicate, long, layered silver necklace. Then he hands me my Tiffany heart bracelet. "For good luck," he says.

"I won't wear it now that it has Jake's initial on it. Yet another thing he's taken from me," I say bitterly.

"Lexi," Simon says, "I'm a firm believer that people make their own luck. You're not lucky because of some bracelet. You're lucky because you've always gone after what you wanted, and good luck has followed." I don't want to argue, so I hold out my wrist. As he slips it on he says, "Who knows? Maybe your luck is changing. Now come on. Let's go."

I look at Marco, who nods his approval and hands me my coat. I put on a pair of Christian Louboutin silver spiked pumps and grab my purse. Simon and I step outside, and the cool air feels good. "We should probably cab it," he says, looking at his watch.

We go back inside, and Roland puts the cab light on for us. He looks at me and says, "You look real pretty, Lexi." I smile at him, and he gives me a wink. A few minutes later, a cab pulls up, and Simon and I get in. Here we go.

Just as the show is about to start, we walk into the auditorium. It's packed, and I don't see any seats. We make our way toward the front, and I hear someone shout my name. "Lexi, over here," says Michelle. "How are you feeling?" she asks, her voice full of concern.

"Better, thanks." I manage a small smile. Simon and I take our seats. Crap, we're in the second row. So much for making an inconspicuous exit once the show ends. The lights dim, and Bill walks up to the podium and gives his opening remarks. I try to pay attention, but my thoughts keep drifting, and I find it hard to concentrate on what he's saying. I glance around and wonder where Jake is. I replay yesterday's conversation in my mind for what feels like the millionth time. The image of him standing there with that look of despair haunts me. Fresh tears threaten to fall, but fortunately a round of applause distracts me; Bill has finished speaking.

"Now I'd like to introduce our next speaker," he says. "He's someone who has helped recharge the agency and give it new momentum. Under his leadership, we've won seven new accounts this year, a record for the agency. He's a tremendous talent, and I'm proud not only of his accomplishments but also the man he has become. I give you our San Francisco office's president, Jake Hartman, to share his last New Business update." Everyone cheers as Jake walks onto the stage while I try to maintain my composure. He shakes Bill's hand, and then Bill pulls him into a hug. Jake then takes his place behind the podium.

I didn't know Jake would be speaking. I'm glad the lights are dim; I hope he can't see me. I stare at his familiar face, perhaps for the last time. I realize I don't even know when he's leaving. My heart aches, and I want to bolt out of the auditorium, but I don't want to make a scene. He looks so handsome in his black suit, and he's wearing the tie I picked out for him the day we went shopping at Bloomingdale's. I close my eyes to block him out, but it's no use; I know every contour of his face. I listen as he gives an update on the agency's success this past year. He's his usual charismatic self, but I can tell he's nervous. I don't think I've ever seen Jake nervous before, especially in this kind of situation, where he's in his element. Then he says, "I want to thank everyone for the well-wishes regarding my new role. As you can see, it's been a great year for me professionally. But it's also been a great year for me personally. You see, I fell in love with the most amazing woman." What? I open my eyes and sit up straighter in my seat. Jake continues, "She's passionate, warm, funny, whip smart, and beautiful, inside and out.

From the moment I met her, I knew she was special. She has an aura about her that draws people in." My mouth drops open in shock. I can't believe what I'm hearing.

I turn to Simon and whisper, "Did you know about this?"

He nods. "I may have known something about it. My job was to get you here, no matter what it took."

I grab his hand and squeeze it hard, attempting to calm my rapidly beating heart.

Jake goes on. "I'm sure you're all surprised to hear me saying this because, as you know, I'm a private person. And I like to keep my private life, well, private. But she makes me so happy that I want to shout it from the rooftops. And I owe much of my success to her because she's made me a better person. I wouldn't be where I am today without her support and encouragement. She challenges me like no one else and pushes me to think the impossible is possible. But I quite possibly screwed up the best thing that's ever happened to me. So I'm putting my transfer on hold. Yes, my career is very important to me, but she's more important. I'm doing what I should have done in the first place. I want to discuss it with her first and come to a decision together." I am shell-shocked. I can't believe Jake is putting his career on hold for me. Even with everything he's worked for, he's willing to put me first. In that moment, all my anger melts away, and I know I forgive him. Fresh tears roll down my cheeks. Simon hands me a tissue, which I gratefully accept.

"You probably all think I'm crazy," Jake continues, "but she never asked much of me other than truthfulness and for our relationship to be out in the open. You see, you all know her because she works here." I hear gasps from the crowd. "I didn't want anyone to know about our relationship—but not because I was embarrassed. That couldn't be further from the truth. I was just trying to protect her. I wanted her to feel she was successful on her own, not because she was dating me. That dynamic changes things, and like it or not, I thought people would think her achievements were a result of my influence. But I shouldn't have worried, because everyone knows she's a brilliant leader with a bright future here."

"Just tell us! Who is it?" someone shouts.

"Lexi Winters," Jake says.

I'm paralyzed in my seat. I can't believe he just told the entire company about our relationship. It's definitely out in the open now. There's a lot of chatter from the crowd, and someone yells, "Way to go, Lexi!" I feel my face burning.

"Lexi, will you please come up here?" Jake asks.

Suddenly, everyone is chanting my name. Jake scans the crowd, looking for me, and everyone around me points to where I'm sitting. He hops off the stage and makes his way over to me, taking my hand to lead me onto the stage. He says softly, so only I can hear, "I'm sorry if I'm embarrassing you, but this was the only way." He takes my hands and stares deeply into my eyes. It's as if we're the only two in the room. "Lexi, I'm so sorry. You've got to know I never meant for any of this to happen this way. As I said yesterday, I tried telling you a bunch of times, but something always seemed to come up. Believe me, I wanted to ask you to come with me on so many occasions, but I guess I was scared that you'd say no. I'm no longer scared of asking; I'm only scared of losing you. You once told me that if someone did something unforgiveable, you'd expect a big gesture. Well, here's mine."

I'm speechless. In my book his outing our relationship to the entire company is a big gesture. I can't believe he did that. I know how hard it must have been, but he did it for me.

"Just so you all know," he says, "this is something I already planned. I just hadn't planned to do it in such a public forum." Suddenly someone brings out a guitar and two stools. Jake motions for me to sit down. "Lexi always wanted me to play for her. Some of you know I was in a band, but not many people know I like to write songs." This is news to me. Of course I knew he played, but I didn't know about the songwriting. How did I not know this? I guess I still have more to learn about him. "I wrote a song for Lexi that I'll play for you now. It's something I've been working on for a while." He gives a nervous smile. "I've never played my own music for anyone before, so here goes nothing." Jake grabs a flask from his jacket pocket and takes a swig. Everyone laughs, including me. "The song is called, 'Forever with You.'"

Jake motions for me to sit on the stool beside him. My body tingles as I sit so close to him. Then he begins to sing.

> *Life was good; I was getting by.*
> *I didn't need anyone; I was flying high.*
> *When you walked in, my walls came crashing down.*
> *My love for you knows no bounds.*
>
> *And when we danced, there was no before,*
> *That life was over; you opened a door.*
> *You light my life like rays of the sun.*
> *My love for you has just begun.*
>
> *You intoxicate me like perfume, heady and sweet.*
> *I didn't have a chance; I admit defeat.*
>
> *Your taste, your touch—I want you so much.*
> *I want to spend forever with you.*
> *Know that my love for you is true.*
>
> *With your easy smile and quiet grace,*
> *You make my world a better place.*
> *You brought color to what was black and white.*
> *Now my world is filled with your light.*
>
> *You captivate me; my heart is whole.*
> *You have all of me, body and soul.*

Out in the Open

I want to drink you in, your taste so sweet.
I'll lay the world down at your feet.

I'll give you my heart and all that's mine.
I'll love you forever, 'til the end of time.

Your taste, your touch—I want you so much.
I want to spend forever with you.
Know that my love for you is true.

Life as I knew it is a thing of the past.
I've finally found a love to last.
As long as I have you and we're together,
I'll give you my heart; it's yours forever.

No matter the cost, whatever the stakes,
To the ends of the earth, if that's what it takes.

You've filled my life with love and laughter.
Let me be your happily ever after.
We're out in the open; I've nothing to hide,
All I want is you by my side.

Your taste, your touch—I need you so much.
I want to spend forever with you.
I want to spend forever with you.

My life is nothing without you in it.

I don't want to waste another minute.
I want to spend forever with you.
Say you'll spend forever with me too.

It's a beautiful song, and I can't believe Jake wrote it for me. No one in my life ever has made such a grand and romantic gesture. I watch him, mesmerized, knowing that everything with Ben was a prelude to this. All the pain and heartache led me to this moment, to this amazing man standing before me, who's baring his soul for all to see. *For me.* My heart is filled with such love that it overwhelms me. Suddenly he stops playing and motions for me to stand up. Then he takes my hand and gets down on one knee. I think I may faint. He sings softly to me, "I want you forever in my life. Make me so happy and be my wife." Then he takes a box from his jacket pocket and opens it. I can hardly see the ring because I'm blinded by the tears streaming down my face. "Lexi Paige, you've brought joy to my life that I never knew was possible. Will you make me the happiest man and marry me?"

I stare into his beautiful blue eyes and know this time it will be forever. "Yes," I say. "Yes, I'll marry you!" The crowd breaks out into thunderous applause. Jake grabs me and pulls me into a passionate embrace that leaves me breathless. As ecstatic as I am, I have to ask the obvious: "What about Bill? I can't imagine he's going to take this well."

"I talked to him last night. He gave us his blessing and told me what an idiot I am, which, of course, you already know."

We are interrupted by a familiar voice calling, and I see Liv and my family make their way toward us from the wings. Of course Jake thought to include them. He sees me looking in their direction and smiles.

"I wanted everyone you love to witness our engagement," he tells me.

"Of course you did. I take back what I said yesterday. There is such a thing as perfection. And he's standing right in front of me."

"No," Jake says, "I'm not perfect—we're perfect together." I smile at him and feel a warm glow that slowly spreads, radiating through me until it feels as if I'm lit from within. "So how does it feel?" he asks me.

"Which part?"

"Being out in the open."

"I feel…complete now that I have everything I've ever wanted. *You're* everything I've ever wanted. And now I can share you with the world, or at least our small part of it."

Jake kisses me again and, with his lips never leaving mine, lifts me into the air as the crowd of well-wishers descends upon us.

CRAVING MORE OF OUT IN THE OPEN?

You've heard Lexi's side of the story. Now get an exclusive look inside Jake's head and his reaction to their initial meeting. Visit jbglazer.com/bonus-chapters to download your free bonus chapters, written from Jake's perspective. Don't miss out on this exciting offer!

Want to hear more from the Winters sisters? Be sure to read on for a sneak peak of *I Should Have Said Yes,* a novel that follows Lexi's sister, Tara, on her journey to finding The One. Cameo appearances from Lexi and Jake included!

A Note from JB

THANKS so much for taking the time to read my book. It means a lot to me as I know there are plenty of options out there. *Out in the Open* is my first novel, and it's exciting, exhilarating, and also terrifying to bring your ideas into the world. As an advertising major, I've always loved the creative process. As much as I dreamed of writing professionally, I didn't think I had what it took to be a copywriter. So I went down the Account Management path because it still gave me an opportunity to be involved in the crafting and selling of ideas. Between work and my young kids, I was busy. Even after a long day, I'd have a hard time falling asleep. I carried my stress from the day with me to bed. Instead of counting sheep, I'd weave narratives. And I realized storytelling was my outlet to unwind.

One summer my husband decided to get his Series 7 license. Night after night, he'd disappear to the office to study. And I thought, if ever there was a time to get these ideas down on paper, this was it. So I started writing. My agency used to have a huge annual holiday party. It was very elaborate with some kind of stage show followed by a big themed bash. And I thought, how amazing would it be if someone proposed at the company party? That thought inspired the plotline for my book, and the rest is history.

Thank you to my husband Josh, for deciding to take that exam. If you hadn't, I'm not sure my book would have seen the light of day. And a shout out to my kids, Maddie and Dylan, for still napping so I could squeeze in more time to write. Thank you to my friends who read my manuscripts and have been my biggest cheerleaders. And to my extended family for supporting me along my journey and helping me to advertise. Even though I work in the industry, that's still the hardest part for me.

While I may not have been a copywriter, I guess I turned out to be a writer after all 😊 I love that books have the power to take people to another world, even if only for a little while. I've always read as an escape, and I hope I've provided that for you. It would mean a lot to me if you could spare a few minutes and share your review at the online store where you purchased from. I know many readers rely on them when choosing whether or not to take a chance on a new book. I love hearing from readers, so feel free to reach out via the "Contact Me" page on my website: jbglazer.com.
Xoxo,
J B

ABOUT THE AUTHOR

J B Glazer developed a love of writing at a young age. She followed that passion to the University of Illinois, where she graduated from the College of Communications. She pursued a career in advertising, a field that provided an outlet to express her creativity. In addition to being a marketer, she's a wife, mom, blogger, chauffeur, referee, short-order cook, maid, chocoholic, shopaholic, and multitasker extraordinaire. She's also an avid reader—Romance is her fave—and is inspired by authors like Colleen Hoover and

Nicholas Sparks. J B has a thing for big, dramatic endings because that's the fun of getting to happily ever after.

Visit www.jbglazer.com for random musings and other inspiration. You can also connect with J B in most of the usual places.
Twitter @JBGlazer
Facebook.com/jbglazer
Authorjbglazer@gmail.com

Read on for a sneak peek of
I Should Have Said Yes.

Available now!

THE INSPIRATION

I attempt to steal a nonchalant glance at my watch. I pick up a sugar packet and sprinkle it into my half-empty mug, giving me a chance to check the time. It's just about half past three. Thank God. My date continues droning on; it's hard to get a word in edgewise. "I'm so sorry to interrupt, but I've got to be going. I'm meeting with a classmate to discuss ideas for our theses."

"Oh, you're in graduate school? What are you getting your degree in?"

"Interior design." *You'd know if you had taken a moment to ask me anything about myself.*

"Wow. That sounds interesting." He starts peppering me with questions, and I try not to let my impatience show. Now I'm going to be late. And I hate being late. He's about to ask me something else, but I cut him off.

"Thanks for the coffee, but I gotta run."

"Nice to meet you, Tara. Text me if you want to meet up again."

"Yeah, sure." I give him a smile and delete his number the second I'm out the door. I quickly make my way a few blocks south to another coffee shop where I'm meeting my classmate Caitlin. This one is much more crowded, and I scan the room until I spy her sitting at a coveted booth. Flustered, I make my way to her table.

"Hi. Sorry I'm late," I say as I slide in across from her.

"No problem. Do you want to grab a coffee before we get started?" she asks, eyeing the reusable mug I've just set down.

"No, thanks, I'm not finished with this one yet."

"Let me guess, another coffee date?"

"Yep."

"Isn't that the third one this week?"
I shrug. "I think so, I've stopped counting."
"You date more people than anyone I know. What's your secret?"
"I say yes to anyone who asks me."
"Really? Why?" She looks at me curiously.
"It's a long story."
"I've got time."
It's because of goddamned D. J. Parker.

I'll never forget the first time I laid eyes on him. It was my third day as a high-school freshman. I was walking to third-period English with my friend Jordan when I realized I had left my book in my locker. Panicked, I dashed back to get it because I didn't want to make a bad impression my first week of class. In my haste to make it before the bell, I threw the book in my bag and attempted to zip it while I walked. And instead, I walked straight into the guy in front of me, causing both of us to stumble. He turned around to find out the responsible culprit, and my dark-brown eyes locked with his: a bright, brilliant blue. I was so mortified that I couldn't speak. He extended a hand to help me up, and I mumbled an apology.

"Hey, D. J., you'd better head to the gym. You were almost knocked out by a girl," one of his friends jeered. He looked into my flustered face and smiled at me, revealing a row of perfect, white teeth. I self-consciously closed my mouth, not wanting him to see my braces.

"You seem like you're in a hurry. You'd better get going or you'll be late to class." I didn't know if he was teasing me or being kind, but all I could do was nod as I hurried down the hall to safety. I slid into my seat just as the bell rang. As it turned out, there was no use in getting the book. All I could think about for the duration of our lesson was the dark-haired boy named D. J. with the bluest eyes I've ever seen.

"Hello, Earth to Tara," Jordan said during lunch.
"Sorry, what did you say?"

"I just wanted to know what you thought of Mr. Stern's tie. What's up with you?"

"Nothing. I like only made a complete fool of myself before English today."

"What happened?" She leaned in conspiratorially.

"I was rushing to get to class and barreled over a guy named D. J. Do you know him?"

"D. J., as in D. J. Parker?"

"I dunno. That's why I'm asking you."

"He's the only D. J. I know of. Hot, senior, student council member, soccer star. It must be the one."

Go figure, he had to be a senior. Like I even had a shot, not to mention his other stellar credentials. I was an average, uninvolved, awkward freshman who'd never been kissed. What are the chances he would ever take an interest in me? But I sure took an interest in him.

"So what happened? I assume you were wrong?" Caitlin looks at me expectantly, waiting for an answer. I've pondered this same question, replaying our relationship and that fateful day over in my mind, wishing for a different outcome.

"Let's just say we became friends, and I think we had a real shot at a relationship. But I ruined it."

"How?"

"We kissed once. A life-changing kiss that I still use as a basis of comparison. As in, does so-and-so's kiss measure up to D. J.'s? But when D. J. confronted me about it, wanting to know if the kiss meant anything, I said no. When in fact it meant *everything*. I was just too scared to admit it, and after I said the words aloud it was too late to take them back. I realized by his reaction it was the wrong answer—the hurt in his eyes told me he was hoping for something more. So the kiss of my dreams became my worst nightmare, and we never spoke again. And I was always left wondering, what would have happened if I had just said yes? Damn it! I should have said, 'Yes, it meant something.' To this day I still live with that regret. So I made a pact with myself that I would say yes from then on."

"Wow! Do you still think about him?"

"From time to time. I used to think he was just a crush, but I've come to realize that he was my first love."

"Where is he now?"

"I think he lives here in Chicago. I've looked him up on Facebook, but I don't think he has an account."

"Now you've got me all depressed. I hope you run into him someday so you can change the ending to your story."

"Me too. I'm a sucker for happily ever after."

"You should write a book about this stuff. Use him as your inspiration. You can talk about how an incident with a past love shaped the future course of your dating experiences. I wouldn't dwell on that too much, though. Your dates are so entertaining—they are the real highlight."

"You know, that's not a bad idea. I don't know that I have the drive or talent to publish a book—that's more my older sister Jules's territory—but I could create a blog." I'm always sharing funny anecdotes about my love life. Why not create a forum where I can share my tales of woe with friends and family?

When I get home I check out sites like Tumblr and WordPress and read up on the basics of blogging. After doing some research I decide to go with WordPress, sign up for an account, and choose a template. I surf the site for inspiration then spend hours customizing the design. I also create a screen name, which is how I'll show up to others when I like or comment on the site. I decide to go with "Unattached T." I think it has a nice ring to it, plus it encapsulates what my site is about: my life as a singleton. Now all that's left is to come up with a name for my site. I play around with a number of options, but I don't like any of them. So I decide to sleep on it. As I'm getting ready for bed, it hits me. When I was growing up we had a babysitter, Abby, who made up elaborate bedtime tales about a babysitter and her big adventures in the city. My sisters and I found her stories mesmerizing, and I couldn't wait for her to sit for us so I could find out what happened next. We told my mom about it one morning and she said, "You know, that sounds a lot like the movie *Adventures in Babysitting*." My mom rented it for us at our insistence, and it was a direct lift. But we never held it against Abby. I still relished those nights, huddled together under the covers in Jules's room, listening to Abby in her hushed voice relaying the next adventure. We had other babysitters since, but she was always my favorite. So I'll draw inspiration from my youth and call it: "Adventures in Dating." Satisfied, I send an e-mail to my friends inviting them to follow my updates. I immediately get a lot of replies about what a great idea it is and how they can't wait to live vicariously through my experiences. I guess I can add blogger to my résumé. This will be interesting.

I log off, and my thoughts drift to D. J. I think about him from time to time, but telling the story to Caitlin today stirred up many powerful memories. I can picture his face so clearly and wonder what he's doing now, and more importantly, if he's happy. As they say, your first love is the hardest to get over, and I don't think I've ever really gotten over D. J. Parker.

It's a Saturday morning, and I'm lounging around my apartment. I should be doing schoolwork, but I'm procrastinating. My cell phone rings, and I see that it's Jordan.

"What are you up to today?" she asks me.

"Not much. I have to get some work done for a project. What about you?"

"I'm going to the gym and have a free guest pass. I wanted to see if you wanted to come and then we could grab lunch."

"I don't know. I was planning on being productive today. Although I probably should get in shape considering Lexi's wedding is in a few months. Not to mention the fact that I'll be in a swimsuit." My sister Lexi and her fiancé, Jake, are getting married in Aruba. She was engaged once before and decided she wanted to keep things simple this time around and do a destination wedding. They went there on vacation together and fell in love with it. They'll have a reception here afterward because they're just inviting close friends and family, which suits me just fine. Now I'll have double the reason to celebrate. I'm really looking forward to the wedding, plus it will be like a mini vacation.

"Tara, just come with me to the gym."

"You know I hate working out around other people. Why do you think I have a stash of Jillian Michaels DVDs?" I've never liked working out in public. I'm a major sweater, plus my face gets beet red when I overexert myself. I just don't see a need to subject myself to the embarrassment.

"Please, just this one time. Who are you going to run into that we know?"

"I don't know, but why chance it?"

"If you come with me, I'll buy you lunch."

"What's the deal? Why do you want me to come with you so badly?"

"OK, there's this cute guy there. He's a personal trainer, and I haven't worked up the nerve to talk to him. If you come with me, I have an excuse. I can tell him you're interested in a membership and some training sessions."

"What do you need me for? Can't you just inquire for yourself?"

"I could, but they're too expensive. I'd feel weird asking him about it and then having to see him but never following through."

"OK, I'll do it just this once. For you. But you owe me."

"Deal, thanks. Meet me there at eleven?"

"Fine."

I throw on my gym clothes and then go in search of a headband. I can't find one so I pull my hair back into a tiny ponytail. I've had the same hairstyle for years—it's kind of my signature. In high school I used to have really long hair, but my freshman year in college I cut it into a graduated bob. The front hits just below my chin and it tapers shorter in the back. It's much easier to maintain, plus I love the sleekness of it. When I pull it back I notice my roots are growing in and sigh, knowing it's time for a highlight appointment. I swear that's where all my extra cash goes. I splurge and do it at the salon—I've tried doing it myself, but I like a specific caramel tone that's hard to replicate at home. I grab my gym bag and throw in an extra deodorant for good measure. Then I fill up my reusable water bottle, hook it on my bag, and I'm out the door. I don't see why anyone should buy plastic water bottles these days. It makes me enraged when I think of all that waste going into the landfills. And why pay for a natural resource when it's free and available? Last I checked, they have water fountains at most places, and many now come with a separate faucet where you can refill your bottle.

At 10:40 I hop on the Blue Line to meet Jordan at the gym. I live in Bucktown, an artsy Chicago neighborhood, but she recently moved to River North. When I arrive I see that she's waiting for me out front. We head inside and the woman at the front desk has me fill out some paperwork. I give a false e-mail address because I don't want to get on their distribution list.

"OK, let's go find your trainer," I tell Jordan. We do a lap but don't see him.

"Let's get a workout in and then we can look for him." Jordan goes off in search of a free elliptical machine. I decide that simple is best and mount a stationary bike. The seat is way too high for me, so I attempt to adjust it.

"Need a hand?" someone says over my shoulder.

I turn and there is a cute guy smirking at me. "Sure, that would be nice."

"How tall are you?"

"About five foot four on a good day."

He laughs and fixes the seat for me. "How's that?"

I try it out. "Much better, thanks."

"I'm Owen."

"Tara."

He takes a seat on a free bike next to mine. So much for not letting anyone see me sweat. I'll have to take it easy. We chat while we ride and he asks me a lot of questions about my workout routine. I notice that he's not the least bit winded even though he's set his bike to a high resistance.

Jordan spots me and mouths, "I found him." I say good-bye to Owen, and she says, "Twelve o'clock, by the water fountain."

I wait until he finishes refilling his water bottle so I can get a better look. "He's got a great ass," I tell her. When he turns around I say, "And a face to match. He's definitely cute. Do you know his name?"

"Nope. Let's go find out."

We make our way to the front desk, and I tell the woman I'm interested in signing up for personal training sessions. She gives me her standard spiel, but I tell her I have a bunch of questions that I'd like to address with him directly. "Hold on, let me see if one our trainers is available."

"Shit, I didn't think about the fact that they have a lot of trainers here," says Jordan. "Let's just hope he's free."

"It didn't look like he was working with a client," I respond. "And let's just hope it's a *he*."

Luckily, the woman comes back with Jordan's crush in tow. He introduces himself as Connor. I BS my way through what I'm looking for with the sessions. I ask for a rate and tell him I'll think it over.

"What about you?" he asks Jordan.

"I'd love to, but it's a bit out of my budget."

"That's too bad. You two can consider splitting a few sessions. Or I'd even make a special exception if you want to get a small group together."

"Thanks, we'll think about it," I tell him.

We say good-bye, and Jordan begs me to do the sessions with her.

"First of all, this gym isn't remotely close to my apartment. And secondly, I can't afford it either."

"I know." She sighs.

Just then, Owen comes over.

"Hey, Tara, are you leaving?"

"Yeah, I'm headed out."

"Oh, meet me back here on Thursday. Say, seven o'clock?"

"I'm actually not a member here."

"Don't worry about it. I can get you in as a one-time exception."

I'm about to say no, but then an image of D. J. flashes through my mind. I sigh and say, "OK, seven it is."

On the way out, Jordan says to me, "How is it that we came here looking for a guy for me, but you're the one that got picked up?"

"I don't know, luck, I guess. But you can come with me on Thursday. Maybe you'll run into Connor again."

"I would, but I don't want to crash your date."

I can't believe I agreed to a gym date. It's like my worst nightmare. I hate working out as it is, let alone having to do it with someone else. Not to mention my sweating issue.

I head into work the next morning and swing by Whitney's office, but she's not there. When I first started working here I never thought Whitney and I would be friends. She's the owner's daughter, and I was immediately intimated by her. She's five eight and very blond, and she always looks flawless. I can definitely pull myself together, but she's on another level. Our styles are also very different: she's classic whereas I'm more bohemian chic. Not hippyish—think Serena van der Woodsen on a budget. I'll admit it: I used to love *Gossip Girl* and was bummed when it went off the air. Anyway, I love mixing different pieces together and have a slight obsession with jeans and accessories. I make jewelry in my spare time—I actually find it very relaxing. Some people do yoga; I string beads. I think it's what landed me the job.

I work at Kellerman and Associates, an interior design firm specializing in the hospitality industry. I used to work for my mom's firm, but she felt it was important that I gain some outside experience as well. She's known Linda Kellerman for years and got me the interview, but the rest was up to me. Linda really liked my portfolio, but she couldn't get over my necklace. After I got the job I made her a similar one, and she's loved me ever since. She was overseeing an installation the day I started, so she asked Whitney to help me get settled. Whitney came to greet me from reception, and I remember feeling very inadequate even though I had a fresh haircut and highlights. She was wearing a fabulous Diane von Furstenberg patterned dress that I had seen recently in a Barneys catalog with a pair of strappy Jimmy Choo heels. Her blond hair was swept back in an immaculate low ponytail, revealing what looked to be five-carat diamond studs in each ear. And I noticed a ring on her left hand to match. I expected her to be elitist, but she was very nice to me. Once I got past the exterior, I discovered she's hilarious, wildly quirky, and not the least bit snobbish. I guess it's true that you can't judge a book by its cover. And she once revealed to me that she's jealous of my olive complexion. She has very fair skin that burns easily, so she's crazy about wearing sunscreen. I never would have guessed she'd ever find any of my qualities enviable, so it only goes to show that even those who seem like they have it all always want more.

Whitney's gone for a good portion of the day at a client meeting. I spend most of my morning looking for sustainable dining chairs. I find a ton of really cool options, but I'm also looking for comfort—people will be sitting in them for the duration of their meal, so there has to be a practical element. Whitney finally strolls in at two o'clock and I tell her about my gym date. Whitney is married but loves hearing all my dating stories. She tells me she's living vicariously through my experiences, although her husband absolutely adores her, so I have no clue why she'd want to relive the dating scene. I have a huge crush on her husband, Chip. He's your typical all-American boy, which is normally not my thing, but he's just so charming. He's very athletic and is involved in a number of sports leagues. Whitney keeps telling me to come to some of his games because there are a lot of eligible bachelors, as she likes to put it. I don't know why I haven't taken her up on her offer. I guess between work, school, and dating, I'm plenty busy, plus I really don't have a hard time meeting people on my own.

I leave work at five on Thursday so I have time to eat dinner and let my food digest before my big gym date. I pack a bag with extra clothes and some toiletries in case we go out to grab a drink afterward. I take the El to Downtown Fitness and realize I have no clue how I'm going to get in. I don't even have Owen's number, so I can't call to ask him. Worst case scenario, I'll get turned away, which wouldn't be such a bad thing. I walk in at seven on the dot, and Owen is waiting for me up front.

"Tara, you made it."

"I said I'd be here."

"Great, follow me."

"So what kind of strings did you have to pull to get me in?"

He looks at me, confused. "None. I just told them you were here for a trial class." Now it's my turn to be confused. "You do know I work here?"

he asks. And here I was thinking he was flirting with me when he was just trying to hit me up for business. I feel like a complete idiot. He leads me past all the equipment into a dance studio, where a small crowd of women await.

"Hi, Owen," they greet him.

"Hi, ladies. This is Tara. She'll be joining us tonight."

I give a small smile and wonder what the hell I've gotten myself into.

"So Owen talked you into coming, huh?" one of the girls says to me.

"Yeah, but what has he talked me into?"

She looks puzzled and says, "Boot camp."

What the fuck? This is an absolute nightmare. I contemplate leaving, but he blows a whistle and starts shouting instructions. He breaks us up into three small teams and informs us we'll rotate stations every three minutes. My group starts at the cardio station doing jumping jacks. This isn't so bad, I tell myself. The whistle blows, and we move to the resistance strength training area, which Owen is leading. I soon discover he is a drill sergeant, and he scares the crap out of me. He makes us do wall squats and expects us to hold it for the full three minutes. After about thirty seconds, my legs feel like Jell-O. My whole body starts trembling, and I finally give up.

"Tara, down and give me twenty."

"What?"

"You heard me."

I drop down and do the twenty pushups, working as slow as I can to shave time off the next station. He's on to me and tells me for that I can do twenty more. By the end of the class I worry that I may vomit. I haven't worked out this hard in a long time, and it feels like every muscle in my body is punishing me for it. I'm about to grab my things, but Owen stops me.

"You did great, Tara. Sorry I was hard on you, but we've gotta push people to their fullest potential. I hope to see you here next week at boot camp."

I'd love to tell him where he can shove his boots, but all I want is a long, hot shower.

"This was an enlightening experience. Thanks, but I think I've reached my full potential." I go to grab my bag, but I can't seem to find it. There is one that looks similar to mine and with a sinking feeling, I realize someone took my bag by mistake. My bag with my change of clothes, toiletries, and cash to get home. At least I had enough sense to keep my phone out. I go to the front desk and explain what's happened to a fresh-faced, perky girl wearing a staff shirt that's two sizes too small. She offers me a sympathetic smile as I launch into my tale of woe. She asks me to wait a few minutes because the other party may realize she grabbed my bag by mistake. Ten minutes later, it still hasn't shown up.

"I'm sorry, she must have gone to work out. Why don't you leave me your information, and I'll call you when it turns up." Great, an insane woman has my bag. What kind of person thinks she needs more exercise after doing boot camp? I call Jordan and tell her she has to pick me up.

"I'll be there in ten minutes," she says.

I stop in the restroom and glance at myself in the mirror, which was a mistake. There is sweat coming out of every pore, and my face is beet red. I splash cold water on my face and the back of my neck, cursing the bitch who stole my bag and my chance at a shower. Thank God there is no date with Owen; I don't think I've ever looked worse. To avoid further humiliation, I head outside and call Whitney because I know she'll appreciate the story. I recount the evening's events, which she finds very humorous. Perhaps I can laugh about it tomorrow.

"And then he said, 'Tara, drop down and give me twenty.'"

"Shut up; he said that?"

"Uh-huh, and I was like—"

"Tara? Is that you?" a male voice says.

I turn and look up into a very familiar pair of blue eyes. Brilliant, bright-blue eyes framed by dark, curly lashes. I watch his mouth as he says my name again, but I'm shocked into silence.

"Tara, I almost didn't recognize you."

I'll bet. A million thoughts are running through my mind, but I can't manage to get one word out. He smiles and says, "Remember me? D. J. Parker."

Like I wouldn't know those eyes anywhere. "D. J., hi! Whitney, let me call you back. I'm sorry. I didn't recognize you," I lie. He's even better-looking now than he was in high school. His dark hair is still a bit unruly, and I just want to run my fingers through it. He looks super sharp in a pinstripe suit, and then I notice his arm candy. I don't know how I could have missed her—tall, bronzed, and sophisticated, in a gorgeous white eyelet dress and dangerously high heels.

"Tara, this is Brynn," D. J. says. I'm about to extend my hand, but she gives me a smile instead. I realize she probably doesn't want to engage in any kind of contact with me. God, I pray I don't smell. Once again, I curse the bitch who stole my bag with my extra deodorant. "So do you live around here?" he asks me.

"Bucktown, actually. I was just meeting up with a friend for a workout. What about you?"

"I'm in the South Loop. I work at Boeing so it makes for an easy commute. This is actually my gym—do you belong here?"

"No, it was kind of a one-time trial class." Note to self, never come to this gym again.

"Oh, bummer. I've been hoping I'd bump into you one of these days." *Really?* I could be blushing, but my face is still so damn hot it's hard to tell. "So, what do you?" he asks me. "Wait, let me guess. You're an artist."

I smile at him. "Not quite. I'm working at Kellerman and Associates while I'm finishing up my master's. It's an interior design firm."

"It suits you. You were always so talented."

"Thanks. And why am I not surprised to hear you're at Boeing? You were always a genius."

He laughs, and I hear a beep, signaling Jordan's arrival. "That's my ride. Good to see you, and nice meeting you," I say to Brynn.

"It was great seeing you, Tara."

I get in the car and Jordan says, "What happened with Owen?"

"Forget about Owen. Do you know who I just ran into?"

"Who?"

"D. J. Parker."

"Seriously?" She offers me a sympathetic look.

In my countless fantasies of running into him, I was always wearing a fabulous outfit and looking my absolute best. Never in a million years would I have anticipated bumping into him under these circumstances. I pull down her visor and flip open the mirror. It's worse than I expected. When I rinsed my face, the water made my mascara run, so now I have raccoon eyes. "I must have been a terrible person in a former life," I wail.

Jordan tries to console me. "It's not that bad."

"Tell me, what could be worse?"

"You could've had a case of bad acne." I burst out laughing. "So what did he say?"

"I talked to him for all of two minutes. He lives in the South Loop and works for Boeing. And he was with an Amazonian goddess."

"Well, at least you know he lives here. That's been confirmed."

"I guess. But what are the chances I'll run into him again?"

"You never know. Perhaps you need to start frequenting some places near Boeing's offices. So I take it things didn't go well with Owen?"

I fill Jordan in on my night and thank her for bailing me out. We say our good-byes, and I let myself in. I take a hot shower, then turn the TV on and mindlessly flip through the channels, not absorbing what I'm watching. I can't believe that I ran into D. J. after all this time. And I can't believe that I ran into D. J. looking like a hot mess. I really wanted to catch up with him more, but I was so taken aback. And I guess the circumstances didn't call for it. I debate about pouring myself a strong drink. Instead I decide to channel my energy into writing my first blog post for *Tara's Adventures in Dating*. I brainstorm a few ideas, one of which is a true/false format for the headline. I like the idea of being nontraditional and having a consistent formula for each post, something unique that my readers can come to expect. A few drafts later, I've finally come up with a fitting introductory post.

True or false: I thought I was going to shake my booty on a fun night out, but instead I got my booty kicked at boot camp.

Welcome to *Tara's Adventures in Dating*! For those of you who know me, I go on a lot of dates. It's not because I'm especially gorgeous, rich, or famous, although I wouldn't mind being any of the above. I'll let you in on my secret: I say yes to any guy who asks me out. Now you're probably thinking, "She's desperate!" But here's the thing. When I was in high school I had a crush on someone, and in hindsight I think we had a real shot at a relationship. But I let my pride and, above all, fear, get in the way. So when he wanted to discuss our relationship, instead of telling him how I felt, I said no, he didn't mean anything to me. But what I really wanted to say was yes. I vowed never to make that mistake again. And so my dating pact was born.

Now here I am years later, a serial dater, yet no step closer to finding the One. Hence, I go on a lot of dates. A wise friend of mine suggested I should start documenting my experiences, so my blog was born. I hope that you'll find my stories entertaining. But I also hope that you'll learn something. Knowing me, it will probably be a lesson in what not to do. Rule number one: never walk away from a chance at love. Trust me from a girl who's still searching.

Now that you know my backstory let me tell you about a recent date. Or shall I say, "nondate." A guy picked me up at the gym earlier this week. Let me preface this by saying I don't do gyms but went to support a friend of mine so she could land a date with a crush. I was invited back to the gym by Owen, Mr. Nondate, who struck up a conversation with me while I was on the bike. Turns out he was an employee of the gym—a personal trainer, to be specific—and our date was actually boot camp. How I get myself into these situations is beyond me. Oh, and the highlight is that on my way out I ran into my high school crush who inspired this dating pact of mine. Did I happen to mention I don't do gyms? Let's just say I had sweat coming out of every pore imaginable and looked like I had spent about five hours too long in the sun. And I could've used extra deodorant. I wanted to die of embarrassment. And for the record, he looked good. *Really good*. Let's hope things can only get better from here on out. Until the next adventure. Ciao for now!

26 Likes 12 Comments

THE ONE THAT GOT AWAY

I'M a bit wired after reading all the comments in response to my blog post. And I now have a handful of random followers, something I wasn't expecting. I've already spent way too much time engrossed on the site, so I crawl into bed. But my mind is still racing, and I have a hard time falling asleep. I decide to call my friend Andy, who's a night owl, so I know he'll be up. Andy is my best friend from college. We met my freshman year at the University of Wisconsin-Madison. I was in the Design Studies program (yes, there is such a thing) majoring in interior design, and he dated my roommate for all of a minute. I'm surprised we met because I was rarely in my dorm room. It was partly because of my demanding schedule, but I also wanted to avoid my psycho roommate. Psycho may be a bit harsh, but she was a definite whack job. For starters, she was a nudist. I'm not a prude by any means, but I'd come home from class, and she would be sitting butt-naked on the couch. And I mean that literally. It's a good thing it was her couch, because I refused to sit on it after that. She also had weird body hair issues. She didn't shave under her arms, but felt the need to shave her bikini line. I'd be in the bathroom brushing my teeth, and she'd literally put one foot up on the counter and have at it with her razor. The final straw for me was that she felt the color red had bad *chi*. (I know; the razor sounds much worse.) She said that it was the color of the devil and refused to eat red foods or have anything red in our dorm. But then she threw out my new red leather iPad case, which I had custom embossed with my initials, and that put the nail in the coffin for me. I can deal with gross behavior, but not shelling out my hard-earned cash. So I requested a transfer. There weren't any open dorms, so I ended up crashing at Andy's a lot because his roommate often slept at his girlfriend's place.

I remember the first time I saw him, or rather, the back of his head. I walked in on him and psycho girl making out on the infamous couch—she was naked, of course; he was not. I was surprised to see that she was with a guy because her sexuality was a bit questionable. I turned and walked right out because I didn't want any further scarring. A few minutes later he ran out of the apartment, chasing after me.

"Is that your roommate?" he panted.

"Yes," I replied questioningly.

"She scares me," he said. "She wanted to burn my boxers when she saw they were red."

"You have red boxers?" I asked.

"Not solid red. They're more of a plaid pattern."

I laughed and told him I'd treat him to a cup of coffee. We've been close ever since. My friends always say we'll end up together. He's adorable, and I love him dearly, but we've always had a platonic relationship. Although we do have a pact that if we're both still single by the time we're thirty, we'll get married. He wanted to go with thirty-five, but I want to be a young(ish) mom. And those five years could just zap all my energy. I was able to negotiate it down by promising him that he could still do his fantasy football league after we had kids. You wouldn't believe how much time he spends planning for the draft. And I think it worked to my advantage that we were both pretty wasted when we made the agreement. I swear I'm not big on pacts. This second one just happened by accident—I blame the alcohol.

As I suspected, Andy answers on the second ring.

"What's up, Tar?"

"You'll never believe who I ran into today."

"Who?"

"D. J. Parker?"

"Seriously? How'd he look?"

"Totally cute. I, on the other hand, not so much."

"Come on, Tar, you're just saying that. You always look great."

"No, I had just come from the gym."

"What were you doing at the gym?"

"A story for another time. But let's put it this way, I had just come from a boot camp class."

"Excuse me, is this Tara Winters?"

"Shut up."

"What the hell were you doing at boot camp?"

"You're missing the point! I was hot and sweaty and looked completely nasty. Of all the times I've looked fabulous and wanted to run into him, this is how it happens."

He's quiet for a minute, and I know he's searching for the right thing to say. "Was it dark out?"

I burst out laughing. "It was dusk."

"Well, that helps. Even sweaty, you still look hot."

"Thanks, Andy, but you're just saying that because you're my friend."

"I'm saying it because it's true. What were you wearing? Those black spandex pants?"

"Yeah, spandex capris and a tank."

"Good, then maybe he wasn't checking out your face after all."

"You're such a guy."

"I'm just channeling how guys think. I'm telling you, he probably wasn't noticing how sweaty you were. And if he did, I'm sure it made him think about how he'd like to have been the one responsible for getting you that way."

Leave it to Andy to think of how to turn the situation around and make it into a positive. That's why I called him. He always knows the perfect thing to say.

"Thanks for cheering me up."

"No problem. Now, going back to my first question, why the hell were you at the gym?"

"Jordan convinced me to go because she wanted my help with a trainer she has a crush on. I ended up meeting this guy who asked me out on what

I thought was a date. Turns out, he was inviting me to a free trial for a boot camp class."

"Classic. I can just picture you." He laughs.

I laugh too. "You can read all about it on my blog."

"Since when do you have a blog?"

"Since just now. Caitlin gave me the idea. I'm going to write about my dating experiences. Or should I say dilemmas?"

"Send me the link so I can follow you."

I pull up his e-mail address while we're talking. "I just sent it." I look at the clock, and it's after eleven thirty. "Shit, I gotta get to bed. I have to be up early for class."

"Wanna meet for a drink on Saturday to drown your sorrows?"

"There's nothing I'd like better." Aside from a do-over for this evening. Even after talking to Andy, I'm still mortified about the whole D. J. run-in. I hope that the gods take mercy on me and allow me another chance when I look like a much better version of myself.

I'm about to turn off my phone when I get a text from Caitlin.

Caitlin: *You up?*
Tara: *Yeah*
Caitlin: *I heart your 1st post. So proud.*
Tara: *I owe you—your idea*
Caitlin: *Then tell me more*
Tara: *More what?*
Caitlin: *About D. J. Intrigued*

I call her, and before she even says hello I say, "Do you really wanna know?"

"Yes. I could use a bedtime story."

"OK." I take a deep breath and let my mind drift back to all those years ago.

I've never been a fan of sports, but the fall of my freshman year I started attending all the varsity soccer games. I loved watching D. J. play, and it was really the only time I ever saw him—until the following semester. It was getting close to Valentine's Day, and the senior class was throwing a Love Match fundraiser. For a one-dollar donation, you could fill out a questionnaire and receive a list of potential matches with similar interests. "Come on, Tara, let's do it," Jordan said. I was not particularly thrilled about the idea, but I filled it out anyway. The following morning, I received a printout in my locker with my top ten matches.

Jordan saw my dumbfounded expression and said, "Who's on your list?" I silently handed it to her. "D. J.'s in your top slot? I can't believe it!" I couldn't believe it either. I wondered if he filled out the survey, and if he did, would my name be on his list as well? Even if it was, I doubt he would know who I was.

That afternoon, I met my older sister Lexi by her locker so she could drive me to an appointment. She was on the dance squad but didn't have practice, so luckily I wasn't stuck taking the bus. We passed by D. J. on our way out, and my stomach started doing flip-flops.

"Hey, Lexi," he called out to her.

"Hi, D. J. Have you met my sister Tara?" He looked at me and I could see the recognition register on his face from our encounter many months before. I guess it's hard to forget being knocked down by a girl. "Oh, so you're Lexi's sister. I've seen you around. Actually, I just got the results from my Love Match survey. Your name is on my list."

"Oh, yours was on mine too."

"That's probably because you lied about your answers," Lexi responded. "My sister's just an innocent freshman. Don't even think about corrupting her."

"Who me? I wouldn't dare."

"I didn't think so," she said with a wink. "You're not one of the guys I should be worried about. So have you decided on a college yet?"

"Yep, I'm going to U of I. I got early acceptance into their engineering program."

"That's awesome, congrats! Well, I've gotta get my sister to an ortho appointment. See you, D. J.," she said.

I just smiled at him as we walked past.

"Really? You had to tell him I was going to the ortho?" I asked once we were out of earshot.

She looked at me and shrugged. "What? That's where we're going."

"Well, you didn't have to tell him. How do you know D. J. anyway? I didn't think juniors and seniors mixed."

"We do some of the time, but I don't know him that well. He's friends with Liv's brother. And I've seen him at a few parties. Why? Do you have a crush on him?"

"No," I said a bit too quickly.

Lexi could have teased me for it, but she didn't say anything else on the topic.

As luck would have it, D. J. was my study hall leader the following semester. While we barely exchanged two words, I always looked forward to seeing him. He even tried talking to me a few times, but I was so nervous I always mumbled some incoherent response. I'd often steal glances in his direction and think, *How could someone be so damn good-looking?* Sometimes our eyes would meet, but I'd quickly look away, embarrassed at having been caught. But one time I allowed myself to hold his gaze, just to see what would happen. He seemed surprised at first, but then he gave me a shy smile, which only intensified my anxiety. One day, he walked by my desk as I was working on a project for art class.

"That's really good. I didn't know you were an artist."

I looked up in disbelief that he paid me a compliment. I tried to play it off and shrugged. "I'm OK, I guess."

"Tara, I'd say that's more than OK. You are really talented."

I loved hearing him say my name. "Thanks. My mom's a designer, so creativity runs in the family."

"Do you have other drawings?"

"Yeah, but they're in the art studio. And a few of them are hanging in the display case outside."

He nodded and continued walking. It took a few minutes for my heart rate to return to normal.

The following day he came by and said, "I saw your other art pieces. I'm really impressed."

"Thanks," I replied, somewhat surprised. The art studio is at the far end of the building, and it's not by any senior classes. I can't imagine why he would have been in that area.

"How's your other work coming along?"

"Fine. I was actually about to start my math homework. I've been avoiding it."

"How come?" he asked.

"I hate math. It's a subject that's never come easily for me."

"Well, you're in luck. Math happens to be my strong suit."

"Really?"

"Scout's honor," he said as he put his hand up. "What've you got?"

I took out my algebra book and showed him my homework sheet. He sat down next to me and I distinctly remember noticing how long his eyelashes were and the way his dark-brown hair fell over his eyes. I did my best to pay close attention as he walked me through how to solve the equation, rather than focusing on his luscious lips.

"Wow, you explained it in much simpler terms than Mr. Gleeson. You should teach the class." He smiled at me, and I felt a pit deep in my stomach. The bell rang, and I was sorry we had to cut our lesson short.

"Thanks for helping me out."

"No problem, Tara. That's what I'm here for."

D. J.'s tutoring became a daily ritual. There were some days when I didn't need the help, but I was not about to turn down spending time with him. I learned that he was really smart and especially good at math and science. I've always been better at the arts. One day, he revealed he'd been struggling with an art history paper.

"I figured that's your area of expertise. Perhaps you can help me out?"

"Sure, I'll do the best I can, but aren't you in AP?" I asked.

"Yeah, but it's not that different."

"If you say so. What's the topic?"

"That's the issue. I have to choose one, and I don't know what to pick."

"Well, what interests you?"

He looked at me in a way that sent tingles down my spine and then shrugged.

"You need to find your inspiration. Have you been to the Art Institute?"

"Not in a long time."

"You should go there. Walk the rooms and see what speaks to you."

He looked skeptical. "Art is art. I don't know that something will speak to me."

"Oh, come on. There are major differences. Take impressionism and postimpressionism, for instance."

"You've already lost me."

"You're the one who's in the class. Haven't you been paying attention?"

"I have. But I need someone who understands this stuff. Will you go with me?"

"Sure." The words were out of my mouth before the meaning sank in. I was going to the city with D. J. Parker. It was by no means a date given it was school-related, but I still couldn't believe it.

"Thanks, Tara. Are you free on Sunday?"

I am now, I thought. "That should be fine."

"Great, I'll pick you up at one o'clock."

I was terrified about how to tell my parents. I knew they wouldn't like the idea of a senior boy driving me to the city. So I asked Lexi for advice. "Just tell them it's for a homework assignment. It is, isn't it?"

"Yes, but it's not my assignment."

"Just leave out that detail. So how did D. J. wind up asking *you* for help?"

"He's my study hall leader. He's been tutoring me in math and saw some of my drawings. He said he could use my help with his art history paper. I guess he figured I was knowledgeable on the topic, so I could help him out too."

"Uh huh," she said and narrowed her eyes at me as I blushed a deep crimson.

I was so nervous I didn't know what to do with myself the rest of the week. Sunday arrived and he picked me up in his navy-blue Ford Explorer. I was disappointed to see his friend, Kyle, in the front seat.

"I hope you don't mind that I brought Kyle. When I told him we were going, he said he could use the help too."

"It's no problem," I said, trying to mask my disappointment.

"Hey, Little Winters," Kyle said as I climbed into the backseat.

It's a nickname that seemed to have stuck with a lot of older guys. But not D. J. He always referred to me by my real name.

We made small talk on the ride downtown, and when we arrived, D. J. paid for my ticket. I tried to give him money, but he wouldn't take it. "You're doing me a favor. It's on me." I thanked him, then asked where they wanted to start. They looked at me with blank stares.

"What's your favorite room?" D. J. asked.

"I like the impressionist paintings."

"Impressionism it is."

We spent the morning walking the different rooms. I shared my perspective on how to view art and discovered D. J. was intrigued by the photography collections. After a while I suggested he and Kyle look around on their own, and we meet back at three o'clock. I wandered the rooms and was studying an abstract painting when I sensed a presence beside me.

"I've never understood abstract art," D. J. said. "It looks like a bunch of scribble-scrabble. I probably could have done that."

"It's very possible, but even though it doesn't look like it, there is a message in this painting."

"Yeah? What's the message?"

"That's the thing about art. Everyone sees something different. This one is called *City Landscape* by Joan Mitchell. I think the vivid colors and her technique represent the energy of a big city. The way the colors are tangled together shows the interconnectedness of the people who live there, helping it to thrive."

"How did you know that?"

"I don't. It's just my interpretation. That's why I love art. It's subjective, and there are no wrong answers. It can be whatever you want it to be, unlike with math. Math is very logical, and you're either right or wrong. With art, you can never be wrong."

"I've never thought about it that way. Are you sure you're just a freshman?" he asked as he playfully nudged my shoulder.

"My mom always told me I'm wise beyond my years," I replied, trying not to focus on the fact that he casually lowered his arm, draping it across my waist.

"Passionate is more like it. You're different from all the girls I know."

I turned so I was facing him. "Different good or different bad?"

"Definitely good," he said, peering at me, looking for a reaction. I felt myself grow warm under his gaze. "Hey, hold still. You have an eyelash."

He touched his index finger to my cheek and held it out for me. "Make a wish."

I felt embarrassed by the intimacy of the gesture, but I gently blew the eyelash while holding his gaze. I swear, it looked like he wanted to kiss me, and for a minute I worried that I'd said my wish out loud. So I was relieved when I discovered Kyle approaching us and figured it must have been my crazy imagination projecting my own desires.

"Why the hell not, Tara?" Caitlin interjects. "You're a great catch."

"Thanks. First of all, I looked much different in high school, and second of all, I haven't gotten to one important detail."

"What's that?"

"He had a girlfriend. A very cliché of a girlfriend. You know, pretty, blond, head-cheerleader type."

"Oh, so what happened?"

I continue to tell her the story.

A few weeks later, my friend Lizzie's brother decided to throw a party while their parents were out of town. I had never been to a high school party before, and I was very excited, but a bit nervous too. I remember the day clearly because I had just gotten my braces off. Lexi was out of town visiting college campuses, so I raided her closet. My friends and I brought a change of clothes to Jordan's and got ready there. I wore a low-cut, black lacy shirt that was roomy on Lexi but showed off my ample curves. I was usually self-conscious about my body, but that night I wanted to be a grown-up. Jordan styled my hair, which I wore long back then, and did my makeup. I couldn't believe the transformation. I thought I looked at least sixteen.

Anyway, we went to the party, and it was mainly seniors. I remember feeling very out of my element. I hadn't tried alcohol yet, but the beer was flowing. I accepted a cup and pretended to drink it because I hated the taste. I spied D. J. across the room, and we made eye contact. He looked at me with surprise but otherwise didn't acknowledge my presence, so I just gave him a little wave. To be honest I felt hurt that he ignored me, which he continued to do for the latter part of the evening. We exchanged looks from time to time, but he didn't come over to speak with me. And I sure as hell wasn't going to initiate conversation. It's like we had this separate reality where things were great when it was just the two of us. But when other people were there, I wasn't sure how to act around him. And if he wanted my company at all.

After a while, some guy whose name escapes me started hitting on me. I was flattered, so I flirted back with him, perhaps hoping to make D. J. jealous. But then he became aggressive and asked if I wanted to go upstairs. I felt uncomfortable, so I made up a lame excuse. He yelled that I was a tease and caused a scene. D. J. came over and told him to chill out and that I was just a freshman. The guy was real pissed, and I was worried a fight was going to break out.

"Come on," D. J. said to me. "I'll drive you home." I tried to protest, but he was pretty adamant, and frankly I was embarrassed by the whole situation. So I gathered up my friends, and he played chauffeur, dropping each of them off. Even though it was out of his way, he took me home last. He pulled up to my driveway and turned the engine off.

"What were you thinking going to that party?" he asked me.

"I don't know, it seemed like a good idea at the time. I didn't realize it would be mainly seniors."

He studied me and said, "You look different. Going out dressed like that will get you in trouble."

"What are you, my dad?"

"No, it's just that guys have one thing on their minds. And you're an easy target."

"Why would you say that?"

"Because you're too trusting."

"I didn't realize that was a bad thing, but I'll try not to be. And thanks for the help, but I didn't need it."

"It looked like you did."

"Well, maybe I wanted to kiss that guy."

"Did you?"

"I don't know. I just wanted to get it over with."

"Get what over with?"

I was beyond embarrassed. "My first real kiss."

He looked at me silently for a full minute, his eyes sweeping over my body and resting on my lips. I could feel a slow heat creeping into my cheeks under his scrutiny. "You've never been kissed?" he finally asked, his eyes dark, his face dangerously close to mine.

I shook my head and turned away, not wanting him to witness my mortification at this revelation.

"Tara, look at me." I slowly turned my face to meet his gaze, and what I saw in his eyes was pure desire. He pulled me toward him and kissed me, tentatively at first, but then more hungrily once he saw my response. It's like every hormone I had was on overdrive. It was a spectacular kiss—I still remember it vividly. Anyway, we started making out, and it was like he unleased this unbridled passion within me. I think he was shocked but very encouraged by my response. He reclined the seat so he was lying on top of me, and the next thing I knew his hands were all over me. At first I let him take the lead, given he was older and more experienced, but I wanted to know what he felt like. I pulled his shirt off and glided my hands down his chest, my fingertips like whispers against his hot skin. I eased my hands lower, feeling his hard abs and moved them lower still until I reached his waistband. I could feel his breath catch as I unbuckled his pants, placing my hand over his erection, and I was shocked that I could make him feel that way. At my touch, he let out a satisfied sigh that mirrored my own. He pulled away, and I was momentarily confused, but then he indicated that I should raise my arms up. He pulled my shirt over my head and then attempted to unhook my bra without success. We both laughed, and I whispered that it was a front clasp and helped him finish the task. I pressed myself closer to him and the sensation of skin-to-skin contact only intensified the heat that was raging through me. He slid his hand down and caressed me on the outside of my jeans, filling me with need. He unzipped my pants and when he touched me I felt a deep longing that I didn't know existed. Then, my porch light went on.

"Well shit, Tara, you were just getting to the good stuff," Caitlin groans.

"Tell me about it. I totally panicked, shimmied back into my clothes, and told him I had to go. It turns out it was my older sister, Jules, home that weekend from college, who turned the light on."

I continued sharing the sordid details.

"Dad will be home soon. I thought you'd better come inside and get changed," she said as she looked me over.

"How did you know?" I asked her.

"I was your age once. And you'd better put that shirt back in Lexi's closet where you found it." I started upstairs, grateful to be away from her scrutiny. "Oh, and Tar," she called out behind me, "make sure when you hang it up it's not inside out." Shit. At least it was just Jules. I carefully replaced Lexi's shirt, inspecting it to make sure that nothing was out of place. I studied it on the hanger, nestled with her other black shirts—Lexi color-coded her closet—and there were no telltale traces of what just happened. But I could still feel D. J.'s touch on my skin, his kiss on my lips. As I lay in bed that night, I replayed what happened between us and wondered how far we would have taken things had Jules not been there. And it scared me how far I'd have been willing to go.

I didn't hear from D. J. the rest of the weekend. At first I was elated about our encounter and what it meant for our relationship, but as time passed and I didn't hear from him, that feeling turned to dread. My stomach was in nervous knots by the time study hall came around on Monday. But he wasn't there, and I couldn't help feeling like he was avoiding me. The next day after school, I was walking down Student Hall and saw him talking to Sherry. His back was to me, so I stopped and pretended to rummage through my backpack so I could eavesdrop. I couldn't hear what they were saying, but they were deep in conversation. He turned slightly and his profile was visible, so I quickly ducked my head. After a few minutes I allowed myself a glance in their direction. I saw the way he looked at her and knew I didn't stand a chance. Hurt flooded through me, and I stumbled to the bathroom to get a hold of myself. I took some deep, steadying breaths, and when I came out he was alone.

He spotted me and said, "Hey, Tara. I've been meaning to talk to you."

I attempted to keep my expression neutral. "Oh, what about?"

He looked at me incredulously. "About Saturday night."

"Oh, that."

"Yeah, that." He smiled nervously. "I figured we should talk about what happened."

"I really don't see a need to talk about it. It was a mistake."

He looked surprised, then his blue eyes darkened like an oncoming storm. "Is that the way you saw it? It didn't mean anything to you?"

Yes! I wanted to shout. It meant everything to me. But how could it mean something to you? I'm just a nobody.

"No," I found myself saying. "It didn't mean anything. I just wanted to experience my first kiss. So thanks for that."

If I thought his eyes were dark before, there wasn't a speck of blue left. He looked at me through his narrowed gaze and said, "Glad I could help you check that off your list. It's good to know where things stand between us. See you around." It took me a moment to register the anger in his voice. I wanted to call out to him, but he was already halfway down the hall, leaving me in his wake without as much as a backward glance.

"You know the rest. That was the last time I spoke to him before he left for college." I glance at the clock, and it's almost one o'clock. "Sorry for talking your ear off."

"Tara, that is such as tragic story. But maybe it happened so you'll say yes to some guy who you wouldn't have otherwise. And he'll be the one you were meant for."

"I sure hope so. 'Night, Caitlin."

I close my eyes and hope to God she's right. Let it all be for something.

Made in the USA
Monee, IL
19 February 2024